PRAISE FOR

"It's sort of Hunter S. Thompson meets Stephen King. *Fear and Loathing at the Drive-in.*" —*Mystery Scene*, Charles de Lint

"Anything with this guy's name on the cover is most definitely worth your time . . . this is one writer who demands greater acclaim." —*Fangoria*, Stanley Wiater

"*The Drive-in* serves as a great introduction for those unfamiliar with Lansdale. It is abounding with the outlandish charm and style that is uniquely his own." —*Sun-Sentinel,* Michael Sellard

"Joe R. Lansdale's *Drive-in* novels make for a classic American trilogy. If your Americans happen to be George A. Romero, Roger Corman, and Stuart Gordon." —Rick Klaw

"This is what a Twilight Zone episode directed by Herschell Gordon Lewis might have been like." —*Thrust*, Howard Coleman.

"*The Drive-in* has that rare combination: fear and laughter. It is a quick read that will have readers alternately chuckling and shivering. And as one must expect from Lansdale, it is utterly tasteless." —*Rocky Mountain News*, Mark Graham

"It's a gross, funny, fascinating book." —*The New York Review of Science Fiction*, George Alec Effinger

"For the uninitiated there is only one piece of advice that needs to be heeded with regard to The Drive-in [novels]: READ THEM NOW! Brilliant in vision and scope . . ." —*The Cabinet of Dr. Casey*, Tony Gangi

"A horror novel for the Roger Corman crowd, a Troma film for the literate, that was nevertheless nominated for both the Bram Stoker and World Fantasy Awards." —*Green Man Review*

"This is bold stuff, not for the squeamish, and it rivals the work of Stephen King on *The Stand* in the scope of its visionary, apocalyptic nature. It's horror on an epic scale . . . with a measured East Texas drawl." —David Rosiak

The Complete Drive-in
Copyright © Joe R. Lansdale 2009

Names, characters, places, and incidents are the product of the authors' imagination and are used fictitiously. Any resemblance to events or persons, living or dead, is coincidental.

All rights reserved. No part of this publication may be reproduced or transmitted in any form or by any means, electronic or mechanical, including photocopy, recording, or any information storage and retrieval system, without permission in writing from the publisher.

Requests for permission should be emailed to underland@underlandpress.com

Underland Press
www.underlandpress.com
Portland, Oregon

Illustrations by Nikita Knatz, Copyright © 1989 Silver Sphere Corporation
Cover design by John Coulthart
Book design by Heidi Whitcomb

ISBN13 978-0-9802260-4-1

Printed in the United States of America
Distributed by PGW

First Underland Press Edition: May 2010

10 9 8 7 6 5 4 3 2

Printed in USA

THE COMPLETE DRIVE-IN

Three Novels of Anarchy, Aliens, & the Popcorn King

BY JOE R. LANSDALE

UNDERLAND PRESS
www.underlandpress.com

OTHER BOOKS BY JOE R. LANSDALE

Hap Collins and Leonard Pine mysteries
Savage Season
Mucho Mojo
Two-Bear Mambo
Bad Chili
Rumble Tumble
Veil's Visit
Captains Outrageous
Vanilla Ride

The Drive-In series
The Drive-In: A "B" Movie with Blood and Popcorn, Made in Texas
The Drive-In 2: Not Just One of Them Sequels
The Drive-In: A Double-Feature
The Drive-In: The Bus Tour

The Ned the Seal trilogy
Zeppelins West
Flaming London
The Sky Done Ripped

Other novels
Act of Love
Texas Night Riders
Dead in the West
Magic Wagon
The Nightrunners
Cold in July
Tarzan: the Lost Adventure
The Boar
Freezer Burn
Waltz of Shadows
Something Lumber This Way Comes
The Big Blow
Blood Dance
The Bottoms
A Fine Dark Line
Sunset and Sawdust
Lost Echoes
Leather Maiden

The Drive-in novels had their own original dedications, including dedications to the drive-in theaters, now gone, that inspired them. For this new edition, however, I have a new dedication, and, ladies and gentlemen, this is it:

This is for my son, Keith Lansdale, of whom I am intensely proud.

THE COMPLETE DRIVE-IN

Three Novels of Anarchy, Aliens, & the Popcorn King

BY JOE R. LANSDALE

CONTENTS

A "B" Movie Night with Popcorn and Water Moccasins

by Don Coscarelli

It all started with an afternoon trip to my local horror bookshop in Sherman Oaks, California. It was a cool little place called Dangerous Visions which, unfortunately, is now long gone. I was chatting up the guy behind the counter and casually asked him what was new and cutting edge in horror. He said, "Follow me." He led me to the back of the store, to the "L" fiction aisle. "Joe Lansdale," he said, and stuck a paperback in my hand. (I think it was *The Nightrunners*.) "Good storyteller," he said, and, as I read over the back cover, he followed up with, "Joe Lansdale always has a high body count."

Well, I went home with that copy of *The Nightrunners* and one other book, something called *The Drive-in*. I don't know exactly why I immediately gravitated to *The Drive-in* as the first one to read. Was it that subtitle on the cover, "*A B-Movie with Blood and Popcorn Made in Texas*"? Probably.

I dove right in to the horror, humor, and overall freaky audacity that was, and still is, *The Drive-in*. Joe writes his books like movies, he sets up the bizarre scenes, populates them with memorable characters, and then lets them talk in that amazing Nacogdoches dialect of his. Then Joe cranks up the suspense, action, and humor. Another amazing talent Joe has is a phenomenal ability to mix up genres. In *The Drive-in*, he got me started with what seemed like a traditional coming-of-age story, then effortlessly moved into post-apocalyptic survival and finally an out-and-out horror monster tale! I was halfway through the book when I realized this will make for a frickin' fantastic movie!

I have a friend named Jeff Conner who was once the publisher of that terrific, and now-extinct, small publisher Scream Press. Since Jeff was the only person I knew in the publishing business, I asked him to track down Joe's phone number for me. Jeff immediately began working his contacts and got me Joe's home phone number. I called Joe up and got him on the phone.

The first thing I noticed in that call was that Joe speaks in this amazing East Texas accent. It's a lingo that is really unique, strange (to me), and wonderful. For the first few moments of our conversation I was so taken with his language that I wasn't really responding. Joe inquired politely if I was still on the line, so I got right to the reason I had called. I told him I was a fan and wanted to make his book *The Drive-in* into a movie. Joe was very nice, but told me there were a couple other people interested and gave me his agent's contact information.

I then did two things. The second thing I did was to call up Joe's agent and make my pitch. But the first thing was a bit unconventional. I hired a brilliant Russian-born illustrator, Nikita Knatz, to help me visually conceptualize what a movie of *The Drive-in* might look like. Nikita had done some epic visualizations for me on my film *The Beastmaster*. Nikita had a knack for the weird and strange and I commissioned him to do a series of illustrations of *The Drive-in* world. I probably should have waited to secure the movie rights but back then I was a guy in a hurry. Imagine my surprise a couple months later when I learned that Joe's agent had optioned the rights to somebody else! Nikita had just finished his work and it was immediately destined to go into my file cabinet for the next couple of decades.

Later I called Joe up, still despondent over the loss of *The Drive-in* movie rights. Joe's response was to invite me down to Texas. He was certain that once we met in person we'd be able to cook up something for us to work on together.

About a month later I arrived in Houston and took the two-hour drive north to Lansdale country. Anyone who gets to know Joe Lansdale knows that his hometown of Nacogdoches informs his entire being. This small town and its residents have had a tremendous influence on him and his work. As he showed me around, Joe told me how Nacogdoches was the first town in Texas and that later it was the last stop on the vaudeville circuit for legendary comedians like Buster Keaton and the Marx Brothers. As it is just a few miles from the Louisiana border, Nacogdoches has a distinct Deep South conservative sensibility, yet Joe is one of the most progressive guys you'll ever meet. Joe happens to be a martial arts master and, coincidentally, the few other liberal-minded citizens of the town all happen to be martial arts experts also. I hear they all like to hang out at Joe's martial arts studio and are happy to talk politics with their right-wing neighbors as long as it's in the dojo and on the mat in the event discussions get hot.

In addition to the tour of Nacogdoches and meeting the entire Lansdale family, including Joe's terrific wife Karen and their two adorable kids, Keith and Kasey, I had the distinct honor of attending a "B-movie night with popcorn" in Joe's den. Later I was to learn that the movie night with popcorn was a coveted invitation and a notorious rite of passage for many of Joe's author friends. It's a little known secret that many of Joe's greatest writerly inspirations came to him in the middle of the night after watching a B-movie and eating the special Nacogdoches popcorn.

The VCR cranked up and *Killer Klowns from Outer Space* started to play. Karen was in the kitchen getting the popcorn popping. During a lull in the Klown action, I looked over my shoulder into the kitchen and saw Karen preparing the popper. She had hold of an ice cream scooper and put several large scoops of what looked to me like vanilla ice cream into the popcorn kettle. I'm thinking to myself, "Now that's a novel way to cook up popcorn—with an ice cream flavor."

A few minutes later Karen came into the den and presented each of us with a monster bowl of the famous popcorn. It was fantastic! I started wolfing the stuff down as Joe told me how he got inspiration for his stories from eating the popcorn, watching the B-movies, and then enduring the fever-induced dreams those two things created in him. I was a bit skeptical that popcorn and B-movies would create a peyote-like experience, but what the hell, I still ate two full bowls of the stuff. I then asked Karen where she got the idea of putting ice cream into the popcorn. It wasn't ice cream, she informed me, they made their popcorn the old-fashioned way, with scoops of *lard*! No wonder it tasted so good! But if I'd known the key ingredient, I would have paced myself a bit and not quaffed it down whole hog, so to speak. The rest of the movie was a hallucinatory blur as the popcorn rumbled its way through my digestive system. It was definitely having an effect as I started hearing a ringing in my ears and the Killer Klowns were actually terrifying to me.

After the movie ended I shakily followed Joe downstairs and across the yard to his office where I would be bunking for the night. I was going to be sleeping in the same bed that such literary luminaries and friends of Joe's had slept in, including Lewis Shiner, Richard Christian Matheson, and David Schow. I was wondering if those gents had eaten the popcorn too and what kind of effect it had on them.

As we moved through his yard in the dark, Joe warned me to watch out for the water moccasins that would slither up from the creek at night. He said something about pitying the poor fool who would step on one of those poisonous critters. I was sweating profusely and my eyes were darting around looking for water moccasins in every shadow.

I fell into the bed and spent the rest of the night in a popcorn-induced fever dream chock full of water moccasins. Every half hour I'd wake to see shadows on the blanket and would flail at them, trying to get the snakes off my bed. I was dreaming of water moccasins on the bed, under the bed, on the floor, in my shoes. Flying moccasins, swimming moccasins, you get the picture. If I were Joe, I would have jumped up the next morning and put those visions to paper in the form of an audacious short story.

A few years later I heard that, due to an interest in a better diet, Karen would not allow Joe to eat the popcorn anymore. I will leave it to the biographers and literary researchers to one day go back and analyze Joe's body of work "pre-popcorn" and "post-popcorn" to see if there is any difference. Sometimes I wonder if Joe just made that whole story up. He is a terrific storyteller and how could an author like Joe pass up one about magic popcorn that, combined with B-movies, generates strange stories in a writer's mind? Stories like *The Drive-in*, contained herein, where the protagonists are literally torn to shreds by "The Popcorn King."

I've been back to Nacogdoches a couple times since then but never slept at Joe's again, never watched B-movies with him again, and never, but never, allowed myself to eat any of that Lansdale popcorn. I guess I am a witness that Joe's claims may be true. For me, there is no question that the trip to Nacogdoches and the B-movies with popcorn were a source of hallucinatory night-sweats and nightmares. Unlike Joe, I was just too lazy to put it down on paper, until now.

Book One

THE DRIVE-IN

A B-Movie with Blood and Popcorn, Made in Texas

INTRODUCTION

Back in the eighties I kept having this dream.

Every night, as soon as I drifted off I found myself at a giant drive-in theater. I could tell, even though I was dreaming, that I was putting together all the drive-ins I had ever attended and was combining true experiences with dream experiences.

The dream got weirder. It was like a movie serial. Every night I was excited because I got to see what happened next. What happened in the dream was I was with some friends, and we got trapped in the drive-in by a big black acidic blob that surrounded it and we couldn't get out. Contained in the drive-in without food and rules, people turned to murder and cannibalism and not washing their hands after peeing.

Anyway, the dream stayed with me, night after night, even though it got to a point where it was no longer advancing; it started repeating itself. I was on a weird drive-in loop.

Then I got a call from T. E. D. Klein at *Twilight Zone*. He asked if I would write a non-fiction piece for the magazine. They had run other articles by other writers, and they wondered if I had something. I don't know why I was chosen. Maybe it was because I had sold them a few stories and Ted—as he was known to most, not T. E. D., even though that was his writer tag—got along with me pretty well, and we had had a number of conversations. On the other hand, maybe I was the last pick in the bag. I don't know.

But I decided to write an article about drive-ins. It contained some drive-in history, and my feelings about drive-ins, and Joe Bob Briggs let me quote him at the front of the article. I then added my dream to it and turned it in.

It really went over well, not only with the editor, but the readers, and one of those readers was my editor at Doubleday, Pat LoBrutto. Pat is one of those unsung heroes of the field. He published dozens of writers on their way up, and dozens on their way down. Good writers who were starting out, or who no longer had a solid home in the publishing industry and should have.

Anyway, he asked if I'd write a book based on the dream.

I said okay, and started writing away. I wrote *The Drive-in* in a little over two months, if memory serves me, and as soon as I finished, I started writing *Cold in July*, as I had a contract for that one at Bantam at about the same time.

I hated *The Drive-in*. I found it hard to write. I wanted it to read simply, and fun, but I had a dark sort of message inside of it, and it weighed on me. I don't say this with any great feeling of philosophical superiority. I just feel a book is at its best when it has subtext. I felt I had perhaps missed the boat on both humor and philosophical underpinning.

I tried to write what I thought was a kind of loving satire of horror films and the stupidity of man. The desire to believe almost anything if it made them feel better. Religion. Astrology. Numerology. You name it. I thought the book was quite serious, and I hoped funny in a kind of biting, satirical way.

The book came out with a cover that didn't fit it at all. It was more of the kind of cover reserved for Ron Goulart's humorous S.F. I liked Goulart's work, by the way, but this was a totally different kind of animal. It wasn't actually S.F., though it used some S.F. tropes. It wasn't exactly horror, though it certainly used elements of that. And it wasn't exactly a mainstream novel because it was too weird. Perhaps it was weird fantasy? I don't know. I didn't care. It was mine.

Anyway, the book came out. It acquired a readership and a kind of underground following. A lot of writers have told me that it was a big influence on their decision to become a writer or that it influenced the way they wrote, or the things they wrote about. That's pretty high praise.

But I'm getting ahead of myself. I often do.

Anyway, backtracking, I hated writing the book and thought it was awful, but when they sent me the galleys, and I read them, I was surprised and pleased. I felt I had done what I started out to do. The problem was the book was written quickly, but intensely, and the things I was writing about, humor or not, underneath were dark and unsettling. At least to me. So, the writing had been tedious and painful, but the reading of the book was not. I am one of those writers who loves writing, not having written. I believe the act itself is what matters most. But for this book, I didn't really enjoy the act at the time or finishing it either. I thought I had written a loser. I wrote much of it sort of free associating, and just going where it wanted to go, no matter how wild it seemed. I let my subconscious lead the way.

It wasn't, as I said, until I held the galleys in my hot little hands that I realized I had done something unique. To this day a lot of people tell me how much they love the novel. Many say they love it because it is light and fun. Well, yeah, if you look at it from one angle, that's true. Some say they think it's the darkest thing I ever wrote. Yep, so do I. The humor is nothing more than a clown suit on a corpse. The important thing is, for whatever reason, it endures, and so does its influence.

Simply put, I'm proud of it. The book has been back in print before, but not as much as I would like. Not considering it is to my way of thinking one of my more unique and important novels. That, of course, is ultimately for the readers to decide.

I'm excited and pleased that it, and its companions, are being brought out in this form and fashion. I hope this volume brings new readers of the novel into the Drive-in fold. I'm glad to see it have a new life and for it to be presented in this respectful and attractive manner.

Enjoy.

—Joe R. Lansdale, 2009

Fade-in Prologue

I'm writing now about the time before things got weird and there was high school to kiss off, college to plan, girls, parties and the All-Night Horror Show come Friday night at the Orbit Drive-in off I-45, the largest drive-in in Texas. The world, for that matter, though I doubt there are that many of them in, say, Yugoslavia.

Think about it for a moment. Set your mind clear and see if you can imagine a drive-in so big it can hold four thousand automobiles. I mean, really think about it.

Four thousand.

On the way to the Orbit we often passed through little towns with fewer people listed on the population sign than that.

And consider that each of those cars generally contained at least two people, often more—not counting the ones hiding in the trunks—and you're talking a lot of cars and people.

And once inside, can you imagine six monstrous drive-in screens, six stories high, with six different movies running simultaneously?

Even if you can imagine all that, there's no way, unless you've been there, that you can imagine what goes on inside come Friday night and the tickets are two bucks each and the cars file in for The All-Night Horror Show to witness six screens leaking buckets of blood and decibels of screams from dusk to dawn.

Picture this, brethren:

A cool, crisp summer night, the Texas stars shining down like rattlesnake eyes showing in a deep, dark wood. A line of cars like a tacky necklace trailing from the paybooth to the highway, stretching alongside it for a mile or better.

Horns are honking.

Children are shouting.

Mosquitoes are buzzing.

Willie Nelson is singing about blue eyes crying in the rain from a tape deck, competing with Hank Williams, Jr., Johnny Cash, ZZ Top, The Big Boys, The Cars and Country Bob and The Blood Farmers, groups and singers you can't identify. And it all rolls together into a metal-velvet haze until it's its own kind of music; the drive-in anthem, a chorus of cultural confusion.

And say your car is about midway in line, and clear as your first good wet dream, standing tall, you can see the Orbit's symbol—a big silver globe with a Saturn ring around it, spinning on a gradually tapering concrete pole jutting up to over a hundred feet above the concession stand; little blue and white fairy lights flittering out of it, alternating colors across your windshield. Blue. White. Blue. White.

God Almighty, it's a sight. Like being in the presence of The Lord of Razzle-Dazzle, The Dark Crown Prince of Blood and Mayhem and Cheap, Bad Popcorn. The All-Night Horror Show God, his own sweet self.

You drive on into this Friday-night extravaganza, this Texas institution of higher partying, sex education and madness, and you see people dressed out in costume like it's Halloween night (and it is Halloween night every Friday night at the Orbit), yelling, talking, cussing and generally raising hell.

You park your car, go to the concession stand. Inside it's decorated with old horror-movie posters, plastic skulls, rubber bats and false cobwebs. And there's this thing called bloody corn that you can buy for a quarter more than the regular stuff, and it's just popcorn with a little red food coloring poured over it. You buy some and a king-size Coke to go with it, maybe some peanuts and enough candy to send a hypoglycemic to the stars.

Now you're ready. The movies begin. B-string and basement-budget pictures. A lot of them made with little more than a Kodak, some spit and a prayer. And if you've watched enough of this stuff, you develop a taste for it, sort of like learning to like sauerkraut.

Drooping mikes, bad acting and the rutting of rubber-suited monsters who want women, not for food, but to mate with, become a genuine pleasure. You can simultaneously hoot and cringe when a monster attacks a screaming female on the beach or in the woods and you see the zipper on the back of the monster's suit winking at you like the quick, drunk smile of a Cheshire cat.

So there you have it. A sort of rundown of The All Night Horror Show at the Orbit. It drew me and the gang in there every Friday night like martyrs to the sacrifice; providing popcorn and Coke instead of wine and wafer.

Yes, sir, brethren, there was something special about the Orbit all right. It was romantic. It was outlaw. It was crazy.

And in the end, it was deadly.

PART ONE

THE ALL NIGHT HORROR SHOW

With Popcorn and Comet

1

I suppose, ultimately, this will read like a diseased version of those stupid essays you're asked to write in school each fall after summer break. You know, "How I Spent My Summer Vacation."

Guess that can't be helped.

This is where I think it begins.

It was Saturday morning, the morning after a night at the Orbit. We drove back to Mud Creek smelling of beer, popcorn and chocolate bars.

Our eyes were cloudy, our minds more so. But we were too wired, or maybe just too stupid, to go home. So we did what we usually did. We drove over to the pool hall.

The pool hall, or Dan's Place, as it's called, is an ugly joint in an ugly section of an overall pretty nice-looking town. It's the area where you hear about knifings and the lowlife congregating, twenty-dollar women, bootleg whisky and Mud Creek's drug deals.

Dan's was a beer drinker's pool hall, had a bar along with the tables. Theoretically the place didn't serve beer until after noon, but Dan and the guys who came there were real short on theory.

There were a few men in there when we went in that morning. Most of them were in their forties or older, and they were sipping long necks, their hats on their heads or on the bar or the stools beside them. Those without cowboy hats and boots wore blue and gray work clothes with worn work boots, and it seemed that no matter how quietly you came in, they always heard you and turned to look with disapproval.

The place was supposed to be off limits to minors, but who were we to tell, and Dan wasn't telling either. Not that he liked us, but he did like our money for the pool games, and once in a small while, when he felt brave and we did too, he'd let us buy a beer, just like he didn't know we were underage.

But there was this: he always had a look about him that let us know he'd take our money, but for little or no reason wouldn't mind killing us for the fun of it. And he looked quite capable of killing us without breaking a sweat. He was kind of fat, but it was hard-looking fat, like there was a great iron wash pot under his too-tight T-shirt. And his arms were big and meaty. Not bodybuilder arms, but workingman's arms; arms that had done real work: bounced drunks, and, from what I'd heard, slapped wives. He also had funny-looking knuckles; knuckles that had remolded facial flesh as if it were silly putty, and, in turn, had been remolded themselves.

Still, we'd go in there like men born for a suicide mission. There were things we wanted out of the place. Attractions. It was forbidden, for one, and that was appealing. Gave us a sense of manhood. Danger hung in the air like a sword on a hair, and as long as the hair didn't snap and the blade didn't fall, it was stimulating.

Dan's was where we met Willard. Saw him there the first time we went inside, which was about the time we started going to the drive-in. I guess we felt if we had permission to stay out all night, we could go over to the tough section of town and shoot pool. Maybe talk some about the twenty-dollar women we didn't dare actually speak to (we weren't even sure we'd seen any) for fear we'd have to shell out money and perform. Something none of us was sure we wanted. We had heard vague stories about viruses and carnivorous insects that grew like sourdough starter in the pubic thatches of twenty-dollar women, and we felt that they would know so many tricks, and we'd know so few, that the cheap little hotel rooms where we planned to consummate our financial arrangements would ring of feminine laughter instead of the satisfying squeaks of bed-springs.

But the poolroom and the possibility of violent death didn't worry us as much as sexual embarrassment, so we went there Saturdays to play pool and to watch Willard do the same.

First look at Willard, and he seemed downright skinny. But closer examination proved him long, lean and muscular. When he bunched over the table for a shot, let the cue glide over the top of his thumb, you could see the muscles roll beneath his hide, and the tattoos on his biceps popped forward and back so fast they were like billboards viewed on the highway at top speed. The left tattoo read KICK ASS and the right read EAT PUSSY. It was understood that he could do either, and probably quite well.

But Willard was a nice guy in an odd sort of way. Smart, too, if, shall we say, not classically educated. He was three years older than us physically, and about ten years older in experience.

That was one of the reasons we liked to be around him. He gave us a glimpse of a world we didn't normally see. Not one we wanted to live in, but one we wanted to investigate.

And I think Willard liked us for the reverse reason. We could talk about something besides beer, women and the plant where he worked all week and Saturday afternoons making aluminum lawn furniture.

None of us had to work. Our parents provided, and we were all college material. Had dreams and a good chance of seeing them come true, and I guess Willard wanted some of that hope to rub off on him.

We didn't really know much about him. Story was his father didn't think the kid looked like him at all, and had been told by some Louisiana Mojo man that the boy had a curse on him, and since Willard's mother, Marjory, was into weird business, like believing in old gods and voodoo-type stuff, this made him even more suspicious. Bottom line was the father left before the baby could crawl. Baptists around town called Willard and his mother sorry as part of their entertainment, and truth was, his mother was no prize. She later took up with a man who had a bad back and a regular check of some sort, and when he went away she took up with another with ailing posture and a steady government income.

This initiated a pattern. Men with bad backs and checks, and it kept Marjory in cigarettes and Willard in throwaway diapers. But when Willard turned sixteen, his birthday present was goodbye and the street—a place he spent a lot of time anyway. Marjory went away to who knows where—probably a fresh town full of bad backs and welfare checks—and Willard did the best he could. Dropped out of school when he was old enough and got some odd jobs here and there, the best of them being a projectionist at one of the movie houses. When he turned eighteen, he went to work at the aluminum chair factory.

It seemed obvious to me, in the short time that I had known him, that he was hungry for something beyond that, something more substantial, something that would give him respect in the eyes of the Uptown folks, though I doubt he would have admitted that—even to himself.

But to get back to it, we came into the pool hall this Saturday I'm telling you about, and there was Willard in his familiar pose, pool cue in hand, leaning over the table, eyeing a ball.

Shooting against him was a guy we'd seen a couple of times before but avoided talking to. His name was Bear, and you didn't ponder why he was called that. He was six-five, ugly as disease, had roux-brown hair and a beard that mercifully consumed most of his face. All that was clearly visible were some nasty blue eyes and a snout that was garage to some troublesome nose hairs thick enough to use for piano wire. The same gruesome down as in his nose also covered his arms and curled out of the neck of his T-shirt to confuse itself with his beard. What could be seen of his lips reminded me of those rubber worms fishermen use, and I wouldn't have been surprised to see shiny silver hooks poking out of them, or to discover that the whole of Bear had been made from decaying meat, wire and the contents of a tackle box and a Crisco can.

There was something rock 'n' roll playing on the jukebox—a rarity for Dan's, which mostly catered to country and western—and Randy went over to lean on it. Wasn't just because he liked what was playing, it put him closer to the door.

Being black, Randy was a bit uncomfortable about bopping around a redneck pool hall. Even if he was with Bob, who wore a toothpick-laden cowboy hat, dipped snuff and wore snakeskin boots. And me, Mr. Average and All-Around Natural Blender.

Wasn't that Randy was the only black that came into the place (though just about), but he was the only one that was skinny, five-five, with headlamp glasses and an inferiority complex. And, most importantly, he was the only black in there this morning I'm telling you about.

I guess if Bob and I had really thought about what we were putting him through as a member of our "gang," we probably wouldn't have gone in there in the first place.

This is not to say Bob and I weren't nervous. We were. We felt like weenies compared to these guys. But there were those attractions I told you about, and there was also our onrushing manhood we were trying to deal with, attempting to define.

When Willard raised up from his shot he nodded at us, and we nodded back, found places to lean and watch.

Bear wasn't playing well. He had a mild temper on, and you could tell it even though he hadn't said a word. He didn't have a poker face.

Bending over the table, Bear took a shot and missed.

"Damn," he said.

Willard winked at us, shot again, talked as he did. He wasn't a temperamental player. He liked to joke and ask us about the movies we'd seen, as he knew our schedule.

He was also interested in special effects, or professed to be, and he liked to talk to Randy about that. Randy was the resident expert; he wanted to do movie makeup and special effects when he got out of college. And there was something between those two from the start. A sort of bond. I think Willard saw in Randy the intellectual side he wanted, and Randy saw in Willard street savvy and strength. When they were together, I had the feeling they considered themselves whole, and there was a yearning to know more about one another.

Willard shot for a long time before missing.

Bear missed.

"Damn."

Willard continued to talk to Randy, shot three more times before missing, and that one was close. He went around and got his beer off the edge of the pool table and took a long pull on it.

"Do your worst, Bear," he said.

Bear showed a few ugly teeth at one corner of his mouth, took his shot.

He missed.

"Damn."

Willard put the beer down, went around and took his shot, chattering all the while to Randy about some blood-squirting technique he'd seen in some cheap low budget film on television, and Randy explained how it was done. And when those two were talking, no one else existed. You would have thought the yin and yang had come together, that two destined lovers had at long last met and fulfilled the will of the gods.

Willard made one ball, missed another.

Bear grunted, took his shot.

And missed.

"Damn." He turned his head slowly toward Willard as he straightened up. "Hey, Willard. Take your pet nigger somewhere else. I'm trying to shoot a game here and he's talking through it."

There was a long pause in which it seemed the seasons changed, and Willard stood where we was, expressionless, staring at Bear.

Bear wasn't looking at Willard. He was glaring at Randy. Randy's right foot kept turning out and in, like he was considering running for it, but he was too scared to make the break. He was pinned there, melting like soft chocolate under Bear's gaze.

"Maybe I'll rub your head for luck," Bear said. "You know, with my knuckles. Or maybe that ain't enough. Maybe I'll pull it off and wear it on a chain around my neck for luck. How's that sound, nigger? You like that?"

Randy didn't say a word. His lips trembled like he wanted to say something, but nothing would come out. His right foot was flopping back and forth, not quite able to lead him away.

"Kid didn't do anything," Willard said.

"Talked while I was shooting."

"So did I."

"I ain't forgot that. You want me to, best be quiet."

He and Willard looked at each other awhile, then Bear turned back to Randy. "This won't hurt long," he said, and he stepped in Randy's direction.

"Let him be," Willard said, and he was almost polite about it.

"Warning you, Willard. Don't make this your business. Step aside."

The seasons were changing again as they stared at one another, and it was the right time for us to run, but we didn't. Couldn't. We were frozen.

I glanced about for help. Dan was in the back. And though I doubted he would take our side, he was damn sure one to protect his property if he thought it was about to get smashed. I'd heard he broke a guy's jaw once for accidentally shattering an ashtray.

But Dan didn't come out of the back and the other guys at the bar and at the pool tables looked mildly curious, not helpful. They were hoping for a little blood, and weren't willing to let any of it be theirs. Some of them got out cigarettes and lit them, just in case what Bear was going to do might take a while.

Bear doubled up his fist and snarled at Willard. "Well, what's it going to be?"

We held our breath.

Willard smiled. "All right, Bear. He's all yours."

2 Bear showed his ugly teeth and moved forward, said, "Let's see how you bounce, little nigger."

I was going to move. I swear I was. Bear or no Bear, I was going to try something, even if I got my head torn off for the effort. So was Bob. I could feel him tense beside me, about to move. Kamikaze attack.

But we never got the chance to get ripped apart and dribbled out the door.

Willard's pool cue whizzed out and the thin end of it caught Bear across the back of the neck. There was a cracking noise like the report of small-arms fire, then the pool cue splintered, went in all directions.

Bear turned his head toward Willard and smiled. He had kind of a nice smile.

"Oh, hell," Willard said softly, and his face went sad and ash-colored.

"Stepped in it, didn't you, bro"?" Bear said.

But Willard brought the rest of the cue around the thick end hit Bear a solid lick on the nose. Bear staggered a little. Nothing to brag about, but a little.

Willard swung again, and this time it had plenty of hip in it, and when it met the side of Bear's head it was like Reggie Jackson connecting the good wood on a clean fast ball. The blow actually brought Bear up on his toes and leaned him starboard.

But the bastard didn't go down.

Willard let what was left of the cue drop from his hands, shot out a left jab, hit Bear on the point of his two-car garage, again and again.

A tributary of blood flowed out of Bear's nostrils and made thin creeks through his mustache and beard. Bear tried to hit back, but Willard sidestepped a sloppy right, left-hooked one into him, knocked him into the pool table. Bear's big ass worked as a kind of springboard, bounced him back into Willard, and Willard gave him another combination.

When Bear's minuscule brain realized his face was being made into red grits, he tried to unleash a wild right, but it didn't even come close.

Willard ducked that baby and the wind from the swing lifted his hair. He went into Bear then with an overhand right that connected on Bear's already destructed nose, and he followed it with a hooking left to the kidneys that made the front of the monster's pants go wet.

Then came the right again, an uppercut this time, and this one was backed with powder and a fifty-caliber load. It caught Bear on the point of his chin, lifted him onto the pool table.

Bear's feet came up high, then flopped down over the edge of the table as if his pant legs were stuffed with straw. The echo of Willard's punch reverberated through the pool hall even as Bear's chin and half his jaw turned the color of bad fruit. A thick trickle of blood fled out of his nose, over his beard and onto the greenery of the pool table.

Willard thrust his fist into his mouth and hopped around a little. "Damn, that hurt."

Dan had wandered out of the back room about the time Willard threw his first punch, but he hadn't made a move to stop the fight. He'd just stood there frowning with his arms crossed. But now that the fun was over and there was a broken pool stick and a bloodstained table to complain about, he was furious.

"That was a brand-new pool stick," he said, coming over.

"Not now it ain't," Willard said.

"And that big bastard is bleeding all over my goddamn pool table."

"Fix that." Willard reached out, grabbed Bear by a boot and jerked him onto the floor. Bear made a grunting noise when he hit the tile, but that was it.

"Blood'll mop off the floor easy," Willard said. "I'll pay you for the pool stick."

"Damn sure will. Twenty dollars."

Willard took twenty out of his billfold and gave it to Dan. "There."

"Get out," Dan said. "You hadn't brought them boys in here wouldn't have been no trouble."

"We came in on our own two legs," Bob said.

"You shut up, boy," Dan said, and he cast an eye at Randy. "And this ain't no colored hangout. Ain't no good idea to come here, you hear me, son?"

"Yes, sir."

"Don't 'sir' that line of crap," Willard said. "This is a free country, ain't it?"

Dan studied Willard. "If you're big enough, you're free to do most anything. Now you've paid for the cue, what about the table?"

"What about it?"

"Blood'll stain."

"Use cold water on it."

"Go on, you little smart-mouth sonofabitch. Get on out of here and don't come back. Take these jerks with you, and don't none of you darken this door again."

"No problem," Willard said. "I ain't gonna miss this class joint none."

"And it ain't gonna miss you," Dan said, and kicked Bear in the ribs a couple of times. "You too. Get up from there and get out." Bear didn't move. "Sorry trash."

We went out with Dan still kicking Bear and Bear still not moving.

Out on the sidewalk, Bob said, "Sorry we got you thrown out of there, Willard."

"No sweat. I was tired of it anyway. This whole town, for that matter. It stinks. Don't reckon I'll be staying around much longer. I got laid off at the plant yesterday, and I figure that now is as good a time as any to get out of this one-horse town. In fact, I'm glad I don't have that damn job anymore. It was like working in hell. Always felt like I was making lawn furniture for Satan. I'm free now to go somewhere better and find a good job, something with a future. I got a feeling that me losing that job was just a turning point, and that from here on out, things are going to start looking up."

We stood there, not knowing what to say. Willard watched some cars go by, got out a cigarette and put fire to it. He took a couple of drags before he spoke again.

"Before I leave for good, thought maybe I'd take in that drive-in you guys go to. What do you say? Can I go with y'all over there Friday?"

"Yeah," I said. "Sure. Why not? We leave at five. Where can we pick you up?"

"Larry's Garage. He lets me keep my bike there."

"Sounds good," Bob said. "We'll pick you up in my truck." He pointed to it in the lot.

"I know it," Willard said. "I'll be watching for you guys."

"Good," Bob said.

"Willard?" Randy said.

"Yeah, kid."

"Thanks for not letting me get killed, or otherwise mutilated in a hideous manner."

Willard almost laughed. "Sure, kid. Nothing to it. Saw your buddies were about to step into it, and I didn't want them to have all the fun."

"Generous of you," I said, "considering Bear breathes harder than we hit."

"Hell with it," Willard said. "Always figured I could take him. Now I know."

We walked Willard to his bike. He climbed on and flipped his cigarette in the gutter. Randy stuck out his hand and Willard shook it for a long time. Then he nodded at us, cranked his machine and rode off.

Randy stood there with his hand out, as if he were still shaking with Willard. Willard didn't look back to see if we were watching him. Hell, he knew he was cool.

3

Friday morning I awoke and was attacked by the glare off the garish paperbacks in the little space for books at the head of my bed. The sun was shining through the window and making the red and yellow spines on the astrology and numerology books seem brighter yet. This wasn't the first morning I had awakened to see them there and hated them because they had let me down. I had tried to believe in the little bastards, but life and reality kept coming up against them, and pretty soon I had to decide the planets didn't give a frog jump about me and that numbers were just numbers, and when you got right down to it, pretty boring.

It was like I was punishing myself, leaving them there, and it was like my body knew to get twisted to the edge of the bed so I'd wake up with my head turned toward them so I could see their bright spines shining at me, reminding me that I had spent money on them and that some jackass writer was spending the royalties he got off them, partly provided *by* me, to drink beer and chase women while I read his books and made charts and tried to figure out how to use them to find the right gal and divine the secrets of the universe.

I figured as long as I was punishing myself, I might as well sit up in bed and get so I could see all the spines and really feel rotten. There were also books on Eastern religions that mainly had to do with holding your thumb next to your forefinger, wrapping a leg around your neck and making with some damn-fool chants. There was even one of those hip modern books that told me I just thought I was a schmuck, but wasn't really. It was everyone else, and I was a pretty neat fella. I liked this one best until I realized that anyone with the price of a paperback was a pretty neat fella. That sort of let the air out of my tires.

Only book I didn't have up there on my shelf was one on divining the future through chicken guts, and I'd have had it had it been for sale.

I couldn't figure why I was such a sucker for that stuff. I wasn't unhappy, but the idea of everything just being random didn't suit me, and didn't seem right. And I didn't like the Big Bang theory. It was kind of disappointing, came across like a lab experiment that had gone wrong and made something. I wanted things to be by design, for there to be some great controlling force with a sense of order. Someone or something up there keeping files and notes.

I figured I just hadn't found the right book.

I got out of bed, got a trash sack out of my closet and took all those little dudes off the shelf and put them in the sack. I went downstairs and threw them in the main garbage in the washroom, then went into the kitchen.

Mom was in there running that crap she has for breakfast through a blender. It smelled like wet dog hair and mildewed newspapers to me.

"Want some eggs and bacon?" she asked, and smiled.

She was standing there in her tennis outfit, her long blonde hair pulled back and bound with a rubber band. I'm sure some backyard psychiatrist will make an Oedipal thing out of this, but to heck with it. My mom is damn fine-looking.

She started pouring the smelly mess from the blender into a glass.

"Well, I don't want that," I said. "And if I were you, I'd see if a nest of roaches, or maybe a rat died in that blender overnight."

She grimaced. "Does smell bad, doesn't it?"

"Oh yeah. How's it taste?"

"Like shit."

I got some cinnamon rolls out of the fridge. "Let's have these."

She patted her flat stomach. "Nah. Got to keep my girlish figure. Otherwise, I'll die while I'm out playing tennis. Bad form to die on the court."

"You couldn't gain a pound if you were wearing galoshes."

"For that, you may have two bone-building, nutritious cinnamon rolls. And though I wouldn't normally eat that garbage, pollute my body with those foul chemicals and sugars, I will, on this occasion, knowing how you hate to eat alone, make an exception."

"If you ever finish your speech, that is."

"Precisely."

She sat down and ate four rolls and drank three cups of coffee. When she was through she smacked her lips. "God, but I hated every horrible minute of that. Each bite was agony, acid to my lips. The sacrifices mothers make for their children."

Dad came down. He was wearing an old brown bathrobe that Mom hated. She had tried to throw it away once, but he'd found it in the garbage, rescued it and slinked upstairs with it under his arm. Mom had laughed after him and he had looked down at her, hurt.

She had also given it to Goodwill, thinking they'd turn it into rags, but they'd washed it, put it on the racks. And Dad, looking for used paperbacks, saw it, bought it and came home mad. He told Mom never to say his robe had come apart in the washing again.

That robe *is* an ugly thing, tattered and threadbare. He had at least three good ones in a drawer upstairs, but as far as I knew, he had never so much as tried them on. Wearing that old brown one, his feet in house sandals and his hair thinning on top, he always reminded me of Friar Tuck.

He wobbled in sleepily, weaved over to the counter and came suddenly awake when he got a whiff of what was in the blender.

"Goddamn, woman," he said. "There's something dead in that blender."

"That's what I said, Dad."

"Funny," Mom said. "It's just that old robe you guys smell."

"Ah," Dad said. "The melodious voice of the serving wench. Make me some ham and eggs."

"Poof." Mom said. "You are some ham and eggs. Any more requests?"

"None I can think of," Dad said. He got a bowl, spoon, milk and cereal, arranged them at the table and pulled up a chair.

"What happened to the ham and eggs, Your Majesty?" Mom asked.

"Too lazy to fix them myself."

"And I won't feel sorry for you, will I, snookums?"

"Looks that way," Dad said. He looked at me and grinned. "Up early, aren't you?"

"Friday," I said.

"Ah. No school and tonight is the big night. A trip to the Orbit with the boys. You should try going out with girls, son. They're a lot more fun."

"I go with girls," I said. "It's just that the Orbit is special . . . something I prefer to do with the guys."

"I always liked drive-ins with girls." He looked at Mom. "A purely puritan adventure, of course."

"That's not the way I remember you," Mom said. "Aren't you running late this morning, Mr. Big Shot?"

"I own the company, my dear. I can do damn well as I please. Outside of this house anyway."

"Ha," Mom said. She got up and started for the cabinet. Dad slapped her on the butt. She whirled. "Harold . . . could you do that again?"

I laughed. Dad stood up, grabbed her, bent her back like they do in those old movies. "Woman, my little dove. You are the love of my life. Patting your ass is a pleasure unmatched by gold and video . . . And remember, serving wench, no TV dinners tonight or I sell you to the Arab traders."

He kissed her.

"Thank you, Harold. Now will you lift me up. My back hurts."

"When the going gets rough, when it looks like we're not going to make it, I'll save the last two bullets for us."

"Harold, you're crazy. Now pull me up, will you? My back hurts."

He pulled her up. "That's what happens when you get old. Back trouble. And no sense of romance."

"Go shower and shave . . . and for heaven's sake brush that hair off your teeth," Mom said.

"My breath is sweet. I go to bed with sugar breath, and I awake with it even sweeter. I—"

"Go!"

"Yessuh, Massuh," he said, and shuffled off.

When he was gone Mom gave me an exasperated look. "He's crazy, you know?"

"I know," I said.

A little later on, Mom went to play tennis and Dad went to work and I never saw them again.

4

Before we started going to the drive-in, come summer mornings you couldn't get me up if you fired a bazooka under the covers. But now Friday meant the Orbit, and I was usually up early. And there was also The Early Morning

Monster Show that I had acquired a taste for. It showed on Channel 6 at eight and Randy came over every Friday to watch. Bob would have, but he worked half a day at his dad's feed store. As I said, none of us had to work, but Bob was more willing, and he liked having plenty of pocket change.

So Randy came over and the movie was *The Crawling Eye*, and it wasn't bad until the monsters showed up. The wind kind of went out of its sails after that. It was hard to feel threatened by things that looked like large rubber mops. Still, I enjoyed it, and it gave Randy a chance to make fun of the special effects.

He got what I thought was a sort of strange, even perverse, pleasure out of that, considering most of those movies had been made on a rubber-band budget. But I think it was important for him to have something to look down on, considering he felt pretty much low man on life's totem pole. He had brains and he was nice, but there was some invisible thing about him that led others to direct their hatred toward him, the incident with Bear being a case in point. In fact, I sometimes felt that behind that mousy, quiet exterior was a tyrant without courage, someone looking for his edge on humanity.

He was good in school, but he didn't take any particular pride in that because no one gave a damn. He was knowledgeable about film, makeup and special effects particularly, but again, no competition. Bob and I loved that stuff too, but we weren't wrapped up in it like Randy. So the only thing he could measure his knowledge and skills against were low-budget films, mentally playing out in his mind that he could do better if given a chance.

But the thing I remember best about that morning was Randy turning to me while all hell was breaking loose in the movie (admittedly the hell in the movie wasn't as intense as it ought to have been), and saying, "Do you think Willard has a steady girl?"

"Hell, Randy, I don't know. I'm sure he has girls, but I don't think he's the wear-my-ring kind. I think the tattoo on his arm, EAT PUSSY, is sort of a statement on romance, don't you?"

"Yeah," Randy said. "I suppose so."

After that he just watched the movie, but I could tell his mind wasn't on it. He had a sort of dreamy look in his eyes, like he was thinking about something that lived way down deep in his brain.

About noon we ate some ham sandwiches and drove over to Safeway and bought some supplies for the night: Cracker Jacks, chocolate-covered almonds, potato chips, some Cokes and a few bags of cookies. Bob was supposed to get a case of beer; he had connections. Connections that bought it cheap and sold it dear, and didn't give a damn if you were a minor or a warthog. In spite of that, Bob could deal with them better than we could. He dressed the way they did, could talk their line of talk, and the bottom line was he was so damn tight, when he blinked the skin on his dick rolled back. Just the man for hard money dealings.

He had also promised Randy and me that he would bring us some jerky from his dad, who had made it himself from last season's deer. He'd given us some of it before, and it was fine. In fact, last time he'd given us enough to feed an army. Well, mine mostly fed my dad, even if it did give his teeth a workout. He loved the stuff, tried to convince everyone who came by the house they should too. My dad and Bob's dad should have gone into business together. Bob's dad could make it and my dad could hawk it.

I remember passing the kitchen once, and Dad was sitting in there at the table with one of his business partners, and he had pushed a strip of the meat off on him, and I heard the guy say, "I'm not so hot on this stuff, Harold. It's kind of like chewing on a dead woman's tit."

From then on when I ate the stuff, I had to chew it in an absentminded sort of way, not thinking too much about the texture so I could enjoy it.

We took the goodies home, read some *Fangoria* magazines Randy had brought over, and Bob arrived an hour later than usual for our ventures.

Two things were noticeable right off. One was that the fool was fresh from the shower and hadn't bothered to dry off; his shirt was stuck to his back and the hair that hung out from beneath his hat was wet and shaggy. The second thing was that he had been in a fight; he had a black doughnut around his left eye.

"You know that girlfriend I used to have?" he said.

"Used to have?" Randy asked.

"Yep, used to have. Caught her with Wendle Benbaker."

Wendle was about the size of a small camper trailer. He had played tackle for Mud Creek High until graduation, and his hobby, when he wasn't drinking beer and talking about girls, was talking about girls and drinking beer. He was the only guy I knew who moved his lips over the *Playboy* foldout as well as the magazine's text. I think it was the staples that confused him.

And to be honest, Bob's girlfriend, Leona of the Big Tits, didn't strike me as any great loss. Her nickname was how she was known by the staunchest anti-male chauvinist, both male and female. She invited being called that, even liked it, thought it was an honor; she wore those monstrous boobs like war medals on a proud general's chest.

"Reckon this discovery," I said, "caused you and Wendle to fight."

Bob rubbed his sore eye. "Good, Sherlock. You're right. Jake was supposed to meet me out back of the Dairy Queen with the beer, and he did. But after I loaded it up, I saw Leona and Wendle sitting in his car around front. She was sitting so close she might as well have been wearing his pants with him. Burned my ass up. She told me she didn't do nothing on Fridays but watch TV. Told me I could go with the guys, no sweat. Now I know the hell why. She's been letting Wendle check her oil."

"What did you do?" Randy asked.

"Went over there, yanked the door open and called him a sonofabitch, I think. I was a bit under stress right then and don't remember so good."

I nodded at the black eye. "And I take it he wasn't scared none?"

"Not that I could see. And he can move fast for a big guy. Sucker popped out of that Dodge like a ripe zit and hit me in the eye before I could shag it."

"Looks bad," I said.

"You oughta see him."

"You hit him?" Randy said, amazed. "You hit Wendle the tank?"

"No, but I damn sure got some oil stains on his pants. I mean I ruined them little buddies."

Randy and I let that hang, trying to work it into the scheme of things.

"Oil stains?" I finally asked, as if I were delivering the cryptic line "Rosebud" in *Citizen Kane*.

"When he knocked me down, I crawled under his car and he crawled after me. Some car had been leaking oil there—Wendle's, I hope—and he got his white pants all nastied up. Covered both knees. Won't wash out. Them boogers are ruined."

"That's showing him," I said.

"He was so big I got over beneath the muffler and he couldn't get under there after me . . . remember that if he starts for you. You get under his car by the muffler and you're safe. He can't get there."

"Good tip," I said. "Go for the muffler."

"He did kick me, though. He can get his legs under there after you pretty good, so it ain't completely safe. He jammed my little finger some, but he finally gave up, got back in the car and tried to back it over me."

"Looks to me you escaped," I said.

"Rolled out from under there like a dung bug. You remember how fast I could roll in gym when we was doing that tumbling exercise, don't you?"

"You were an ace roller, as I recall," I said.

"Damn right."

"What was Leona doing?" Randy asked.

"She got out of the car, started screaming and cussing—which was a thing that hurt me. She told me a couple of times she was a lady and didn't say them kind of words. Swore she wouldn't say 'shit' if she had a mouthful. But she was out there yelling at Wendle to pull my head off and to kick a turd down my throat.

"When I rolled out from under the car and started running, her and ole Wendle yelling at my back, I knew right then and there that things between us were over."

"Does sound kind of past the patching stage," I said.

"Well . . . I ruined that sucker's pants."

• • •

We put the goodies in Bob's truck, drove over to Buddy's Fill-up to get gas and some ice for our beer chest.

While we were there, I went to the bathroom to take a leak and Bob joined me at the urinal. The two caballeros.

The place was really nasty, smelled awful. The urinal was stopped up with candy wrappers and some things I didn't want to examine too closely, lest I identify them. Over in one corner was a mashed item I hoped was a Baby Ruth.

Most of the graffiti were illiterate and the artist who had drawn naked women on the walls seemed to lack acquaintance with human anatomy. My dad told me his generation learned a lot about sex from writings and drawings on bathroom walls. I hoped to goodness our generation was getting its information from better sources.

"Nice place, ain't it?" Bob said.

"Maybe we ought to bring us some dates in here."

"We could sit on the commodes and talk."

"Bring in some dip and stuff."

"Have some of them little sausages wrapped in bread with toothpicks through them."

"Serious now," I said. "How are you making it?"

"Good enough. Splashed a little on my boots is all. But I ain't having a good enough time to stick around when I finish. Kind of stinks. How about you? What are your plans?"

"That's funny, Bob."

"Okay, I'm doing fine. She was just some ole gal. You worry about other people too much. Me included."

"Yeah, I'm a regular bleeding heart."

"Well, you are . . . but, yeah, I'm okay. I'm going to miss her some."

"There's nothing to miss, Bob."

"I don't know. Them tits were sure nice and warm."

Randy was leaning on the truck when we came out.

"I was about to organize a search party," he said.

"Well," Bob said, "we got to talking, you know, and damn if we don't have all kinds of things in common."

"Yeah," I said. "You just wouldn't believe."

Randy rolled his eyes. "How about we get in the truck?"

We drove over to Larry's Garage, got there fifteen minutes early, but Willard was out front, smoking a cigarette, the damn thing hanging off his lip like a leech. His long hair was clean and combed back and he wore a black T-shirt with a cigarette pack stuck under one short sleeve. He had a faded blue-jean jacket tossed over one shoulder. He looked like he was waiting for someone to come along so he could mug them.

He strolled over to the truck. "Ready?"

"We're always ready," Bob said.

"You look ready," Willard said. "What happened to your eye?"

"A truck named Wendle Benbaker."

"Get in," I said, "and he'll tell you how he ruined Wendle's pants, and how to hide from him under a muffler."

Randy got out of the truck and made Willard take his place at shotgun. He went around to ride in the back, carrying a *Fangoria* with him to read.

"He's a nice little guy," Willard said when he was seated, his arm hanging out the window.

"That's the truth," Bob said, cranked the truck and drove on out of town. As we went, I took the whole place in, noticed for the first time some houses and stores I had looked at before, but hadn't really seen. We drove down the main drag, past the university that I planned to attend, past the big pines that were slowly being thinned by idiots with no concept of city planning but a firm grasp on the concept of greed; drove past the stinking chicken plant and the plywood plant and the aluminum-chair factory, which Willard saluted with an upward push of his middle finger; drove on out of there with me photographing it all in *my* mind, perhaps sensing somehow it was for the last time.

5

It didn't seem like a night for horrors. Least not the real kind.

It was cool and pleasant. We got there a little later than usual due to some bad traffic. Quite a line had formed. You could see the Orbit's Saturn symbol spinning blue and silver against the night.

"I'll be damned," Willard said.

"We'll all be if we don't change our ways," Bob said.

"Wait until you see the inside," I said.

We moved up in line, finally drove by the outdoor marquee. It listed *I Dismember Mama*, *The Evil Dead*, *Night of the Living Dead*, *The Toolbox Murders* and *The Texas Chainsaw Massacre*.

Inside, the big party had already started. There were lawn chairs planted in the backs of pickups, and folks planted in the chairs. There were people on the hoods and tops of their cars. Punkers. Aging hippies. Conservative types. Fraternity and sorority kids. Families. Cowboys and cowgirls with beer cans growing out of their fists. Barbecue grills sputtered away, lifting sweet smoke into the fine Texas sky. Tape decks whined in conflict of one another. A few lovers on blankets were so hot at it, Willard suggested that they should charge admission. Cars rocked in spastic rhythm to the sexual gyrations of unbridled youth. Someone somewhere called someone a sonofabitch. Other people yelled things we couldn't understand. Bikini-clad women walked by. People in monster suits walked by. Sometimes young men in monster suits chased the bikini-clad women by. Dogs, let out of their owners' cars to do their business, pissed on tires or left deposits of another nature in the vicinity.

And, most important, of course, *there was the screen.*

One of six, it stood stark-white against a jet-black sky, a six-story portal into another dimension.

We tried to get as close as we could, but most of the front rows were taken. We ended up in the middle of a rear row.

We got the lawn chairs out, the goodies. Bob and I went to the concession stand and bought some bloody corn for all of us, and by the time we got back with it, the sleaze classic *I Dismember Mama* had started.

We rolled through that one, drinking, eating, laughing, shouting at the gory spots, and finally *The Toolbox Murders* came on, and it was halfway through that one that it happened.

I don't remember any great change in the atmosphere, anything like that. Everything was normal—for the Orbit. Sights, sounds and smells as they ought to be. The bloody corn was gone, so were several Cokes, and Bob and Willard had made good work of the beers. We were about a third of the way through a bag of chocolate cookies. Cameron Mitchell had just opened his ominous box of tools to take out an industrial nailer, as he had designs to use the wicked instrument on a young lady he'd been spying on in the shower, and we were ready, hoping as much for blatant nudity as celluloid gore, when

—there was light.

It was a light so bright and crimson, the images on the screen paled, then faded.

We looked up.

The source of the light was a monstrous red comet, or meteor, hurtling directly toward us. The night sky and stars around it were consumed by its light, and the thing filled our vision. The rays from the object felt soft and liquid, like being bathed in warm milk and honey.

Collision with the drive-in seemed imminent. My life didn't pass before my eyes, but I thought suddenly of things I hadn't done, thought of Mom and Dad, then, abruptly, *the comet smiled.*

Split down the middle to show us a mouthful of jagged saw-blade teeth. Instead of going out of life with a bang, it appeared we were going out with a crunch.

The mouth opened wider, and I was turning my head away from the inevitable, thinking in a fleeting second that I would be swallowed by it, like Pinocchio by the whale, when

—it whipped up and away, dragging its fiery tail behind it, leaving us awash in flickering red sparks and an even more intense feeling of being engulfed in warm liquid.

When the red pupil paint peeled away from my eyes and I could see again, the sky had gone from blood red to pink, and now that was slowly fading. The comet was racing faster and faster, ever upward, seemingly dragging the moon and stars after it, like glitter swirling down a sewerish drain. Finally the comet was nothing more than a hot-pink pinprick surrounded by black turbulence that sparked with blue twists of lightning; then the dark sky went still, the lightning died out, and the comet was memory.

At first, it looked as if nothing had changed, except for a loss of the moon and the stars. But the exterior of the drive-in was different. Beyond that seven-foot, moon-shimmering tin fence that surrounded it was . . . *nothing.* Well, to be more exact, blackness. Complete blackness, the ultimate fudge pudding. A moment before the tops of the houses, trees and buildings had been visible beyond the drive-in, but now they were not. There was not even a dot of light.

The only illumination came from the drive-in itself: from open car doors, the concession-stand lights, the red neon tubes that said ENTRANCE (ƎƆИAЯTИƎ from our angle) and EXIT, the projector beams, and, most brilliantly, the marquee and the tall Orbit symbol, the last two sources being oddly located on a spur of concrete jutting into the blackness like a pier over night ocean. I found myself drawn to that great symbol, its blue and white lights alternating like overhead fan slats across the concession, making the Halloweenish decorations against the window glass seem oddly alive and far too appropriate.

Then I glanced at the screen. *The Toolbox Murders* was visible again, but there was no fun in it. It seemed horribly silly and out of place, like someone dancing at a funeral.

Voices began to rumble across the lot, voices touched with surprise and confusion. I saw a rubber suited monster take the head off his suit and tuck it under his arm and look around, hoping he hadn't seen what he thought he saw, and that it would be some kind of trick due to bad lighting through the eyes of his mask. A bikini-clad girl let her stomach sag, having lost the ambition to suck it in.

I realized suddenly I was walking toward the exit, and that the gang was with me, and Bob was chattering like an idiot, not making any sense. The din of voices across the lot had grown, and people were out of their cars, walking in the same direction we were, like lemmings being willed to the sea.

One man fired up his car. It was a new Ford station wagon and it was full of fat. Fat driver in a Hawaiian shirt with a fat wife beside him, two fat kids in the back. He jerked the car around a speaker post with surprising deftness, pulled on the lights and raced for the exit.

People scattered before the wagon, and I got a glimpse of the driver's face as he raced past. It looked like a mask made of paste with painted golf balls for eyes.

The headlights hit the darkness, but didn't penetrate. The car pushed down the tire-buster spears with a clack and was swallowed foot by foot by the pudding. It was as if there had never been a car. There was not even the sound of the motor retreating into the distance.

A tall cowboy in a Stetson full of toothpicks and feathers sauntered over to the opening, flexed his shoulders and said, "Let's find out what the hell gives here."

He put a boot on the tire-buster spears to hold them down, stuck his arm into the fudge, up to the elbow.

And the cowboy screamed. Never in my personal history of real life or movie experiences have I heard such a sound. It was like a depth charge to the soul, and its impact blew up my spine and rocked my skull.

The cowboy staggered back, flopped to the ground and turned himself around and around like a dog with its guts dragging. His arm was gone from hand to elbow.

We ran over to help him, but before we could lay a hand on him, he yelled, "Back, goddammit. Don't touch me! It runs."

He started screaming again, but it sounded as if his vocal cords were filling with mud. And I saw then what he meant by "It runs." Slowly his arm was dissolving, the sleeve going limp at the shoulder, then the shoulder folded and he tried to scream again. But whatever was eating him from the outside seemed to be working inside him even faster.

His forehead wobbled forward as bone and tissue went to Jell-O, caved in on the rest of his collapsing face. His cowboy hat came to settle on top of the mess, floated in it. His entire body went liquid, ran out of his clothes in nauseating streams. The stink was awful.

Carefully, holding my breath, I reached out and took hold of one of his boots and upended it. A loathsome goop, like vomit, poured out of it and splattered to the ground.

Beside me, Bob let out with a curse, and Willard said something I didn't understand. I dropped the boot and looked at the darkness beyond the tin fence and the strange truth of it struck me.

We were trapped in the drive-in.

6

That we were trapped in the drive-in was realized immediately by most, but accepted slowly by all of us. And there were some who didn't know right off, like the couple in the Buick parked near where a bunch of us had gathered, looking at the hat, boots and empty clothes of the dissolved cowboy. Neither comet nor screams had reached them. They were too wrapped up in their lovemaking. They were in the back seat of the Buick, and the girl had one ankle draped across the seat and the other on the package shelf. We were all watching the car rock, watching it threaten the shock absorbers and test the strength of four-ply tires. And as the car was at a slant, dipping its rear end toward us, we could see a pale butt rising to view, vanishing, rising, vanishing, all with a regular rhythm, like an invisible man dribbling a basketball. It was something we kept our eyes on, something that tied us to our old reality, and I really hated for it to end and for the girl's ankles to come down, and a little later for them to come out of the car with their clothes rumpled, looking mad at first, then confused. It was our faces that did that to them, the way we were bunched up, the rumble of our voices, the fact that more people were walking our way, and, of course, there was the absolute blackness all around.

Someone tried to tell the couple about the comet, the fat folks in the Ford and the brave (or stupid) cowboy who got dissolved, and they just grinned. The guy said, "No way."

"Well," Bob said, waving a hand at the fudge surrounding the drive-in, "I guess we just dreamed all this crap. You think we're giving you a bill of goods, why don't you two just take you a little stroll out in that shit—but don't expect to come back."

The guy looked at the girl; she looked at him; he looked at us and shook his head.

People tried radios, CBs, and some clustered to the concession to make a stab at the phones. But nothing was in order. Just a little static on the radios.

The crowd grew. Must have been over a hundred of us standing around, and more people were coming. They were starting to congregate over in Lot B too, in little spots here and there. Some were driving cars around and around, honking horns, maybe not scared yet, but certainly bewildered. But that didn't go on long. Pretty soon no cars were moving about, just groups of people, talking or looking lost.

A story came to us from Lot B about a motorcycle gang that was over there, about how one of their members panicked and drove his bike off into the stuff, with the same result as our fat man and his calorie-laden family in the Ford station wagon.

The theories started then, those by the loudest and most persistent ones among us being the ones heard. The man with the beer gut wearing a T-shirt a size too small with a mustard blossom on the neck of it, for instance.

"Well, I think it's them men from outer space, whatever color they are. They've done this to us. With us shooting our rockets and stuff up there, they were bound to get sore with us. So they've come down with some of them sophisticated weapons they've got, and they've done this. I don't see how it could be anything else."

"I don't think so," said a guy in a sports coat, his hair neat and stiff as a J.C. Penney model. "I suspect the Communists. They're a lot stronger in this country than most people imagine. And I don't want to open any old wounds here, but maybe McCarthy wasn't as far off as some people thought. These Communists are into everything, and they've said all along that they planned to take us over."

"Why in the hell would they want some Texas drive-in picture show?" Bob said. "They like horror movies, or what? That don't make no damn sense. I like the one about the guys from outer space, whatever color they are, better than that, and that's dumb."

"Hey," said the man with the mustard-colored T-shirt.

"Call 'em like I see 'em," Bob said.

"It's the will of God," said a girl in a long blue cotton dress. "There was so much sinning going on here, God has sent a blight."

The couple who had been practicing the rites of the three-toed salamander in the back of the Buick started shuffling their feet and looking over the heads of the crowd as if they were expecting someone.

"It wasn't God," said somebody at the rear of the crowd, "it was Satan done it. God doesn't punish. Man and Satan punish."

"We're uptight for nothing," said another voice. "Tomorrow the sun will come up and shine through this mess. It's just a freak of nature, that's all."

"No," said a punker girl with orange spiked hair. "It's dimensional invaders."

No one bought that one.

A pretty girl in a pink bathing suit suggested, "Maybe we're all dead, and, like, hanging in limbo or something."

Some consideration on that. A couple of maybes from the crowd; I think it might have edged out the Commie threat a bit in popularity.

"Ain't none of them things," said a fat lady with a nose like a red pickle. She was wearing a pink and green housecoat that could have served as a visual emetic and yellow bunny slippers. She had her arm around her skinny husband's waist and two small ankle biters (a girl and a boy) were at her feet.

"It's the ghost of Elvis Presley. I read about something like this in *The Weekly World News*, and Elvis was involved in that. His ghost came down and did some things to some sinners. He said to them that he wasn't happy with the way people were living on Earth."

"Hell," Bob said. "He's got to be a self-righteous sonofabitch now that he's dead. He wasn't nothing but a fat doper."

"He was the King," the woman said, as if she were talking about Jesus.

"King of what?" Bob said. "Constipation? I heard he died on the floor of his toilet with a turd hanging out of his ass. Report said he died 'straining at stool.' He wasn't any more than the rest of us, except he could sing. And even then, he wasn't any Hank Williams."

"Hank Williams," said the fat lady, taking her arm from around her husband's waist and looking as if she were about to leap. "Now there was a drunk and a doper. And he wasn't near as good-looking as Elvis."

"That may be," Bob said, "but you don't hear of his ghost coming down to bother nobody. He knew to mind his own business."

This went on for a time, not really solving anything, but it was entertaining. I got to thinking about how much time had elapsed, and looked at my watch. It had stopped.

Bob and the lady with the red pickle nose had finally quit going at it, and a black guy wearing a straw hat and a worn-out gray sweatshirt with "Dallas Cowboys" on it spoke up then. "We could be here a time. What about food? We're gonna need that."

I thought about the cookies and junk back at the truck and wished we'd brought something more substantial, but then maybe that was carrying worry too far, projecting this strange situation too distantly in the future.

The manager of the main concession joined us then. "Look, it isn't going to come to that, worrying about food, I mean. This will pass. Whatever it is, it can't last long. But to ease your minds, let me tell you that if we're here awhile, if food becomes a problem, we've got enough back there in that concession, and over on Lot B, to last a long time."

"How long is a long time?" Willard said.

"A long, long time," the manager said. "But let's don't jump the gun here. This'll pass. Maybe some sort of industrial accident put this mess around us."

"And the comet?" Randy said.

"I don't know, but I'm sure there's a logical explanation to it all, and I don't see any need to get worked up over starving to death. We haven't been in this mess but a few minutes, and I can tell you now, it won't last."

"God has spoken," Bob said, and the manager glared at him.

"I think we all ought to hold tight," the manager said. "Go on back to your cars, try to forget all this, get your mind on the movies. Pretty soon someone will come to get us out of this. Some kind of accident happened out there, someone knows about it. Hell, they'll have the National Guard in here pretty soon."

"That makes me feel comfy all over," Bob said. "My uncle is in the National Guard and he don't know dick about nothing, has a belly that hangs down to his knees. Great, the National Guard."

"You boys think like you want," the manager said. "Me, I'm going back to the concession, try the phones again, see if they've got to working. Tomorrow we'll all have something to tell our families about."

"Right," Randy said. "A comet smiled at us, put us in Limbo Land, and the edge of Limbo Land ate a station wagon full of fat people and dissolved a cowboy."

The manager tried to smile. "I'm not saying this isn't a dangerous situation, but I am saying we have to make the best of it. Keep our spirits up, stay away from that gas . . . jell, whatever it is . . . and you'll see. We'll be fine. Now I'm going on back to the concession to try the phones."

The manager went away and Randy said, "Yeah, fine."

"He's right, though," a tall guy said. "We can't do much else. We've got to make the best of it . . . unless someone here has a great idea."

No one did.

One guy went out to the trunk of his car, came back with an old box and a shovel. He scooped up the cowboy and put him in the box. The mess had lost its acidic quality and was congealing. The box remained intact. He used the point of the shovel to scoop up the clothes and the boots, dropped the hat on top of it all.

"I'll just . . . keep him in my trunk," he said. "Wife said she didn't mind . . . seems like the decent thing to do. Maybe we can figure out who he is . . . get his folks to bury him when we get out . . . Anybody here know him?"

No one said they did.

"Guess he came by himself," the guy said, and carried the shovel and the cowboy in the cardboard box away.

"What a way to end up," Bob said. "In the trunk of a car next to a spare tire."

"In a dirty box, no less," Randy said.

Now to make a long story short, or at least this part of it, this went on, this standing around and talking, this looking at the black mess and waiting for the National Guard, but no one showed up to rescue us.

"We've talked and talked about it," Willard said, "but nothing's gotten any better."

"I'm gonna get me a Baby Ruth," Bob said. "It's good for my skin."

"Not much else to do, is there," I said.

"Let's just do like the manager suggested," said the black guy in the straw hat.

We drifted away from the crowd, and the crowd started to break apart, wandering back to their cars with a stunned look on their faces. The immediate drama was over and nothing had changed. We were still trapped in the drive-in, and the adventure of it was old already.

We all went back to the truck, and I took up my position in the chair and recovered my bag of popcorn. I even found I could get interested in the movies again.

Bob came back with his Baby Ruth and smacked his lips over it enough to make me look through our stuff for some cookies. I had eaten so much I was beginning to feel queasy.

We watched the movies, but after they had run through and started over again, I began to lose interest and really worry. With that many movies shown, and them starting a second run, it ought to be getting toward dawn. There wasn't a ray of sunlight, however. Just the same artificial lights. I was getting sick of movies, the drive-in, even the goofballs who were wandering around in monster suits. I couldn't even feel any warmth for the gals in their bikinis. I felt like a roach in a toilet bowl with someone's hand on the handle, ready to flush. I wanted to go home to my nice warm bed, with Mom and Dad down the hall.

The concession manager we had talked to spoke over the speakers. "The phones still aren't on, folks, and we haven't been able to pick up anything on the radio, but I'm sure the National Guard is on this, and we'll be out of here soon—"

"Guy has a hard-on for the National Guard," Bob said.

"—until then, we're going to keep right on showing the movies, and if there's no help by the time of the third one, we'll be serving breakfast here at the concession—on the house. No eggs and bacon, I'm afraid. But we've got hot dogs, fresh hot popcorn, plenty of candy and soft drinks, plus some real good orange drink we got in just for tonight."

The manager went off then, and Bob said, "Here we are surrounded by acidic goo, and all this guy can think about is the National Guard, free hot dogs and good orange drink."

"The odd thing to me," Randy said, "is how come the electricity works here in the drive-in, but radios, things that connect us to the outside world, don't? Hell, my watch has even stopped."

"Mine too," I said.

Bob took out his pocket watch. "This one's dead too. First time ever."

"Bet they're all dead," Willard said. It was the first time he had said a word in some time. He had just been sitting, watching the movies, eating popcorn. "Time is an outside connection too."

"You getting at something, Willard?" I asked.

"Not really. I don't know any better what's going on than anyone else. But this all has a kind of artificial feel to it . . . like, hell, I don't know—"

"A B science-fiction movie," Randy said.

"Yeah," Willard said. "I guess so."

"Personally," Bob said, "I think the lady in the blanket and bunnies was right. It's the ghost of Elvis."

"I just hope the damn bulbs and such in the projectors don't burn out," Willard said. "Or in the Orbit sign. They do, and it's going to be some kind of dark in here."

Willard got out his cigarettes, passed them around. We all took one, just as if we smoked, and Willard put his lighter to them, and we leaned against the truck and puffed them until we coughed.

"That poor cowboy," Randy said. "It melted him like salt melts a slug. Looked like cheap special effects. Like in that movie *The Hydrogen Man*, or maybe *The Blob*."

"And that fat family and their car," Bob said. "Rendered right down, I figure."

So we smoked our cigarettes and the movies rolled on.

7

After a time, I gave it up and crawled in the back of the truck, found one of the bedrolls we kept back there for camping trips, got in it and fell asleep. Kind of sleep you get from depression and absolute exhaustion.

I dreamed about what Randy had said, about this being like a B science-fiction movie, and the dream was very real. It was like I was tapped into some truth somewhere. There was this B-string god and he was making a movie. He didn't have the power to make the Big Movie, so he just borrowed some people (us) and a setting (the drive-in) and made do with that. Real shoestring stuff. There was a bunch of other creatures with him, maybe they were gods too—hell, maybe none of them were gods—and they were like technicians and the like. They were real ugly hombres. They were speaking in a language I had never heard before, but I could understand it. The main ugly was telling them that it all had to be under budget. If it wasn't, it was all over. He wanted them to do it cheap but be proud. Mostly, he wanted it quick. The technicians were very much in agreement. In fact, they seemed agreeable to most anything the main critter wanted.

It all seemed very real.

Then it was like someone was calling me, my dad yelling at me to come eat breakfast, but the voice didn't sound quite right. It sounded far away, filtered.

And when I woke up and ran my hand through my hair I was in the bedroll in the camper, and the voice was coming from the outside, and it was Bob's.

I got out of the bedroll and came out of the back of the camper, still groggy.

"I was about to come in there and drag your ass out," Bob said. "Breakfast, such as it is, is being served."

I sat on the tailgate of the truck and looked at a line forming at the concession. People were talking in a friendly, if not happy, way, but you could feel the tension in the air, like some sort of invisible mesh. Seeing all those folks, thinking about what the line must be like over at Lot B, I realized that big as the Orbit was, it wasn't *that* large, and there were a lot of hungry people here, and when it came to living here awhile, it could get pretty crowded. And fast.

But at this point, things were still not bad. This was the time between hot dogs and horrors. When people were still trying to pull together, stiff upper lip, like all those old science-fiction movies where an alien menace makes them cooperate to thwart it, and in the end Earth overcomes and learns to live as one, and Moscow opens some McDonald's and Disneyland puts in a branch over there.

We got in a breakfast line and went through. There were three people operating the concession stand, plus the manager. I noticed the girl giving out the candy right off, and in time I would come to think of her as the Candy Girl. She was blonde and very pretty. She had cheekbones so sharp you could have picked your teeth with them. It looked fine on her. If she hadn't been so short she would have looked like a model instead of a doll.

"There's plenty of food here," the manager said loudly, trying to keep everyone's spirits up. "Everything's going to be all right. It might take a little time, but it'll all work out in the wash . . ."

I felt sorry for the manager. He was really trying. But Bob didn't give a damn.

"National Guard show up yet?" Bob asked.

The manager gritted his teeth. "Not yet."

I got my hot dog, drink and candy, and up close the Candy Girl was no disappointment. The dark brown uniform dress she wore set her skin and hair off nicely. She had dark brown eyes, pale, clear skin. Her legs looked nice. I wouldn't have minded being strangled between them. She was as delicious as the sweets she was passing out.

I said hi to her and she gave me a quizzical look and said it back.

So our ritual started. We would eat our meals, go back and watch the movies, visit with folks who came by and wanted to talk, mostly speculating on what was happening. Nobody had an idea any better than Willard's and Randy's about it all being a B movie, and nothing as loony as Elvis Presley's ghost, which made all the other ideas a little less loony in comparison.

One guy from Lot B came by regularly. He was tall and lean and probably thirty. He carried all the information from one lot to the other, sort of a town crier. Because of that, we got so we simply called him Crier, and he liked it and adopted the name.

"I used to drive a beer truck for Budweiser," Crier said. "Only Friday, whenever the hell that was, I got in the samples, if you know what I mean, and turned me a corner a little quick and I didn't have the door closed tight, and I slung Bud all over the highway. Bunch of cars behind me had blowouts on the glass, and some other folks grabbed up the crates that weren't broken before I could get the truck braked and run the hell off with them. Budweiser frowned on this and canned me. I got good and drunk and come to the drive-in. I wish now I'd stayed home and watched the Friday-night movie on television. It looked like it was gonna be a good one. One of them Godzilla-versus-another-guy-in-a-monster-suit movies. Before my wife left me for a Miller Lite driver, me and her and our dog Boscoe, he's dead now on account of I backed the beer truck over him, used to sit up on the couch and watch them Jap movies every chance we got. There ain't a comedy good as a Jap monster movie."

"How are things all about?" Willard asked.

"I guess it's better than heart disease at the moment, but it's about to turn real nasty. There are signs. I always had a knack for signs. I could watch the news or read in *People* magazine about something, and I could always project, you know. Meaning I could look at a thing and see where it was really going. It's a gift."

"Well, where's it going then?" Willard asked, shaking us all out a cigarette.

"As I was saying," Crier said, taking a smoke and putting it in his mouth and producing his own lighter, "there are signs. Over in Lot B a man and a woman pulled their car up close to the tin fence, got on the roof of the car and climbed over the fence into that black crap. So long, sweeties. Suckers went out like June bugs on a hot griddle. It was quick, though. I seen a fella fall under one of them rollers they use to flatten out tar on the highway once, now that was tough. And it didn't kill him right away. Can you believe that?"

"Yeah?" Willard said.

"Yeah," Crier said, and he gave details, then went away.

Without clocks, the sun and the moon to measure time by, it was up to the projectionists to mark the hours. They did this by counting the number of movies they changed. They kept them running constantly. Six of them. Three from our concession stand and film house, another three from the concession in Lot B. When one film was finished, they would measure by its reel time. Usually about an hour and a half per flick. That way, when enough films had been changed, they could compute time for meals. The manager would then announce over the speaker: "Snack bar will be serving breakfast now." Or whatever meal was on the roster. Not that it mattered, since it was the same stuff every time.

"Hot damn," Bob would say, "popcorn. They make a mean bag here, don't they? Regular four-star restaurant." And he would always ask the manager about the National Guard.

That Bob. What a kidder.

For a while I tried using one of Bob's old history composition notebooks and a Bic pen to keep time by the number of movies seen, like the projectionists. But I could never remember if the mark on paper was for the previous movie or the one I had just seen. Things ran together kind of rapid like.

I don't think I was the only one having trouble with time. I think the projectionists were missing it now and then too. Certainly, I was pretty hungry a few times, and I think they missed calling us for meals. But mistakes were expected. I could attest to the fact that keeping time by the number of movies shown wasn't an exact science. And I was sick of the movies. I knew them by heart. You could hear people across the drive-in chanting the dialogue ahead of the actors. Sometimes I dozed when the zombies were eating guts, or when Mitchell was using the industrial nailer on the pretty woman from the shower.

People continued to be patient. Or most. There were a few fights. I saw a guy slug a guy in front of us once, but I don't know what started it. It was fast and explosive. But mostly, people were doing pretty good. It was still like what I was talking about earlier, about those old science-fiction movies where we all pull together against the menace. Only our menace was silent and surrounded us, and we didn't have any bombs to throw at it, and the damned old National Guard didn't seem likely to show up.

When we were tired, we slept in the camper using the bedrolls, giving Willard spare blankets and an old backpack for a pillow. Sometimes one of us would sleep in the cab, or lie down on our bedroll under the truck. We didn't always sleep at the same time. Bob especially seemed to have a different body clock. He would usually climb into the camper for a nap when we were waking up. There seemed to be something furtive about this, but I couldn't figure what it was, unless he wanted to masturbate.

We used the bathroom at the concession, but I could see that wasn't going to last. It didn't work well. It was getting so bad I longed for the toilet at Buddy's Fill-up.

My highlights were saying hi to the Candy Girl and eating. It got so I was getting kind of fat. I took up exercising, but I couldn't stay with it. Just too damn tired. Nothing seemed real or important. The idea of being trapped in the drive-in, though depressing, began to seem normal, as if we had always been there. I wondered why ants in ant farms didn't commit suicide.

The weather in the drive-in was fairly consistent. Not too warm, not too cold. Yet it did change occasionally. Wild winds would twist up out of nowhere and tear across the lots, blowing paper cups and popcorn bags before them like frightened coveys of quail. The paper would fly against the wind-rattled tin fences or over them and into the blackness to be consumed. Sometimes the wind was so strong it shook the truck like a mechanical pony ride.

There was also a now-and-then movement in the blackness overhead. It bulged down, made lumps. Fuzzy blue lightning leaped out of it, produced crackling stick figures that danced across the strange sky to the rhythm of metallic thunder and ran together like idiots to explode in dazzling displays of fireworks.

It never rained, however, and it got so the electrical storms were welcome. They were a break from the monotony. They gave more light. People would lie on the ground, or on top of their cars, hands behind heads, looking up, entranced.

And when there wasn't the lightning, there were the meals at the concession, and the movies. The movies, ever rolling: chainsaws and zombies, drills and screams, common as spit.

With all of us so close together, it got so sex was super casual, damn near a spectator sport. There had always been this element at the Orbit, but it was more blatant than ever, and the romance had gone out of it. To the front of us a group formed that participated in orgies. We were hurt no one invited us over. We used to sit in lawn chairs and watch them wallow on the asphalt. Bob would cheer them on and call out points, and I would wonder where they got their energy. Watching them made me tired.

I remember this little girl who used to walk her poodle between the fornicating bodies. She must have been about eleven. The bodies could have been hedges for all she and the mutt cared. The dog had a pink bow, the girl a red one. The dog was too small in its white fur, the girl too small in her dress. The red ribbon against her oily blonde hair looked like a wound.

There were fights. People got mad over very little. Over to our right a fellow wearing a welder's cap got into some kind of shindig with a hatless fella over the quality of the chainsaw Leatherface was using in yet another viewing of *The Texas Chainsaw Massacre*. They did some excellent name-calling. Even Willard and Bob were impressed, and they were well versed in tongue-lashing. Willard had been raised on the streets, and Bob had a dad who thought most of humanity was a sonofabitch, and that the word "sonofabitch" itself was the period to a sentence. "I'll be a sonofabitch. There goes that sonofabitch. You got to watch them sonofabitches. Remember now, boys, folks are just sonofabitches."

The guy with the hat was the sharper of the two, as he had a three-foot length of two-by-four, while the hatless fella had only a popcorn sack, and that mostly empty. Even as Leatherface chased an intended victim across the screen, Hat laid a lick on Hatless's noggin that would have made a sadist wince. Hatless, wobbling a little from the blow, flapped his popcorn bag at Hat, and the bag burst open and sent popcorn bouncing into the night.

It got better than championship wrestling. Folks nearby, maybe friends or relatives, or just interested parties, got in the act, chose up sides, started kicking and slugging. After a while, sides didn't matter. It was getting the good blow in that counted. One guy got crazy, ripped a speaker off a post, went at everyone and anyone with it. He was good, too. Way he whipped that baby around on that wire made Bruce Lee and his nunchukkas look like a third-grade carnival act.

He started coming our way, whirling the speaker fast as a propeller, yelling. He smashed the windshield out of the car next to us.

From my lawn chair I could see him coming straight for me. Bob had already vacated his seat and beat a hasty retreat. He called for me to do the same, but I couldn't move. I was excited and wanted to move, but couldn't quite find the energy to get up. Lately everything was a major chore, even fleeing before a madman. I waited for my destiny. Death by drive-in speaker.

Willard calmly got the baseball bat out of the truck and stepped smoothly over and swatted a home run with the guy's head before he could reach me. The best part of me feared the fella was dead, the worst part of me hoped he was.

"Thanks, Willard," I said. I could have been thanking him for a cigarette the way it came out.

"Hell," he said. "I was going to do that anyway."

The fight was still going on, though it was now moving in the other direction. There was a guy in the car that had gotten its windshield knocked out, and he was sitting there behind the windshield with glass in his hair and on his shoulders. He looked as if he'd tried to ram his head through a block of ice and made it. "Who's gonna pay for all this?" he said. "That's what I want to know."

No one came forward with an answer.

The fight was so far down the lot now, encased in shadow, the grapplers looked like frogs jumping together. After a while, you could just hear cussing, but it was losing some of its originality.

I finally shifted my chair and started watching the next movie, *Night of the Living Dead.* Out of the corner of my eye, I saw the guy Willard had swatted wake up. The side of his head looked dark and pregnant. He had one eye open and he was moving it from left to right, scoping things out.

He rolled smoothly and gently onto his stomach, started to crawl off, dragging the speaker behind him by the wire. He didn't seem to notice it was clattering on the asphalt like a bad transmission. He crawled a great distance down the row of cars and disappeared under a Cadillac festooned with so many curb feelers it might be mistaken for a giant centipede. He stayed there through most of *Night,* and by the time of the next movie, he was brave enough to crawl out from under it, go on his hands and knees for a few yards, rise up to a squatting run and weave off into a maze of parked automobiles, the speaker following him like a tail.

I looked around for Bob, Randy and Willard. They were not in sight. Perhaps they had gone to sleep, or gone off to look around the lots for girls, for action. Me, I didn't want to get out of my chair. I didn't know what was wrong with me, and couldn't seem to concern myself with it. I closed my eyes and thought again of B-string gods. In the dream these gods were made of big eyes and bladders and tentacles. They had a cobbled look, as if a good special-effects man was doing the best he could with leftover parts. They were the same creatures as in the dream before, but they were clearer this time, as if my brain had been focused.

They were up there behind the blackness, and when they writhed across it, it made those bumps we saw from time to time. They had great machines with great cogs and wheels and gears and gauges. They had switches that made lightning. They even had lightning that came out of the tips of their tentacles. They took clubs and beat large sheets of metal for thunder. They talked in that strange language, a noise like a rat with its tail in a fan. Like before, it made no sense, yet I understood it. They were talking about motivation of scene, drama, needing something ugly and special. One wanted some cuts. Another thought there was too much sitting around and it wasn't funny enough. He said something about humor making horror better. The gods argued. Finally they put their misshapen heads together and agreed on something, but whatever it was wouldn't stay with me. I felt as if I had tuned in on them, and was now being tuned out.

Then I wasn't thinking of that anymore. The dream had gone to steak and potatoes, country gravy and toast, a big glass of ice tea. In the background of this dream the speaker coughed out screams from *The Toolbox Murders*, or maybe it was *I Dismember Mama*. It didn't matter. I fell into a deep, deep sleep, the screams my lullaby.

8

Dingo City.

Everything started getting fuzzy around the edges. Sometimes my lawn chair moved through time and space. (Spin me around, Jesus, save me stars, get Scorpio in line with my moon, Lord Almighty, let my good number come up, put some beefsteak on the table and wish me luck.)

It got so about all I could do was eat and sit in that chair. And take care of my bodily functions, and that had become quite a chore. Not only was I weak, but the restroom had gotten so bad I didn't want to use it. The odor waited there for me like a mugger, and inside the concrete bunker the floor had gone so stale and tacky with overflowing toilets and urinals, my shoes stuck to it like cat hairs to honey. I damn near needed skis to get to the john, which was now doorless, the hinges hanging like frayed tendons. And once I made it that far, I would find the commode even more studded with cigarette butts, candy wrappers, used prophylactics and the stuff that was supposed to be there. What the toilet wouldn't hold was on the floor. So going into that stinking pit was rather pointless. I was terrified at the idea of standing over one of those malodorous urinals or johns (this item of wisdom crayoned above the latter: REMEMBER, CRABS CAN POLE-VAULT) and having something ugly, fuzzy, multilegged and ravenous leap out at me.

I took to using large popcorn tubs to do my business in, carried them to the tin fence and used a flat board I had found to catapult tub and contents into the blackness to be devoured.

Take that, B-string gods.

Sometimes I was so dizzy I couldn't even carry the tubs to the fence to launch them, and then Bob would do it for me. He was the only one of us who seemed firm, relatively unchanged. I wondered what his secret was, or if he had any. I kept wanting to ask, but the words hung in my throat like phlegm. What if there wasn't a secret and there was no knowledge that could help me.

I took to sitting in the lawn chair for longer and longer periods, watching the movies. They were familiar and they made me comfortable. I liked the movies better than people. They were so damned dependable. The same ghosts were revived and slaughtered again and again. Leatherface became adorable. He seemed like an action kind of guy. Knew what he wanted and went after it. Didn't sit around in a lawn chair feeling dizzy. He ate good, too.

Bob leaned over the chair and put his face down close to mine. "You know," he said, "you need to get you some focus. Quit looking at them movies, you're starting to drift." He gave me a pat on the shoulder and went away. I fell into the well of film for a time and came out when I heard voices, some laughter.

"What did you think about that?" Willard's voice. I was too weak to turn and look at him.

"Great." Randy's voice. "I hit him right where you said, the way you showed me, right on the button. Did it kill him?"

"Naw," Willard said. "You just decked him. You get a guy on the chin like that, especially when he's not expecting it, and most of the time he'll go down."

The camaraderie in their voices was strange. Like Siamese twins rediscovering each other after a lengthy separation at birth. Maybe meeting at a dogfight, or something bloody.

Randy had gone from quiet and shy to swaggering, and Willard had become content, like an empty cup that had been filled.

And me, I was out in Bozo Land, flying about in a lawn chair, watching stars and planets and hamburgers fly by. Something about that bothered me, but I couldn't nail down exactly what it was. I watched Leatherface for a time, then heard:

"Let's look for trouble," Randy said.

Willard laughed. "We are trouble."

"Maybe you boys are getting a mite out of hand." It was Bob's voice. Calm and in control. "You're not eating good, none of us are, and it's changing us. We're not thinking right. We've got to—"

"Mind your own business." It was Willard's voice, and it was a snarl. "You just take care of the basket case over there and leave us alone."

"Have it your way," Bob said.

I think I flew away in my lawn chair then. I don't know how long I was gone, but when I came back to earth, my chair had been turned around so that I was facing the truck. I think Bob had done that, to keep me from watching the movies.

Randy and Willard were on the hood of the truck. Willard was stripped down to his underwear. Randy had a gallon-sized popcorn tub on his head for a hat. He had poked holes in either side of it and run a piece of leather (probably from his belt) through it so he could fasten it under his chin. He was leaning over Willard, who was lying on his stomach, and he had Willard's knife, and he was using it to cut designs in his back. He'd cut, then use a popcorn bag to sop up the blood. He'd put the bag in his mouth and suck on it while he used the black asphalt from the lot (he had it collected in a large Coke cup) to rub into the wounds he was making. From where I sat I could make out animal designs, words, a bandolier of bullets even. All of the tattoos had the slick look of crude oil by moonlight.

Bob floated into view. "Ya'll ought to quit that. End up getting an infection and ain't a thing can be done about it here."

"I've told you to mind your own business," Willard snapped.

"Yeah," Bob said, "and I said I'd mind it too. So carve away, Randy. It's his skin. But don't screw up the hood of my truck. Blood'll rust it."

Willard, who had raised up on his elbows, relaxed again. Randy looked at Bob for a moment, then looked at me, smiled like a cannibal watching the pot, then bent to his work.

And so it went.

Movies and tattoos.

I got so weak that Bob would have to help me to the concession for my meals. The Candy Girl had lost her smile and a lot of flesh, the sharp bones in her face were like tent poles pushing at old canvas, her hair was as listless as a dead horse's tail.

She didn't put the candy in your hand now; she slapped it down on the counter and let you pick it up. She seldom stood anymore, preferred to roost in a chair behind the counter, just the top of her head showing. I quit saying hi. She didn't miss it.

The manager and the counter boy argued with patrons and with each other. Bob still asked the manager about the National Guard, but now the manager would cry. Finally, even Bob felt sorry for him and didn't mention it again.

When we got our food, Bob would help me back to the truck and feed me by hand. I couldn't make my fingers work, couldn't always keep the food down. It was too sweet. My teeth felt loose and my gums hurt.

And the drive-in changed. People were not so good now. Nobody said "please" and "thank you" anymore. Patience was as hard to find as steak. The fight I'd seen with the welding-cap fella and the others had been just a preview. It was going a step beyond that. There was lots of yelling and fighting now. We heard gunfire frequently over in Lot B and from the west screen in Lot A. When Crier came by he would talk about murder. He had developed a sense of humor about it and was able to mix it in with his telling. It had gotten so nothing was real to me.

I remember seeing the father of the little girl with the poodle come out of their car, butt naked, climb on the roof and hop around yelling, "I feel better now, I surely do, yes, sir." Then he hopped down, ran across the lot, leaped onto the hood of a car, leaped off, repeated the process down the row until, in mid-leap from a Toyota, he was shot out of the air by a big fat guy brandishing a pump shotgun.

The little girl had come out of the car to watch her father's run, and when he was shot, she yelled, "Two points," at the top of her lungs. I thought it was more like four, and something inside me told me I should be concerned about that kind of attitude, but the voice was small and tired.

Later I saw the little girl wearing a ratty white cape held to her neck by a dog collar. The cape had a pink ribbon on it. The little girl was dragging the empty leash around the lot talking to it. Her mother, who looked like a death-camp survivor, was telling her, "Don't tug on it."

All this scared Bob enough to get his shotgun down, and he kept it close by him for a while. Eventually he returned it to the rack in the truck, chained and locked it.

I remember some of Crier's visits. He came by often. He had found a hoe handle somewhere, and he used it for a walking stick. His hair was almost to his shoulders. He said there had been murders again.

"There were these two brothers over in Lot B," he said, "and they got into it over a popcorn kernel that rolled under their truck. The fastest brother dove under after it, and the slower brother cut the quick one's throat, pried his mouth open, got the bloody kernel and ate it. Afterward, he cut his own throat."

"That ain't good," Bob said.

"I'll say. And the brothers' bodies disappeared, and a short time thereafter there were some well-fed folks over there stepping pretty lively, and I reckon what happened with the brothers was what got this couple fired up to eat their baby *raw*."

Crier had emphasized 'raw' as if that were the crime. Smoked, barbecued or plain fried baby was probably all right with him, but *raw*?

Personally, I couldn't see a thing wrong with a raw baby. The idea of eating a baby had certainly not become acceptable to me, but I was beginning to think ahead to the time when it would, and I was quite certain I wouldn't mind my baby raw. Oh, I'm like anyone else, I prefer my meat cooked, but if raw was the only way my baby would come, then raw it was.

"They were out there eating this kid on the hood of their car," Crier continued. "Each one had a leg and was going at it, and the motorcycle gang over there, Banditos, I think they call themselves, seen this and they got some upset, brothers."

"Cause the baby was raw?'" I asked.

"I don't think so," Crier said. "The cycle guys have taken over in B Lot. They run the concession and keep the movies showing. They've appointed themselves the police officers for over there, and I figure this side of the lot is next when they get around to it.

"Anyway, they got this wrecker from somebody over there, took that couple of baby-eaters and hung them one at a time from the wrecker's wench. When that was done, they tore the couple's car apart looking for food. Found some popcorn kernels and a chocolate almond under the back seat. The corker is someone stole what was left of the kid when the bikers weren't looking, and one of their own men got up there on the hood and started licking the spot where the baby had been. The bikers had to take him over to the wrecker and hang him too. Afterward, the bodies of the executed disappeared faster than a horny man's conscience. Oh, they found the clothes, but not the stiffs that went in them. They watched for charcoal smoke around and about from those who brought barbecue grills, but no smoke was detected. You might say Lot B's law enforcement was thwarted."

"When you get some more cheerful news like that, Crier," Bob said, "you be sure and come share it with us."

"I will," Crier said, winking, and he moved on.

"I think he's a little too cheery about things," Bob said. "Then again, maybe my sense of humor is on the blink."

Moment by moment I felt worse. Got so bad Bob had to decide when it was time for me to sleep. He'd come get me from my chair and guide me over to the truck and put me inside to lie down. Randy and Willard had gotten even chummier, and they didn't have anything to do with us anymore. They took to sleeping under the truck.

Willard had given up his underwear and now went around naked. Randy had tattooed Willard's buttocks so that it looked as if black dahlias were blooming out of the crack of his ass. When he walked, the flower arrangement wiggled as if moved by the wind.

Black blooms on a white-marble ass. I should have seen it as some kind of omen.

The last time the concession was open, I almost didn't make it. We were having one of those electrical storms, and it was the wildest ever; blue fuzz-bolts slamming across the sky (what served as our sky anyway), colliding, blowing patterns like neon quilt designs against the blackness.

Bob got me out of my chair, said something to me that I don't remember, and started leading me. All I recall was that there was lots of light from overhead and I was as crazy as a blind mouse in a paint shaker. I leaned against him and walked, tilted my head up to watch the raging electricity. I remembered my dreams about the B-string gods and thought if they were real, they were pretty worked up this time.

Close as we were to the concession, when we got there, a line had formed, and a long one. There were a lot of naked people. It seemed to be the fashion. Not far up in line was Willard, naked, of course, his knife on a strip of cloth around his neck. His black tattoos were flat and dull in the bad light. He had Randy on his shoulders, and Randy was naked too, except for that silly popcorn container on his head.

Since no one was bathing, it stunk there in line and it was hard to breathe. It made me feel worse than I already felt, and I hadn't thought that possible. A moment later, when we actually entered the concession and the stink of bodies was intensified, mingled with body heat, it was even more intense. I kept wondering in an absent sort of way if the air in the drive-in was limited, if, like rats under glass, we could use it all up.

"Breathe through your mouth," Bob said.

I was leaning against him, and he was holding me up. I turned and noticed for the first time that he had a light beard. There was a band of sweat between the brim and the crown of his hat. All the toothpicks and feathers were gone. His face was hard and there was something different about his eyes. I wondered idly what I looked like.

The Candy Girl looked worse than ever, her movements were automatic. Her mouth hung open and there was chocolate drool running out of the corners and a spot of it was beaded between her teeth. She slapped the candy onto the counter with ill humor.

The counter boy seemed to be having a hard time getting the hot dogs on the buns, and he kept squirting mustard on the outside of the bread. After dropping his third weenie, he threw the bread and mustard squirter down, walked toward the back. The manager yelled at him, "You're fired. You hear? That's it. Fired!"

"That's good," said the counter boy. "I won't have to quit. I was looking for a job when I found this one, so it's no big deal." He disappeared into the storage room.

The manager was wild-eyed and his hair looked spiked from having gone greasy and uncombed for so long. His lips were purple, and there was something on his shirt that might have been dried vomit. He was mumbling under his breath about "freeloaders and sorry no-goods."

Willard was next in line with the manager, who was doling out the popcorn, and when he got his little sack handed to him, he said, "Hell, that ain't half what you're supposed to give."

"Think not?" the manager said.

"No, it ain't half."

"That right?"

"Yeah, that's right."

"Yeah," Randy said.

"Who asked you, you four-eyed nigger?"

And then the chili hit the fan.

Willard may have lost some pounds off his frame, but unlike me, he still had some stamina. His right hand flicked out and hit the manager in the nose, flicked out again, grabbed the manager by the throat. Willard applied both hands then, and the bag of popcorn went flying. A woman dropped to her knees and scuttled after it, chased the bag across the floor. A man stepped on her hand, hard, and she screamed. A kid grabbed for the bag, but his foot was ahead of his hand, and he accidentally kicked it, and it was like a hockey puck going into play. The line broke, folks went after the bag. It sailed past us, then sailed back our way. No one could quite lay a hand on it until the girl with the poodle cape nabbed it with "I got it, I got it," but a man behind her slammed a fist into the back of her head and knocked her to the ground. "No you don't," he said triumphantly.

The bag and the little girl both were now in play, getting kicked up and down the length of the aisle. The bag burst and pops of corn rolled every which way. People scuttled after them on their hands and knees, shoving what they could grab into their mouths. I wanted that corn too, but I was too weak to let go of Bob.

Meanwhile, back to Willard, who was choking the manager.

Willard had the guy pulled across the counter, and he quit choking him long enough to grab him by the back of the hair and slam his face into the glass display case. The manager's face went through with a crack of glass and skull, and a shard of glass went through his throat, spraying the candy boxes and wrappers below with blood. The Candy Girl said, "Oh wow."

Randy, who was still miraculously on Willard's shoulders, was yelling, "Four-eyed nigger, my ass. That'll show him, that'll show him."

The little girl with the poodle cape had become open season. She was surrounded by people who were kicking her, including her mother, who was screeching, "I told you not to jerk on that leash."

"Time to shake out of here," Bob said. He grabbed me and steered me away from the line, headed me toward the door. A fist caught me in the side of the head, and it hurt, but I was already so dizzy and messed up, it didn't make much difference.

A woman with a nail file tried to stab Bob, and Bob kicked her kneecap with the toe of his boot. She went yipping and hopping along the wall, past the rows of horror-movie posters. She clutched at a strand of black-and-orange confetti strung across the window and pulled it down, along with some paper bats and skulls. Finally she tripped over a foot and fell down. The crowd that had been kicking the little girl moved in mass over to the woman and went at it. I could see the shape of the little girl beneath her dog cape. Her body was the color of the red ribbon in her hair, but the ribbon didn't flow.

Then I saw Willard. He had his knife out. He was spinning around and around with Randy on his shoulders, slashing out at anyone in reach. For a moment Randy's eyes caught mine, held recognition, then went savage.

Bob pulled me out of there, outside into the storm.

9

Bob sat me on the tailgate of the truck and went away. He came back with the shotgun, pushed me inside, pulled up the tailgate and locked it. He sat me over by one of the camper windows, then hunkered down by me. From there we could see the concession and the lightning that was sparking across the sky. The truck rocked against the wind, paper bags and cups fluttered across the lot. It was the strongest wind yet.

People were fleeing out of the concession, jamming in the door. There were fights out front of the place. Lots of biting and kicking.

Bob moved over to the trap that held the spare tire and pulled it up. There was a cardboard box next to the spare. He took it out, opened it. It was full of homemade jerky wrapped in cellophane. I had forgotten about that. Something tried to click together in the back of my mind. but it wouldn't. All I could do was say "But—"

"Not right now," Bob said. "Take this and eat it. You're hypoglycemic, pal. Bad. You eat this. Chew it slowly and swallow the juice."

I took it and began to chew. It hurt my gums at first, but it was like new blood was being pumped into me. I wanted to gobble it, but Bob kept warning me to suck it, to make it last.

"If Willard and Randy come back to the truck," Bob said, "I'm not going to let them in. No matter what. Understand?"

"Randy's our friend."

"Not anymore. Eat."

I looked at him holding the shotgun. He looked like a young Clint Eastwood, only shorter, ready to step out of a spaghetti Western.

"I've had the jerky all along," Bob said. "I forgot about it at first—all that was happening and it out of sight. I brought it for you and Randy to split and take home, enough there so your folks could have some. I've been slipping in here and eating it from time to time."

It was as if my head were clearing, cotton stuffing was being pulled out. "You should have told us," I said,

"I can tell you're feeling good already. You're starting to get self-righteous again. First thing you've said in a while that makes any sense. You been out in Bozo Land, pal. All you needed was a rubber nose and some flappy shoes."

"You could have told us," I said again.

"Naw. Randy and Willard were out there in orbit, man. If I'd told them about the jerky, it would have been all she wrote. Willard would have taken it from us, and if we'd given him any trouble, he'd have killed us. No, wasn't nothing friendly about it. And telling him about it and keeping him at shotgun point all the time didn't appeal to me none neither."

"It was needing protein that made them goofy," I said. I closed my eyes and chewed the last of the jerky. I had never tasted anything better in my life.

"That may be, but I ain't no hero, Jack. I was watching after me. What can I say? I knew we had us a ticklish situation here, and I wanted to have my strength for as long as I could. More meat I had, longer I could last. I took it easy on the soft drinks and the candy, tried to drink enough to keep liquid in my body, but to balance the sugar out with the meat. I figured if I could stay alive long enough, all this might go back to the way it was."

"So how come you're telling me?"

"I don't know. Worse you got, worse I felt. Hell, we been partners a long time . . . Look at you. You look like crap. It was tough to look at."

"But you managed."

"For a time. My dad always said when it got right down to it, people were sonofabitches. If it was a difference between honor and no food, he said they'd take the food every time. Looks like he was right about that. We get home, I'll tell him so."

"Well, you don't look so good neither," I said. "And to hell with your old man."

"I ain't feeling up to snuff, Jack, but with this jerky in me I could kind of figure which was my left hand and my right, know my pecker from my leg, know what was going on in here wasn't just something to look at . . . Man, this is humanity shredding."

"Randy's been a friend a long time," I said.

"Yeah. I care about him. But you and I been friends a long damn time—since kindergarten. And Randy has gotten real weird, partner. Him and Willard are . . . well, they didn't just get that way from lack of groceries. Those two and this drive-in and the things that have happened go together like bourbon and Coke . . . I think they're happy with the way things are. Hell, I don't know, maybe they're queer and in love and it's all this making them find it out. And maybe it isn't that; maybe they're just super fucked up and this is the straw that broke the camel's back, so to speak."

"It still doesn't strike me as the way you should have handled it," I said.

"No? Here, take another piece."

I took it without argument. In fact, I took it a little too fast. I almost ate it with the cellophane on it.

"You're a nice guy, Jack. Kind of a bleeding heart, but a nice guy. I wanted to tell you about the meat, but I knew you'd tell Randy and Willard. A bite of jerky meat wasn't gonna help them none, so I couldn't have that. Finally, though, I figured, hell, I ain't gonna make this nohow, no matter how much meat I hold back. So, I thought, me and Jack, we'll split it, last as long as we can. I mean . . . well, guess I still got some kind of hope in me, just like that manager. Maybe down deep I think the National Guard is going to come through too . . . You see, I had to choose between Willard and Randy and you. And I took you."

"Am I supposed to feel flattered?"

"Be nice if you were. You been fucked up so long, you ain't really got a grip on your thinking. Look out there."

He slapped his hand against the camper window and I looked. People were fighting. They were on their hands and knees going at it. They sounded like rabid dogs.

"It's like I was saying, Jack, you're kind of a bleeding heart. If I'd told you about that jerky a time back, when you were feeling good and full of all that social morality shit, you'd have wanted to share with Randy and Willard . . . maybe even invite Crier, some of the others over for lunch. Make a picnic out of it. Sing a few songs. We'd have been out of that stuff faster than a whore's out of pride. And I'll tell you again: Willard would have killed us."

"He seemed all right to me."

"He was. He was good to us because he needed friends. In spite of that tough-guy stuff, he was lonely. I've thought on this some, had time to. But he's a survivor, and Randy's a needer. Them two are together now and they ain't two people no more, they're one."

"So what if I want to share with them now?"

"I don't know."

"Would you shoot me?"

"I might. I could eat you then. That seems to be the trend around here. But I don't think so. But I might. Just look at it this way, Jack. Randy and Willard are out there—way out there. Twilight Zone theme time. You can forget them two boys unless the manager is right and the National Guard comes in here and rescues us and we all get turkey sandwiches and some rest. Otherwise, you ain't seen nothing yet. People ain't nothing but animals, Jack. You and me too. Things get bad enough, like animals, folks are gonna eat what they can, do what they have to."

I thought about those books I'd garbaged. All of them were junk, but the basic theme to most had been that man was better than the animals, had something inside him that blossomed like a rose and never died, even when the physical body decayed.

I looked out at the fighters in the lot. A guy in a werewolf costume with the mask missing was rolling around on the ground with a fraternity-type guy whose pants had lost their razor crease sometime back.

"And you're saying we'll end up like that too?"

"Could. We last as long as we can, though. Build up some hope. Gets too bad . . . there's always the shotgun."

I thought about Dad kidding Mom about the last two bullets back . . . when? Christ, who could know? Yesterday? Today? A century ago? What exactly was it he told her . . . ? "When the going gets rough, and it looks like we're not going to make it, I'll save the last two bullets for us."

I looked out the window again. There were people lying on the ground, not moving. A naked man was taking a swift kick in the nuts from a near-naked girl with a punk haircut. There were other people on the ground, on their hands and knees, grabbing for spilled popcorn and candy. One woman was lapping a spilled soft drink like a dog. She had her rear end to me and her dress was hiked up and she didn't have on any underpants. It was far from sexy. She looked like a desperate, dying animal. I felt sorry for her. For them. For us.

"Maybe you're thinking about going out there and giving a speech on the unity of mankind?" Bob asked.

"No," I said. "Guess not."

"That's wise. Now take one more piece of meat, chew it slowly, and be a happy animal."

10

We sat there for a time, not talking. I was thinking, watching the storm out there, and the people. I didn't want to watch them fight and kill one another, but I couldn't take my eyes off them. It was sort of like watching the Dallas Cowboys play when they were bad. You hated looking at it, but you had to see it through.

Physically, I felt better. Not ready to do any hurdles or anything, but it seemed my senses had floated to the top once more. A lot of things I'd seen while lost in the ozone clicked together now, and I could see them in a truer light. The little girl with the cape getting kicked to death, for one. Seemed to me I had wanted to kick her too. I could remember thinking that, but for the life of me couldn't remember why. Had I really watched her father get shotgunned out of the air and thought it funny? And hadn't there been something about eating a baby? (Raw as opposed to grilled.)

I thought about the jerky I had eaten and remembered what my father's friend had said about it, how it was like chewing on a dead woman's tit. The thought of that and what was happening out there, people eating one another now and then, made me feel weak and dizzy.

Maybe Bob was right. Animals. That's what we were. No different from the animals except for an opposable thumb and a desire to make popcorn and hit each other over the head with rocks, or whatever instrument was available.

Outside, it looked as if things had calmed down. No one was fighting and there were only gawkers. Standing and looking at the bodies on the ground (there were a few of those) and maybe considering them as steaks, but not quite ready to make the move.

But the calm didn't last long. A guy came walking up, and he had a revolver in his hand, a .357 Magnum. He had a big, loud voice and he was using it.

"Can't do this crap to Merve Kinsman. Merve Kinsman don't take this off anybody. I come here to get my food, real polite like, and I'll be damned if a punk without any drawers with a nigger on his back is gonna tell me dip. I don't take that crap, nosireebob. I'll blow their heads off, is what I'll do. Knife or no knife. I'll not have it, I tell you."

Merve didn't seem to be speaking to anyone in particular, but he was turning his head from side to side as he talked, as if those who were still milling about were hanging on his every word.

I looked at the concession itself. There wasn't any more activity there, and I hadn't seen Willard or Randy come out. It seemed pretty obvious that they were the "punk without any drawers" and the "nigger."

Merve Who-Didn't-Take-That-Off-Anybody stopped outside the concession and waved the revolver and talked to the air some more. "Ain't nobody gonna talk to my ass like that, you hear. I'll pull their damn head off and piss an ocean down their throat is what I'm trying to tell you."

Merve looked at one of the closest bystanders, an aging hippie dressed in old blue jeans and high-top tennis shoes and no shirt. The hippie tried to look casual. He tried a friendly smile.

"Don't you be looking at me like that, you weird little fart." Merve grabbed the hippie and gave him a rapid pistol-whipping about the head and ears and threw him down on the ground. The hippie lay on his side and tried to look dead, but I could see he was blinking. Blood was dribbling down his face. This was a long ways from sixties flower power. I imagined he was trying to figure exactly how he had looked at Merve, so if the situation came up again be could play his cards differently.

Merve pulled open the concession door and put a foot in there quick as a door-to-door salesman. He threw his chest out and stepped inside, saying, "Got some bullets here with your names on them, assholes. Come and get 'em."

Then he moved to the right inside the concession, out of view. Patrons who had been hanging around, and still had enough functioning gray matter, sauntered briskly off. A few lay down on the ground like whipped dogs. The aging hippie remained stone-still.

A shot was fired inside the concession.

More patrons scrambled. More briskly this time.

When no more shots followed, the hippie rolled quickly to his right, came to his feet and darted off. He looked to have been taking lessons from the guy Willard had hit with the baseball bat.

The moments moved by slower than dental work, then Merve Kinsman made his appearance. He came out of the concession walking like a drunk trying to look sober. He had Willard's knife in his right eye. It was buried halfway to the hilt. Merve Kinsman Who-Didn't-Take-That-Off-Anybody was complaining, though not as loud as before. He was now Merve Kinsman Who-Would-Not-Be-Messed-With, By-God, and he wanted every damn one of us to know it. He said something about hell to pay when he found his gun, then he went face down on the lot, the knife point punching up through the back of his head.

Willard came out then. Randy was still on his shoulders, wearing the popcorn container. Willard had to duck to let Randy through the door. Willard had the .357. He looked real happy. He smiled. There was blood on his teeth (or maybe chocolate). Maybe he had been hit in the mouth or had bitten somebody. (Or had eaten an Almond Joy.)

"The concession is ours, you sapsuckers," Willard screamed. "Hear me? Ours!"

Nobody made with an argument. A few people who had been too dull to run shuffled their feet.

Merve Kinsman Who-Didn't-Take-That-Off-Anybody, alias Merve Kinsman Who-Would-Not-Be-Messed-With, By-God, didn't come back from the dead to debate the point, and I figured if anybody could, or would, it would be that guy.

Willard stepped forward a couple more steps, waved the .357 around. Randy beat his chest and let out with an anemic Tarzan yell. Away from the direct light of the concession, shadows falling across them, it was hard to see where one body quit and the other began, especially with Willard covered in those asphalt-black tattoos.

"We're in charge now," Randy screamed.

Willard waved the .357 around some more, turned, ducked back through the concession door and closed it. He pressed his nose against the glass door and looked out. You could only see Randy's legs. The rest of him was above the door, behind solid wall, that popcorn-cup hat damn near scraping the ceiling, I imagined.

Willard went away; the smudge circle of his nose remained to mark his passing.

"Reckon that concession is theirs," Bob said, "until someone with more firepower shows up."

"You got intentions?" I asked.

"Not me, but you can bet someone does."

The blackness above grew cluttered with electric blue veins, and pretty soon there was more blue than black, and the thunder and the snake-hiss of lightning was tough on the ears, even inside the camper.

Bob got brave enough to open up the back and look out. He said, "Will you look at this?"

I did. The Orbit symbol and the marquee were drawing lightning like decay draws germs. The lightning was hopping through the symbol, kicking out dark blue lights that mingled with the fairy blue and white. The marquee's red letters looked like bright blood blisters about to pop.

We watched as the electric bolts from the symbol expanded, reached out toward the concession and touched it (like God giving the spark to Adam). The concession glowed blue and white, and those bat and skull symbols in the windows looked almost alive.

"Look at that," Bob said.

He was referring to the symbol again, or rather what was above it. Sticking out of the black was what looked like a green-black tentacle, though it could have been a trick of the lightning, a dipping rent in the blackness like a tornado tail. Out of the tentacle (I preferred to think of it that way as it went along with my dreams of *something* up there, something in control) the lightning was flowing faster than ever, zeroing in on the Orbit symbol, jetting from that to the strained marquee. The word "Massacre" exploded in a flutter of glass, fizzled. The rest of it looked ready to go, but held.

Now another tentacle shape dropped down, twisted in the air and gave lightning from its tip, and this lightning went through the symbol and the marquee, and it made the marquee blow the word "Dismember." And that damn symbol began to spin, rapidly, kicking out more and more bolts of energy, all of it going straight to the concession.

One of the black bats in the window flapped its wings and flew away into the depths of the concession. A paper skull twisted and fell to the floor, out of sight. The lights in there were blinking like a strobe show. They went out. But there was still plenty of light from the energy bolts, and it was a strange light, and it lit the concession up inside and out, bright and garish as a cheap nightclub act.

Then I saw Willard and Randy on the roof of the concession. Willard was still carrying Randy and Randy still had that damn container on his head. Willard had the .357 in his hand. They were spinning around up there in the blue glow, raising their hands, cussing, most likely, though there was too much thunder and hissing lightning to hear.

"Must be a trapdoor up there," Bob said.

"Yeah, but what the hell are they doing up there?"

"Believe me, they don't know."

Willard raised his pistol and shot at the Orbit symbol, and, almost as if in answer, a thicker strand of lightning leaped out of it like a hot, bony finger with too many joints and hit Randy on top of his popcorn container hat, turned him and Willard the color of the bolt, and made them smoke. Willard did a kind of funky chicken dance across the length of the roof and back again. The lightning made him look like he was moving very fast. Randy stayed in place, didn't even wobble.

Willard heel-toed it over to the trapdoor, and with the two of them glowing like a nuclear accident, they dropped through the hole.

The concession was lit up like blue neon. The original lights did not come back on. The movies, defying electrical logic, continued to churn.

I looked to see if there were still any paper bats and skulls decorating the window. Nope.

11

Things went from sho' is bad to sho' is rotten.

The lightning continued to shoot out of the blackness overhead (though the greenish-black tentacles were no longer visible), strike the Orbit symbol, and in turn strike the concession, and shower blueness over it.

Word of what had happened spread pretty fast through the drive-in, and in less time than it took for a messy dismemberment, the bikers showed.

They spun their bikes around in front of the concession and yelled some things. They roared around Bob's truck a few times.

Most of them had guns: shotguns, revolvers of all kinds. A few had knives, chains and tire irons. They looked nasty. There were twelve of them, and I couldn't figure exactly what had prompted them to show up, unless it was the idea of some guy with a gun and another guy on his shoulders taking over the concession that warmed their blood. Or maybe they had planned to take the concession over themselves and were just now getting around to it, mad because some chump had beaten them to it.

I tried to compute when they had taken over B concession, but couldn't. Time was just too screwed up. It could have been yesterday, last week, a month ago, a year back. No idea.

Whatever, they were here now, riding their bikes and yelling, shouting for the "sumbitches" inside to come on out and take their hanging like men.

To accommodate the hanging, one of the bikers showed up in a wrecker, which I'm sure didn't belong to him. He was more the wind and bugs-in-the-teeth type. There was a noose made of barbed wire fastened to the wrecker hook, and it looked ready for occupancy; one size fits all. I wondered where they had gotten the barbed wire, but not much. People carried everything in their pickups, wreckers and car trunks; all the tools of Texas trades.

There were also a barbecue grill and a bag of charcoal on the back of the wrecker. Not standard equipment. That made me think cannibalism wasn't a crime in the biker book anymore.

The biggest and ugliest of the bikers pulled up in front of the concession door, lifted one hip, farted, and yelled for whoever was in there to come out. Everyone else had quit yelling, and now he was giving it the "I'm the boss" tone. The others stopped their bikes, just sat on them and watched.

The one talking, calling out for Willard and Randy to give it up, was three hundred pounds if he was an ounce. A lot of that poundage was stomach, and it stretched his yellow T-shirt (I think the coloring was due to sweat, not dye) to the point of bursting. He, unlike most of us in the drive-in, didn't seem to be missing any meals. I wondered how big he had been before all of this. For that matter, all the bikers looked pretty good.

But this guy wasn't just a fat boy. He had arms big around as my head, a head a little bigger around than my arms. His hair was long and greasy, tied back with a piece of black cloth. He was wearing leather pants, chain-strapped boots, and an open leather jacket with BANDITOS on the back of it. Part of the jacket had been cut away, and it gave the impression of being too small; it was about halfway up between his waist and armpits.

I noticed the other bikers had done a similar thing to their jackets, or, if they had leather pants, to the legs of those. It hit me that they were cutting the leather off to eat. Maybe boiling it down in Coke so it wouldn't be so tough; making their own kind of jerky.

Though, after looking at the wrecker with the barbecue grill, I assumed they were willing to try more exotic fare. And that being the case, I sat real still in the camper, looking out of those windows that were blacked on the outside so you couldn't see in. I sat there glad that Bob had the shotgun. I had gone duck and squirrel hunting with him, and he knew how to use it.

I fretted over Willard and Randy. Knew they didn't have a chance against these guys, even if Willard was a bad ass and had a gun. There were just too many men out there with weapons and a bad attitude.

For that matter, I didn't even know if Randy and Willard were alive. We had seen them take lightning, lots of it, and walk away, but that didn't mean they were okay. They might have died from it; lying in there now on the floor, Randy's popcorn-container hat still on his head, Willard still gripping the gun.

The fat guy used his feet to push his bike forward, but when he reached the blue aurora around the concession, he backpedaled. It gave him such a shock that the handlebars and his hands smoked. He shook his hands rapidly and frowned.

"Damn you, in there, come on out and take it like a man. That 'lectricity ain't gonna keep you safe. Ain't nothing gonna keep you safe from the Banditos."

"That's right," one of the lackeys behind him said, and the big guy turned to look, as if the agreement had been unnecessary and off-key. The guy who had chimed out smiled wistfully. The big leader didn't smile back. "Shut up, Cooter," he yelled. "I'm the president of this here club, and I'll do the—"

But he cut short when he saw the look on Cooter's face, realized Cooter was looking at the concession.

The leader turned his head forward again, and there were Randy and Willard. They had come out of the concession, and Randy was still on Willard's shoulders and he was still wearing the popcorn-container hat. But the lightning had melted the edges of the container, dripped it down over his head. His features had run together in such a way that one of his eyes was gone and the other had shifted to the center of his forehead. His legs had fused to Willard's shoulders, his knees sticking up like pathetic knots on a charcoaled stick.

Willard's tattoos were crawling all over his body like worms, in and out of his empty, blackened eye sockets. His nostrils had become two large round holes in his face, and his lips were gone, showing a wide mouth with smoldering teeth. Willard still had the gun, but there in the blue lightning you could see that it had fused to his hand, become one with flesh and bone. The tiger Randy had tattooed so lovingly on Willard's stomach was poking a three-dimensional head out and was growling; flesh-colored whiskers twitched against its dark face.

"Man," said the Bandito leader, "you are one geeked-out sucker. But we can fix you."

With that, the biker reached inside his jacket, under his armpit, and pulled out a pistol (also a .357) and snapped off a professional shot that hit Willard between the ears of the tiger tattoo on his stomach.

When the load hit, Willard flinched a bit. The shot went into a rare pink space on his skin, and the flesh puckered up like a roughed mouth, spat the projectile out with a sputter. An ooze the color of Coke syrup boiled out of the hole momentarily, then the wound closed up.

"That's different," Bob said, his nose pressed to the glass.

Willard raised his revolver and grinned. Randy's mouth grinned too. For a man without eyes, Willard was unerringly accurate. His shot hit the Bandito leader between the eyes, and the biker's brains left home through the back of his skull with a slushy rush, came to rest on the sleeve of the one called Cooter.

"Man," said Cooter. "Radical."

All the bikers with guns opened fire. Slugs hit Willard and Randy repeatedly, but their flesh spat out the buckshot and revolver loads. Even that damn popcorn tub on Randy's head had become flesh, molded into Randy's skull, and it too regurgitated lead.

Willard raised his revolver and emptied it. Hitting a biker each shot, killing two of them, wounding one. He was empty now.

Or would have been, except for the tattooed bandolier across his chest. He reached up, pinched six dark loads from it, shoved the fleshy projectiles into the revolver, which puckered open to receive them.

This was the bikers' clue to zoom out of there. Motors roared, bikes whirled, and they were off. The one called Cooter made a quick turn in front of Bob's truck and Willard fired in the general direction. The bullet came out of the barrel, hung there a moment, then it was a streak and gone. It went around the edge of the truck in hot pursuit and I heard Cooter yell.

I went across the camper, shared a window with Bob, who was also checking it out, and there was Cooter's bike still going down the row, veering slightly to the left. But the biker lay on the ground, face down, the top of his head gone. The bike hit a speaker post, went up it a foot, turned sideways in the air, came down, slid across the path and slammed up against the back of a Ranchero, bounced back into the row and lay on its side like a small foundered horse.

I rushed to the other side to take a look at Willard. He was still firing his flesh bullets. They sought out their targets like heat seeking missiles.

When he was through firing, Willard lowered the gun and looked down. His stomach bulged. The tiger tattoo stretched its neck. Shoulders appeared, then a foreleg poked out. It was as if the tiger were climbing out of a deep, inky well. Another foreleg showed. The cat leaned forward, touched both feet to the ground, pulled the rest of his body out of Willard's stomach, growing in size as it did. It stood momentarily in front of Randy and Willard and swished its tail. Then, with a roar, it went after the biker who had been injured early on, grabbed him around the head with its jaws and bit down with a sound like a duck egg being swatted with a mallet. That was all for the biker.

The tiger pulled the biker inside the concession by what was left of his head (pieces were dropping here and there like china fragments) while Willard held the door open. The tiger deposited the stiff inside, came back out licking its lips. A paper bat exited with it, fluttered up beyond the blue glow, then flapped down again and went back inside the concession. Two skulls rolled into the doorway, looked out with empty eye sockets, chattered their teeth like sidewinder rattles, then rolled out of sight, not even venturing out of doors.

The tiger, as it moved outside the influence of the blue light, softened in color until it was almost light gray; it looked weaker. Then, as it returned, dragging another body by the noggin, it would gradually darken and hold its head higher, and finally, within the confines of the blue glow, it would turn its true color and look strong again.

As each corpse passed through the doorway, I became aware of a black dot, like a bee that had been in hiding, leaping from the bodies and going into Willard's bandolier—little bullets returning to their nests.

Finished with its work, the tiger jumped at Willard and it was as if someone had tossed a can of black paint. The beast splattered against Willard's stomach, made a blot that dripped like hot tar. Its whiskers twitched and it showed its teeth, then it went still and was nothing more than a vivid tattoo.

The other tattoos on Willard's body (they had been thrashing and lashing about) followed suit. The last of them to lie down were EAT PUSSY and KICK ASS. They had been walking across Willard's upper arms like tall, stiff ants.

Randy continued to look peaceful up there on Willard's shoulders, like a real estate agent who had just closed a big deal. I looked for a sign of my friend in that wrecked one-eyed face, but saw not a clue.

Willard and Randy lifted a hand and waved to the left, then to the right. From my position I could see a few people waving back—reflex reaction, or maybe after seeing what these guys could do, they just felt friendly.

The mouth that belonged to Randy opened and a powerful voice came out. "I am the Popcorn King, and my rein has begun. I will take care of you."

"That's damn nice of him," Bob said.

Then the King ceased to wave and went inside the electrified concession. And so began the reign of the Popcorn King.

Part Two

THE POPCORN KING

With Scabcorn and Other Bad Stuffs

1

The Popcorn King was happy.

He was a smiley kind of guy—with both mouths and he could talk that trash. I mean, say you're in this little universe of the drive-in, and maybe we should say the smaller universe of your car or truck, and all you've got is movies. You got no real food, and you got soft drinks for liquid, you're hypoglycemic to the max and your hope don't work no more. All you got is this voice, sleek as a starlet's thighs, soft as duck fluff, as intoxicating as rum and honey. A voice that oozes out of the speaker and flows in your ears, jells around your brain like candied fruit.

The voice of the Popcorn King, telling you how it is, offering you *truth*, telling you he loves you and will feed you and take care of you, and all you've got to do is love him back, and all you've got to do is understand that what you see on the screens are the visions of gods, the way it is, ole buddy, and the manner in which you should live, for so speaks the messiah, the Popcorn King.

Yeah, the Popcorn King was happy.

And he was crazy.

And he helped make everyone else more crazy than they had become.

Back up.

Speculate.

This is how I think it came about; the birth of the Popcorn King.

So Willard and Randy go up on the roof during the storm, wandering up there because they are nuts on junk food and high on a kind of love for one another that isn't quite homosexual, nor exactly the passion of friendship. They're parasites feeding off one another, trying to make something whole out of two halves.

They wander up there on the roof after they have cleared out the concession with the knife, after they have killed. And maybe somewhere deep down, they realize this is something they don't like, this killing. Or maybe, like me, they're so high on sugar it all seems okey-dokey. Or maybe they just didn't give a fuck all along.

Well, you add all that together, toss in their insecurities, and what you have here are a couple of buddies a couple bricks shy a full load. Or to put it in Yankee terms, "They are on the verge of a nervous breakdown."

There's this storm, and it crackles and hisses and fizzles and pops, brightens the sky. Sheet-metal thunder rolls. And these guys up there on the roof are working off little more than the impulses of the primitive brain; that part that takes care of raw survival.

And so they yell at the storm (they don't like the noise, see), call it names. And perhaps by design, because the B-string gods up there are looking for a twist in the plot, or maybe they just don't like being talked to like that . . . and maybe there are no B-string gods and my dreams were just dreams and Bob and I only thought we saw tentacles poking out of the blackness and it's nothing more than an accident that this bolt pops out and zaps the living shit out of our boys, makes them one creature full of power.

Down through the trap they go, smoking like bacon too long in a pan. And they are no longer angry and confused, but they're not just well done either. They have been given power, and this power has straightened their confused asses right out. It has moved through them like a quick, happy cancer, spreading little roots of energy from head to head, from toes to toes.

They are one sho'-ugly critter now, but they are not aware of that. They feel pretty. In their mind's eye they are darling. So sweet with that one eye in the center of the top forehead, and the other head without eyes, just two gaps dripping ooze, puffing smoke.

Their brains no longer work independently of one another; this happy cancer has spread its tendrils through them so that their gray matter operates as one. Randy's eyes are Willard's eyes. Willard's muscles respond to Randy's needs. So, instead of *they* and *them*, these two are now one, and say at his feet are a few stray popcorn kernels that are blossoming in the electrical current, popping high up to greet him ("take me, take me"), and he thinks, uh-huh, happy little subjects, these popcorns, and he names himself the Popcorn King.

The Popcorn King is very happy because he feels as if he has been told the ultimate joke by the ultimate jokester, and he has understood the punch line perfectly.

He knows now he is the Chosen One. Feels that what led him up that ladder, onto the roof, was more than just confusion. It was ordained. Destiny.

Yeah, that's it. He thinks it again. Destiny.

He can feel a network of raw power spiraling through him, replacing the blood and bones inside him with something new; something that makes him master of his flesh (tattoos wiggle like maggots in dung).

The air around him hums (no particular tune) with that blue electrical current. (And while I'm hypothesizing here, sports fans, let's have some of those paper bats—now real—flap around his head, let's have some paper skulls—now real—roll at his feet and nip at his heels like happy pups.) He walks among the carnage of the concession, sees:

the manager with his face through the counter glass, his blood having splashed the wrapped and boxed candies and congealed like cold gravy;

the little girl that was kicked to death, looking like strawberry pulp;

other dead folks, including the Candy Girl (later I would see her corpse in the window, hanging there like a prize cold cut in a butcher's display);

and he moves through the blue air, into the film room, (the bats at his head, the skulls at his feet), sees that there are three projectors, pointing like ray guns in three directions at three six-story screens.

He goes over to one of the little slots by one of the projectors and looks out, sees *The Texas Chainsaw Massacre.* He goes to another and looks out, sees the tail end of *I Dismember Mama.* He examines the last projector slot, sees *The Toolbox Murders.*

He sighs contentedly. This is his domain. His throne room. His damn concession stand. And all those people out there watching those movies are his subjects. He is their King, their Popcorn King. And he is a fun kind of guy.

But what's this? A bunch of fat men on motorcycles are riding around and around in circles out front of his palace, calling him names (had one of them actually called him "dog puke"? Sure sounded like it), yelling for him to come out.

The little people are upset. A rebellion is brewing. The peasants are revolting.

Time to nip this crap in the bud.

So he steps out with the gun fused to his hand, the tattoos shucking and jiving like snakes on hot glass . . .

And from there, I have given you an eyewitness account.

When it was over and the tattoos had settled down, and the King had waved, he went inside the concession and closed the door. And Bob went out of the back of the camper, sneaky-like, cranked the truck, turned right, bumped over the dead biker and his bike, worked us to the far end, turned right at the fence, found a front row in what was called the East Screen of Lot A. We parked in a slot next to a big yellow bus with CHRIST IS THE ANSWER IF YOU ASK THE QUESTION, THAT'S WHAT I'M TRYING TO TELL YOU written messily on the side in what looked like rust-colored paint. And underneath in dirty-white letters, much smaller, was AIN'T BEING A BAPTIST GRAND?

On the other side of us was an old Ford. It looked empty. The occupants were probably dead, or had joined up with some others and gone to a new location.

Bob got a speaker off the post, more out of habit than anything else, put it in the window, turned the dial high as it would go, and we watched, or rather looked at, *The Evil Dead.* Ash, the character in the movie, was sticking his hand into a mirror, and the mirror had turned into some kind of liquid.

We sat there feeling numb until Bob said, "I don't think coming over here is going to help much, but I'm sort of in the mood for a change of scenery . . . Maybe out of sight, out of mind . . . And I don't think his tattoos can come this far . . . too much distance between the concession and us."

"Agreed," I said.

It wasn't much, but comparatively, this was the best part of the drive-in for us to hide out. For some reason, East Screen had had a lot less badness going on. There had certainly been some stuff happening over there; Crier, who knew everything had told us about it, but compared to the rest of Lot A, and certainly B, it was pretty tame business.

The movies changed as usual, and I could imagine the Popcorn King in the film room, going from projector to projector, switching them as needed. (Didn't he need sleep?) That part of Willard that had been a projectionist was coming into play; he knew how to keep things going.

Bob and I dozed a lot, and when we were so hungry we couldn't take it anymore, we'd go to the camper and lie down and eat, chewing slowly, sometimes talking if we had something to say, listening to the movies filtering into the camper from the speaker in the cab window. It got so I was having a hard time remembering what life was like before the drive-in. I could remember Mom and Dad, but couldn't quite see their faces, recall how they moved or talked. I couldn't remember friends, or even girlfriends whose faces had haunted my dreams at home. My past was fading like cold breath on a mirror.

And the movies rolled on.

At certain intervals, the old yellow bus next door to us would crack its back door, and out of it would come this rail-thin man in a black coat, white shirt and dark tie, and with him was this bony, broad-shouldered, homely woman in a flowered housedress and false leather slippers. She walked without picking her feet up much.

They'd walk toward the center of the row, and there would be others there, and they would form a crowd, and the man in the black coat, white shirt and dark tie would go before them and talk, move his arms a lot, strut back and forth like a bantam rooster. He'd point at the movies now and then, then at the group. He'd hop up and down and stretch his facial muscles and toward the end of this little exercise he'd be into much hand-waving you'd think he was swatting marauding bees.

When he tuckered out, everyone would gather around him in a team huddle, and stay that way for some time. When they broke up, they all looked satisfied. They'd stand around while the rail-thin man bowed his head and said some words, then each went on about his limited business.

Every time this little event occurred, the couple coming out of the bus, I mean, and Bob saw them, he'd say, "Well, gonna be a prayer meetin' tonight."

It got so it irritated me, him making fun of them, and I told him so.

"They've got something," I said. "Faith. It's been ages since any of these folks have eaten . . . not since the King took over the concession, and look how they act. Orderly. With strength and faith. And the rest of the drive-in . . ."

You could hear screams and chainsaws frequently, and not just from the screen. Now and then a shot would puncture the air and there would be the sounds of yelling and fighting. But not here at East Screen.

"They've got food somewhere, Jack. Faith ain't gonna take care of an empty belly. Trust me on the matter."

"You'd have to have faith to know anything about it," I said.

"And I guess you do?"

"No, but I'd like to."

"It's all a lie, Jack. There ain't no magic formula, no way to know how to go. Astrology, numerology, readings in tea leaves and rat droppings, it's all the same. It don't amount to nothing. Nothing at all."

Crier came by to see us.

We were out leaning on the front bumper of the truck, watching the people over at North Screen running around like savages, killing one another, wrecking cars. Bob had his faithful twelve-gauge companion by his side, just in case radical company from over there should come by and want to kill or eat us.

None did.

I figured the reason for this was threefold. Each screen had sort of become its own community,and strange as it was, each tended to stick together; they liked killing and eating their own. Least at this point. Two, Bob had the shotgun and he looked like a man who would use it, and there was the fact that the Christians, as I had come to think of them, had formed their own patrol. The patrol walked around the perimeters of East Screen regularly, armed mostly with tire irons, car aerials and the like, but also a gun or two. The third reason they left us alone was just a surmise on my part. I figured they were patient and were saving us for dessert.

Well, anyway, as I was saying, we were out leaning on the bumper of the truck, and along comes Crier. He looked bad. His lips were cracked and his eyes had a hollow look, as if they were shrinking in their sockets. He was using the hoe handle to keep from falling over. He seemed to concentrate heavily just to put one foot after another. I wanted to give him a piece of jerky bad, but Bob, anticipating my thinking, looked at me quickly and shook his head.

Crier came up and sat on the bumper next to Bob, let his head hang, got his breath. "I hope you boys aren't going to kill and eat me," he said almost pleasantly.

"Not today," Bob said.

"Then you wouldn't have anything I could eat, would you? I feel like fly-blown shit. You boys look pretty good. Maybe you got some food."

"Sorry," Bob said. "We did have, but we ate it. We saved a little of what we got at the concession each time, but now that's gone. No more stash."

"Well," said Crier, "I always ask. It don't hurt to do that. Getting so there ain't no use my doing this anymore, this walking around to report the news. Everyone is news now, and no one wants to listen anymore. They just want to kill or eat me. This hoe handle has saved my life a dozen times. Maybe more. I did get beat up pretty bad, though. My ribs are cracked, I think. Hurts when I breathe too deep or walk too fast."

"What can you tell us about the Popcorn King?" I asked.

"He went in there and he hasn't come out. Nobody can get in there neither. That blue light around it would fry an egg. I know, I seen an old boy get his hand burned off trying to go in there after the King and some food."

"Then why doesn't it kill the King?" I asked.

"Don't get me to lying. I ain't got the slightest," Crier said. "Maybe conditions were just different then."

"So, that's it on the King," Bob said.

"Well, almost," Crier said. "Those bodies his tiger dragged inside . . . He's eating those. Got them hung up in the window there, and every time you look, there's less meat on them."

That would be right, I thought. Willard and Randy showing their power, showing that they have food, that it's behind glass, hung up nice and neat, and that the rest of us are lowlifes scrounging for popcorn kernels, killing one another and tearing the flesh off the bones like hyenas. But not him, not the Popcorn King. He's got it all fine and clean and well lighted, and he probably slices his meat off with a knife. Has soft drinks to go with it. Maybe some chocolate almonds for dessert.

"The concession at B?" Bob asked.

"Taken over again," Crier said. "But there isn't any food left. Those Banditos had already cleaned it out. Did I tell you I found a third of a bag of popcorn under a car a few movies back? Over at North Screen too. Just lying there, and hadn't nobody seen it. Kind of in the shadow of a tire, part of the way under the car. I ate that sapsucker on the spot . . . Man, you boys got it made in this section."

"Right now," Bob said.

"Why don't you stay over here then?" I asked.

"Got to keep moving. It's my way. Besides, I don't know that your neighbors would want me moving in. I've been coming and going as I please so long, they let me do that, but I don't know about moving in."

"A word from us wouldn't do you no good," Bob said. "We're sort of low man on the totem pole here."

"Don't need a word. No matter what happens, got to keep moving. I used to drive a beer truck, you know. Always on the road . . . Got divorced twice because I couldn't stay still. Had to stay on the go. Get home and I wanted to drive around. One reason I liked drive-ins. You came and sat in a car, and when you watched the movie it was like you were driving through a new world or something. All you had to do was put your hands on the steering wheel and imagine. . . Sure you boys haven't got a thing to eat?"

"Nothing," Bob said.

"Then I'll hobble on. Take care. Hope the next time I see you ain't neither one of us so bad we want to eat one another."

"Same here," Bob said.

Crier climbed the hoe handle and started off again, moving down the row of speakers, heading for the pathway between East Screen and North.

"We should have fed him," I said. "He looks bad."

"Everyone here looks bad, Jack. It ain't practical to go feeding folks. Even Crier. He gets good and hungry, he might conk our noggins and take what we got. He's all right, but he ain't nothing more than a human being."

"Which as a group you don't nave a lot of respect for, do you?"

"It's damn near got so I don't have a drop," Bob said.

I thought about the Christians, their meetings, their faith. It gave me moral strength. Their attitude assured me that there was more to humanity than a good meal, a cold beer and a roll in the hay. There was something strong and noble there too, something that, like a seed, needed fertilizing, and I told all that to Bob, and he said he thought beer, a good meal and a roll in the hay were just fine, and as for the seed that needed fertilizing, he had a strong suggestion for the type of fertilizer that would best be suited for such a seed.

You just couldn't talk to Bob. He was too narrow-minded.

And so we got worn down and went to sleep, the speaker rattling movie dialogue and sound tracks through the camper as we drifted into nocturnal lands of cold shadow and dark dreams. And it was then that the Popcorn King came to us over the speaker, oozed into our brains and outlined his plans for us, told us how we fit into the scheme of things. And I will admit, they sounded inviting, these plans. He would be there to watch over us, feed us, give us a point on which to fix our wretched lives. And finally there was that voice, that lovely voice that was kind of Randy's and kind of not; that other voice that was kind of Willard's and kind of not, the one that hummed softly, shucked and jived, put a word in edgewise in just the right place. Those voices, those honey-poison, hot and cold voices of the Popcorn King.

2

So spake the Popcorn King—first one mouth and then the other:

My little dearies, my little popcorn eaters and movie lovers, my little heathens and mortals, you who take dukies beside your cars, how are you, babies, how are you? And listen up tight now, 'cause you done gone and went and got yourself the Popcorn King here, and I want to whisper to you, tell you some secrets, make your life complete, and talk on a subject that is dear to both mine and your hearts.

Popcorn.

Food, my subjects. Chow. Grub. Chewables. Hit it, mouth number two.

(chuckachew, chuckachew, chuckachewchewchew)

Yes, brethren—

(pseudo organ music from other mouth)

—I am here to talk to you about how things are going to be. How things are, in fact, though you may not know it yet. But before I do, let me tell you about the corn, about the sweet, popping corn, hot and fine and ready to melt in your mouth; good ole popcorn the color of fresh bird shit, but the texture and taste of life.

Corn, babies, corn.

Hit it again, mouth number two.

(chuckachew, chuckachew, chuckachewchewchew)

So I come off the roof, and I'm feelin' wild, walk in the house, jive down the aisle. There's some blue air here, some blue air there, lots of dead bodies shoo everywhere

(chuckachew, chuckachew, chuckachewchewchew)

—blood on the candy, blood on the door, dried and gone nasty, and there'll be more.

(pappa pap, pappapap, pappapap, papachewchewchew)

Yes sir now, babies, friends and pals, gonna tell you a story 'bout the Popcorn King, how he rolled and walked and talked so clean, yessire billy, I'm the Popcorn King.

(chuckachew, chuckachew, chuckachewchewchew)

Put your ears to the speakers, put your brain on hold, listen up, honeys, and don't get bold, popcorn's the magic and that's no load.

(jujujujujujujujuju-pap, pap, pap, pap, yeah, chuckachew, chuckachew, chuckachew chewchew)

Yeah, Popcorn's the magic, it's the tiny bomb, when it sees your insides goes off like a four-alarm.

(chuckachew, chuckachew, chuckachewchewchew)

Now if you been eatin' your kids, dead dogs too, licking cold shit off the bottoms of your shoes, this oughta thrill you, oughta make you feel grand. I'm here to tell you Popcorn King is a friendly man—

(boop, boop, boop-tadtadtadtadachew, chuckachewchewchew)

—gonna offer somethin' special, offer somethin' fine, gonna tell you a story of the popcorn kind.

(chuckachew, chuckachew, chuckachewchewchew)

Listen up tight, don't stray on me, keep them ears wide open and I won't tell you no lie.

(jujujujujujujupap, pap, pap, yeah, chukachew, chuckachew, chuckachew chewchew)

You ain't gonna make it, you don't be my friend, so better do what I'm askin' then.

(boop, hoop, boop-tadatada, tadachew, chuckachewchewchew)

Now we gonna close up shop with the rappin' man, gonna take us a trip to the Promised Land.

(bringing in the sheaves, bringing in the sheaves, we'll all come rejoicing, bringing in the sheaves)

Yes sir, brethren, I have come to you today with a line of pure truth. I come to fill your hearts with love or panic or hate or blood, whatever it takes. Listen up, sinners, let me tell you about the Lords of Popcorn. Let me tell you that those movies are lights from the very eyes of the Lords.

(amen, brother, amen)

Was a time, though I can only distantly remember it and can't make sense of it, when I was a man like you. Two men, to be exact. And sinners in the eyes of the Lords of Popcorn.

(amen)

Yes sir, a sinner, I surely was, a great sinner . . . a damn big sinner. Where's the amen corner?

(amen, brother, amen)

I didn't know the laws of popcorn and soda, of hot dogs and chocolate-covered almonds, didn't know blood and death were the paths to destruction, didn't know that the very flesh of man was salvation and that all we could do was to please our needs and instincts and all else was out the window. Yeah, didn't know love and beauty when it was looking me in my own eye.

(no you didn't, brother, no you didn't)

That's right, I didn't, so the Lords of Popcorn in their ultimate wisdom—blessed are those Lords—seen this, and chillun, they saw I was trying to live like everyone else, and they brought me here.

(yes they did, brother, yes they did)

And I was picked by those Lords as your messiah, your grand executioner, your grand lover, your Popcorn King. They gave me the lightning and the lightning gave me the powers, and these powers made me better than you, and that's all there is to that tune.

(tell it like it is, Brother Corn)

But I come down off that roof a new man made of two, and I come in here and I saw these movies and I knew the truth, seen it was all a sign.

(come to you in a flash of light, this sign)

That's right, it did. Say amen.

(AMEN)

Man but I feel good, sanitized and homogenized. Say it again, good brother.

(AMEN)

Oh, but I like the sound of that. One more time.

(AMEN)

All right, glory hallelujah, popcorn and corpses be praised.

(amen on that popcorn and dead folks)

You see, I saw these movies were the juice of the Lord's brains, the very juice done squirted out of their heads and onto them big white things we call screens. There is the way to live, brethren. It's a dog-eat-dog, folk-eat-folk world, and ain't nothing matters but one thing. That you ain't the one that gets et, if you know what I mean.

(that's the truth, Brother Corn, ain't no denying)

And I said aloud right off the top set of my lips—

(yes, you did)

—I have been sent down here from that roof a changed couple of individuals to make sure those little people out there who are not nearly as neat as I am have an example, someone to follow . . . someone with the corn. 'Cause this place is full of corn, my friends. You too can eat again, and not your neighbor. I'll eat your neighbors, just bring them to me when they go belly up . . . get tired of living, bring your own self, I'll be glad to kill your ass dead.

(be thrilled to do it, yes, he will)

And now you say, but what is the point of all this? It is confusing, Brother Corn.

(was gonna ask that)

Sure you were. And the point is I do as I like when I like and you do what I like when I like. And there is just really very little that I want.

(ain't asking much)

No I'm not. Just that meat I told you about, alive or dead. And another little thing. The most important thing. I want you to know the movies to be real.

(just as real as can be)

They are the reality and you are the non-reality. You cannot prove your reality by touching yourself. That means nothing.

(go on, touch yourself, don't mean a thing)

It's what you can't touch that's real.

(can't touch reality, no matter how hard you try)

If you want to become as real as the lights on the screens, you have to give yourself to them, do as they do, live as they live. They are the scripture and I am their voice.

(talking for them just as plain as can be)

So come on over to the other side, Reality City. Embrace the truth of the flickering dream, hold on to reality and let the non-reality flow out of you like piss from a bladder. Take the first step toward gratification, toward becoming real. All you got to do to have this thing and the popcorn—

(bless that popcorn)

—is listen to me, dear hearts, the voice of the scripture. All you got to do is listen, and give me what I want.

(amen, Brother Corn, amen)

3

What the nutcase in the concession wanted was simple.

Power.

For the King, power was the end and the beginning—the snake biting its tail. There was nothing else. For in his brains were the distant and confused memories of Randy and Willard. Two people who had seen themselves as outsiders, felt like hitchhikers on the road of life, forever watching fast cars pass them by.

But now, *they* were the drivers, hands firm on the wheel. It was *they* who drove with the pedal to the metal, smiling, looking out at the pedestrians, passing them by, shooting them the finger, giving them a rude honk and a flicking wave.

And if you could have heard the King's voice, that incredible voice massaging your brain like a cat kneading a pillow, you could understand a little how he suckered those folks in, gave them the religion of violence and greed to believe in.

And if Bob and I hadn't had the jerky, the juice of it giving fuel to our thoughts, keeping our brains clearer than the masses (but not as clear as the Christians fueled on the higher octane of faith), we would have joined right up with old King, praised him on high, begged for the corn, worshiped the action on the screens and tried not to think about the time we would die.

And it must be said that the Popcorn King not only had the voice, he had presence. He'd stand out in front of the concession with smiles on both his faces, plastic bags of popcorn in all of his hands (both of Randy's and one of Willard's—the other being permanently full of .357), and he'd close his eyes and flex his body, and the tattoos would quiver, and he'd open his eyes, and the popcorn would begin to pop in the bags, bursting them, and the King would toss the bags forward, beyond the blue glow, and it would snow corn onto the asphalt and fights would begin (the King would chuckle) as people tried to secure the puffs. But there was always plenty—least at this time I'm telling you about—and the fights were more ritualistic than desperate, like punk rockers slam-dancing.

Then would come the buckets of soft drinks carried by the King. Big buckets with paper cups floating in the liquid. People would form unruly lines, come forward one at a time, take a cup, dip from the buckets and drink the syrupy drinks, increasing, more than satisfying, their thirst. But that was the thing that bothered me most as Bob and I stood at the back of East Screen looking over the hood of an abandoned car, those people lifting those cups and seeing little drips of liquid running down their chins. All we had for liquid was the juice from the jerky, but it wasn't water, and we were feeling the slow effect of dehydration. But still, we held out.

Then the weak and the dead would be brought to the King, laid before the blue glow like sacrifices, and the tiger tattoo would leap from the King's stomach, finish off the living, then drag all the bodies inside, where later they would appear in the window, gradually losing flesh in strips.

These eaters and drinkers were not only from Lot A, but B as well. They would all come to eat the King's corn and drink his soft drinks, and afterward go back to their cars and sit on the hoods or roofs and quote the lines in the movies. Quote them with the reverence of holy scripture.

And ole Popcorn King, from inside the concession, using the intercom, would talk to his congregation via the speakers, that hot-cool voice fogging their brains. He would quote the movie lines with them. He would turn the sound down, preach at them, rap at them.

This version of loaves and fishes continued for a time to the happy contentment of the followers, and then the popcorn stopped.

Zip.

Nada.

No corn.

The King did not appear in front of the concession, and his voice did not grace the speakers. There were just the movies rolling on and on, giving evidence to the fact that someone was changing them, keeping them in order, but the King did not make an appearance.

The faithful continued to gather outside the concession, and they would call to the King, but he would not respond. The calls turned to chants, and finally to angry cries, but still no King. The meat in the window gradually disappeared. Someone was eating it. (The bats and the skulls? Nope, cut off cleanly from the bone.)

Bob and I got brave, and we'd go over there for a look, standing behind that same abandoned car, but there was never anything to see besides that confused crowd and those pathetic bodies in the window. People looked at us, but they looked at the shotgun too. Bob made sure they saw it, displayed it like a proud rooster tossing his comb.

I always carried the baseball bat. I liked its weight. It was my friend, Louisville Slugger.

One time we're up there standing behind that old car (a Fairlane Ford with the windows knocked out, I might add), watching, not really expecting anything, but maybe hoping for something. Standing there with our mouths and throats dry as kitty litter, our bellies howling and rolling like a storm, thinking maybe how it would be to have something warm to eat and sweet to drink, thinking hard on that meat in the window there, when out of the concession steps the Popcorn King.

The King had turned quite a bit darker, both Randy's naturally dark flesh and Willard's. They had blended together to make a charcoal hue, except in spots where Willard's original flesh tone swirled amid the darker skin like twists of vanilla in a chocolate Bundt cake.

The popcorn tub hat was now amalgamated with Randy's head, and veins like garden hoses stood out from it and extended down his forehead and came to rest above the single eye. The eye itself reminded me of that old Pinkerton ad with the bloodshot eye and the slogan that read: WE NEVER SLEEP.

Randy's knees had blended almost entirely into Willard's chest and shoulders, and the back of Willard's skull had nestled deeply into Randy's crotch like a large egg in a nest. Willard's blinded eyes had sealed over, and there were holes where his nostrils and mouth had been. Even Willard's sex had dried up and fallen off, like the shriveled stem of an overripe apple.

The tattoos, as usual, were quite busy. The animal designs made the appropriate, though diminutive, noises, fussed and snapped at one another like ill-tempered neighbors. The rude arm remarks (KICK ASS and EAT PUSSY), the bandoliers and the like moved about as if looking for better terrain. The tiger on Willard's stomach was silent, however, and, except for the lazy blinkings of its eyes, remained stationary.

An involuntary cry went up from the crowd, and it was a ragged bunch. They reminded me of those photos I had seen of starved, mistreated Jews in books about the war. Some of the women had little round stomachs, and it struck me that they might be pregnant. My God, had we been in the drive-in that long?

The King held up both hands like a victorious prizefighter. His mouths smiled. And out of the top mouth came: "I have returned. I offer you manna from the bowels of the messiah."

With that he opened his mouths phenomenally wide, the teeth folding back against the roofs of his mouths like tire-buster spears, and with a rumble and a methane-ish stink we could smell from where we stood, out came *popcorn.*

Sort of.

The velocity of the vomit was tremendous, the well from which it gorged endless. The content of the vomit looked to be cola and popcorn. It hit the crowd like a fire-hose blast, dispersed them, knocked them down. It spewed all the way back to Lot B.

Then it ceased. The shaken crowd found their feet.

Again the King opened his mouth, and once more the vomit spewed. More powerful than before. And when it ended this time, the King said, "Take of me and eat."

The crowd, somewhat recovered, examined the corn, looked at it long and hard. And then one man picked up a big puffy kernel and closed his eyes and put it in his mouth and bit down. You could hear his sigh of contentment throughout the Orbit.

Everyone, as of old, began to shove and fight for the corn, and a stray kernel, perhaps launched by an excited foot, came rolling our way, went under the Fairlane and lay between mine and Bob's legs.

We looked at it.

We looked at one another.

We looked at it again.

It looked back.

It was the general shape of popcorn, slightly off white in color with a sort of scabby look between the creases, along with thread-thin veins that pulsed . . . and in its center was an eye. A little eye that had no lid, but was instead a constant thing that matched the eye in the center of the King's top forehead.

Bob put his foot on it and pressed down. It was like stepping on one of those big dog ticks that are flat and gray until they've fed and dropped off their hosts to lie big as plump raisins.

"It moved under my boot," Bob claimed. "I felt it."

"Jesus," I said, and it sounded like a plea.

We looked back at the people. They were popping the corn into their mouths, oblivious of its appearance, or not caring. Blood oozed from between their lips. I could see their bodies rippling as if a sonic wave were passing beneath their flesh. Their grunts and cries of satisfaction and anxiety came to me like hyena barks, their squeals and lip-smacking like the sound of hogs at trough.

And a part of me, the hungry part, envied them.

The King looked at us over the top of the Fairlane. It was a decent distance away, if not outstanding, and I couldn't determine with his features the way they were, if he recognized us. I doubted it. Least not in a way that really mattered.

"Come," came that sweet-sour voice, "join us, brothers. Eat."

"Not just now," Bob said. "Maybe later."

And we turned and walked quickly away, back to the camper. When we got there, Bob took some wire cutters out of his toolbox, went out and cut the speaker wire off at the post, flung the speaker far away from us.

• •

4 That's when I made my decision to join the "church."

If I was destined to go down before evil, or simply to starve to death, I wanted to make sure I would be embraced by the arms of our Savior, the Lord Jesus Christ.

It was odd that I hadn't seen this obvious truth before. Odd that it had always been right before me, and I had denied it. But now it was all very clear, as if a visionary light had opened from the blackness above, a light unlike the fuzzy blue lightning, but instead a warm yellow light that struck me on the top of the head, penetrated my skull and filled me with sudden understanding.

Shortly thereafter, for it took little to tire us, we climbed into the back of the camper to sleep, and when I heard Bob's breathing go regular I got up and snuck out and went over to that bus.

As I was nearing it, the back door opened, and the contents of an improvised bedpan went flying. I was glad I wasn't along a little farther when this happened, or my first meeting with them might have been less than auspicious.

Watching where I stepped (for this bedpan procedure had been followed for quite some time), I went over and called just as the door was closing.

With the door half open, the woman of the bus stuck her head out and looked at me in the same way all the Christians looked at me. With that cold stare that told me I was an outsider. She had her hair up, and some of it had escaped over her face like spider legs, She was wearing an ugly duster and pink house slippers I hadn't seen before. They had MEXICO written across the top of the insteps.

"I want to be one with the Lord," I said.

She just kept staring.

"I am not a Christian, and I see that you folks are, and I like what I see. I want to be one of you. I want to join in salvation, and—"

"Hold it a minute," she said, turned back into the bus and yelled, "Sam!"

After a moment the door cracked wider and the scrawny man stood there. Behind him it was dark, but there was enough light from the storm overhead that I could see the bus's walls were lined with shelves and the shelves were full, though I couldn't tell with what.

I noticed the man's tie wasn't a real tie at all. It was painted on. He eyeballed me for a long moment. "Whatchawant, sinner?"

"I want to be a Christian:'

"Say you do. Want to be baptized and the like?"

"If that's what it takes."

"Does."

"Then baptize me,"

"That's the spirit. Come around front of the bus, I'll let you in."

"Sam?" the woman said.

"Now, don't you worry," he said. "This here's a nice boy. Besides, he wants to become a Christian. Right, son?"

"That's right," I said.

"See, there you are," he said to the woman. Then to me: "Come around front."

They closed the door and I went around to the door at the front side of the bus, and Sam opened it. I stepped inside and saw that a blanket curtain had been put behind the driver's seat, blocking off the rest of the bus from view. The woman was still back there.

There was a special seat bolted to the floor next to the one behind the steering wheel, and hanging from the mirror was a plastic Jesus that glowed in the dark, one of those things you buy across the border in Juarez. I had never wanted one. Lastly, in upraised rainbow stencil on the dash was this message: GOD IS LOVE.

"Sit down, boy." He patted the seat beside him, and I took it. "Now," he said, pursing his lips, "you want to become a Christian, do you?"

"I've been watching you folks . . . your meetings going on . . . Well, I like what I see."

"Don't blame you . . . I was a plumber, you know."

"Beg your pardon?"

"And a painter. Did plumbing and painting. Paint a little, plumb a little. Mostly plumbing, 'cause I'm kind of wiry, you see. Get up under them houses like a snake, fix them pipes. Some of the other plumbers called me that—Snake, I mean. They'd say, 'Snake, you sure can get under them houses,' and I'd say, 'Yeah, I can.' 'Cause I could."

"I see," I said.

"Painting now . . . that was different. I did it, but I didn't care for it. All them fumes make you sick, real sick. I'd sign on to paint a house, and I'd be sick through the whole thing. Not a minute's peace, just queasy and kind of headachy all the time. Even at night when I was away from it, after I'd cleaned up, I could smell that paint under my fingernails. It kind of hung on me like a cloud, it did. Much preferred plumbing. Sewer smell ain't nothing to a paint smell. Sewer smell is good honest smell. Human smell. But paint . . . paint is just paint, you see what I mean?"

I had begun to sense a parable. "Well . . . I suppose so."

The blanket moved then and the woman came out from behind it. She had put on another duster, not any more attractive than the first. She had on the same house shoes. I noted that she kept the backs broken down so her heels could hang out.

"It was just awful when he was painting," the woman said, picking right into the conversation. "He wasn't no fun at all. Grouchy all the time, like a poisoned dog. Hi. My name is Mable."

"Glad to meet you," I said. "I guess this is your seat."

"Oh no," Mable said. "You just keep it. I'll stand right here. I'm fine. I used to say to Sam about the way he acted when he was painting, 'Now you gonna act like that, you go out and sleep in the yard.' Didn't I say that to you, honeybunch?"

"Yes, you did, dumpling. She'd just say it right out, and mean it too. 'You gonna act like that, Sam,' she'd say, 'then you go out there in the yard and sleep. Take your piller with you, but get on out of this house.' That would straighten me right up, it would. Couldn't stand to be without my dumpling."

I was beginning to suspect this wasn't a parable.

The woman moved close to him, and he reached up and put an arm around her waist. She patted him on the head. I thought maybe she would give him a dog treat next.

"Painting is why I got preaching on my mind," Sam said. "They used to say, 'Be a Baptist preacher and you don't have to do no work,' and that sounded good to me. So, I started trying to teach myself about it, just so I could quit painting, you see, and you know what, son?"

I said I didn't.

"The call come over me. I'd been reading the Bible, trying to get a handle on it, trying to get all them names separate in my head, you know, and one night I'd just finished all that—I'd been painting earlier in the day—and I was dozing, listening to the radio, one of them country and western stations, and God, the Big Man himself come to me over that radio and told me some things he hadn't told none of them other preachers. Gave me some insights into His ways."

"Hallelujah, honey," the woman said.

"His name be praised. So God come to me over that radio, and I remember it was right in the middle of a pretty good ole song too, and he said, 'Sam, I'm giving you the call, and I want you to spread my word.' That was it. He didn't layout no details or nothing, just matter-of-fact about it, and I packed up our things, built us a traveling home out of this bus—"

"They come and took our house 'cause we couldn't pay for it," Mable added.

"Yes, they did, didn't they, dumpling. And I got this bus fixed up, and we started traveling around the country, doing a little fixing here and there, plumbing mostly, little painting when I couldn't get out of it and we needed the money, and I did a lot of preaching."

"It paid better than the plumbing or painting," the woman said. "It was just a sight to see how full that offering plate would be after a night of Sam's preaching. People just loved him."

"But the money wasn't the important thing. The thing was, I was reaching people with the Lord, taking the offering to keep this bus running, to feed our faces and keep us at the Lord's work."

"Sam made so many conversions," Mable said.

"Yes, I did. And one night while we was traveling, we come by this place, seen all those cars in line, and I thought, now wouldn't this be a golden opportunity?"

"Them's the exact words you used, sugar," Mable said. "You turned to me and said, 'Wouldn't this be a golden opportunity?'"

"I thought during intermission I might turn on my loudspeaker and start preaching. Try to bring some souls to God. But then this thing happened, this thing of the Devil. He'll do that every time, son. You got some good designs, well, ole Devil will come right in there on you, trying to mess things up. Even Oral Roberts, and you know how close he is to God, has problems with the Devil. Ole booger come right in Oral's bedroom once and tried to choke him, tried to choke the life out of him."

"But his wife run the Devil off and saved him," Mable said. "She come right in there and ran him right off." She patted Sam on the head. "I'd do that for you, wouldn't I, sugarbunch?"

"Yes, you would, dumpling, you surely would. But now, what we got here is a boy that wants to join our flock. Am I right, boy?"

'That's right," I said.

"Good, good . . . You ain't got no food on you, do you?"

"No," I said. I thought about the jerky back in the camper, but it was really Bob's and I couldn't offer it without his permission. Besides, I was afraid he'd shoot me.

"Well, let's get the baptizing part over with." With that Sam spit on his fingers and rubbed them across the top of my head. "I baptize you in the name of the Father and the Son and the Holy Ghost. Amen. Okay."

"That's it?" I asked.

"You were expecting a tub?"

"No . . . I mean, I guess it's okay."

"Sure it is. You feel any different?"

I thought about it. "No, not a thing."

"Just a little tingle or something?"

"Nope."

Sam looked distressed. "Well, sometimes it takes some time, so you give it some. Thing I'm gonna want you to do is go to the services a little later on. You come to that, son, and I'll hand you the Lord on a silver platter. Mable, bring the sand, will you, darling?"

Mable went behind the blanket curtain and came back with a big hourglass. The sand in the top half had almost run out.

"This here has come in handy. It was just one of them things we picked up once and hadn't never used, but since we been here in this outdoor picture show, we've used it quite a bit. It's an eight-hour hourglass. When it runs through twice, we have services. Unless we forget to turn it or we sleep through, but that ain't often."

We sat there a minute and he told me a couple of plumbing adventures, then he said he had to go get ready and he went behind the blanket curtain and left me with Mable, who took his seat in front of the steering wheel. She looked at the rainbow GOD IS LOVE on the dash for a while, then put her eye on the Jesus hanging from the mirror, and finally looked out at the wing mirror as if she might find a revelation there. Things being as they were, I was kind of short on small talk, and as the weather was constant, that was out. I was beginning to feel like an enormous jackass.

"You know," Mable said out of the clear blue, "wish I had me some ham bone and some dried beans, pintos. I think I miss that the most, ham bone and beans. I can make the best pot of beans. I just take me some pintos, the dried kind, and soak them in a pan of water overnight, then the next morning I start cooking them, making sure I don't let all the water boil down. I chop me up a bunch of onions, put some salt and pepper in there, and that ham bone, and just cook and cook and cook till that water gets real soupy. You fix you some cornbread with that, even hot-water cornbread, and I tell you, you've got major eating, mister. I just dream about food all the time. How about you?"

"I think about it a lot," I said. "Mostly hamburgers. Sometimes pizza."

"You do like pinto beans and cornbread, though?"

"I've got no complaints against it. Right now most anything sounds good."

She seemed to consider that for a moment, then she said, "You know, this is all the work of the Devil. And we can beat the Devil if we try. My next-door neighbor back when Sam was plumbing all the time was named Lillie, and she had these Hell's Angel types move in across from her. Drove them motorsickles, you know. And she said they were worshiping the Devil, 'cause she could hear that loud rock music, you know. The stuff where you play the records backwards and it's got some sort of ooga-booga about the Devil on it. And she started praying, and darn if they didn't move. Just up and moved six months later, and she said it was on account of her praying all the time. The Lord heard her prayers, and those Hell's Angels just up and moved."

Right. Up and moved six months later. I wondered if Bob would do me the favor of kicking my butt around the camper a few times.

In the middle of an apple-pie recipe, Sam returned. He had on his coat; it sagged badly. He had on a different shirt, and though it was in pretty tough shape, it did look better than the other one. Even the tie was painted on better. It must have been the shirt he used for Christmas because the tie was bright red.

Mable went behind the curtain then to do "a little touchin' up," and Sam sat down behind the steering wheel and looked at me like a loving, but stern father.

"Son, I want you to know that now, no matter what happens, you are in the hands of the Lord. If something really ugly should happen to you . . . if a ton of bricks fell out of the sky and crushed you flatter than a pie pan, you'd be one with the Lord. He's waiting on you, son. Waiting for you to join His kingdom. What do you think of that?"

"It's a comfort," I said. I wondered if Bob would loan me his shotgun so I could shoot myself. I had been a bean head to see anything wonderful about these people and their way of life. The truth was I was going to die, and there wasn't any heaven to go to. Unless it was some sort of B-string heaven for extras in bad movies. That's what this all had to be. A bad movie.

When Mable came back she had on a long overcoat, and I could tell the pockets were filled with something, but I had no idea what.

"Well, how do I look?" she asked Sam cheerfully.

"Like a million dollars, sugarbunch, like a million dollars." He smiled at her, then looked at the hourglass. "Almost time. I got to go next door and tap on Deacon Cecil's car window, get him to get everybody ready for tonight's services. You're gonna like this, son. It's gonna put you straight with God."

I was beginning to doubt that. If these were God's chosen people, He had poor taste, and if I wanted in with them, then I had even poorer taste. But as it stood, in for a penny, in for a pound. It wasn't like I had a pressing engagement elsewhere, but I was beginning to plan one. Maybe Bob would like the idea. We could maybe find a hose somewhere and run the exhaust fumes into the back of the camper. Just go to sleep and not wake up. It sure seemed like a good proposition to me.

Sam got up and I let him pass by me and out the door to get Deacon Cecil. When he was gone, Mable shrugged and said, "Well, here we are."

She told me a story about how she'd won a baking contest in Gladewater, Texas, once, and by then Sam was back.

"Are things ready?" Mable asked.

"Ready," he said, and looked at me and smiled.

I smiled back.

We went out of the bus, and as we walked, Sam put his arm around my shoulders and told me about the Kingdom of Heaven. None of it was particularly inspiring. The smell from his armpit kept my mind off what he was saying and made me woozy.

As we neared the selected spot, I could see a number of the Christians strutting rapidly toward it. They really seemed worked up and excited this time, like they'd just arrived at the company picnic.

On the other hand, I was considerably less than worked up. My entire religious experiment so far had been a vast disappointment. Sort of like when I found out my pet gerbil wouldn't live forever, and later, after I'd cleaned the little turds out of his cage for what seemed like an enormous period of time, thought the little fucker would never die.

When we were all gathered there, Sam introduced me as a "boy who wants to join God," and the others told me how nice that was, and a girl who might have been pretty, had she not been so thin and her hair so greasy, said, "A fresh one, huh?"

"You know," Mable said, looking up at the lightning flashing across the blackness, "this reminds me of when we used to camp out, and sometimes it looked like it was going to rain. And we'd build us a big fire anyway, and we'd take some coat hangers and straighten them out and roast wienies over the fire. It was so much fun. We'd just let them cook until they were black, and they tasted so good. That just don't make sense really, 'cause if you burn them at home they aren't any good at all, but out there on an open fire you can cook them black as a nigger, and they're just as fine as they can be."

"We'll start the services with a little round of prayer." Sam said, "then we'll have communion."

At mention of the word "communion," a collective sigh went up from the crowd. These were some communion-loving folks. I remembered the sighs from the Popcorn King's followers when they were eating the results of his vomit. There hadn't been a lot of difference in sounds.

"God," Sam said, "you sure have allowed some odd things here. In fact, I would say you have outdone yourself. But if that's your will, that's it. Still, sure would like to know the why of it . . . We also have this young fella amongst us, just baptized and craving the Lord, and we thought we'd bring him to you . . . It would certainly be nice if you'd do something to that old Popcorn King, by the way. Like maybe kill him. And it wouldn't hurt my feelings, or the feelings of anyone here, if you'd make this black mess go away and give us back our highway and things. Amen—"

"Amen," said the crowd.

"Bad as things *is*," Mable whispered to me, "you got to be thankful. Things will work out, I know they will. I had a cousin, her name was Frances, and she didn't have good thoughts on nothing or nobody, and she got this rash on her foot and it got infected, and she wouldn't do nothing but wear this old sock on it, day in, day out. It just stunk something awful. I'd say to her, 'Frances, you need to go and pour you some chemicals on that thing. It's done gone and got infected.' But you know, she wouldn't listen, and her foot got so infected they had to cut it off. Had a foot one day, next she didn't. Just had this little stub and they got this leather thing they put over it, and she had to put on this artificial foot, and she'd pull a stocking over that and she could slip a shoe on, you know, and it looked almost real. But when she walked, she walked something like this." She showed me how her cousin Frances walked. The congregation and Sam had stopped to look at her, but she didn't seem to notice.

She did a sort of stiff step with one foot and dragged the other after it. "That's how she looked. And there's some little ole mean kids that live down the block from her, and they'd get up behind her when she was walking to the store, and they'd all walk like her." She showed me the walk in more exaggerated form. "It was just like a bunch of crippled ducks following their ole crippled mama. They'd been my kids I'd have worn their little hind ends out so bad they couldn't have sat down for a week. But the reason she got her foot rotted off like that and got mocked by them children is because she didn't have no faith and doesn't look on the bright side of things. God keeps score on them kind, you can bet he does."

"Mable," Sam said patiently, "if you're through with the story about your cousin's rotting foot, we'd like to continue."

"Oh, I am sorry," said Mable. "Don't you pay me no never mind. Ya'll just go right on with your rat killing and I'll hush and listen."

"That would be nice," Sam said.

Then came the sermon. It had a lot of storm clouds, sinners, fire and brimstone and the work of the Devil in it. Sam hopped around and waved his arms a lot. But somehow it wasn't very exciting. There were quite a few references to plumbing and painting and a parable about a little girl that got hit by a truck, which I couldn't seem to work into the rest of the sermon or find the point of.

A man beside me leaned over to another and said, "I'm really sick of this crap."

"It's a thing to get through," the other man said.

Finally Sam's sermon sort of petered out, like maybe he couldn't keep it on his mind anymore. He said "amen" and called his flock to him. This was the huddle I'd seen, and Mable put her arm around me and pushed me toward it. In the huddle it was hot and full of sweaty pits, unwashed clothes and bad breath; all this ganged up on me and I felt dizzy and weak, and before I knew it, I was in the center of the huddle and hands were touching me, then suddenly Sam stepped forward and kicked my feet out from under me. I went down hard and hit my head, tried to rise, but Sam shoved me down with his foot, and the next thing I know there's two guys holding my arms, and the girl with the greasy hair has one of my legs and Mable has the other.

"What in hell are you doing?" I yelled.

"Communion," Sam said. He took a tin of sardines out of his rumpled coat, and that made me aware suddenly of what was filling that shabby coat of Mable's. More sardine tins. "We been sharing these with the congregation," Sam said. "Folks have been real nice about it too, especially since they know I got the bus rigged up with a bomb, and they mess where they ain't supposed to be messin' when we're away from there, and BLAM!"

"That's got nothing to do with me . . . Tell these people to let me go."

"It's got everything to do with you. We also drink a little of each other's blood."

"Like this," Mable said, and she put her knee over my ankle to hold me down and produced a penknife from the pocket of her coat. She opened it smoothly and drew it across her palm. A line of blood appeared there and she held her hand up without looking and a man who was standing above her grabbed it and put his mouth to the wound and sucked. He trembled he was so excited. Mable's tongue worked from one corner of her mouth to the other and her eyes closed.

A man in the crowd began speaking softly. "Yeah, brother, get it, get it, go, go."

"Oh yes," Mable said, "Oh yes, yes, yes. Suck, suck, oh God in Heaven, suck, yes, oh yes."

Then other knives and razors flashed and flesh was opened and mouths were pleased. It sounded like a convention of leeches, or an orgy—or, to be more precise, both.

Sam squatted down close to my face. There was blood on his lips. "You see," he said, patting my chest. "We made a pact. We wouldn't let nobody else in. We would convert them if they wanted, but they couldn't join us, and we'd eliminate competition. It's a tough thing to do, but the Lord moves in mysterious ways his miracles to perform . . . and food lasts longer this way."

A man took Mable's place holding my leg and she inched down to me and held the penknife where I could see it. "And we have to take advantage of any food that comes our way," she said. "It would be sinful to waste . . . and we've had our eyes on you and your friend for a while."

"We just didn't want to get shot," Sam said. "Your pal never seems to leave his shotgun."

"But you're Christians," I said.

"That we are," Sam said, "and that should make you feel proud and special. You'll be with God in Heaven in a short time now. He'll embrace you and—"

"Then why don't you go join him," I said. "You're holier than me, you should go first."

Sam smiled. "It isn't my time."

"It's a little thing," Mable said. "Nothing to it, really. We got to do this thing, and you've got to accept it . . . And this here knife may be small, but it's sharp. It won't hurt much. They say the blood goes out of you fast when it's done right, that you just get terrible sleepy, then it's all over. I've cut many a hog's throat in my day, and though couldn't none of them tell me if it was sleepy or not, they seemed to go pretty peaceful, wouldn't you say, Sam?"

"I would," Sam said.

"But I'm no hog," I said.

"Cut the gab," a man said, and he dropped a rusty looking hubcap beside my head; it clanged, rattled, stopped.

"Turn him," Sam said.

The two holding my legs let go, and the men who had my arms flipped me onto my knees, pulled my arms back so hard behind my back my shoulder blades met. They pushed me forward so that my face was over the hubcap.

"Won't none of you waste," Mable said. "I thought you'd like to know that. We'll take the blood to drink, then we'll have us a little ole cookout with the rest of you."

"Mable can cook like the dickens; don't matter what it is, she can cook it."

The greasy-haired girl who had held one of my legs earlier came around and bent down to look me in the face. "I'm gonna love you, sugar. I'm gonna just love you to death. Gonna wrap my lips around you, and chew and chew and chew."

"Get on with it, for Pete's sake," the man who had dropped the hubcap said.

Mable grabbed my hair. "Just think about something pleasant, like good ole turnip greens and black-eyed peas. It'll be over quick-like."

I closed my eyes, but I didn't think of turnip greens and black-eyed peas. I tried to remember how things were before the drive-in, but nothing would come. There was only the dark behind my eyelids, the sound of all those hungry Christians breathing, the smell of their bodies. Mable lifted my head more to expose my neck. I hoped it would be quick and that I would not have to hear my blood draining into the hubcap for very long.

And just when I expected to feel the blade, there was an explosion, a thud in the hubcap and I was warmly wet from chin to forehead.

Part Three

THE ORBIT MUST DIE

Death and Destruction and School Bus-Fu

1

I thought my throat had been cut and the blood from the wound had sprayed my face, and that simultaneously there had been a loud clap of thunder, though it didn't sound right, not even for the artificial thunder of the drive-in.

Against my will I opened my eyes, saw lying in the hubcap beneath me a hand, and lying next to it in a little pond of blood was the penknife.

The men had let go of my arms and I was able to rock up on my knees and see Mable. She was still on her knees, but now she was holding her arm in front of her, minus her hand, and watching blood leap from the wound like freshly tapped oil.

Mable looked at me and said, "Oh my."

A number of the congregation dropped down to try and suck at the stump of her arm, and the girl with the greasy hair began lapping at the blood that had sprayed my face. Her tongue was rough and dry, like a cat's.

"Who's next?" a voice called, and I turned to see Bob standing there with the shotgun, a wreath of gunsmoke about his head. With his hair and beard grown long, his sweaty hat drooping, he looked like an old-time desperado. At his feet two men lay holding their heads. He had apparently cleared himself a path into the huddle with the stock of his gun.

"Mess with me," he said, "and I'll shoot you just to check the pump action on this baby."

Mable said, "Sam, Sam, my hand's done come off. Do you think we can get me an artificial one?"

"They cost too much," Sam said, and Mable fainted forward on her face. The stump-suckers stayed with her, working on her arm, pushing and shoving each other out of the way, tongues darting and colliding as they pursued the taste of the hot blood.

"Quit that sucking on her," Bob said. "Get away from there." He stepped in and gave one of the lappers a quick kick to the seat of the pants. "Spread the hell out."

They did.

"And you," he said, giving the greasy-haired girl a kick in the ribs, "you quit licking his face."

She scrambled away. I sort of hated that. I was beginning to like her.

A guy tried to pull a pistol on Bob, and Bob saw him out of the corner of his eye and gave him the stock of the shotgun to eat. The man went down and the gun slid across the asphalt. Bob looked at the greasy-haired girl and said, "Do me a favor, sugar, hand me that gun. Easy-like."

She gave it to him without protest and he put it in his belt.

"All right, all other weapons hit the deck," Bob said, "or I'm gonna start opening up heads."

Another pistol dropped to the ground. Can openers, knives, clubs, coins in socks. A condom full of marbles.

Bob nodded at the pistol. "I'd like that one too, sugar. Okay?"

The greasy-haired girl gave it to him. He put it in his belt next to the other one. Now he did look like a desperado.

The crowd had spread out, and I got up. I felt a little on the limp side.

"Take off your belt, Jack," Bob said, "and give it to that preacher fella to put on the woman. He doesn't make her a tourniquet pretty quick, she's gonna die."

"She's gonna die anyway," a man in the crowd said. "Why don't you just let us go on and eat her, and you two can join in. Hell, you can go first."

"That's a good idea," the greasy-haired girl said.

"No thanks," Bob said.

I took off my belt and gave it to Sam. He got down on his hands and knees and applied it to Mable's arm, about six inches above the wound. It cut off most of the bleeding.

"I think you're supposed to let that off now and then," Bob said. "You don't, she'll lose her whole arm . . . if it don't kill her."

"I got some idea how to do it," Sam said. When he leaned over to make an extra adjustment on the belt, a can of sardines tipped out of his pocket. All eyes went to that can.

"They've got a lot of those," I said to Bob. "That's how they've been holding things together. And nobody's tried to take it away from them because they've got the bus rigged with a bomb."

"You don't say?" Bob said. "And here I was thinking this was all just the power of the Lord, and it's cans of sardines."

"You mess with that bus," Sam said, "it'll blow you out of this drive-in,"

"That's an idea," Bob said. "Okay, Mr. Preacher, get your wife there. Jack, give him a hand. Ya'll come with me. Rest of you Christians just sort of lick up here while we're gone."

Sam and I got our arms around Mable and got her up. She came to briefly, but she couldn't walk. We dragged her away, the toes of her house shoes scraping the asphalt. I looked back over my shoulder as we went away from there, and the greasy-haired girl grabbed the sardines and tried to make a run for it. She was swamped. At the bottom of the mound of thrashing arms and legs you could hear her yelling, "Mine, mine."

The guy who had dropped the hubcap snatched Mable's hand from it, sprinted off tearing at it with his teeth. He rounded an elderly Chevy, practically leaped from one row to the other, weaved into some other cars and disappeared into shadows, perhaps to lie under some automobile and chew on his prize like a contented terrier.

A middle-aged woman in jean shorts and a red blouse dove down on the hubcap and began to lap at the blood there. A man dropped to his knees to join her. They growled at each other like Dobermans.

"Praise the Lord," Bob said.

"Oh, shut up," I said.

When we came to the bus, Bob made Sam put Mable down and give him the key. Sam said he would give him the key if he was going to be so foolish, but he would rather be shot point-blank with the shotgun before he would open it himself. The results would be too terrible, and the death of all of us would be on his hands.

Bob put the key in the lock and opened the back door.

He looked at us and smiled. "Boom," he said.

"Well," Sam said, "it worked up until now."

Bob climbed inside and we went after. The bus had shelves and the shelves had wire over them, and behind the wire were oodles of canned goods, mostly sardines and Vienna sausages. Two of my all-time non-favorites under normal conditions. Right now they looked rather attractive. My stomach growled like an attack dog.

"Comfy in here," Bob said.

Sam and I helped Mable over to a bed that folded away from the bus wall, and Sam got a bucket and put that by the bed and took the pressure off the tourniquet. Blood shot out of the wound and into the bucket. "We were afeared of a nigger takeover," Sam explained as he tightened the tourniquet again. "Figured it came down to us or the niggers, we'd have this food put back, and that would hold us for a time."

I looked around more now that my eyes were adjusted. There was all manner of stuff in there. Plumbing tools, carpentry tools, painting equipment, even a welding torch and the tanks to go with it arranged on a dolly.

"Guns?" Bob asked.

"We hadn't gotten around to that," Sam said. "That was next."

"Wouldn't lie to me, would you?"

"I'm telling the truth . . . Damn you, why'd you have to shoot Mable's hand off?"

"Seemed sort of necessary," Bob said. "She was about to cut my buddy's throat. "Though I figure the dumb sucker deserved it. Christians, my ass."

"Watch your language," Sam said. "If it had been her foot, that wouldn't have been *so* bad. But her hand. She likes to cook and give me back rubs, and she needs two good hands to do them things right."

"She wasn't holding the knife with her foot," Bob said. "Just be glad I'm shooting slugs, or you'd have all got peppered."

I looked at Mable. Her face was as pale as a baby's ass, and her eyes were foggy. I figured she wasn't going to make it.

About then she opened her eyes and said, "You know, the thing that would do me some good right now is a chicken fried steak. Maybe some mashed taters and cream gravy and rolls with it. Big ole glass of ice tea."

"Rest now," Sam said.

"It's the batter does it on them steaks," Mable said. "Don't got that right, it ain't worth eatin'. You dip the steak in the milk-and-egg batter, then into the flour, then back into the milk and egg, then back into the flour. Makes it extra crispy."

"Ssshhhh, now, sugar bee, you rest."

"Don't do it that way, you don't get that good flaky crust, and I do like a good flaky crust."

She passed out again.

Bob came over and gave me one of the pistols from his belt. "Here, you might want to shoot someone later."

I took it and walked to the open door at the back of the bus and looked out. The Christians were fist-fighting, probably over drops of blood on the asphalt, or what was left of the sardines Sam had dropped. I could see the greasy-haired girl lying on her side with her eyes wide open. There was a young man with a knife cutting strips of meat off her legs. I took a deep breath and closed the door.

2

Bob and I ate sardines while Sam lay asleep on the floor near Mable, who now and then came awake and gave us in great detail one of her favorite recipes. We had been through cherry pie, buttermilk biscuits, chili and hominy cakes.

"I feel kind of bad eating another person's food," I said.

"They were going to eat you," Bob said. "Look at it that way."

"A point," I said, and ate a little faster.

"You're going to need your strength when the Christians come for us. They're not going to be worried about the bomb anymore. They'll have it figured now, since we didn't get blown up."

"How'd you know the bus wasn't rigged with a bomb?"

"Just figured . . . didn't know for sure . . . Hell, Jack, I don't care anymore. If this is life, it ain't worth living. I think what you and I ought to do is something real foolish. Otherwise, we'll end up licking blood out of hubcaps."

"What you got in mind?" I asked.

"Destroy the Orbit symbol."

I mulled that over awhile. "It has a ring to it. Any reason?"

Bob looked back to make sure Sam and Mable were still sleeping. "Come with me." He pulled the lever and opened the door and we went outside, "You've been a mite busy to notice, but when I woke up and seen you were gone, I figured you'd joined the Christians."

"Okay, I was a jackass. Happy?"

"It's just your way, Jack. I'm used to it. Anyway, I woke up and come out of the camper and the first thing I seen was that."

He pointed at the Orbit symbol. "And it's worse now than when I'm talking about."

"God Almighty," I said.

The Orbit symbol had turned a hot blue, so blue it hurt my eyes. It was getting the juice from the tentacles—there were twelve of them now and I couldn't think of them as anything other than tentacles—and they were twisting and lashing across the blackness, spitting lightning from their tips like venom, and this lightning no longer ran the length of the pole, but just gathered in the symbol alone, and the symbol was spinning very fast, hurling more lightning than ever from it, striking the concession. The concession glowed so violently that at any moment I expected it to move, like amputated frog legs hopping in response to a live wire. The marquee was no longer there. I figured it had exploded and crumbled down, like a charcoaled stick.

"I figure something new is about to happen," Bob said, "and I'm not sure it's worth waiting around for. Last time we had something like this we got the Popcorn King."

I agreed with Bob. I felt it was gearing up for something bigger and more catastrophic. I tried to figure exactly what it was with the symbol and why the power from the lightning concentrated itself there before going to the concession. A number of B-movie possibilities presented themselves: The symbol had accidentally been made from smelted iron ore that had been mixed with some strange and horrid sentient metal that had come to earth in a meteor, and once it had been converted to the Orbit symbol it had awakened from a long sleep and was now tormenting us earthlings for lack of anything better to do. I figured being a chunk of rock, or even a sign, could get pretty boring. It was the sort of thing that could give you a bad attitude. And I thought again of the B-movie gods, and that idea appealed to me most of all. Their motives seemed to fit in with those of most low-budget moviemakers. Bring it in on time. If it doesn't make sense in spots, well, make it pretty or exciting. Don't let them think about it too long.

"You getting hypoglycemic again," Bob said, bringing me up from the pit of my thoughts.

"No," I said. "I was just thinking."

"About what?"

"About rewriting the script."

"The script?"

"Let's just say this is a movie and those tentacles—"

"Just drips of goo, Jack."

"—belong to the B-movie gods, and they're manufacturing all this, using us as actors, only we're not acting, and they're making up the script as they go. They've isolated us, they've given us our monster, the Popcorn King, and now they're looking for the big finish, and I don't think they've planned a heroic ending. I think this is one of those downbeat films."

"Always got to have something to believe in, don't you, Jack? Astrology, Christianity, now B-movie gods."

"Give me something to blame all this on. A random universe with no god, evil or otherwise, is just too much for me. Just let me say it's the B-movie gods and they have this bad scenario planned, and you and me, we're not going to stand for it. We're going to destroy the symbol . . . Hell, let's do something even if it's wrong."

"Believe the ghost of Elvis is doing it if you like," Bob said. "It don't make a hang to me. But I've got a plan for taking that symbol down . . ."

Bob woke Sam up when we got back to the bus. He pulled him up front and said, "You know how to use that torch and stuff?"

"I don't just carry it around, boy. Sure, I know. But I aint' got a hankering at the moment."

"I'm going to give you a hankering," Bob said. "We're going to cut the Orbit symbol down."

"Have at it," Sam said.

"We want you to do it. You know how to use the equipment."

"After what you done to Mable, you think I'm gonna help you? You shouldn't oughta shot her hand off, little buddy."

I thought he might add "nahnuhnahnah," but he passed on that.

"We want to cut that sucker down and drop it on the concession," Bob said. "See if we can smash the Popcorn King . . . Christ, we want to do something besides wait to get eaten, or end up eating one another. What say, Sam?"

"Don't use the Saviour's name in vain . . . I don't know. You have to cut it just right, get it to fall that way."

"That's why we need you," Bob said. "You're the expert."

"Well," Sam said, rubbing his lingers along his chin, "it might not change a thing, but it sure could give a man peace of mind for trying, now couldn't it?"

"Our point exactly," Bob said. "You'll do it then?"

"All right, but this don't mean we're friends."

"Wouldn't think of it. One more thing. We're gonna need this bus, and when we finish with it, it won't be in any shape at all."

"No sir," Sam said, "you ain't gonna . . ." Then he looked hard at Bob and the shotgun. "It don't matter what I say, does it? You'll take the bus anyway."

"We'd like to have your permission," Bob said, "just to be sociable."

Sam nodded wearily. "Well, tell me what you're gonna do to it."

The bus was part diversion, part weapon.

We tore the wire off the shelves, took the food and put it in a couple of blankets and tied it up, pulled it to the rear of the bus. We took the wire outside and Sam welded it into a kind of pen on the hood of the bus while Bob watched with his shotgun, just in case we had visitors. When Sam finished, I brought all the cans of paint thinner he had and put them in the wire enclosure, made sure they fit snug by pushing a couple of moldy pillowcases in between them.

"When the front end hits that electrical field," Bob said, "it'll blow. And if we can get enough momentum behind this baby, really put the hammer down, it'll run on into the concession and the gas tank will go. We're lucky, that'll get the Popcorn King. Or the symbol will when it comes down. The idea here is to try and hit him with both things at once. I've got a flare gun in the camper, and I'll give that to one of you. When the symbol is about to drop, shoot off the flare and I'll put my foot through it, put this sucker in his lap."

"And how will you get out?" I asked.

"I'll jump. I'm a jumping sonofabitch, didn't I tell you?"

"No. I knew you could hide under mufflers good, but I didn't know about the jumping."

Bob smiled. "If Wendle was here right now, big guy or no big guy, I'd kick his butt . . . after I had me something to eat, that is, like about ten cans of those sardines in there."

"I don't doubt it," I said. "But right now, let's kick the King's butt."

"I'll get the flare gun," Bob said.

Bob got the flare gun, then we took the blankets of food over to the camper, trying to make sure no one was watching, but not worrying too much about it. It was most likely a formality anyway. I didn't really expect to be coming back. If our plan failed, the Popcorn King would have plans for us—lunch, probably.

Fact was, I figured our time was running out anyway. So far the King had been patient, waiting for us to get hungry enough to join his flock, or maybe not thinking about us at all. He didn't seem to have any master plan. Feed the flock, and gradually feed on the flock. An insane demigod without true design; a voyeur of human destruction; the Jim Jones of Popcorn.

When we got back to the bus Sam was sitting on the bed beside Mable. "Died," he said. "Just gave her buttermilk-biscuit recipe and died. Didn't quite make it to the part about how long to keep them little buddies in the oven."

Bob nodded and went to the front of the bus.

"You did this, cowboy," Sam yelled at Bob's back.

Bob pulled the door lever and went outside. I went after him. He was leaning against the bus, the shotgun cradled in his arms. He was watching the movie. It was *The Toolbox Murders.*

I went up and leaned beside him. "You saved my life. I'm sorry you had to shoot the woman, but thanks for saving my life."

"I never said I was sorry for shooting her," Bob said, but he didn't look at me.

We leaned that way for a time. "Movie any good?" I asked.

"It's all right," Bob said, "but I've seen it."

I laughed and clapped him on the shoulder. "Come on," I said. "We've got things to do."

We went back inside the bus.

Sam looked at me and snarled. "Damn you, if you'd just gone on and cooperated, we'd have eaten you and things would have gone on like they were . . . least for a while."

"I have days when I'm obstreperous," I said.

"To hell with this talk," Bob said. "We're going on with it, Sam, with or without you even if I have to teach myself how to use that torch by trial and error and let Jack drive the bus. So how's it going to be? You in or out?"

Sam turned to look at Mable. He closed her eyes with his fingertips, then looked at us. "I'm in," he said.

Bob nodded. "Now . . . what would you like to do with her body?"

There was no way to bury her, and options were few. We could toss her into the acidic blackness or we could leave her on the bus to burn when it exploded. (If it exploded. Just because we had a plan didn't mean I had a lot of faith in it.)

Sam preferred to leave her on the bus. He got some cans of sardines out of her overcoat pockets (he wasn't so sentimental as to leave those), and put some old clothes on top of her to help her catch fire. He took some plastic plumbing pipe, couplings and pipe glue, used a hacksaw to make her an artificial hand. Or that's what it was supposed to be. It looked like a dull garden rake to me. He tied it to the stump of her arm with some rounds of twine and a twisted coat hanger.

Finished, he put a blanket over her and tied it and Mable to the bed with some strips of old sheet, changed out of his festive-tie shirt and put back on the one with a black tie. He said some words over her, then changed back to the shirt with the red tie painted on. I presumed that was also his welding shirt.

"Sam," I said, "I'm not one to meddle, but I've been meaning to ask you. Why do you paint those ties on your shirts?"

"Can't tie the knots," he said.

Made sense.

We ate some sardines, talked the plan over one more time, then Sam and I lowered the dolly with the welding equipment on it out the back of the bus.

"Go for it," Bob said. We shook hands and he gave me the flare pistol. I slipped it into my belt next to the revolver.

"Let's get on with it," Sam said. "I ain't gonna shake hands with nobody."

I took hold of the dolly, cocked it back and started pushing it across the lot at a dog trot. Sam ran alongside me, wheezing like a tire going flat.

3

We weren't too worried about the Popcorn King noticing us. We were a good distance away, and hey, it wasn't like there wasn't something strange going on all the time anyway.

But the closer we got to the little fence that led out to the stretch of concrete where the Orbit symbol was, the more nervous I became. My courage began to falter, and I wanted to go back to the truck and get into the sardines and eat those, and just hope for the best.

Still, I kept running, and Sam was staying up with me. We saw the Christians here and there, standing around, watching, wondering, I suppose. None of them waved. Stuck up.

I looked toward the concession. It glowed beautifully against the blackness, like some exotic gem on black velvet. One of those little winds that kicked up out of nowhere from time to time started going and it carried the stink of the no-longer-used toilets to me, and the smell was as hard and mean as a head-on collision.

In the window of the concession I could see the bodies hanging, like big fish in a market. Some of them were little more than skeletons.

We came to the wooden fence and Sam got up there and straddled it, and I pushed the dolly up where he could get hold of it and twist it over, lower it to the other side.

Sam followed after it and I took his place, straddling the fence. I looked out at the great tin fence surrounding the drive-in (except this area that led out to the Orbit symbol), and saw the cruel blackness beyond. I saw some of the screens and their movies and wondered how they had gone on so long without being destroyed. But then I knew. They were light. They were holy shrines to a mad god. I wondered how it would be if we managed to destroy the concession here in Lot A and the three movies went out. Once in darkness, would it all end, like bad dreams tumbling down the throat of sleep?

Nope. Lot B would be the center then, for however long that lasted. Lot B with its empty concession and its manned film room, carrying on with or without the King until there was mass murder and/or starvation and finally over there the lights went out as well.

I could see people moving around the drive-in, a number of them moving toward the concession. Probably time for the next meal of popcorn vomit. I figured some of the patrons could see me up there, but it most likely wouldn't excite them much. Many had gone over the fences and out into the blackness, and in their eyes I'd just be one more quitter.

"You gonna lay an egg up there, or what?" Sam said.

I went on over and took hold of the dolly and started pushing it out on the spur toward the symbol. It was brighter out there because of the lightning, and the ozone was so thick it smelled like a wound being cauterized.

The spur narrowed as we went and the ebony pudding was close on either side of us, and I thought about how easy it would be to end it all. I mean it was right there taunting me, inviting me to freedom. But I kept pushing.

When finally we made the tall, tapering pole that held the symbol, I looked up at the tentacles (liked to think I could see suckers on one side of them, like on an octopus) and the lightning coming out of them, watched the bolts strike the symbol, spin off and engulf the concession. Looking up at that great light, those tentacles, made me feel small and weak and hated.

Sam tried to arc a spark on the torch, but wasn't having much luck. He talked to it. "Come on, now, be good. Come on. Hot A'mighty, that's the way."

A spark jumped to the torch and he turned it up and the flame licked out and he put it to the pole, began to cut through. "Might as well get comfy," he said. "This is going to take a while."

I remembered it was not wise to look at a torch without goggles because a spark could jump to your eyes, and I didn't want to watch Sam work without goggles. The way he was squinting at the flame made me ache. I turned and looked at the blackness, but that was too dreary and it had a siren's call, so I turned and looked at the fence and the back and top of the concession. I could see the upper half of one of the screens beyond that and I tried to watch the movie, *Night of the Living Dead*, but it seemed too much like reality and I knew all the lines by heart. I closed my eyes and tried to think of nothing, but there was just too much in my head for that. I wondered what Bob was doing and how he felt sitting there in the bus, waiting for our signal. I wondered if he really would jump.

I figured he might have already turned the bus toward the concession, and he would be watching the symbol, waiting for our flare. God, I hoped the bus would start.

Then I didn't think about that anymore. I thought of Randy and Willard and I felt pity, something I was afraid I might have lost, then there were tears in my eyes and they might have been for Randy and Willard.

"Getting there," Sam said.

I thought, no, the tears are not for Randy and Willard, they are for all the good dreams I've dreamed, for all the good gods, who do not exist, for all the good in man that is only social conditioning to keep the bigger man from breaking his head. Yes, that was what I was weeping for: mankind. The fact that *man* is not *kind* at all. But then I knew that was malarkey and that I was weeping for myself, all my loneliness, disappointment, the awareness of my mortality, the realization that the universe was a dark, empty place and life was nothing more than a carnival ride and that when the bell sounded to end the ride and you got off, you stepped out into nothing. It was all over then, all there was was ended, flesh and soul might as well have never been.

Even the B-movie gods could not be proved except in my dreams. Maybe they were not gods at all but some sort of life-form that was far enough advanced that they served the purpose of god counterfeit deities. Alien filmmakers. Youthful aliens who have had an interesting accident with their chemistry set. Or nothing more than my need for there to be reason and design where there was none; I so desperately wanted there to be gods and magic, even if they were bad.

"Timber," yelled Sam.

I turned and looked up and the pole was starting to go, dragging its lightning after it.

"The flare," Sam said.

I pulled the flare gun, lifted it and fired at an angle, not knowing the height of our sky. The flare went bright red and pretty against the dark and the strands of blue lightning. I dropped the gun and started running for the fence, Sam behind me, wheezing. Before we made it there, the symbol came down, and it lost its lightning; it was like the lightning was bubble gum and it had been stretched too far and had popped free. The symbol came down on the concession with a crunch, and there was a momentary crackling and sizzling that hurt my ears and made my flesh feel warm, then debris flew and the lights of the projectors went out.

I got hold of the fence and pulled myself up, straddled it. There was still plenty of light from the lightning overhead, and I could see that Bob had gotten a late start, but was coming. The old bus whined like an unpleasant child, the lights shone like miniature suns. The bus hit the concession with a screech and a blast, and a rush of flame went through it, blew the windows out and wrapped around the roof, kicked the back door open. All manner of crap propelled out the open door and went sailing, including the bed Mable was strapped to. It skidded across the asphalt, twisted sideways and struck a Volkswagen, ricocheted back toward the burning bus, stopped spinning halfway there, sat smoldering like a cheap cigar. The blanket had been torn partially free, and Mable's arm with the plumbing-pipe hand came out from under it and struck the ground, lay there like a stiff white spider unable to run. The recipe cards had also escaped from beneath the blanket and they were fluttering down. Some had been flame-kissed and were nothing now but blackened wisps.

I saw Bob. He had jumped. He was on his feet and limping toward me. He had the shotgun and he was still wearing his hat. I felt like cheering but before I could celebrate, the debris shifted, boards lifted and dropped as the Popcorn King stood up out of the rubble. He was charred from head to foot. That part of his head that was the popcorn cup had a lick of flame fluttering out of it like a feather in a fez. A board had gone through his top chest. Glass poked out of his flesh. He looked very unhappy, and he was looking directly at me.

He reached up with his top right hand and pulled the board out of his chest and tossed it aside. He started walking out of the debris, toward me.

"Get away from there," Bob yelled. "Run."

But I was frozen, watching the King. He was moving slowly, staggering. He no longer had the blue glow. He looked more like a bad acrobat act, a little guy on a big guy's shoulders.

The King opened his mouth and coughed out smoke. He fell to his knees and the tattoos dripped off him like melting licorice and formed a dark pool on the ground. The King lay face down and quit moving.

I got down off the fence and went over there. I could hear Sam calling to me to help him over, asking what was happening. I could hear Bob telling me to run, but I didn't pay either of them any mind.

I bent down to the King and whispered, "Randy?"

The head lifted slightly. The single eye looked at me. I couldn't tell if there was recognition there or not. Maybe it was just confusion. A tooth fell out of his mouth and clinked on the asphalt, was followed by a little lake of vomit in which one of the cyclopean popcorns floated; the eye was dead and filmed over.

"Eat and be fed, brother," the King's upper mouth said.

"I don't think so," I said.

"Turning down a sick man," the King said, and it was the lower mouth this time. "That's a hell of a note."

He laid his head down gently, his face in the vomit. His head was turned so I could still see the single eye. He opened his top left hand and there was a crumpled paper skull in it. "Second-rate materials. Second-rate effects," Randy's voice said. "I could have done better with household supplies."

The one eye closed. The Popcorn King was dead.

But Mable wasn't. About that time she screamed.

---

4 When I turned, I saw that at Mable's scream Sam had made it over the fence and sprinted over to her. Bob was ahead of him, tearing off the smoldering blanket. Sam and Bob got arms around her and lifted her up and Sam said, "Oh, honey bugs, I thought you were croaked. Done gone to be with Jesus."

Mable was clutching one of the recipe cards in her good hand. She looked at it there in the light of the burning concession and the lightning overhead. "Polk salad," she said. "Now that's a good one, if you get it when the shoots are young. Don't, you might as well cook you up a mess of Johnson grass."

I started over to join them, stopped. The patrons of both lots were coming out of the shadows, into the light of the great fire, coming toward us. A more unpleasant crowd I'd never seen. The patrons from Lot A no longer had their movies, and neither lot had their King and their popcorn.

Sam and Bob saw me looking, and they swiveled Mable around so that they were all facing the crowd. I pulled the pistol from my belt and held it against my leg and walked over there.

Bob and Sam gently lowered Mable to the ground. She sat there reading the pork salad recipe, nodding over it.

"It ain't over," Sam said. "It ain't never over."

"The King," went the cry from the crowd. "The King."

Then they swarmed us. I heard Bob's shotgun roar and I got off one shot—and missed. In a crowd, no less. Jack the deadly gunman. Sweaty, hot bodies piled on me and I struck the ground hard and someone said an obscenity in my face and some other smart aleck twisted the gun out of my hand and hit me with it, which is kind of humiliating, getting clubbed with your own gun, I mean. Next the crowd started dribbling me around the lot with fists and feet and I got beyond pain and entered into nice, dark, cozy unconsciousness.

But that didn't last long.

Lot A built a bigger and better fire out of the smoldering lumber of the concession stand so they would have plenty of light to work by, but they managed to save enough of the lumber for cooking and building.

What they built was crosses.

They got some nails out of the wreckage and someone had a hammer, and they stripped us naked and held us down and crucified us. That hurt bad enough, but when they dropped our crosses into the holes the concession pilings had been in, that was real pain. It shook my entire body until I felt as if the tips of my teeth would bulb up and squirt blood.

They packed the holes tight with junk from the concession, then piled lumber around the bottoms of the crosses and looked up at us like chefs contemplating the larder.

The nails hurt something awful, but worse was the racking pain throughout the body and the pressure it put on the lungs. Now and then I had to make my legs work so I could force myself up on the nail through my feet and get some good breaths. I'd stay that way long as I could until the muscles in my feet cramped and I had to let go. Then I'd have trouble breathing again, and I'd get my strength back just enough before my lungs collapsed, and I'd push up once more. I had just thought Coach Murphy's calisthenics in PE were tough.

They got the Popcorn King's body, put it on a pole and stuck it upright in that part of the wreckage that wasn't on fire. The King had gone seriously ugly. The tattoos had fallen off him and lay like ink pools on the ground where he had lain. That part of the body that had been Willard was pink again; he had even lost the tattoos he had come to the drive-in with.

Members of the crowd took a blanket and put it over the King's head so his face would show, and they took a nail and nailed through it into the top of his hat so it wouldn't fall off. Then they stretched the blanket behind him so that he looked like he was standing there wearing a hooded robe. One young woman with spiky hair claimed she had been possessed by the King's spirit, or some such thing (I wasn't in the mood to take it all in, actually), and she wandered around and did a kind of Jezebel dance by the body, and after a while she let her voice go deep, though it cracked some, and she gave the impression the King was talking through her. The crowd liked that, and she got behind the body, under the stretched-out blanket, and patrons would come by and ask the King questions and she'd answer for him and everyone was pleased with this oracle. They did this until it got boring and they turned back to us and started piling more lumber. One of the pilers was especially annoying. He kept singing "Mama's Little Baby Loves Short'nin' Bread," and he couldn't carry a tune in a safety-deposit box. It just wasn't the way for a man to die. On a cross, about to be cooked, with some idiot singing "Short'nin' Bread."

I could turn my head and see the others to my left. Sam, Bob and Mable. Mable, who had lost her plumbing-pipe hand, had gotten nailed through the wrist a couple of times and I think she was bleeding worse than the rest of us. She cashed in early, her last words being something about how to wrap tamale meat in corn shucks. I kept expecting her to come alive again and start on some other recipe, but this time she was dead for real. Her shapeless white body hung out from the cross like a swollen grub.

When Sam knew she was gone he went to preaching. Said something about Jesus and the thieves on either side of him.

"Ain't stole nothing in my life," Bob said. "Cept maybe your bus and sardines, and I don't think that counts."

Sam went on with his story, said those suckers on either side of Jesus had repented and Jesus had saved their lives and they went on to Paradise. Being as I was in the thieves' position, I could sympathize with their line of thinking, but just having had a rather uninspiring religious experience, I declined to join Sam in Paradise.

But Sam kept at it. I couldn't figure where he was getting the wind. I could hardly breathe at all. I reckon he felt like a big wheel because he was in the middle. He preached for quite some time before his mouth went dry and he couldn't say anything else, which I was grateful for.

I blacked out off and on, and once I had what might have been a dream. In the dream the lightning overhead ceased and out of the blackness came a face, an indescribable face, but a face that had the look of someone, or something, with a mission. He opened his toothy mouth and roared, "Over budget, you fools. Over budget. Cut. Wrap." Then the face withdrew into the black and there was light. The dream ended.

I opened my eyes and saw below that the patrons were piling more wood around me, and that one of them had a piece of board wrapped in a shirt and it was on fire. He was about to put it to my pile of lumber. I hoped fire was quick. I had read somewhere that it was a tough way to go, and that smoke inhalation killed you first. I decided I would breathe a lot of smoke quickly, get it over with.

And then there was a change. I looked up. The lightning was still there and so was the blackness, but there was something bright moving behind it, a red glow that was expanding.

I looked down at my captors, at the faces of those close to the fire and at the shadowy shapes of those beyond; the more clearly outlined, if distant, shapes over in Lot B, where the movies still rolled. They all seemed to be looking up.

I lifted my head again. It wasn't just delirium. It was lighter up there and growing lighter still. Then it looked as if a great apple broke through the chocolate pudding, but it was the comet tearing through the poison sky. Down it came, dragging daylight behind it, white clouds, the sun.

The drive-in went red and the comet smiled.

Up it whipped again, this time pulling the blackness with it. Up, up, up and away, until it was not even a speck against the bright blue sky, and there was nothing left but a fine warm day with the smell of trees in the air and the touch of hot sun on our faces.

It was nice, but I didn't feel like a picnic or nothing.

The patrons just sort of stood there for a while, marveling at the world beyond the tin fence. There were lots of trees visible. Big trees. The guy with the burning board dropped it—not on the wood pile, fortunately. People began wandering off, some began to run. Cars were cranked. Engines seemed to be working fine. Like a line of insects the cars and trucks rolled out of the drive-in. Some people whose cars had been totaled walked. Some hot-wired and took other cars. Everyone was in a hurry to get out of there. They didn't mention getting us down. No one waved or shot us the finger as they went by.

A tall, skinny man with long hair and a hoe handle for a cane came up. He looked up at Bob. "How's it going?"

"Hanging around," Bob said, not missing a beat.

"Maybe you'd like down?" Crier said.

"That would be right nice," Bob said.

Crier got down on his hands and knees and started pulling the junk out of the piling holes and pretty soon the crosses were wobbling and then Crier pushed us down. When I hit the ground I thought my arms and legs would come off.

Crier went away for a while and when he came back he had a hammer. He used the claw end to free us. It hurt like hell. He got Mable free last, since she wasn't in any hurry.

"I broke into your camper to get this hammer," Crier said to Bob, "I figured you'd have one. Hope you don't mind."

"Nah," Bob said, "it's insured."

My hands and feet hurt so bad I couldn't move them and I couldn't walk, least not without help. My legs seemed to have died. Sam looked walleyed and had gone to singing "The Old Rugged Cross" in a whispery kind of voice, and that wasn't helping my nerves.

"What you driving?" Bob said.

"Well," Crier said, "this is kind of odd, but I can't remember what car I came in. Can't remember who I came with."

"Don't matter," Bob said. "We'll take the camper. You can drive, can't you?"

"Is it an automatic?"

"I thought you said you were a truck driver," Bob said. "I figured you could drive anything."

"Well, I may have exaggerated. A whole lot. I drove an ice cream truck, actually."

"An ice cream truck!" Bob said.

"Yeah. But sometimes I drove it real fast. And it was an automatic. Which brings me back to the question. Is your truck an automatic?"

"Yep." Bob said.

"Then I can drive the hell out of that. It's been awhile, but I reckon I remember that much. But you don't look like you got a key on you."

"There's one underneath the dash in a magnetic box. Doors aren't locked."

"Okay," Crier said. "I'll drive it over here and pick you up."

"You wouldn't just drive off and leave us, would you?" Bob said.

"Gone this far for you, might as well go the whole hog."

When Crier came back with the truck, Bob said, "There's some blankets in the back. There's a knife back there too. We can cut a hole in the blankets and slip them over our heads."

"Why the trouble?" Crier asked. "You boys got dates?"

"Just a thing I prefer, if you'll do it," Bob said.

Crier found the blankets and the sardines and the knife. He brought the sardines out and we ate all we could stand, Crier feeding them to us, as our hands didn't work so good.

He cut the blankets and pulled them over our heads. Sam didn't even notice. He was trying to sing "When the Roll Is Called Up Yonder."

"What about her?" I asked, nodding at Mable.

"Dead, ain't she?" Crier said.

"Maybe you could pile some boards on her or something, set her on fire if you had a mind to. She ought to have some kind of burial."

"Ain't you something," Crier said.

"And the Popcorn King," I said. "He ought not just be left."

"You're kind of tight with everybody, ain't you?" Crier said,

"Before he was that, he was two friends of ours," Bob said. "I know it's a bother, but could you?"

"Hell," Crier said. "Good thing you boys are paying by the hour." He piled some boards on Mable and set fire to her and she caught poorly at first, but after a time was blazing away. It didn't take so much to get the Popcorn King burning. He caught quick and flared like a torch, the blanket whipping to flame immediately. Black smoke churned up from the corpses and floated up into the clear sky and faded.

"Now," Crier said. "Any little ole chores you boys want performed? Just anything would be all right. Maybe you'd like to see if I can make a few laps around the lots."

"Would you?" Bob said.

"You know what you can do," Crier said.

Crier helped Bob and Sam into the back of the truck and led me around to the cab. It seemed to take forever and my feet felt like raw stumps. I had Crier on one side holding me up, and the truck on the other. I touched the truck with my elbow because my hand wouldn't take it. I still couldn't open or close either one of them. They looked like talons.

Inside the cab, Crier started the truck again, leaned on the wheel and looked around. "Strange, I feel funny leaving."

"Maybe you can get over it," I said.

"Maybe."

"One thing, Crier," I said. "You saw what that crowd was about to do to us. I know you couldn't have stopped them, but would you have helped eat us? Could you have done that?"

"Been the first in line if I could have. No sense missing a free meal, even if it is made up of a couple of guys I kind of like."

"Well," I said, "that's one way of looking at things."

EPILOGUE

I leaned against the door and kept my sore hands in my lap. As we started rolling, I looked around at all the vacant cars, many of them wrecked. There were also lots of bones. You could see that clearly now. We drove by one car with its roof decorated with human skulls wearing popcorn sacks, and there was another car with a baby seat sitting on top of it with a little skeleton in the seat holding a rattle.

I glanced through the gun rack and the back glass, saw Bob and Sam stretched on the floor of the camper. Bob was up on one elbow, gingerly managing sardines from a can Crier had opened and left for him. Sam wasn't moving. Later Bob told me he died before we got out of the lot.

We went through the exit, and though the highway was there, the yellow line had faded and the concrete had buckled and grass grew up through it in spots. Nothing else was remotely familiar. I wasn't in the least bit surprised. I remembered what Sam had said: "It ain't over yet. It ain't never over." No, it wasn't over. It was time for the second feature. A lost world movie. As we drove, a massive shape stepped out of the jungle foliage at the right of the highway and Crier eased on the brake and we watched. It was a Tyrannosaurus Rex covered in bat-like parasites, their wings opening and closing slowly, like contented butterflies sipping nectar from a flower.

The dinosaur looked at us in a disinterested way, crossed the highway and was swallowed by the jungle.

"I don't think this leads home anymore," Crier said, and eased forward again, started picking up speed. I looked in the truck's wing mirror and I could see the drive-in in it, one of the screens in Lot B. The projector might still be running back there, but if it was, I couldn't make out a picture. The screen looked like nothing more than an enormous slice of Wonder Bread.

CUT/FADE-OUT

Book Two

THE DRIVE-IN

Not Just One of Them Sequels

INTRODUCTION

The Drive-in 2: Not Just One of Them Sequels, wasn't a book I expected to write. I didn't have plans. I had a few ideas left over from the first book, and I from time to time thought about what to do with them, but nothing came to mind. And then, my editor, Pat LoBrutto called.

He wanted a sequel.

I've always balanced my career between art and pragmatism. If I want to write something, I generally write it, no matter what. Sometimes, I'm asked to do a project I didn't originate, but that doesn't mean it's necessarily a project I wouldn't like to do. Often I pass on things I'm offered. But when Pat LoBrutto asked me to do another novel about the Drive-in world, needing to keep my career going, needing money to pay bills, and liking the challenge. I went for it. The first time had been a tough experience that turned out well, so I thought, been there before, so this one will be more fun to write.

It wasn't. It too was hard. There was something about telling these kind of stories, making them seem simple, and sliding in the ideas I wanted to portray at the same time. But, I had a sense this one was good, even though it was tough. I chose to let it end in what for some might be an anticlimactic manner, but was for me, the perfect ending. As always, I go my own way.

It was received with a little less enthusiasm, but over the years the fans for it have grown, especially those who have read the first book.

I like it quite a bit. I think it has some of my best satirical work. It's also weird with a side of weird. The first novel had a character called the Popcorn King, who I believe to be as unusual an invention as I've ever come up with—or at least I thought so until I wrote *The Drive-in 2* with Popalong Cassidy.

No doubt all of these books seem to have at their core a love–hate relationship with the entertainment media, TV, movies, etc., as well as a love for false profits and a strange desire to identify with pretty horrible people.

The novel, like the first, was written quickly, though perhaps a little less quickly. Like the first, I was uncertain what I had wrought. Upon reading it in galley form (I don't think the term galley is used so much these days), I found myself pleased with it. The first is somehow more powerful, if for no other reason than it's the first, but this one is highly inventive and as a writer, I got to explore the Drive-in world some more and find out what was out there.

What was out there was pretty weird.

Here, let me invite you on the journey. Keep your hands and feet inside the car, and if you think you see something weird, it is weird.

Enjoy.

—Joe R. Lansdale, 2009

"Everything human is pathetic. The secret source of humor itself is not joy but sorrow. There is no humor in heaven."

—Mark Twain, *Pudd'nhead Wilson*

Fade-in Prologue

Pay attention. When I'm through there will be a test.

One day suddenly you're out of high school, happy as a grub in shit, waking up with a hard-on and spending your days sitting around in your pee-stained underwear with your feet propped up next to the air conditioner vent with cool air blowing on your nuts, and the next goddamn thing you know, you're crucified.

And I don't mean symbolically. I'm talking nails in the paws and wood splinters in the ass, sore hands and feet and screams and a wavering attitude about the human race. It's the sort of thing that when it happens to you, you have a hard time believing ol' Jesus could have been all that forgiving about it.

It hurts.

Had I been J.C., I'd have come back from the dead madder than a badger with turpentined balls, and there wouldn't have been any of this peace-and-love shit, and I would have forgotten how to do trivial crap like turn water to wine and multiply bread and fishes. I'd have made myself big as the universe and made me two bricks just the right size, and I'd have gotten the world between the bricks, and *whammo*, shit jelly.

It wouldn't do to make me a messiah. I've got a bad attitude.

I do now, anyway.

It isn't that I expected life to be so sweet and fine that I'd grow up sweating pearls and farting peach blossoms, nor was I expecting to live to be three million and have endless fan mail from long-legged, sex-starved Hollywood starlets telling me how they'd like to ravish my body and bronze my pecker. But on the other hand, I was expecting a little better than this.

Me and my friends went to the drive-in to see movies, not to become part of them.

The evening we drove into the Orbit things started going to hell in a fiery hand-basket. We had just gotten settled in, and this big, red comet came hurtling from the sky like a tomato thrown by God, and then the comet split apart and smiled rows of saw-bladed teeth at us.

And when I thought the comet would hit us and splatter us into little sparklers of light, it veered upwards and moved out of sight. What it left in its wake was some bad business.

The drive-in still had light, but the light came from the projectors and the projectors didn't seem to have any source of electricity. We were surrounded by a blackness so complete it was like being in a bag with a handful of penlights. The blackness beyond the drive-in was acidic. I'll never forget what it did to that carload of fat people that drove off into it (or what I assumed it did), or the cowboy who put his arm into it and got his entire self dissolved.

Anyway, we were trapped.

Things got nasty.

There was nothing to eat in the drive-in besides the concession food, which was bad enough, but when that got low, people started eating one another, cooked and uncooked.

Then two of my friends, whacked out from lack of food, got hit by this strange blue lightning; (Randy was riding on Willard's back at the time) and it fused them together and made them uglier than a shopping mall parking lot and gave them strange powers and they became known as the Popcorn King. They weren't friends of mine and Bob's anymore. They weren't anyone's friends. They were now one creature. A bad creature.

Hello, permanent blue Monday.

The Popcorn King used his weird powers and unlimited popcorn to control the hungry crowd, and Bob and I might have joined them if it hadn't been for the jerky stash Bob had in his camper truck. The meat kept us from having to eat the King's popcorn, which had grown kind of funky, and from having to eat other folks, which was a thing the King encouraged.

But me and Bob were realistic enough to figure eating other folks and each other was just on the horizon, so to speak, so we decided, live or die, we were going to destroy the Popcorn King, and we did, with the help of this evangelist named Sam and his wife, Mable, who we thought was dead at the time. But that's another story and I've already told it. Let me just say that Sam and Mable together probably had a lower IQ than the foreskin on my dick.

To shorten this all up, we killed the Popcorn King, smashed him with a bus and blew his ass up, and for our efforts, Samaritan as they were, the King's followers stripped us naked, called us some real bad names, crucified us and started building bonfires at the bottom of our crosses so they could have us for lunch.

Then the comet decided to come back.

The big red bastard couldn't come back before we were crucified. No sir. It had to wait until we were up on those crosses with nails in our hands and feet and our bare asses hanging out before it chose to make an appearance.

But, I suppose I shouldn't complain. The bonfire didn't get built, and consequently, we didn't get eaten.

The comet did what it had done before, only this time when it went away the blackness around the drive-in went with it and folks got in their cars and trucks and drove off.

A fella named Crier, who was kind of a friend of ours, but who was planning on eating us if we got cooked, took us down from the crosses. Mable, who got crucified with us and was really dead this time, wound up burned and buried under some lumber left over from where the concession exploded while we were in the process of killing the Popcorn King. Sam died shortly after all this, about the time he got loaded in the back of the camper, but I didn't know this at the time.

Crier had to help me and Bob to the truck, and Bob got put in the back with Sam, and I rode up front with Crier, who did the driving. My feet weren't in any condition to push pedals. Getting crucified is not like stepping on a sticker or having a splinter in your palm, I'll guarantee you. It takes the rhythm out of your step and saps your will to clap to inner music.

So Crier drove us out of there, and at first things looked fine as the missionary position, but when we saw that the highway was buckling and cracking and grass was growing up between the cracks and on either side of the concrete was thick jungle, none of us had to be a nuclear physicist to know things still hadn't gone back to normal. And while we were contemplating this, letting those old inner wheels turn and squeak, a Tyrannosaurus Rex came goose-stepping out of the jungle on one side of the highway, looked at us with contempt, and disappeared into the foliage on the other side.

It was an exhilarating experience. Scary too.

And that's where this part of my story takes up.

SHOWTIME

FIRST REEL

A Burial, a Tree House, a Burned Man, and Titties Close Up

1

There was some nice scenery out there. Big trees that climbed to a sky bluer than a Swede's eye, and next to the highway was some grass growing so tall and sharp it looked like green spikes.

After being cooped up in that drive-in for who knows how long with the tar-colored sky overhead and people so close together you couldn't scratch your ass without elbowing your neighbor, I suppose I should have been grateful. No one was trying to crucify and eat me, and that was worth something, but even with everything so pretty, it had a sort of landscaped look about it that I couldn't explain. You know, like a movie set that could afford to use real trees and grass and what looked like a real sky but struck me as a little too blue and perfect. It put me in mind of an old woodcut I saw in an art magazine once. The woodcut was from the sixteenth century, I think, maybe earlier, and there was this monk on his hands and knees and he was poking his head through the fabric of a night sky and looking at all manner of gears and machinery on the other side, stuff that made the world work, that swung the sun and moon across the sky and popped out the stars and turned things light or dark.

As we rode along, I thought about the dinosaur, and the way he walked, and thoughts spun through my head like pinwheels in a blue norther. The Tyrannosaurus Rex had moved smooth, all right, but slightly mechanical, and had I heard a sort of hum as he crossed the road, like the soft buzz of a battery-powered watch?

Probably not. But I had dreamed off and on that there were these many-tentacled, bladdery, eyes-on-stalks aliens that were doing this to us, making us the stars of low budget movies they were filming. And if my dreams were, as I suspected, more than dreams, were in fact my tapping into their thought processes, then they could be doing to us again what they had done with us in the drive-in. Didn't low-budget movies nearly always show as part of a double feature?

Odder than the dreams was me wanting to see someone. Meaning not someone from the drive-in. They were on my shit list. But I wanted to see someone out there, someone who could make me feel this was more than a movie set. I think I might have felt better if I'd at least seen some beer cans or Frito wrappers lying out beside the road or thrown up in the trees. It would assure me that humanity was out there, ready to start fucking up anything it could get its hands on. There's nothing like pristine wilderness to incite in human beings the need to start chopping down trees, tromping grass, killing animals and throwing down beer cans, so I was pretty certain there wasn't a human being within a hundred miles of us.

Not counting the folks who left the drive-in ahead of us, of course. They hadn't had time to respond to natural tendencies, and after our ordeal, it was doubtful anyone had a beer can or a wrapper to toss. Everything that could be eaten or drunk had been consumed at the drive-in and the containers and wrappers tossed down there.

So the people ahead of us were forced to fight their instincts to litter, though I figured in time the urge would become too strong, and they'd start throwing their clothes out, or pulling over to the side of the road to bum their spare tires and leave the blackened, rubber-dotted rims to mark their passing.

We drove on for quite a time, and when it was getting near dark, Crier said, "Think we ought to find a place to hole up for the night?"

"I doubt we're going to come across many motels," I said.

The sun was going down in what struck me as the north, and I mention this because when we went into the drive-in the highway ran north and south, and when we came out we were heading in what was formerly a northerly direction. But being a creature of habit, and not wishing to give any alien movie-makers the satisfaction of letting on I noticed, I reoriented myself and called the direction in which the sun was falling west.

Besides, you never knew when someone might ask you directions.

Crier found a place off the highway where the jungle cleared out and there was some tall grass that went on for a ways, and he pulled over and parked, came around and helped me out of the truck.

My feet were sore and stiff from the crucifixion and I couldn't walk, but I could lean a little when propped against the camper.

As our duds had been stripped off us by the mad drive-in crowd, Crier had cut holes in blankets for me, Bob and Sam, and slipped them over our heads to serve as clothes, and I took this moment to lift my stylish wardrobe's hem and take a whiz.

Crier went around and opened the back of the camper and helped Bob out, and that's when Crier and I found out about Sam.

"We hadn't no more than gotten started back there," Bob said, "when he snorted once, shit on himself and went on to glory. Or wherever assholes like him go. I won't miss him."

Bob was sentimental like that.

When Crier got Bob propped up next to me, Bob lifted his blanket and took a leak too. If I had waited a minute or two, we could have gone together.

Crier had gone back to the rear of the camper, and Bob called to him, "I know it's a bother, and I hate to ask, you having been so nice to us and all, but—"

"Would I clean Sam's shit out of the back?" Crier said.

"And they say there's no evidence for ESP," Bob said.

Crier took Sam by the heels and dragged him bumpity-bumpity out of the camper and onto the ground. Sam hit hard enough to make me wince. Crier pulled him over to the grass and dropped his hold on the old boy's heels. He peeled Sam's blanket off and went back to the truck and used it to clean the mess up as best he could. It still wasn't going to smell like the perfume counter at J.C. Penney's back there, but it had to beat leaving things the way they were.

Bob began to ease down so he could sit, and I did the same. We managed our legs out in front of us without wincing and moaning too awful much.

Bob looked over at Sam's body in the grass and made a clucking sound with his tongue. "Hell of a thing, ain't it Jack? Life's hard, then you die, then you shit yourself. There's just no dignity in dying, no matter how you look at it . . ."

"Might not be any dignity," I said. "But at least you don't have to get phone calls from aluminum siding salesmen anymore."

"Got news for you," Bob said. "We won't be getting those anyway, and we're alive."

"It's because we don't have a phone," I said. "If we come across a phone, you can bet we'll be hearing from them."

Bob called to Crier. "You're gonna bury the old fart, ain't you?"

Crier came around from the back of the camper. He was a sight. He was scrawny as a month-old corpse, but didn't have as nice a complexion. He still had his clothes and shoes, but they seemed to be held together by little more than body odor and hope. His hair was long and shaggy and thinning. His beard looked like a nest. He had the shit-stained blanket in his hand, and he gracelessly tossed it into the grass, an act that gave me some hope. Humanity was once again on the roll.

"You're kind of pushy, Bob," Crier said.

"I ain't saying you have to bury him—"

"That's big of you."

"—I'm suggesting it. If I had two good hands and two good feet, I might do it."

"Uh-huh."

"Let your conscience be your guide."

Crier said something under his breath, then went to the back of the truck and came out with a tire tool.

"Hey, forget it," Bob said.

Crier used the tool to pop the hubcap off the rear right tire. He took the cap out to the grass and tossed it down next to Sam. He began pulling the grass and cussing while he did it. It was pretty interesting to watch. Once in a while he'd toss a wad of grass, dirty roots still intact, toward Bob, and it would land near his sore feet or slam into the truck beside him. Bob started moving his head like a nervous anaconda.

Actually, I think Crier could have hit him if he'd wanted to. It wasn't that far a shot. Instead, he was trying to make Bob nervous, which I could kind of understand. Bob didn't always bring out the best in a person.

As for me, I tried to sit casual with my punctured biscuit hooks in my lap, looking at the crusty wounds on the backs of my hands where the nails had come out and gone into the wood of my cross.

When Crier had a good patch of grass pulled, he took the hubcap and used it to dig with and his mouth to cuss with. He worked the dirt between his legs like a dog burying a bone.

It was almost solid dark when he finished the grave. It wasn't much, more of a shallow trench, really. The moon came up in the north, right where the sun had gone down, the place I had decided to call west before, and I had a vision of my real or imagined multiple-eyed, many-tentacled, bladder-shaped aliens pulling levers and pushing buttons and causing gears to creak and crank and start the final descent of the sun and the rise of the moon, which spilled its light into Sam's final resting place like thin cream.

Crier hooked his hands under Sam's chin and pulled him over to the trench. Sam's body rustled through the grass like a snake. Crier rolled him into the hole face first. Sam's legs stuck out at one end, and his left arm flopped from the grave and lay in a manner that suggested he was about to push up and get out of that hole as soon as he gathered his strength.

"You're gonna have to dig some more," Bob said.

Crier turned slowly and looked at Bob. The moonlight on his face made him look like the man most likely not to give an ax. I hoped he knew that Bob's sentiments were his own and that I was an independent.

"Maybe not," Bob said. "Hell, just throw some of that grass over the spots that don't fit, and fuck it."

Crier turned back to his work, took hold of Sam's free arm and brutally twisted it behind Sam's back like a kid working his end of a wishbone. When the arm cracked loud enough to run a cold tremor up my spine, Crier pushed it down against Sam's back and put a foot on it and pressed, rocking back and forth on it until it stayed in place. He bent Sam's overlong legs at the knee, folded them to where the soles of his feet touched the back of his naked thighs, sat on them and bounced hard.

Every time Crier got up to examine his handiwork, the legs would creep up slowly. Finally Crier had had enough. He hopped on them one last time, got up and grabbed the hubcap and started scraping the dirt into the trench and topped it off by tossing loose grass on it.

I guess it was an okay grave, in that it beat lying naked in the grass with a blanket full of your shit nearby, but it was disconcerting to see the top of Sam's feet and part of his ankles sticking up in the moonlight. If any of Sam's relatives had been around, I don't think they'd have liked it.

I suppose it got to Crier too, because he took the hubcap and set it on the soles of Sam's feet as a kind of marker. And though it wasn't perfect, it did sort of tidy things up.

Without saying a word, Crier went around on the other side of the truck and got in. I could tell from the way the truck moved he had lain down in the seat.

Bob leaned over to me and said, "Think it would be okay if I asked him to help us into the camper?"

"Maybe not just now," I said.

From inside the cab we heard Crier say something about "goddamn ingrates," and Bob and I went very, very quiet.

2

We crawled under the truck and tried to sleep. The grass made it pretty soft, but there were bugs crawling on me and it began to get cold and I was feeling stiff in the hands and feet. One thing I had gotten used to in the drive-in was the constant moderate temperature, and that made the chill seem even chillier.

I got one of the larger bugs off of me and crushed it with my thumb and forefinger, a movement that made my sore hand throb. The bug's body collapsed like a peanut husk. I tried to look at it closely, but under the truck with only a stray strand of moonlight, there wasn't much to see. It looked like a crushed bug. Maybe I was expecting little silver wires and a battery the size of a pinhead.

I suppose Crier started feeling guilty, because in the middle of the night he came and woke us up and pulled us out from under the truck and helped us into the camper, which he had, in fact, cleaned out quite well, though the odor of Sam's last bad meals clung to the interior like moss.

Still, it wasn't cold in there and the bugs, real or synthetic, weren't crawling or biting.

After we lay down, and Crier was about to shut the back of the camper, Bob said, "No kiss and story?"

Crier held out his hand, palm up, made a fist and let the cobra rise.

Bob looked at Crier's stiff middle finger and said, "That's not nice."

Crier shut the back of the camper and went around to the front seat and lay down.

Bob managed to get up on his knees and thumped his forehead against the glass that connected the camper to the cab.

Crier sat up and turned to look. I've seen more pleasant faces on water moccasins.

"Night-night," Bob said.

Crier did the trick with his finger again, only with less flourish this time, then lay down out of sight.

Bob wiggled onto his sleeping bag, got on his side and looked at me and said, "You know, I like that guy, I really do."

That night the dreams came back, the same sort I'd had in the drive-in. They seemed more like visions than dreams, like I had tapped into some consciousness that controlled things. Bob and Crier didn't have the dreams, so I could only guess that through some quirk of fate, or by alien design, I had been given this gift. Or, I was as crazy as a cat in a dryer.

Hot-wired to aliens or not, the dreams/visions were clear. I could see the aliens in them, their bulbous heads sporting wiggling tendons tipped with eyes, tentacles flashing about, touching gears and punching buttons. Lights and buzzers and beepers going off and on around them. And them leaning forward, conversing with one another in a language that sounded like grunts, squeaks, burps and whines, and yet, a language I could somehow understand.

And some of the things they were saying went like this:

"Slow, uh-huh, uh-huh . . . that's it."

"Nice, nice . . ."

"Very pretty, oh yes, very pretty . . . tight and easy now."

"All right, that's it. CUT!"

Then the connection was cut as well, and the dream or whatever it was, ended. The next thing I knew it was morning and Crier had joined us for breakfast, such as it was: a can of sardines that we had taken from Sam's bus before we blew it up.

Afterwards, Crier got us out of the back of the camper and made us take turns walking, him supporting us, so that we could exercise our sore feet. Mine had started to curl like burned tortillas, and Crier said if I didn't make them work, they'd quit on me, and that at best, I'd end up having a couple of lumps that had all the mobility of potted plants.

I believed him. I exercised. So did Bob, though he grumbled about it.

Worst part about the exercise, worse even than the pain, was the thirst. It had been a long time since I had had a drink of water, and of course, this was true of Bob and Crier too. In the drive-in, for a time, we existed on soft drinks, and later on, Bob and I had nothing but the juice from jerky, and now the liquid from sardines.

If that doesn't sound so bad, go out some summer evening and do some kind of hard work, like say hauling hay, then try quenching your thirst with a big glass of soy oil or meat broth.

The bottom line was we were dehydrating, starting to look like flesh-colored plastic stretched over a frame of coat hangers.

"I figure," Crier said, after we got through exercising and were sitting with our backs against the truck, "any place as full of trees and grass and critters as this, ought to have water."

I wasn't so sure. I wouldn't have been surprised to come to what looked like a stream only to discover it was colored glass or rippling cellophane.

We were looking at Sam's grave while we talked, examining his ankles sticking up, his feet wearing the hubcap, and all of a sudden, we grew silent, as if possessed of a hive mind.

"I could have at least spoken some words over him," Crier said.

"And who the hell would you have been talking to?" Bob said. "Sam? He don't give a damn about nothing no more. God? Personally, I'm not real fond of the sonofabitch. Or wouldn't be, if I thought he, she, or it, existed."

I didn't say so, but I was in Bob's camp. Like the drive-in patrons, God was on my shit list. I had tried religion during our stay in the drive-in, and it hadn't exactly been a rewarding experience.

I had decided that if there was a God, he was a cruel sonofabitch to allow the things he allowed. Especially since he claimed his name was synonymous with love. It seemed to me that he was little more than a celestial Jack the Ripper, offering us, his whores, rewards with one hand, smiling and telling us he loved us, while with the other hand he held a shiny, sharp knife, the better with which to disembowel us.

"I don't know what I believe anymore," Crier said, "but I feel I owe the boy some words because he's a human being. It doesn't matter if I'm talking to the wind, or just myself. I didn't give him the best kind of burial, so it's the least I can do. And who knows, if there is some God out there, maybe he'll be listening."

Crier said this soft and solemn like, and you could almost hear the organ music in the background. I think Bob was as affected as I was by Crier's remarks, because he didn't say anything rude, and something of that sort was always on the tip of his tongue. A lump, like a crippled frog trying to make it downhill, moved in my throat.

Crier went over to the grave and looked at the hubcap, picked it up and looked at the soles of Sam's feet, put the hubcap back, sighed, looked at the jungle.

"I'm here to say some words about this man, but nothing much comes to me. I didn't really know the poor bastard, but from what I could tell, he was about the dumbest sonofabitch that ever shit over a pair of shoes.

"Still, he was a man, and he deserved better than this. I'm sorry I couldn't get him buried proper, couldn't get his feet to stay down, but I did get his ass in the grave, and that was a job. I hope he rests in peace.

"I'm sorry about his wife, Mable. She wasn't any better or smarter than he was, from what I could tell, maybe a damn sight dumber. But I guess she did the best she could, like all of us. She's back at the drive-in, burned up under some lumber pieces, just in case you care.

"And listen, God, if you're out there, how about some relief around here? Lighten up. Things are multiple-fucked-up, and if anyone can put things straight, it ought to be you. Right? I mean, you hear what I'm saying? Give us some sign of good things to come. It would be appreciated. Okay, that's it. Amen."

Crier walked back to the truck, and about the time he reached it, the jungle parted and out stepped a nasty red-and-blue dinosaur that was probably a baby Tyrannosaurus Rex, or something close enough to be a double cousin to one.

Whatever it was, it stood on big hind legs and held two puny forelegs in front of itself as if pleading. Its face was mostly teeth.

Toothy sniffed the air delicately, scampered over to the grave, snapped at the hubcap with its mouthful of big, sharp teeth, and managed to gulp it and Sam's feet down with very little chewing.

After a moment, Toothy coughed and spat out the hubcap, which now resembled a wad of aluminum foil. He used one clawed foot to scratch Sam out of the grave the way a chicken might scratch a worm from the dirt, bent and bit into Sam's corpse. With a series of rapid head-flipping motions, he proceeded to gobble the old boy so viciously that pieces of Sam flew out of Toothy's mouth and sprinkled the grass.

Finished with his repast, Toothy eyed us, as if giving the dessert counter a once-over.

We stayed very still. Rocks couldn't have been that still.

He let out a little honk that shook the truck, then started to turn toward the jungle.

A weight watcher, to our relief.

But before he could make a complete turn, he froze, turned his head slightly to the side and acquired a look akin to that of a patient who has just experienced the greased finger of the doctor up his ass. Then with a grunt, Toothy leaned slightly forward and cut a monster fart that was reminiscent of an air horn, but with more tonality.

When the fart was finished and Toothy had adopted a more satisfied and comfortable look, he moved into the jungle and out of sight.

After a moment of silence, Bob said, "Well, Crier, hope that wasn't the sign from God you were waiting for."

3

We drove along for a while, and finally Crier, who had been looking pretty distressed for a time, pulled over and killed the motor.

"What's up?"

"Sam," he said. "I can't get him out of my mind."

"Hell, you buried him, didn't you? Wasn't your fault all you had was a hubcap. And that dinosaur even gave him a musical salute after he ate him. Tomorrow sometime, Sam will be fertilizing a patch of ground. What more could you ask for?"

"Fuck Sam. It's me I'm talking about. I don't want to end up buried alongside the road like that."

"You aren't dead, Crier."

"But I might get that way, and I don't want to end up in some trench next to the highway where something can dig me up and eat me."

"Something doesn't dig you up, the worms are going to take care of you, so what's the difference? Maybe we could just leave you where you lie and save the dinosaurs some digging."

"That's nice. I'm pouring out *my* heart here and you're making fun. I don't want to be left beside the road and I don't want to be buried beside it neither."

"Perhaps we could arrange for you to be whisked away to heaven."

"I want to be carried to the end of the highway."

"Keep driving, and if we don't run out of gas, that's a wish you'll get. You don't even have to be dead. Have you noticed the gas mileage we're getting? It's got to be super or the gas gauge is fucked."

"Forget the goddamn gas gauge and the mileage, I'm serious here. I get croaked, you guys make sure I get to the end of the highway. Something about that appeals to me. I like the idea of finishing things. Dinosaur eats me there, so be it."

"Crier, if you're dead, it doesn't matter if fifty naked girls with tits like zeppelins are at the end of the highway ready to suck your dick until your balls cave in. You'll still be dead."

"Promise me that should something happen to me you'll make sure I get to the end of the highway to be buried."

"Okay."

"Okay what?"

"If you get killed. I'll see you get to the end of the highway and get buried or cremated or something."

"Not cremated, I don't like that."

"Tried it?"

"Just bury me. I'll make you the same promise if you like."

"Something happens to me, leave me in the bushes. I'll be past caring."

Bob rose up in back and tapped on the glass with an elbow, held out his hands to question why we had stopped.

Crier waved him down, started up the engine and pulled back onto the highway.

"I'm going to talk to Bob about it too," Crier said. "Think he'll do it?"

"Who knows about Bob?" I said.

• • •

We finally came to a clearing on the right-hand side of the highway. There was grass, but it wasn't high, and I figured a lot of critters had been grazing on it. In the distance I could see the blue of a great lake. Or what looked like a lake. I still felt as if I were on a movie set. Reality was not to be trusted.

Crier turned off the highway and drove over the grass, and it seemed like it took forever to reach the lake. He parked about six feet from it, jumped out and went belly down on the bank and stuck his face into the water and began to drink.

It was real water.

I opened my door and tried to get out, but it was too far a step and too much pressure on my feet to manage it.

I sat and waited for Crier to finish drinking. If there had been any moisture in my mouth I would have salivated.

When Crier was done he came over and got me out of the truck. The grass was soft and I found I could hobble across it without too much support from Crier.

"I couldn't wait," Crier said. "Sorry."

"I'd have done the same," I said.

The water was cool and sweet, and pretty soon Crier had Bob beside me, then all three of us were lying there on our bellies drinking. I was the first to overdo it. I puked up the water and the sardines on the bank, and Bob and Crier followed shortly thereafter.

We finished puking and went to drinking again, slower this time, and when we were finished, we pulled off what we were wearing and went into the water, Bob and I entering it on elbows and knees, looking like pale alligators.

Waterlogged, we climbed on the bank and lay on our backs and looked at the sky. The sun went down—in the south, go figure—and the lake went dark and the moon rose up—in the south, go figure again—and the water turned the color of molten silver.

After we had talked a while about this and that, Crier said, "I'm one tired sonofabitch, boys. Let's call it a night."

Crier got us in the camper and stood at the tailgate. He said, "I'm in no hurry to leave. I like that water. What say we stick around a while? The highway's out there when we decide to try it again."

Sounded good to me, and I said so.

"Yeah," Bob said. "The idea of going off and leaving all that water doesn't excite me right now. Maybe just because I been thirsty for so long. But yeah, let's wait a while."

Crier nodded and went around to the cab to sleep. I lay down on my bedroll, and for the first time since before the big red comet, I felt a stirring of hope. Or maybe I had drunk too much water.

Whatever, it wasn't so exciting it kept me awake.

4

Next day Crier drove the truck to the other side of the lake, near the jungle, and that became our home. In spite of the water, we hadn't planned to stay as long as we did, but one day rolled into the next.

The jungle provided all kinds of fruit, and in defiance of the age of dinosaurs, all manner of recognizable animals from rabbits to squirrels to monkeys to snakes. All of these were good to eat, but in the beginning we left them alone. Not out of any respect for the lesser species, but simply because we couldn't catch the little bastards and had nothing suitable to kill or trap them with. Also, Bob and I were still crips, and you've got to have legs to run critters down.

Crier made a spear by breaking off a long, thin limb in such a way that it left a point. He put fruit rinds in the lake and stood in the water with them floating around him. He waited for fish to come and nibble at the rinds, then he tried to spear them.

Sometimes it took all day for him to get one, but he stayed with it. He was so determined that sometimes dinosaurs would come and stand off in the distance and watch. I think they were amused.

As time went by Crier got better, and later he changed to a more successful method. He got some strong vine and whittled a hook out of wood with a beer can opener he flattened and sharpened with a file from Bob's tool box. He used bugs and worms for bait. By the end of the day, he'd have a pretty nice mess of fish.

I was the fire builder. I'd pull grass and let it dry for a day or two, always keeping the supply ahead of the demand. When the grass looked brittle, I'd take two files from the tool box and knock them together until they made a spark, which I directed into the grass. By blowing on the spark, I could get a blaze going, and then I would feed it twigs, then larger kindling, and finally big hunks of wood. Before long, I'd have a good fire going.

Bob cleaned the fish and cooked them by spitting them on a green limb and hanging the limb between two upright forked sticks. The fish tasted pretty good. Every night, before bed, we ended up with a pile of fish bones and fruit rinds around us.

In time, Bob and I healed, and once we could get around, we turned industrious.

With what we had in the toolbox, we managed to make some simple tools for cutting and splitting wood. And damn if we weren't making crude lumber, notching it and pegging it and building a two-story house at the edge of the jungle. It wasn't anything to impress *Better Homes and Gardens*, but it was all right. We managed to use the limbs of this big tree as part of it, and the tree's foliage was so thick the house blended into it. We christened the place Jungle Home. It made me feel like I was a relative of the Swiss Family Robinson. A poor relation, to be sure, but a relation.

The upper floor was the sleeping nest, and by stuffing it with leaves and dried grass and putting the sleeping bags and blankets on top of that, we had a pretty comfortable place,

We also built a deck of split wood and bamboo on either side of the top floor, and it gave us a place to sit and feel the wind.

It wasn't paradise, but it beat being jabbed in the eye with a number two pencil.

But, as a great philosopher once wrote over the urinal in Buddy's Fill-up, "Things will go and change on you."

Crier and Bob had gone off hunting, since Crier had finally made a bow and a few arrows, and from here on out the animal populace was no longer safe. It was going to be roast rabbit and roast squirrel to go with the fish from now on.

Or so said Crier.

I had my doubts, since I had seen Crier practicing with that thing. It didn't look to me that he could have hit the side of a barn with a cannon, let alone a squirrel with a dull arrow. Still, I was hoping for him. I was beginning to tire of fish and fruit, fine as it had once seemed.

Isn't that the way of humans? They're never happy. One day I'm living off sardines and jerky with no water, and the next thing you know, I'm complaining about having fresh water, fish and fruit. Before long, I'd probably want a sauna in Jungle Home and someone to cater my meals.

Anyway, Crier and Bob went off on safari, and I was home filling some water containers we had made out of thick cylinders of hollowed-out bamboo.

I finished the job, stripped off my blanket, and went out and sat on the deck and dangled my feet over the edge.

I had no more than gotten comfortable, when I heard a car out on the highway, the engine straining and knocking as if it were about to explode.

I found me a good spot between the limbs and leaves, zeroed in on the highway, and saw a battered green Galaxy. It was coughing gouts of black smoke from under its hood and puffing a matching concoction from its tailpipe.

The driver hit down on the horn for some reason, and the horn hung.

This wasn't the Galaxy's day.

It slowed, turned off the highway onto the grassland, started weaving and picking up speed again.

I could see a figure in the front seat, fighting the wheel as if it were some rare breed of poisonous hoop snake. Then the driver lost it or quit, because the Galaxy veered to the left toward the lake.

The closer it got to the lake, the more speed it lost. It got down to a crawl. But it still made the water and dipped its nose in. Hot black smoke hissed up in a cloud, and the Galaxy began to slide languidly into the water.

And I was moving.

I had minded my own business so long, I was somewhat surprised when my Good Samaritan urges came back to me like a return bout of malaria fever. I went down the ladder two steps at a time and started running across the grassland toward the lake.

Owing to the gradual slope of the shore, the Galaxy had still not eased all the way in. The back right window was open, and I climbed through that.

The backseat was little more than springs and foam rubber. On the floorboard was something that looked like burnt sticks and brush. Another look and I knew it was human. Its skin was burned the color of neglected bacon. There was no hair, features or genitals. One of its arms was lifted, fingers extended and frozen in a pose that made the hand look like a miniature weed rake.

Water began to trickle in the back window. Already the front seat was filled. The thing on the floor didn't look alive, so I was about to go over the seat for the driver when the garden rake took hold of my ankle.

I jerked and flesh came off of the ruined hand and ran down my ankle like dirty Jell-O. I looked at the thing and it opened its mouth, made a croaking noise that sounded like "Kill me."

The water would take care of that. I couldn't. I went over the seat and into the water and found the driver, fearing he or she would be like the burned creature on the floorboard.

I got the driver's head out of the water, saw it was a woman. I started pulling her into the backseat by the chin. The rising water helped me.

The car was going under now, and I had time to get one deep breath before the whole kit and caboodle sank to the bottom of the lake.

The mud was stirred up down there and it was like being in creamed coffee. Somehow I got out the open window and tugged the woman after me, tried to kick to the surface.

The woman was deadweight and I couldn't get us up. We sank to the bottom. Since we were near the edge of the lake, it wasn't too deep, so I buried my toes in the sand and flexed my knees and shot us to the surface.

I managed her on shore, rolled her on her stomach, got hold of her arms and worked them some, pausing to push in the middle of her back. She puked.

I turned her over, cleared her mouth with my fingers and started mouth-to-mouth. It was a stinky job and tasted of vomit, but after a short time she coughed hard once and started breathing regularly.

She blinked at me. "Timothy?"

"He the burned guy?"

She nodded.

"He's still down there."

"Best," she said, and tried to get up on her elbows. She looked at that part of my body I least wanted her to look at.

"Small," she said.

"It's cold, for Christsakes."

But she wasn't listening. She had fallen back and was out of it.

5

Considering the way she had insulted my anatomy, I wasn't in any rush to pick her up and carry her to Jungle Home, but I finally gave it a try. She was a pretty hefty gal.

I put her down, went back to Jungle Home, found the keys to the camper and drove over there and got her, loaded her into the back, letting her head bump the tailgate only a couple of times.

When I got her stretched out, I moved her hair out of her face and took my first good look at her. She wasn't bad looking. Somewhere between eighteen and twenty-one. Guessing ages is not one of my better attributes.

Under the wet clothes her breasts looked nice and so did the width of her hips and the shape of her thighs. I thought about getting her wet clothes off to make her more comfortable, but I feared an ulterior motive.

I left her there in a puddle and went back to Jungle Home, stopping on the way to look at myself in the truck's wing mirror. My hair was wet and twisted and my scraggly little beard looked like a smear of grease. If I was going to have whiskers, why couldn't I have a full set like Bob and Crier.

I did the best I could combing my hair with my fingers, then went on up to Jungle Home and put on my blanket and tied it around my waist with a belt I had made of vines. Then I lay down on my sleeping bag and found that all that exertion had worn me out. I went right to sleep.

Next thing I knew, Bob and Crier were back. They had a vine basket of fruit, but no game.

"The great hunters return," I said.

"He saw a bunny," Bob said, "and couldn't shoot it. He got all dewy-eyed."

"It had a little pink nose," Crier said. "After all that's happened, I just couldn't kill something."

"Think those fish you catch live happily ever after in our bowel movements?"

"They aren't cute like bunnies," Crier said.

"Boys," I said, "there's a girl down in the camper."

"Don't joke me," Bob said. "I see a fork in a tree and I get hard."

"I'm not joking," I said, and told them the story.

We brought the basket of fruit with us, and when we got around to the back of the camper and looked inside, it was empty. There was a pool of water where she had been and her clothes and tennis shoes were laid out on the tailgate.

"Melted, I figure," Bob said.

"I'm right here."

We turned. She was about ten feet away, wearing only faded blue bikini panties. Her blonde hair was dry now and somehow she had combed it out. It fell to her wide shoulders and tumbled over them and, much to our happiness, stopped just before covering her breasts, which were firm and full with areola the size of half-dollars and the color of warm beef gravy. The nipples were thick and firm, like the tips of pointing fingers. She had a narrow waist and her ribs showed from having lost too much weight. There were faint, pink bands here and there on her body, as if she had been lashed with something. She had her hands on her hips and was looking right at us. If she was embarrassed, I couldn't tell it.

"Christ," she said. "Haven't you boys seen titties before?"

"There's titties," Bob said, "then there's titties."

"This is my first time, ma'am," Crier said. "I've heard of them, of course."

"Fuck with me, any kind of way," she said, "and I'll break your legs off and shove them up your assholes."

"Me first," Crier said.

But the way she looked at us then made us step aside. She came over and got her clothes and started putting them on.

"You boys enjoying the show?"

"Very much, yes," Bob said.

She finished dressing, sat on the tailgate, and looked at us. I guarantee we weren't as pleasant to look at as she was.

She said, "Had a cousin told me about a boyfriend she'd had. Said he was so horny he'd go to the ocean and fuck the water in case there might be a shark out there that had swallowed a girl. Know what she meant now. You could at least close your mouths."

"We're not so bad," Crier said. "We brought you some fruit."

She eyed the fruit we had left on the tailgate and said, "It isn't full of dick holes, is it?"

"Oh, come on," I said, "we're not that bad. All things considered, we're doing okay. We're not trying to rape you, are we? Look here. I'm Jack, this is Bob, and this is Crier."

Her face changed a little then and there was something behind that pretty skin and those green-gray eyes that wasn't so pretty. But whatever it was went away as quickly as it had arrived.

She took a plum-like fruit from the basket and bit out of it. The juice leaped from it in gold beads and flecked her lips and cheeks and she began to chew. After a moment, she spat out the seed, and went deeper into the fruit like a lion biting the innards out of an antelope's belly. When she finished that one, she ate another.

Somehow, watching her eat was as good as a peepshow. None of us said a word.

When she was finished, she said, "Now you've had a look at my tits and watched me eat. I hope you're happy. Had you showed five minutes earlier, you could have gone off in the bushes with me and watched me pee."

"You could have called us," Bob said.

"Nice dresses," she said, nodding at Bob and me.

"Let's not talk fashion," I said. "Tell us about yourself. Before the drive-in and up to now."

"Why would you want to know?"

"Entertainment," I said. "It's not like we have a pressing social calendar. We know more than we want to know about each other. Give us something new to think about."

"All right," she said. "Sit down and get comfy, because this is going to take a while."

SECOND REEL

Grace Talks About Frat House Fires, Raw Liver, and a Nine Iron to the Noggin

1

My name is Grace, and I come from a little burg called Nacogdoches. It's supposed to be the oldest town in Texas. We got a sign that says so, but it doesn't look that old—the town, I mean, not the sign.

The place is still kind of neat, but it's going to hell fast, and when I look at photographs Mom and Dad have of it twenty-five years ago, it really chaps my highly attractive ass.

It's one of those towns where the fine old houses and the massive trees have been torn or cut down so progress can slither in. You know progress. Burger King, McDonald's, and all manner of plastic eateries where the wrappers for the burgers and the lettuce inside them taste pretty much alike, and it's my opinion the wrappers have a more natural tint than the lettuce and are probably more nutritious.

These days the old houses are gone and you can stand in the parking lot of McDonald's on fourth Street and toss a dried Big Mac underhanded and bounce it off the front glass of Wendy's on the other side of the street. Or you can go over to University Drive and toss a pepperoni pizza, no anchovies, out of the driveway of Mazzio's Pizza and wing an innocent bystander on the table-laden deck of Arby's.

I went to high school and college in good ol' Nac. The college is called Stephen F. Austin University, and it's named after one of the guys that helped con Texas from Mexico.

I was majoring in anthropology/archaeology, but what I really wanted to be was a karate instructor, since my dad, who was a black belt in kenpo, had been teaching me ever since I was five. If it matters, I'm first degree brown belt now.

But like Dad, I couldn't see any real future in martial arts. Or to be more precise, I think I let Mom convince me there wasn't any future in it. She talked Dad into being a manager of an optical store and she wanted something like that for me, or as she always put it, "Kicking people is all right, but you can't make a decent living at it. You got to have something to fall back on."

Well, I had been hearing this speech since I was old enough to know which was the business end of a tampon, so when I saw this *National Geographic* special on archaeology on television, I thought it might be just what I was looking for.

There were these folks with tans about the color of fresh walnut stains applied to burnt mahogany, wearing khaki shorts and pith helmets, and they were swarming over these ruins. Fire ants couldn't have been any busier.

They were doing a lot of pointing and writing in notebooks and looking intelligent. There were close-ups of pottery shards from pots that had been made before Jesus was old enough to suck Mary's tit, and there were skull fragments and pieces of bones from the guys and gals that had made the pots.

The show ended with a close-up of this woman with sweat running from under her pith helmet and onto her face and mixing with the sand there, out over these little fragments of walls, looking soulful as a Baptist preacher, contemplating the past and all the great civilizations that had arisen there and folded back in on themselves like a card table.

It was inspiring.

Thinking back on it now, she may have been looking out over that sand waiting for somebody to pick her up in an air-conditioned truck and drive her over to a Mideast Hilton.

But the desire to dig holes in the ground and hold the bony remains of ancient pottery makers in my hands had come over me like the Holy Ghost. I couldn't think of anything else. I checked out archaeology books and read them cover to cover and started envisioning ancient civilizations marching ghostlike through Nacogdoches, throwing down pots and bowls and breaking them so I could find them a zillion years later.

What I didn't get from those books, or refused to get, was how goddamn hard archaeology is. And it's dirty work. Those people on *National Geographic* weren't just deeply tanned, they were downright filthy.

At the end of a day, having sifted through enough sand to fill Galveston Beach, the sun burning through my clothes like an X-ray, it was hard for me to take a whole lot of pride in a few broken pieces of pottery that some prehistoric dude had marked on with a pine needle.

Looking back on it, it was pretty wonderful stuff, I guess, but I don't like working in the heat and getting so dirty you have to use a putty knife to get it off your elbows. And I didn't even have a pith helmet. Just a cap that said Nacogdoches Dragons on it, and they weren't winning many ball games.

If someone from *National Geographic* had showed up right then, I'd have stuffed a year's run of magazines down their throat and kicked them until they shit a single bound volume.

It's not that I'm a weak sister. I'm not. Karate gave me patience as well as determination. But it's mostly clean work. A little sweat and dirty feet is all. And I did my workouts in our air-conditioned garage or the college gym. If you have to use martial arts on the street, it doesn't take but a few moments to open up a can of whup-ass, then you can find some air-conditioned building to cool off in when it's over.

Even indoor archaeology is hard.

On one dig I found some pottery pieces, and I was assigned to try and reconstruct them. That's like giving a blind, crippled monkey a hammer, a bag of nails, and a pile of lumber and telling him to build an A-frame. I'm the gal who still has an unfinished fifty-piece puzzle of a white cat in my closet at home, and I got that puzzle for my tenth birthday.

I'd go to the lab every night and try to do that pottery, and I'll tell you, after fifteen minutes of that I was dangerous. I wanted to kill something and drink a couple of bottles of Nervine.

Bottom line is, I quit. And that was the turning point. Had I stayed in archaeology, I'd probably have been home studying, or up at the lab, destroying my nerves with that pottery instead of meeting up with Timothy and Sue Ellen and tooling on over to the Orbit Drive-in that weird Friday night.

2

So, on the night after I'd given up archaeology and my chance to have something to fall back on, I was out riding around in my old Chevy Nova trying to figure out what I was going to do with the rest of my life, and I'll tell you, what I was coming up with was not pretty.

I thought about all those stories I'd heard about college dropouts and how they spent their lives working behind the counter at K-mart or pulling the train for the football team during off season. I could envision myself standing on the corner of North and Main with a cigarette jutting out of my mouth, one side of my lip pulled up in a permanent snarl, and me thinking how I can get a few dollars so I can go over to the 7 Eleven and buy me a bottle of Thunderbird wine. Nothing would be too low for me to do: prostitution, theft, drug-running, murder, working as a used-car salesman. In time I would be shunned by winos and Baptists alike.

On the other hand, I was also thinking about whoever had inherited my prehistoric pottery shards, and I felt a wicked elation that while I was out tooling around, someone was hunched over those shards with their eyes twitching, their hands shaking, wishing I had quietly pushed those fragments down a gopher hole.

Anyway, I was riding around, taking back streets mostly, thinking, and I came up on this fire.

There were cars pulled over the curb and people were standing on the sidewalk and out front of their houses, watching a frat house burn down.

I pulled across from the house, behind the string of parked cars, got out and leaned on the Nova and watched.

The fire department was there and the firemen were jerking hoses, yelling and hopping on the lawn like grasshoppers. Every now and then one of them would erupt from the doorway of the burning structure like the end result of the Heimlich maneuver, land in the yard on his hands and knees, and crawl about feebly, coughing smoke like a little dragon.

I had never seen a fire like that before, and it didn't take Smokey the Bear to tell me it was some kind of serious. A blazing paper hat would have been easier to save.

While I was watching the frat joint burn up—hating that it was an old house of the sort the city council loved to see go so an aluminum building the shape of a box could take its place, or some concrete could be laid down for a car lot—a tan van came down the street and stopped at the curb and three guys fell out of it yelling. Frats, I figured. Most likely they had gone for a six-pack, or to work their version of heavy machinery, a Trojan dispenser, and had come back to find they had forgot to turn the fire off from under the chili, and now their pad was on its way to becoming air pollution.

Two of them sat on the curb and started crying and the other one rolled around on the lawn and whimpered like a dog with glass in his belly. A fireman came over and yelled at him and kicked him in the butt. The guy crawled off and joined his comrades at the curb and they cried in trio.

I hoped like hell there wasn't anyone inside that house. If so, they wouldn't be graduating.

I was about to leave when I was touched lightly on the elbow and a voice said, "You start this one, baby?"

"Nope. I'm all out of matches."

"Then you got nothing to worry about."

I turned and looked at Timothy. I had known him all my life, had been over to his house to play when we were kids, and he had been over to mine. There had never been anything romantic between us, though when I was twelve I talked him into playing doctor and discovered what I'd heard about boys was true: They were fixed up different from girls.

"Good to see you," I said. "It's been a while."

One of the firemen came coughing out to the curb across from us and sat down next to one of the frat boys. The one who had been rolling on the ground sobbed and said, "They gonna save it?"

The fireman took off his smoke-stained hat, coughed, and looked at the frat the way some people look at retarded children. "Son, we'll be lucky if we save the mineral rights on that sonofabitch."

The three frats really started to cry.

The roof collapsed then and the sparks from it rose up to heaven and turned clear like the souls of fireflies gone off to meet their just rewards.

"Last time I heard," Timothy said, "you were digging holes in the ground or something. Had some night classes too."

"A lab," I said. "Archaeology in the daytime, labs at night. I had to let it go."

Then I told him the whole story.

"I quit too," he said.

"I never knew you started."

"It was the math fixed me. Never could understand how X could be some other number. It always looked like X to me. I couldn't make sense of it. If X was ten one time, how could it be fifteen the next? Who the hell could keep up with what X was if it could be anything?

"What I should have taken was all P. E. courses and majored in golf. I can't make X and Y add up, but by God, I can knock those little white balls to Dallas."

And he could. I had played golf with him before. My golfing style was akin to a frightened matron trying to beat a rat to death with a curtain rod, but I had played enough to know the good stuff when I saw it, and Timothy had the good stuff. A number of pro golfers had made the same observation, and Timothy had mentioned more than once that he was thinking about taking his clubs on the road and seeing what he could do.

"We're on our way to the Orbit," Timothy said. "Want to go?"

"We?"

"Sue Ellen. She loves that horror stuff."

Sue Ellen was Timothy's little sister. She was twelve. Last time I'd seen her was two years back, and she wanted me to explain why Barbie and Ken were smooth allover. I didn't remember having any answers.

"I doubt she even remembers me," I said. "She might feel uncomfortable."

"She remembers you quite well."

"She's sort of young for blood and guts, isn't she?"

"Tell me about it. Mom and Dad think I'm taking her over to see *Bambi*, *Cinderella*, *The Fox and the Hound* and assorted cartoons in a Disney dusk-to-dawn extravaganza."

"Wonder how they got that idea," I said.

I took my car home, told my parents where I was going, not mentioning that Sue Ellen was waiting in the car with Timothy, and we went over there in the Galaxy.

When we got there, the line was as long as the Macy's Thanksgiving parade, and, of course, we got a place near the end of it. The flashing blue-and-white Saturn symbol of the Orbit was far enough away to look like a Ping-Pong ball with an oversized washer around it.

It was warm and the air was full of mosquitoes. Rolling up the windows made you hotter, and rolling them down fed you to the mosquitoes. Timothy talked about giving it up and going home, and I was for it. But not Sue Ellen.

"You promised me, Timmy. You said you'd take me. You know I want to see *The Toolbox Murders.*"

I turned and looked at Sue Ellen perched in the middle of the backseat. She was blonde and fair and had moist blue eyes and a freckled pug nose and a red bow mouth. Course, it was dark enough you couldn't see all this, but you knew it was there, and telling her no was a lot like kicking a puppy for licking your hand.

"We'll be miserable," Timothy said. "Besides, *The Toolbox Murders*? How'd I let you talk me into that?"

"You promised, Bubba. And if any of it bothers me, you can explain it to me."

"That's choice. I might need you to explain it to me."

"See, I'm old enough."

"One word about mosquitoes, one complaint, and we're out of here."

"Deal."

Had the weather been hotter, the mosquitoes thicker, or if Sue Ellen had had all the charm of Dr. Frankenstein's hunchback assistant, we might have cut for home right then. Sue Ellen would have grown up to break hearts, Timothy would have gone on to hit little white balls across great expanses of greenery for unreasonable amounts of money, and I might have ended up with my own karate studio.

3

All right, I'm going to stop with Grace's story now. For all you dipshits in the back row who haven't been listening—Leroy, quit playing in *that pile of shit. Put that stick down. Yeah, well, screw you too, little buddy. I hope your balls get covered in ants.*

Now, all you bozos keep interrupting my relating here and I'm tired of it. *You all keep saying, "What about the comet? What about the comet?" Well, I've got no new news on the comet, okay? You've heard it all before. I've told you that story half a dozen times. I started this story with the comet. Remember?*

No, I don't change it as I go along Leroy. Look, I don't make you come and listen, do I, huh?

Why did all this happen?

We've been over this part, Leroy, back when I read you the first half of this story, the one I call THE DRIVE-IN, A B-MOVIE WITH BLOOD AND POPCORN. *Yes, the one written on the Big Chief tablets. But to answer your question why . . . I don't know. It's like why do turds come in different shapes and colors. I can't answer that. It's one of life's big mysteries, and the comet is an even bigger one.*

Here, listen. Do you remember those sayings I taught you? The ones the Christians are fond of. Remember, we talked about Christians. Good? Now those sayings. Let's use them to get things on the roll and because they're all purpose. Repeat after me: THERE ARE SOME THINGS MAN WAS NOT MEANT TO KNOW, and I FEEL IT IN MY HEART. *Later I'll teach you about Faith, that way if you don't know how to explain something, say, you've got faith. That covers a lot of bases and cuts down on argument.*

What do you mean that doesn't work for you? Is this going to be like yesterday's conversation, Leroy? The one about Why Is There Air and Why Do Boys Have a Pecker and Girls Don't? Good, because I'm not going to get into that. I've got a story written down here and it's the story I'm going to read. It's a good story and I've recorded it as best I can, and it's almost the truth. If you want to hear it, fine, if not, I'll read to myself. I do this for me, not you, so you want to hear the story you got to listen. What, Leroy?

Uh huh, that's right. Why don't you go ahead and find your stick again and stir the shit pile. At least you were quiet. I wish I hadn't disturbed you.

Yeah. That's okay, use your finger. Let me get back to Grace—

Okay. Maybe I don't remember what Grace said word for word, but this is pretty close. Trust me.

Food started running out at the concession, so we used Timothy's pocket knife to cut strips from the leather seat covers. The leather must have been coated with something (a dirt-resistant spray?), because it made us sick at first, though after a while we got used to it. When we still had Coke from the concession, we'd soak it in that and chew on it, maybe finish off with a few chocolate almonds. But when everything was gone at the concession we had to eat the strips straight out.

All around us people were losing it, going nuts for food, killing one another and eating one another. Sue Ellen wasn't doing so hot either. She seemed addled most of the time and kept insisting we take her home, that Mommy and Daddy would be worried. She said she didn't like the movies anymore. She missed her dog. She said lots of things.

I had to use my martial arts a few times to keep from being hurt by nuts who wanted me for either sex or food. We never got the situation clear; I pounded their heads briskly and they went away. But in time I got too weak for the martial arts, and a lot of the folks around us were too weak to do much of anything either. I guess you could say it was a kind of trade-off. I didn't feel so good, but the folks that might have done me, Timothy and Sue Ellen harm weren't exactly up to the Boston marathon either.

Then along came the Popcorn King.

Now he was one weird sonofabitch, looking back on it, but I'll tell you, when those two guys were fused together by the lightning and they had all those powers, tattoos coming to life and running around and the like, I wasn't even surprised.

Weird was the status quo, right?

What did surprise me was when he used those powers of his to supply us with popcorn and Coke, and he started talking that stuff about how he was our savior and that the movies were reality and murder and mayhem were okey-dokey and our salvation, and by the way, got any dead bodies, bring them on over to me and I'll eat them. You know the rap.

When he stopped giving out the popcorn and disappeared inside the concession stand for a time, like Jesus gone off into the wilderness, I'll tell you true, I was some depressed. It was back to eating seat covers.

When he finally did reappear, he no longer had popcorn to give us. Least not the real stuff. Now it was that substitute crap he was vomiting up. And that had bloodshot eyeballs on it.

Weirdness suddenly re-identified and redefined itself. I wasn't going to eat that junk, no way, no how. And neither was Timothy.

Sue Ellen ate it. There wasn't any way we could stop her from it. We tried at first, but she got away and got to it anyhow. She said it was sweet as candy and ran around inside your head like a hot lizard; said looking out of her eyes was like looking through a projector, like becoming the light and sound that shot out of the projector and hit the screen; like being everything fast-moving and bright that ever existed. Stuff like that, not twelve-year-old talk. She said when she looked at us she saw little screens on our faces instead of eyes and on the screens she could see little picture shows of our past, and I guess maybe she could, because she told us some things we hadn't told her about the two of us, like about the time we played doctor.

Mysterious stuff. Popcorn magic.

And in time the eyeball corn didn't seem so odd. So what, big deal, the popcorn had eyeballs and it came from the King who vomited it up? So what?

The idea of crunching down on those eyeballs wasn't so weird anymore. I thought maybe in texture it might be like damp Cracker Jack. Was it the vomit that made it sweet? Did lights and shadows and sounds run around in your head like a hot lizard, as Sue Ellen said? Was it really like that? Would I know new and wonderful things?

I looked around at the others. They were eating the corn, but they didn't seem to be cruising through life any better than I was. They were weak and sick and malicious, always hungry. They were dying same as me except they were hiding behind the veneer of the King's chemistry, mixing it with his jive religion, but they were going to die same as me.

Still, you can only hold out so long. Hunger is the biggest monkey ever made. It can make heroin addiction seem like a Coca-Cola habit.

Timothy caved in. He got tired of chewing seat covers and listening to his belly rumble. He went the way of Sue Ellen and ate the vomit corn. First time he had it he came back talking about the color of lies. His breath was sewerish and his eyes were dull; I wondered what movies were showing on the backs of them.

I used my martial arts to keep me away from the corn. I was too weak to practice it, but I did the movements in my head, tried to fill the hungry thoughts with visions of me nude and strong and practicing every technique I knew, fast and slow and medium.

It worked well, but not well enough. In time my belly started to win over, and I would have gone for the corn had the man not come along.

This is hard to talk about, but it seems to me, bad as this was, it was better than the corn. The corn would make me sing the King's song; I wasn't ready for the color of lies and movies on the backs of my eyes.

Okay, here goes. Straight plunge.

Timothy and Sue Ellen were just back from the concession, sitting in the car, eyes closed, seeing whatever it was the corn made them see, and I was sitting there thinking of stripping off another piece of seat cover to chew on. There wasn't much left and it made me ill to think about chewing on that nasty stuff, but what else was there to do? So I'm thinking about this, trying to get the will to do it, when this man staggered by on my side, put his hand against the door frame, said, "Shit, this ain't heartburn," and fell over.

I got out of the car and looked at him. He was about thirty with long, stringy, grayish hair and he was lying on his stomach with his head turned to one side, his eyes open. But he wasn't seeing much. He had been correct. It wasn't heartburn. He was as dead as a dodo's agenda.

Sue Ellen and Timothy got out of the car and came around and looked at him, then looked at each other, and finally me.

We didn't say a word. We got hold of him and put him in the backseat and Sue Ellen got back there with him, and Timothy and I got in the front.

Of course, I knew what we were doing. We were saving him for food. I hadn't been willing to eat popcorn with eyeballs on it, but somehow this was different. It would have been a shame to let him go to waste when we were starving. And if we didn't eat him, someone else was going to come along and drag him off for just that purpose.

Hell, it wasn't like we'd killed him.

I remember sitting there thinking about this, turning from time to time to look at the body on the backseat, and finding that each time I looked, Sue Ellen had removed yet another article of his clothing. When he was completely stripped, she called for Timothy's knife, and he gave it to her.

My next memory is of holding the corpse's still-warm liver in my hands and rubbing it into my face, then eating it. Strength flowed back into me immediately, and for some reason my legs began to jerk spasmodically and my knees hit the bottom of the dash and caused the glove box to knock open.

Timothy kept a little mirror in there, and it was at an angle, and by the light of the pulsating Orbit symbol, I could see myself. My face was stained a rust color from forehead to chin, and my eyes were little pits.

I looked at Timothy and Sue Ellen.

Timothy was chewing on a bone with a few chunks of meat on it. He had his eyes closed, and when he chewed he made little orgasmic noises deep in his throat.

Sue Ellen was on her hands and knees straddling the body, and she had half her head buried in an opening she had cut in the man's stomach. She was rooting around in there like a pig.

I opened the door and fell on the ground and threw up.

I don't think Timothy or Sue Ellen noticed. They were too busy with lunch.

I crawled under the Galaxy and tried to wipe the blood off my face with my forearms, then lay on my side with my knees pulled into my chest, and shook.

A young man so thin his pants flapped around his legs like flags on poles, came by, dropped to the ground, and made a meal of what I'd thrown up. His face was turned toward me as he lapped. When he saw me, he lapped faster. Maybe he thought I wanted it.

He finally staggered off. Where my vomit had been was a damp spot.

I rolled on my back and looked at the underside of the car and tried to think about nothing, but all I could see was that man gutted from throat to crotch and Sue Ellen with her head dipped into him. And lastly, my own face in that mirror, smeared with blood from hair to chin.

Bones were dropped out of the Galaxy's windows on the left side, and I turned my head and looked at them and tried to determine if they were rib, forearm, or leg bones. I couldn't make a decision.

As I watched, people came along and snatched up the bones and ran off with them.

I lay there for the longest time, feeling very sick to my stomach and my soul.

When I heard Timothy and Sue Ellen getting out of the Galaxy, I refused to watch their legs go by. I knew they were going to the concession to get their vomit corn from the King. I had decided I would starve to death before I did that.

I don't know how long this went on, my lying under the car hoping to starve. It could have been thirty minutes or it could have been days. But Timothy and Sue Ellen came and went several times and I always felt dizzy, as if I were in the middle of some huge platter that was being spun.

But my starvation plans weren't working out. The hunger had a mind of its own, and finally I crawled out from under the car and tried to stand up. But couldn't. I was too weak. I got hold of a door handle and pulled myself up and looked in the window at the body on the backseat.

There was hardly anything left of the man. Even his eyes and genitals had been eaten. Only his pelvis, ankles and feet had flesh on them, and it was turning black.

I felt hungry enough to bite the toes off his feet, one at a time, and would have tried, but about the time I started to go after him, the concession stand blew up.

4

That was us that did it, of course, and no use going into that again. Anyway, we smashed the concession, killed the King, and for our fine work, the crowd got hold of us and crucified us. But I told you all about that too.

Summing up this part of Grace's story, she didn't see what happened to the concession, but when she turned around it was in shambles and on fire. Of course the movies from the concession were snuffed too, though the projector over in B section of the lot was still pumping. But the thing is, we killed the King.

Grace's dizziness subsided and she managed to walk toward the flames. She saw what was happening to us, but later when she met us, she didn't remember our faces. The crowd was about to put fires under the crosses and cook us, and the comet came back. The black goo went away, and the drive-in folks were out of there.

Grace wanted to help get us down. Her dizziness had passed, and she tried to talk Timothy and Sue Ellen into helping, but they had come back to the car and they were ready to leave.

Anyway, Grace said—

I got the keys from Timothy and pulled the body out of the backseat. Doing that made me dizzy again, but I put a hand on the side of the car and stood that way until it passed.

I went around back to the trunk and opened it. I wanted to find something I could use as a tool to get those people down off those crosses, but there wasn't much there. A tire tool, a spare, and a bag full of golf clubs. I leaned down deeper, seeing if maybe there was something way in the back, and when I did, my head felt as if it were flying apart.

And as they say in the old detective movies, I fell into a deep, dark pit and it closed around me.

"I didn't mean to hit you that hard," Timothy said.

"Someone meant to," I said. "What did you use?"

"A golf club."

It was bright daylight and I was stretched out on the ground beside the Galaxy, which was parked on the grass next to the highway. I felt a little too warm.

Timothy helped me to a sitting position and gave me a piece of fruit. After what we'd been eating, it tasted like heaven. I began feeling better immediately. Which is not to say the golf-ball-size lump (which was appropriate) had gone away.

"I panicked," Timothy said. "I was afraid it would go back to how it was. I'm thinking better now that I've had some food."

I looked for Sue Ellen and spotted her sitting in the shade of a big tree, eating fruit. She was rocking a little and humming to herself.

"She's not doing so good," Timothy said.

He got an arm under me and helped me to my feet. I looked down the highway and saw nothing but more highway bordered by jungle and topped by blue sky.

"I've got to go back to the Orbit," I said.

"I can't do that," Timothy said. "Neither can Sue Ellen."

"Just take me back. You don't have to go in."

"We've come a long ways since I hit you."

"You owe me, Timothy."

He drove me back and waited while I went inside the drive-in. I thought maybe I could find something in a car there to use as a tool to get those fellas down, if they were still alive. But when I got inside, the crosses were down and they were gone.

I didn't stick around to look at the empty cars or the bones. I went outside to where the Galaxy was waiting, and we started on down the highway.

Okay, gang, I'll interrupt here to say that we stopped Grace's story and told her that Bob and me were two of the folks on the cross, and Crier was the one that got us down. And when we finished that, she picked up with her adventures.

But before we get to those, why don't we take a brief intermission. My tongue is getting tired.

THIRD REEL

Grace Tells of Tremendous Gas Mileage, Shit Town, and Popalong Cassidy

1

So we went on down the highway, traveling only a few miles a day, stopping to look around, relieve ourselves and search for fruit and berries.

I was amazed at the way the gas held out. It was like when we were in the drive-in and the electricity worked for no logical reason, and now here was the gas gauge showing us to be getting incredible mileage. It was going down all right, but slowly compared to the miles we were racking up.

Still, gas was going to be a problem eventually. But it was a problem that was solved when we came to a place with lots of cars pulled off the highway and parked along its edges and out in an area that had been partially cleaned by nature and partially by human beings.

A crude sign had been painted on a big, split limb and stuck up in the ground beside the road. It read:

S
H
I
T

T
O
W
N

People were living in their cars and crude huts. There was a river nearby and they were getting fish out of it. And, of course, there was abundant fruit.

You wouldn't call it a harmonious little town, but it seemed to be doing well enough, considering a canopy of doom hung over it; a canopy knitted stitch by stitch by dark experience.

We stayed on a while, living out of our car, watching the place try and become a real town.

One night this guy about my age got a rope from somewhere and went out to the edge of town and picked this big oak and threw the rope over a limb and fashioned a noose and hung himself.

Next morning he was dangling there, purple-faced, looking like some odd-shaped, overripe fruit about to drop from the vine. The log he had stood on and kicked away at the last moment was about six feet from where his feet dangled. I wondered if in his last painful moments he had looked down at the log with regret.

Timothy and I helped get him down and some others got rid of the body, and the next night a girl of about twelve went out there and climbed up on the limb and put the rope around her neck and hung herself.

In the morning she was discovered. Sue Ellen went over to look at her. Neither Timothy nor I tried to stop her from seeing the body. She had seen much worse than that, and keeping her from it was akin to shutting the barn door after the stock have run off. Still, the way she looked at the dead girl's face made me shiver. You'd have thought she was gazing on the countenance of the Madonna.

No one cut the rope down. I think it was a way out everyone liked knowing was there, even if they never actually planned to use it.

New people joined the community regularly. They had all been down the road a piece and they had given up and turned back, coming rolling into Shit Town in cars propelled by little more than fumes. Or they walked in, weary and defeated.

I was still thinking about the end of the highway, so I talked to as many newcomers as I could. No one I spoke with had made it to the end. They said it got rougher and stranger as you went, and some of them felt certain the highway never ended.

The town grew and the rope became more popular. Sue Ellen spent a lot of time looking at it. I decided it was time to move on.

Timothy agreed. He spent his days gathering stones and taking them out to the middle of the highway and putting them on the fading yellow line and swatting them with a golf club. His strength, like mine, had come back, and he could knock them real far. He did that day in and day out until it was too dark to do it. He didn't talk much.

I talked to people in the town that had cars, asked if I could have their gas. A lot of them said they had gone all they intended to go, and they gave it to me. I managed to get a can and a hose. I siphoned gas from the cars into the can and transferred it to the Galaxy.

While I did this, Timothy golfed and Sue Ellen looked at the rope.

I put a can of gas in the trunk and some fruit too, then I got Timothy and Sue Ellen and drove us out of there. Timothy wasn't shit for driving anymore. He couldn't keep his mind on it, and the King's popcorn had done something to the both of them. They had flashbacks of a sort. Recited lines from the movies back at the Orbit. Sue Ellen could even do the nail gun noise from *The Toolbox Murders*.

Anyway, we drove on out of there, and I put the pedal to the metal and kept my eyes ever forward, searching for the end of the highway.

2 We went along quickly, stopping only to sleep and get fruit from the trunk of the car, but after a few days, things began to change.

It was getting along night when I first noticed it. As it grew darker the jungle grew thicker and great roots cracked the concrete and coiled onto the highway along with vines that twisted and knotted like threads in a complex tapestry.

When the Galaxy's tires went over the big roots, the shocks throbbed, and when they went over the larger vines, the vines exploded like garden hoses full of black water.

The sun, like a head full of fire, nodded out below the pinprick of the highway's horizon, and the moon rose up in the same spot like a mean little kid giving us a bent-over view of a pockmarked ass.

I turned on the lights and the trees on either side of the highway leaned forward and touched overhead making a tunnel of foliage down which the Galaxy was shooting like a bullet out of a gun barrel.

The wind picked up and leaves churned across the road and popcorn bags and soft drink cups and candy wrappers joined them and made a little twister that fell over the windshield of the Galaxy like an avalanche. I beat the refuse away with the wipers and went though another twister of the stuff, and yet another, each gaining strength and causing the car to shake violently.

I thought I could see drive-in screens, or fragments of old drive-ins, on either side of the road, but I couldn't be sure because of the shadows.

Something came blowing toward me and plastered to the windshield and there was no way I could make out for sure what it was before it blew away, but it looked like a movie poster, one of those garish ones you see in the horror movies.

I glanced at Timothy, but he had passed out some time back and was leaning against the door, snoring softly. Sue Ellen was stretched out on the back seat asleep.

Goose bumps went up my back, but I didn't slow down and I didn't pull over. I didn't know what I'd find out there if I pulled over, and the idea of slowing down bothered me, especially now that the shadows were growing thicker and looking funny, and I use the word funny in the loosest sense, because I wasn't laughing about anything. I wasn't even cracking a smile.

The shadows fluttered and rolled across the road like tumbleweeds and hit the car with a sound like wet blankets. They were very odd shadows indeed. Shadows of trees and leaves and men and women and giant apes and dinosaurs and flying things bigger than a double-decker bus.

I couldn't see the source of any of the shadows, but I had a feeling if they had a source, they lived lives contrary to the movements of their origins.

I thought I saw movements in my mirror, faces, reflections of things in windows, thought I heard whispers, laughs and sighs.

Then it started to get really bad out there. The wind picked up and gathered all the shadows, the popcorn bags, candy wrappers, cups, and posters (I was sure now), all this stuff, and it began to hit the Galaxy and whirl about it and the wind sucked at the car and lifted it up and dropped it down, lifted it up and dropped it down, and once when it went down, the back right tire went with a noise like a six-gun shot.

The car swerved and I tried to turn in the direction of the skid like the handbook says, but the skid said "Fuck You," and the shadows sacked up the car and took away the light.

Round and round the Galaxy went, over and over. Timothy flew into me and we banged heads and the darkness outside became the darkness in me.

3

I woke up and found that the car had righted itself and that I was lying on the front seat alone. The door on the passenger side was open.

I sat up and clung to the back of the seat until I felt focused. I could see Sue Ellen's shape in the back, draped partially on the floorboard and partially on the seat. I reached back and touched her and she moaned and sat up slowly and held the side of her jaw.

"You okay?" I asked.

"The movie over yet?" she asked.

"Not yet," I said. I took her hand gently from her face and saw a thin cut running from the corner of her mouth to her chin, a scratch really. She didn't seem to be in any real pain.

"Wait here, okay?"

"You going to the concession stand?"

"I'll be right back."

"Where's Timmy?"

"I'm going to get him."

"Have him bring me a large popcorn, will you?"

I couldn't tell if the wreck had banged her around and thrown off her timeframe, or if she was having another of those pop-backs. Maybe she was seeing a movie through the windshield of the car.

The wind was still high when I got out of the car, but not as bad as before. I held on to the door handle for a moment, edged my way to the rear of the car. The trunk was open and the keys were in the trunk lid. Timothy had gotten the keys and gotten back here. Maybe he wanted some of the fruit.

I got the keys and put them in my pants pocket and saw that his golf bag had been pulled from under all the fruit. It was sticking out of the back of the car by a foot. I knew then that he had gotten one of his golf clubs. If Sue Ellen was still at the drive-in watching movies, maybe Timothy thought he was participating in the Bob Hope Open, or whatever that golf thing is called.

There was mashed fruit all over the place and the gas can was hanged up, but not open. I set it up and got a piece of fruit and ate a few bites out of it, and started looking for Timothy.

The wind passed on by, and the last of it let popcorn bags and debris flutter onto the car and ground. Plastered across the rear of the windshield was a poster. The moon was brighter, now that the shadows had fled, and I could read the printing on the poster. *Texas Chainsaw Massacre.* The words looked as if they had been written in blood.

Out in the trees I could see big hunks of whiteness. I decided they were fragments of drive-in screens—chunks of white painted wood.

Draped between the trees like Christmas decorations were lengths of film, the moonlight sticking through the sprocket holes like long, bright needles, and a sort of mist swirling about the film itself.

I didn't see any videotapes, and I didn't see Timothy.

I went around the car a couple of times, examining it. Except for a lot of bumps and a hairline crack in the windshield, it looked all right. It was no more than ten feet from the highway, and the ground between it and the highway looked firm enough to drive on.

I wanted to look for Timothy, but I didn't know if we might need the car in a hurry, and I wanted to be ready. I dug around under the fruit and the golf bag and got out the tire iron and the spare.

The jacking up and the tire changing went pretty quick, and I rolled the old tire off beside the road, tossed the tire tool in the back and closed the trunk.

I started looking for Timothy.

Out to the right there was a trail. Maybe dinosaurs had made it. Maybe cars had made it. There was no rhyme or reason to this place.

I went down the trail calling for Timothy. As I went the wind picked up again and it started to rain and lightning began to crackle in the heavens. Still, the moon held bright.

Something moved in the jungle, and I found a good-sized stick and carried it with me. Martial arts or not, another equalizer never hurts. Course, if it was a Tyrannosaurus Rex, something like that, it would eat me and pick its teeth with my stick.

As I went along, the trail widened. I went over a little rise and down into a clearing. There was a lot of grass there were posts for drive-in speakers, and a few of them still had speakers on them. There were rusted cars dotted about.

At the back, almost integrated into the jungle, was a drive-in screen. It was split open in spots and limbs poked through the splits and twisted upwards and spread out in leaf-covered branches that looked like bony fingers from which dangled tufts of dark flesh.

About ten yards in front of the screen, golf club in hand, on the tail end of a classic swing, was Timothy.

I stood and watched a while. He was golfing up dirt and leaves.

I called to him. He looked up, went back to golfing. I walked over and waited until he finished a swing, then I stepped in and took hold of his elbow.

"This is a tough course," he said.

"You can say that again."

"I don't think I'm doing too well."

"You're doing fine. That was the last hole."

"Yeah. How'd I do?"

"You beat the competition hands down. Come along, Sue Ellen is waiting for us."

I led him along and the wind picked up and the trash twisters coiled at our feet.

4

Serious rain.

Serious wind.

Serious lightning.

Serious lost.

"Where the hell are we?" Timothy asked.

"Well, Toto, I don't think we're in Kansas anymore."

"Kansas? We've been in Kansas? Who's Toto?"

"Just close your little mouth and walk."

Sometimes it doesn't pay to read or watch old movies. No one knows what you're talking about.

"Goddamn," Timothy said. "This is a weird course. What's that?"

It was shadows. They had collected in our path. On either side of us the trees whipped their heads up and down like drunk women with the dry heaves.

I threw my stick at the shadows and the stick went into them and was not seen again. The shadows flowed over us with a howl of the wind and they felt like wet felt where they touched us. But there was nothing more to them. They went through us, and I turned to watch them blow on down the trail like ink-stained ghosts.

The trail disappeared. It was as if the trees had pulled up by the roots and repositioned themselves. Nothing was familiar. Strips of film dropped down from the branches and clung to us, and when I tore them off they ripped my flesh.

Timothy swatted at them with his golf club. The film wound itself around the club and jerked it away from him. Last sight of it was a silver wink in the moonlight as it disappeared into the rustling leaves of a dark, gnarled tree.

I grabbed hold of his wrist and tugged him. We went between trees and shrubs, wherever there was a space. Film ran along the ground and dropped out of the trees and tried to grab us.

Lightning flashed. I got a glimpse of the highway through the trees. Not much farther.

Timothy was pulled from me. I turned. The film had him by the feet and more of it had dropped down from the trees and coiled around his arms and pulled them up. A thin strip of it was twisting around his leg and working up his body. By the time I reached him, the end of it was tight around his neck.

I tried to pull it off of him, but more of it came up from the forest floor and snapped around me like the business end of a whip. Then my feet were held and my arms went up and more of it wrapped around my body. Where it touched my bare skin I could feel a sensation like dozens of tiny needles.

From where I stood, immobile, I could see a clear spot in the trees, and when the lightning flashed. I saw the highway, and out there on the highway was a black wrecker with its light on. A man was standing by the wrecker looking at the jungle and the wrecker door was open and I could see a naked butt rising and falling, and there was something between the butt and the seat, white-legged and thrashing, and I knew instantly that it was poor Sue Ellen.

And I knew too that the same lightning that had flashed and allowed me to see the man by the wrecker had allowed him to see me.

5

A flashlight bounced like a great firefly toward us. When the light reached the edge of the jungle I could see the outline of a big, broad-shouldered man and the outline of another behind him. Their shadows leaned together behind them like two happy thugs. When the men moved, the shadows moved of their own accord.

As they entered into the jungle the film crept out and grabbed at them and the biggest of the two men yelled, "Edit," and produced some large scissors and snipped at the film. The man behind him did the same with a smaller pair.

They clipped their way through, and one came up to me, the other to Timothy.

The one with the big scissors and the flashlight was the one in front of me. He put the light in my face and said, "How would you like to be cast in the part of prime pussy?"

Film crawled on his legs and he bent casually and clipped it. "Damn stuff," he said.

"This one looks like a dumb asshole," said the other.

Some of the old Timothy came back, and it couldn't have been a worse time. Timothy said. "Fuck you."

The man hit Timothy in the side of the head with the little scissors. Timothy nodded forward, made no further sounds.

The little scissors went to work on the film that held Timothy, and when it was snipped, Timothy fell down. The man picked him up and tossed him over his shoulder and headed toward the highway, kicking at the film as he went. Once he squatted with Timothy balanced on his shoulder, and used the scissors on a swathe of film.

"Snip, snip, snip, you little motherfuckers," he said. Then he and Timothy were out of the jungle, being pursued by both men's shadows; they moved out into the brighter moonlight which had replaced the dark and the lightning. Out on the highway the wind made little plumes of trash jig all around the wrecker.

The man in front of me cut a coil of film from around my neck and snipped an even smaller piece from that, held it three feet from me. It dripped blood.

"They're like leeches. They show best when they've eaten." He put the flashlight against the strip from behind and two hands holding a chainsaw came out on my side and ballooned to full size and the chainsaw buzzed and the hands shoved it at my face.

He turned out the light just in time. The buzz of the saw died, and where the hands and saw had been, were drops of falling blood. I felt them bite my shoe.

The man cocked the flashlight and said, "Good night, moon," and he hit me.

I was still bound when I awoke, but I was no longer in the jungle. I was tied to the wrecker, facing out. The wrecker was off the highway and a tarp had been stretched over it and the end visible to me was stretched down tight with stakes, and the center of it was poked up high with an antenna stalk that bloomed into a clutch of silver quills at the top.

It was warm under the tarp, and the warmth came from fires built in the husks of a dozen television sets. Rain pounded the tarp and scratched at it like harpy claws. Some of it came through the holes in the tarp and hissed in the fire and hit my face and ran down it like tears. The televisions gave off greasy smoke and it fouled the air and made me woozy.

The side of my head hurt. It should. I had been knocked on it enough. But considering all that, I was lucky. My dad always said I had a hard head. On the other hand, I have dizzy spells from time to time even now. My vision gets screwy.

But as I was saying. My head hurt. Where the film touched me stung.

To the rear of the tarp, squatting in a semicircle, facing me, were four men. They were all dressed in ragged clothes and jeans. They were close-shaved and had bushy flattops that looked as if they had been cut with dull knives. They looked strong and well fed, or maybe just fed. Two of them were the men who had taken Timothy and me out of the jungle.

Behind them on the tarp were their shadows, The shadows were moving in defiance of the motionless posture of the men and the flickerings of the firelight.

I looked to the right of me and saw Timothy. He was tied to the wrecker by blue and red electrical wire. I assumed the same thing held me. Where the man had hit him with the scissors his skull had cracked open and a coil of his brain was leaking out like congealed oatmeal escaping from a crack in a bowl. Suddenly it was very hot. I thought I was going to faint. The wire was the only thing holding me up; there were no usable muscles left in me.

I took a deep breath and pulled some strength back into me from somewhere and looked to my left and saw Sue Ellen. She was tied to the wrecker by wire too. She had her clothes on now. Both her eyes had been blacked and her bottom lip was puffed. The front of her pants was dark with blood. She had her eyes open and she was looking straight ahead, but she wasn't seeing what was there. She was tuned in to something else. Maybe a flashback of one of the movies she liked. I hoped so. This little scenario was certainly a stinker.

Then the four in the back rose and their shadows went still and rigid. They were staring at me, or so I thought at first, but realized that they were in fact staring at something behind me. I could sense the presence of that something, and I heard movement on the wrecker and I could hear a sound like breathing through a bad drive-in speaker, puff and crackle, puff and crackle.

Goose bumps rose along my arms and ripped up my back and down my spine, felt as big as blackberries. They were even on the backs of my calves. Then the sensation passed and the wrecker creaked and I knew that whatever had been behind me had moved.

I watched the heads of the men in back turn; watched the heads of their shadows turn. The fires flickered and popped when the cold rain came through the holes in the tarp and went into them and was turned to steam.

There was movement on the wrecker again, then whatever it was jumped to the ground between Sue Ellen and myself, and I got my first look at the thing I would come to know as Popalong Cassidy.

6

Leave It to Beaver was playing on his face and his face was a sixteen-inch screen with one of those old-fashioned glow lights trimmed around it, and this was all encased in a cheap brown wooden case. The character on the screen,

Ward Cleaver, closed a door and said, "Honey, I'm home," and this was all faint, this dialogue, because there was lots of static right then. And behind all this, in the depths of that tube-face, I could see two red glows that might have been little tubes or eyes.

The television set was wearing a tall, black hat. There was a white scarf around a very human neck, and the rest of the figure was human too, and it was dressed all in black, drugstore-cowboy attire. The pants were stuffed into some tall, black boots and there was a black glove on either hand. He wore a black gun belt with some metal studs on it and there was a holster on each hip and in the holsters were pearl-handled, silver-tooled revolvers.

Television Face came and stood in front of me, and I saw below his screen, on the cheap wooden frame, two rows of knobs and dials. They divided suddenly so that they looked like top and bottom teeth, which in a way they were.

The thing was smiling. The wood was not wood.

A tongue made of tangled blue and red wires licked from left to right and disappeared. In its place came a voice full of static and high of tone. "Hi. My name is Popalong Cassidy, and I bet you think we are mean."

The hat lifted and I saw a set of rabbit ear antennas were responsible. They wiggled out cautiously, as if testing the air for radiation. The hat tipped way back but didn't fall off; it fit there like a flap of skin.

A blue arc jumped from the tip of one ear to the other and the arc rode down the middle space between the ears, then back up. *Leave It to Beaver* went away and on the screen there was a dumpy, ugly man down on one knee next to a Highway Patrol car. The car door was open and the man reached inside and took a microphone from off the dash and pulled it out until the wire was stretched. He said something into the microphone I didn't catch, ended it with "Ten-four." I realized then that he was down like that because on the other side of his car, way off the highway, hid out there in the brush-covered hills, there was supposed to be a bad guy with a gun.

I recognized the television series. It was an old black-and-white one I had watched on occasion. It was called *Highway Patrol* and starred Broderick Crawford.

I didn't get to find out if Crawford went after the culprit in the brush or not, because Popalong darkened his face except for a little yellow dot in the center, and that grew rapidly smaller until it too was gone. The rabbit ears slid back into the set and the hat fell back into place.

"It's okay if you think we're mean, you know. I don't mind." And with that Popalong backed away from me until he was up against the big antenna that punched up the middle of the tarp. There was a bar that ran through the bottom of the antenna, about four inches off the ground, and Popalong back-stepped onto that and reached his arms up and draped them through the antenna rods, hung his head to the side and let his body droop. Presto, a media Christ.

The rain plummeted the tarp and slipped through the holes and sizzled in the popping fires. Nobody said a thing or moved a muscle.

After a while, one of the men got up and raced to the wrecker and climbed on it. When he jumped off he had a big load of magazines under each arm. He went from TV to TV and put magazines into their blazes. I saw the covers of some of the magazines before the flames devoured them. *TV Guide*, *People*, *Tiger Beat*, *Screen Gems*, all of them decorated with the faces of movie stars and fading celebrities. I thought: Where in hell did that stuff come from?

When the fires were really popping and the air was tinged with smoke, the man darted back to his place with the others, and Popalong lifted his head and looked at me and turned his face on. A test pattern filled it. The dials below the screen split apart again and the tongue of tangled wire presented itself briefly and disappeared. "Don't think there's any hatred in my heart for you or anyone," Popalong said. "My heart has no room for that. It's full of electromagnetic waves and they jump about like frogs."

He got down off the antenna and came over and bent forward and looked at me, as if hoping to find something reflected in my eyes. The rabbit ears poked out from under the hat and touched my hair and I felt a faint electric sizzle ride the circumference of my skull. "You have no shadow, you know. It's because you haven't learned to belong. That's what I think. I think when you belong here you have a shadow. I think you earn it. You haven't earned anything. When you're like us you'll have a shadow, a familiar made up of the absence of light.

"Pay attention. Keep sharp. I jump around a lot. It's the sign of a good mind. I'm trying to tell you there's a confusion about good and evil. We worry about which is which way too much. Let me just say that good is too easy. It requires nothing. No real commitment. You can't get the real good out of goodness until you know darkness. Death. Pain. These are instructive tools. Or as Dr. Frankenstein said in *Andy Warhol's Frankenstein*, 'To know death, you have to fuck life in the gall bladder.'

"I know this now, but all my life I have been looking for this truth and it's been under my nose all the time. The images taught me where it was at. There are good images and there are bad images, but the bad images make the best show, so I've opted for the bad images. I praise the Orbit for leading me to the truth. I praise the night I went. The Popcorn King was right. Movies are reality and everything else is fraud. But the King was not the Messiah, as I thought. He was John the Baptist. I'm the Messiah. I was given powers and position by the Producer and the Great Director, and they wanted a sci-fi horror picture. We're number two of a double feature.

"Why me, you ask? Because I have seen more hours of television than anyone. I can quote commercials by heart. I know the name of the Green Hornet's secret identity, the name of the sleek, black car he drives. I know the name of Sky

King's niece and what Batman eats for breakfast. Everything that is important is in this square head.

"Let me tell you too, I was made for it. I'm a preacher's son. I grew up with fire and brimstone and channel nine, the only channel we could get at that time.

"My father spoke savagely to us from the pulpit and every Sunday afternoon after church he beat my mother with his thick belt, then came downstairs and beat me too. I never ran. I took it. He would beat me until his arm got tired, then he would switch arms and wear down. He left welts on my ass.

"When he was finished, he would become remorseful and read the Bible to me and pray. Then he would tell me to turn on my television set and watch it. That I was redeemed. That the sin was cast out of me by pain.

"My mother went away when I was eleven. I thought about her a few days after she was gone, but I never missed her. She had been nothing more than someone around the house, going this way and that in a plaid housecoat and slippers with the backs broken down. She ate a lot of sweets and drank lots of coffee and sipped Nervine that she poured from a bottle into a great big spoon. She seldom spoke to me and never fixed meals. I took care of myself. I grew up on Cokes and Twinkies. The characters on TV spoke to me in her place.

"When I graduated, passed more out of courtesy than from any other reason, my father took his belt to me and beat me until I couldn't get off my knees. He gave me a new Sylvania set and told me to be gone by morning and to never come back. He had taken care of my raising until I was a man, and now I was a man, and to go.

"I went. I couldn't get a good job. The people out there were cruel. Unlike TV, they expected things of you. They wanted college educations. I wanted a satellite dish and more channels. The chance to see time and again *Apocalypse Now*, *Taxi Driver*, *The Andy Griffith Show*. It really didn't matter. Just images. My images. Part of my holy communion. Kurtz and Opie, Leatherface and Lassie, side by side.

"I ended up working at a filling station. I could never get the work straight. I mostly put nozzles in gas tanks and dreamed of *Gilligan's Island* and a trip on *The Love Boat*, of chain-sawing pretty people and stripping their flesh so that I could wear it, jacking air in a gutted corpse. I missed my father's belt. Gasoline ran over my shoes."

As he talked, silent scenes from films and TV shows and commercials ran across his screen like track stars. I couldn't take my eyes off of them. Something about them tugged at me. I felt drunk. I wanted Popalong to turn his face off and shut up. I wanted a hot bath and a good meal and a hot fuck. I wanted to be home in Nacogdoches, tooling down Main Street with the car windows down and a hot wind in my face, looking to see what historical house or building they would tear down next.

But what I got was more of Popalong.

7 POPALONG'S STORY

But the boss kept me working even if I wasn't any good. It wasn't a place that got much business and nobody else wanted to work there because the pay was cheap. Lucky for the boss, I didn't need much and no one else would have me. He let me watch television there at the station between cars. I was between cars a lot.

The money I made kept me in Twinkies and Cokes, *TV Guide* and the cable. I saved up and bought a VCR. I bought a belt like my father used to beat me. I was cozy. I lived in a one-room, walk-up apartment that smelled like the winos in the doorways below. I often saw them when I was walking to work, shuffling ahead of me in search of a bottle. For some reason they made me think of Henry Fonda in *The Grapes of Wrath.*

At night I would take the belt like my father's and slap my naked back with it. I did this while I watched tapes of Hopalong Cassidy reruns. Hopalong had a face like my father's. Watching him made the beltings work all the better. I slapped myself until I bled. I tore pages from the *TV Guide* and stuck them to my back to stop the blood. Sometimes there were not enough pages.

When I finished, I would put the videotape of *The Bible* into the VCR and watch a few minutes of that while I knelt and held the box the tape had come out of. I prayed there would be no electrical blackouts while I was watching a movie, I prayed my television would not wear out until I could afford a big-screen TV. I prayed I would someday have a place of my own away from the noise of the winos, a place where I could have a satellite dish and fill my head with channels. I wondered who I was praying to.

So it went until a week before Halloween. I was on my way home from work eager to get my belt and put in the Hopalong tape, and what do I see in the window of the costume shop between Sylvester the Cat and a pirate outfit but a Hopalong Cassidy costume. I felt weak in the knees.

I went in there and blew all the money I had. I knew I would have to buy some cheap brand of soft drink and some sort of pastry that wouldn't match Twinkies, but I had my Hopalong suit, complete with hat and boots and holsters, though the guns in it were cap pistols.

When I got home I put the outfit on and looked in the mirror. I was disappointed. My shoulders were not as broad as Hoppy's and my face was nothing to look at. I didn't look like my father who looked like Hoppy. I looked like a weasel staring out of the woods.

I took off the suit and hung it in the closet and put the boots below and the hat on a shelf above. I discovered if I left the closet door cracked and turned on the end table light, or if the moonlight came through the window just right, it looked like Hoppy was standing in there, hiding, waiting to come out and beat me with a belt or shoot me with his pistols.

I liked that. The suit was not a total loss.

Then about Christmastime I saw this special on random killers. I noted that most of them had sad little faces like mine. But here they were with their sad little faces going out to millions while I lay in bed holding my dick. They had done things like pump hot lead into warm bodies, and all I could do was shoot a pathetic wet bullet onto my sheets. What they had done brought camera crews out, and they got their pictures taken. Got seen by millions. Got to be stars. What I had was more laundry.

But when the special was over, I knew what I wanted to do.

I had to save my money again, and this meant I didn't eat very much, but I never really cared that much for eating anyway. The more I thought about what I wanted to do, the more excited I got, and the more I took the belt to myself. When I showered it looked as if red paint were running down the drain.

I took to wearing the Hopalong outfit. I didn't look any better in it, but I didn't care anymore. I knew what I wanted now, and knowing made me feel better about myself.

First I bought a car from my boss for three hundred dollars. A white Ford Fairlane. I was not a good driver, but I knew how. I could get from one place to the next if I could get my mind off television. I tried to pretend that I was part of a television show like *Miami Vice*, and I was patrolling the streets for crime. I drove every day so I could get better at it, but I never learned to like it.

Then I saved up enough to get the rifle. A Winchester with an old-fashioned lever. I had it replaced with a loop cock like the one John Wayne had in *Stagecoach.* It was no big problem to get the rifle. I merely had to sign some papers. It didn't matter to me that later they would be able to trace it. I wanted them to.

By the time the summer came around I was able to buy two pearl-handled, silver-tooled pistols and enough ammunition for them and the Winchester. Again, I merely had to sign some papers.

I went home and took the cap guns out of the holsters and put in the real .45s after I loaded them. I loaded the Winchester and put it in the closet. I watched a video of *The Wild Bunch.*

Next afternoon after work, I put the rifle in the trunk of my car and went back in and put the Hopalong outfit and gun belt on. The real guns weighed more than the cap pistols, but I liked their weight. It was like waking up and having muscles.

When I went out to the car the second time, a wino saw me. He said, "Man, who you supposed to be, Hopalong Cassidy?"

"That's right," I said, and pulled one of the .45s and shot at him. I missed him by a mile. The bullet went past him and smacked into the doorway of the apartment house. The wino ran around the corner, and I shot at him again. This shot wasn't any better. He got away. My marksmanship worried me some.

I drove out of town, and by the time I got to the overpass, it was starting to get dark. I pulled over next to the concrete wall and unlocked the trunk and got the rifle. It was dark now. I could see the lights of the cars, but to see who was in them I had to let them get pretty close to the overpass so the lights there would shine down on them and give me a look.

I watched a few go by before I shot at anybody. Guess I was getting the feel of things.

I picked one out and aimed between the headlights, then lifted the rifle barrel above that so I could center on the windshield, then I moved the barrel to the driver's position and pulled the trigger.

First time didn't work because I had the safety on. The car went beneath the underpass and on.

I took off the safety and waited for another car, remembered to cock the lever and jack a shell into the chamber. I felt like Lucas McCain, the Rifleman.

Next car that came I shot at, and I don't know if I hit anyone or not, but it veered off the road, then back on, and went under the overpass and kept going, very fast. Next car I hit someone because it went off the road and through a barbed wire fence right before it reached the underpass. I saw a man stumble out of it and fall down in the pasture and get up. I took a couple of shots at him, and I guess I finally hit him because he fell down and didn't get up. I shot once more in his direction, then went back to watching cars.

A station wagon was next, and I put a shot into it and it ran into the side of the overpass and a woman opened the door part of the way and fell out. The lights from the overpass were bright on the windshield in the car, and I could see a child in a baby seat on the passenger's side. I could even hear it crying.

I leveled the rifle and fired until I finally hit it and it shut up. I figured I had done enough then. I was a celebrity, though no one knew it yet. I could just imagine being apprehended and handcuffed and the television cameras coming out and taking my picture in my Hopalong outfit, and then taking pictures of my pistols and my loop-cock Winchester. I hoped they'd let me see myself on television in the jail. But just knowing I was going to be there was a great thrill. I was, for the first time in my life, somebody.

At first I thought I should turn myself in, but this seemed too easy. I would let them come for me. I might take a few shots at them, then, if they fired back, I would toss out my weapons and say I quit; I had watched that sort of thing on television more than once. They didn't kill you if you quit. After I got on television, I didn't care what they did with me.

I put the rifle in the trunk and drove away. I drove until I came to a little serve-yourself gas station and grocery. I was very hungry and I needed gas.

I went in there and got a Coke and a Twinkie and the girl behind the counter stared at me. I liked that. I felt like a movie star. "Who are you supposed to be?" she said.

"Hopalong Cassidy," I said, and pulled out my pistol and reached across the counter and put it next to her nose and fired just as she screamed. Blood went all over the cash register. I went around and opened it and got some of the money just to have something to do, got my Coke and Twinkie and started to leave.

A man in a big black wrecker drove up then, and he walked inside just as I was about to go out. He looked at me and I saw his head jerk a little. He knew something wasn't right. I pulled the revolver and shot him in the chest and he went back against the glass door, hitting it so hard it cracked. It swung open and he fell out on the ground. I bent over him and shot him twice in the head.

Something about the wrecker appealed to me. I put my Coke and Twinkie in the wrecker's seat and got my rifle out of the Fairlane and put it in the floorboard of the wrecker. I had some trouble driving the wrecker at first, but I knew how. I had learned how to drive a lot of things at the station so I could put them in stalls to have flats and oil changed.

I drove along not thinking about much, and I saw the Orbit drive-in. I couldn't pass that up. I had been away from a screen too long and had begun to feel unreal. I drove in there and watched the movies and waited to be arrested. I thought I might not even wait. I thought I could get my rifle and go behind one of the screens and poke a hole in it and start shooting at people in their cars like the guy did in *Targets*. Maybe Boris Karloff would show up to stop me. I would have liked that.

But before I could do anything the comet came and trapped us all in the drive-in. I wasn't going to be arrested. I wasn't going to be on TV. It was depressing at first, until I realized an incredible truth. I was living a movie. This wasn't like working at the filling station. This wasn't like walking home and seeing the winos. This was even better than watching television. It was like when I was shooting from the top of the underpass, only more so. This was constant, and everyone had to be involved, like it or not. The movie owned us all and you couldn't change channels or turn it off. Here was a movie with blood and guts and a wild monster, the Popcorn King. He was wonderful. He preached violence and religion. If he could have gotten wrestling into his talks he would have covered the three manias of television. I loved him. I wanted him to beat me with a belt. I quit wearing the Hopalong outfit. I stripped off and went around naked like a lot of the others. I was not ashamed of my body now. Everyone looked awful. The comet and the Popcorn King had made us all alike. My constant fear was a happy ending, which meant, of course, everyone would go back to what they were before. And for me, that wouldn't have been much.

But things did not last. The comet came back. I put my Hopalong outfit on and drove out of the drive-in behind the others. I figured the old world would be out there and the only thing I could think of that was positive about that was that I would eventually be arrested and my picture would be on TV, and I would be recorded on video for all time.

But the old world wasn't out there. There was this world. This double feature.

I became determined to drive to the end of the highway. Things got weirder as I drove along, and I wanted to see just how weird they would get. I wanted to be part of the weird.

Once, when I stopped to find fruit, I saw a crowbar lying on the bed of the wrecker, and I got it and used it to break the padlock of the big metal box welded below the back window. Inside was a tarp, flares, knives, electrical wire, miscellaneous items. I knew these would come in handy later.

The gas in the wrecker lasted a long time, and when I got to this place with the film draped in the trees, I knew I was on the right track.

I pushed on. I felt like Humphrey Bogart in *They Drive by Night.*

Though the shadows and the storms and the crawling film persisted, I began to see new things. Solid things. Munchkins from *The Wizard of Oz*, for example. I never saw a live one, just dead ones. They were lying beside the highway or in it, obviously having been hit by cars. They were smashed and/or bloated. Their little caps lay beside them like markers. I passed one that someone had propped up with a stick. They also had a stick down one of his sleeves and had rigged it so his arm stuck straight out; he looked as if he were thumbing a ride.

I passed cars beside the road. Empty. Came to one where a body was wrapped like a mummy in film; the film was pulsing like a tumor.

Cars passed me on their way back. None of the drivers waved.

Beside the road I saw what looked like a collapsed water tower, but it was one of the Martian stalking machines from *War of the Worlds.* A squid-like creature was dangling out of an opening in the top of the machine, limp as spaghetti.

When the storms came now, they were more violent than ever. The blue lightning flashed through the films and the images on the films were cast onto the ground and into the trees and onto the wrecker. They lived and breathed during those brief moments of lightning.

The wrecker was rigged with an auxiliary tank, and I switched that on and kept at it. I finally had to stop and use the hose from the box on the wrecker bed to siphon gas from a couple of dead cars, which turned out to be the last ones I saw on the highway. What gas I got from them you could have put in a paper cup. But it was gas that got me to the end of the highway.

I got closer looks at the Munchkins. They were solid all right, but they weren't real after all. They were elaborate dummies. As I went, there were more of these, and not all of them were Munchkins. They were the sort of dummies they used to use a lot in old movies, when they wanted to have a body tumble over Niagara Falls for instance. I stopped in the daylight and looked at the Martian machines. Cheap wood painted silver. The Martians were rubber octopuses.

I liked that.

Finally I came to the end of the highway.

And there was the Orbit.

It was different in many ways, but it was the Orbit. The highway was a snake biting its tail.

Amid the wreckage that had been made by the fools who killed the Popcorn King were strips of film, more dummies, props of all kinds, lobby cards, TV sets and fragments of antennas. In several spots there were piles of TV sets; piles that made pyramids that tipped through a continuous bank of dark clouds.

At night there were really violent storms. Worse yet. The wind blew popcorn bags and movie posters and soft drinks and movie magazines against the wrecker with a sound like wet towels popping.

When it rained, it rained chocolate almonds and popcorn and soft drinks—every kind imaginable: cherry, orange, Coke, Dr Pepper, Pepsi. I recognized the taste of these and more by drinking from puddles in the blacktop. Later I sat cups out at night and in the morning I drank from these, picked up chocolate almonds and popcorn and the occasional unwrapped Snickers for my breakfast. I confess, I longed for Twinkies.

I learned that the busted television sets grew up from the ground like sacrificial potatoes. Once birthed, the ground healed up behind them like a sore.

I checked out the concession over in Lot B, but though it was intact, it was a shambles inside; there wasn't anything of use in there. The projectors looked okay, but unlike when the Orbit was in that black stuff, they didn't work without electricity. It was a depressing discovery. All those films and no way to show them.

The lightning gave me glimpses of films, because of the way it made images jump, but it was really more of a tease than anything else. What I would have given even for a complete dog food commercial.

I picked magazines—*Screen Gems*, *TV Guide*, and the like—off the windshields of the cars and off the ground, and spent my days shaking the soft drinks out of their pages and reading them carefully. It was okay at first, but a lot of the magazines were the same. I began to get bored. This place was certainly like a movie set, but it wasn't as satisfying as before, not the way it had been when it was at the other end of the highway. Then it had been more than a set. It had been a movie that I was part of. There was action and drama and comedy, and now there was just me. I didn't care much for me.

I decided to climb one of the pyramids and go up into the constant cloudbank. I doubted it was high enough for me to need an oxygen mask up there, and then again, I didn't really care. I wanted to see where all the chocolate almonds and soft drinks came from, and it was something to do that was like being in a movie.

I started up by sticking my feet into the busted faces of the sets, clutching them like lovers. After a time I realized the pyramid was much higher than I thought. I began to get frightened. I was reminded of the movie *The Bible* and the scene concerning the Tower of Babel. Was I defying the gods? Or was it a test?

Once again, I decided it didn't matter. I was living a movie and that was what counted. I would rather die as part of a movie than live as part of the normal world.

When night set in with its storms of papers and its rains of soft drinks, chocolate almonds, and popcorn, I was not even halfway up. I found a twenty-three-inch television with the tube busted out and I crawled into the opening and pushed out the back and found myself in a den of sets and movie magazines. It looked like someone or something had been living in there at one time. I crawled back through some more sets and found a comfortable spot with plenty of room and stretched out on top of some magazines and tried to pull a few over me. I lay there pretending I was Stewart Granger and I was trapped in King Solomon's mines.

When I awoke the next morning, I felt awful. I let down my pants and took a shit, got out of there and started climbing. I went like that for three or four days, sleeping in what TV caves I could find, traveling as long as I could take it each day.

Finally I came to a wisp of cloud. I was right, the clouds were low. They were also made of cotton and they bunched tightly around the top of the pyramid. I pulled the cotton away to make the going easier, and kept climbing.

As I went up, I saw there were hundreds of thin, white strings holding the dark clouds up on either side of me.

I didn't go much farther before I came to a spot where the blue lightning jumped and crackled constantly and swarmed around my head like a halo. The electricity made my hair stand on end and pushed my hat up so that it seemed to be supported by porcupine quills. The hair on my body poked through my clothes like tacks.

Above me I could see an opening in the blue sky. I went up through that and felt my hair go soft and my hat settle down on my head. When I got through the hole I was at the top of the pyramid and I stepped off of it and found myself inside a tremendous room full of gigantic cameras, sound systems, and gadgets I couldn't identify. None of it looked designed for human hands.

Leaning against a distant wall was a backdrop. It was of the Orbit, and it was the Orbit when it was acidic and the Popcorn King had ruled. My favorite time.

I took the long walk over and touched it. It rippled under my hand and I was able to move into it. It was suddenly real. On the screen nearest me, *Night of the Living Dead* was playing. It wasn't one of the good parts. No one was getting ripped apart or eaten.

There were people moving about among the speakers and cars. They looked stunned, mechanical, thin and wasted. But they didn't look as bad as they were going to look.

When I turned, I expected to be trapped in the Orbit, and I wouldn't have minded too terribly, but behind me was a backdrop of the room full of equipment. I reached out and touched it and walked forward, and I was out of the Orbit; it was a backdrop again. I was a free agent.

I looked around.

There was this hallway, and on either side of the hallway were painted backdrops. I went down the hallway and stopped to look at some of them. One that caught my eye was of a jungle.

I stepped into it. Immediately I was very hot and the air was full of the stink of mold and plants, and the trees were dripping water. I thought maybe this was a backdrop of the jungle below; maybe by stepping into this one, I was down below again.

I heard a cracking of trees and brush, and a red, blue and yellow Triceratops poked its head through some greenery and looked at me. I know they're supposed to be vegetarians, but I wasn't in the mood to find out. Besides, he looked as if he might charge. I wondered if he could charge right out of the backdrop. I turned quickly and stepped back into the hallway. When I looked at the backdrop, it was just a jungle. No Triceratops.

I walked down the hallway until a Western backdrop caught my eye. I stepped into a dusty street and began walking between rows of clapboard buildings. At the far end of the narrow street, a tall fellow with a gun on his hip began walking toward me.

I was dressed for the part, but I didn't like the looks of this. I turned around and walked back up the street and stepped back into the hallway.

When I examined the backdrop, there was just an empty street, of course.

The backdrops came to an end, and in their place were mirrors that distorted my appearance. No two had me looking the same. It seemed to me there was some great cosmic truth in this, but try as I might, I couldn't put my finger on it. I kept walking.

The hallway became filled with a large red ball. It towered high above me and touched the walls of the hallway. I put my hand against it and it felt as if it were made of cardboard. I pushed and it rolled back to reveal a split that widened and showed me several rows of jagged, poorly painted, cardboard teeth.

It was the comet that had smiled and turned the Orbit into a horror movie. I pushed the ball hard and it went rolling down the long hallway very fast and disappeared into the distance like the sun falling down the dark shaft of the universe.

I noticed now that the floor beneath me had changed and that I was standing on a dark rectangle and it was in turn linked to another and a series of these went on down the hall and disappeared into the same distance the comet had fallen. On either side and between the rectangles were gaps and out of the gaps poured a bright yellow light that hit against the ceiling.

The light became stronger and warmer. It worked through the rectangle and it worked through me. I fell face forward, went stiff and was enveloped by the flooring.

The light went out.

Lines I remember from my father and his Bible:

In the beginning God created the heaven and the earth. And the earth was without form, and void; and darkness was on the face of the deep. And the Spirit of God moved upon the face of the waters.

And God said, Let there be light; and there was light.

I don't know about the waters, but there was certainly light, and plenty of it. It was stronger than before and warmer than before; it went through me like new blood. I felt as if I had never lived, except I had memories, and these seemed to belong to someone else and loaned to me. I felt as if I were a new creature in the eyes of the God (or Gods) of film; I was nothing more than a flat lifeless piece of celluloid with a great yellow light shining through me and the light was giving me life.

In other words, I was on a filmstrip.

I could hear gears grinding, sprockets turning, and the rectangle that was my home began to move. It rolled through what must have been a projector, because at some point the bright light became brighter and I hit a white wall and—

I was animated, cartoon style. I held my hand in front of me, and it was black-gloved like it was supposed to be but the hand was puffy and silly, as if it were really nothing more than a glove filled with air.

I was in a little room sitting on a stool, and all around me were white walls, and there were whisperings from somewhere, and occasional shadows. Then in front of me was this little blue glow. The glow died down and in its place was a short, dumpy cartoon woman wearing a blue-and-white dress tied in back with a white cloth belt. Her hair was silver and done up in a bun. She was holding a wand tipped with a silver star and she was using it to scratch her ass.

In a voice that had been worked over with Brillo pads, she said, "I think it's the riding around on the film or the light that leaves you the itch, but whatever, it's some kind of itch. Lots of us have it. But listen, kid, I'm not here to talk to you about ass itch. We know what you want and we want you to have it. You're made for the part, and I ain't blowing smoke up your ass. You're perfect. You see, the Producer and the Great Director want a show down there and we think you're the one can give it to us. Kid, we're gonna make you a goddamn star."

She took a pack of cigarettes out from under a roll in the sleeve of her dress, shook one out and lipped it, replaced the pack. "We give a man a job, we like to give him the full run of things, see, and while we're talking here, let me tell you something. You're ugly, kid. With a kisser like that if you was a chicken you'd have to sneak up on a pile of shit to peck a corn kernel out of it. But that's not your fault. It's something we can fix."

She brought out a box of wooden matches and struck one on her hip and lit her smoke. She puffed and tossed the box on the floor. She pinched the cigarette between thumb and forefinger and held the flame toward her palm.

"Tell me what face you want, kid. I want to show you what we can do. Naw, don't tell me a thing. I know the face, and it ain't pretty and it ain't ugly. It ain't really a face. You want something everyone will look at. You want it so when you step into a room all eyes go to you. Well, in the name of the Producer and the Great Director, by the power vested in me, and all that stuff, I give it to you."

She waved the wand. "The stuff dreams are made of, kid."

I felt a rush of energy. I was a thermometer and I was overheated and my mercury was about to explode out the top of my head.

Next thing I knew, I was on the floor, then I was coming out of darkness. I blinked and found myself next to the hole that let in the tip of the TV pyramid.

I looked at my hands. They weren't animated now. A big-handled mirror lay next to me. I picked it up and looked at myself.

What I had for a face was a TV, and that suited me fine. And my face operated like one. Inside my head was the mental switch, and with a twist of my mind I could tune into any movie, television show, commercial, or personal video I wanted.

And I could play it on my face and see it at the same time.

I was proud.

I tossed away the mirror and started down. I felt like Charlton Heston playing Moses in *The Ten Commandments*. But I wasn't coming down from on high with the Ten Commandments. I had something better. Every movie, show and commercial ever made was tucked tight in my head, ready to explode onto my face at a whim.

It took me some time to get down, of course, but when I did, the drive-in was full of people. They had been wandering in for a time. They had built a stage of TVs in front of one of the drive-in screens, and they were taking turns going up there and acting out scenes from movies, quoting dialogue they remembered. They also did sound effects and screams. They weren't too good at it.

When they saw me they stood open-mouthed, and when I turned my face on and filled it with *Night of the Living Dead*, their expressions turned to rapture. I sat down on a TV set and crossed my legs and leaned forward and they gathered before me and squatted down and watched. And when *Night* was over, I gave them *The Texas*

Chainsaw Massacre and then *The Sound of Music* intercut with *Zombie.* Now and then I gave them a commercial for GI Joe action figures and accessories, tossed in a California Raisins commercial, and one for some kind of shampoo. Things got cozy.

They loved me, and it was then that I gave myself a new name. I was in Hopalong gear and I had a TV face and my idol had been the Popcorn King, so naturally, I came up with Popalong Cassidy. I told my audience that was what they should call me, and they did. They would have called me anything to keep those images coming; they had learned that the images were the reality and all else was an illusion they had to work to invent. My face did all the work for them. It gave them all the reality they needed to know, minus the effort.

I found that I no longer needed to eat food. All I needed were the eyes and minds of those people on my face. That kept me full.

In time, more people came to the drive-in, and they too sat before my face and worshiped it, and I pulled energy from them and felt fuller and stronger than ever before.

I was loved. Loved by those who sat before me and ate the popcorn and candy that fell from the sky, drank the drinks it rained. Loved, goddamnit, loved. Me, Popalong Cassidy. Loved and admired and revered.

Course, there were some nonbelievers. They wanted to stay away from my face. They saw it as bad. They blamed the movies for what had happened to them.

This was nonsense.

I had my followers rip them open and eat their guts and act out *Night of the Living Dead.* Then the heads of those stupid dissenters went up on tall pieces of antenna and we placed them all around the drive-in as a warning to the non-viewers who might come, and as an inspiration to the rest of us.

I had my followers strike sparks and set the TV pyramids on fire. They would have no other gods before me. I was it, and I didn't want competition. No one else would be climbing up there to see my Fairy Godmother; no one else could have my prize.

This kept the drive-in a happy place. A new era had dawned. I was its messiah. Offspring of the Producer and the Great Director, whoever they were, and it was my job to make sure they were entertained. And I planned to give my heavenly parents a really big show.

Now let's pause for this brief commercial message.

8 GRACE TALKING

All the while Popalong had been talking, images were flashing on his face. Clips from movies and television shows. Now a series of commercials went lickety-split across the screen; everything from exercise machines to Boxcar Willie's Greatest Hits. Damn if I hadn't always wanted to try Boxcar Willie's stuff, though I hated to admit it. If I ever got home, I was going to order his album.

I suppose there were subliminals at work under all that film stuff, but maybe not. I like to think it had no effect on me because I'm just too much woman to be taken in by a subliminal message; I like to think Mom and Dad raised a pretty stubborn girl and that my martial arts training allowed me to maintain my focus on who I was and what I thought.

Course, maybe the only subliminal in the whole mess was for me to buy a Boxcar Willie album, and that seemed to be working. Maybe all those people who had fallen for Popalong's line of corn were just stupid. My dad always said, "Grace, most people are idiots."

It was kind of cold-blooded, but life seemed to sort of be bearing him out.

The commercials wrapped up, and in spite of myself I liked the last one. It had to do with these carrots, potatoes and bell peppers with stick legs and shoes and stick arms and gloves. They were hopping off the face of a box and dancing across a kitchen table on their way to leap into a pan full of water resting in the mouth of an open stove.

"My message is simple," said Popalong. "There is pleasure in darkness and pain. The light cannot be appreciated without the dark. Entertainment is where it's at. At the end of the highway I have formed a humble Church of Darkness and Pain. Services every day. It all plays on my face. And when someone, shall we say, becomes a star at the church, like those nonbelievers I told you about, we record their acting and play it again and again for our pleasure. No special effects. No wooden lines. No one pretending to eat guts. The real thing. It's addicting, I kid you not."

He leaned close to me. "Revolutionary, don't you think?"

"It bites the moose," I said.

"Now that's ugly," Popalong said. "After all I've shown you and told you, you're still an asshole. I'm afraid you'll have to be edited out of what you call life. But don't worry, I'll make you a star. I'll make sure your agony is recorded forever in the only way that really matters. On film."

He turned to Sue Ellen. "Her, I think she's got potential. I think she can see the light of my face and know it for what it is, don't you? I think she's rather pretty. She might make me a nice queen. I'd like that. I mean I may be a messiah, but to hell with this Jesus stuff where you don't get any pussy. I'm a new kind of messiah, and I say hey, what's the point in being a messiah with all kinds of control, if you don't throw some pork to the women. You see, I can give them any face they want while I make love to them. Whatever star they want, man or woman, hell, Lassie or Rin Tin Tin, I can call them up on my screen, and presto, I'm who they want me to be."

The rain had stopped and daylight was creeping beneath the tarp and poking through the holes where the rain had come through. The fires in the television sets were dying down and the smoke from them was thinning and becoming lighter, going as soft and gray as the cottony strands of an old man's hair.

The shadows huddling against the back of the tarp were fading. Popalong's shadow was seeping into the ground at his feet like motor oil.

"They're fraidy-cats of the light," he said. "Roy, would you please get the gasoline."

The man who had cut me free climbed on the wrecker and came down with a five-gallon can.

"You should feel honored," Popalong said. "Rare as gasoline is. You know, this will be our last trip out from the church in the wrecker. When we get back we'll be near empty. It's a pisser not to be able to go out and spread the word, but what's a fella to do?"

"You're no fella," I said.

"You know, you're right. Soak her, Roy."

"Don't we get to fuck her first?" Roy asked.

"Now that you mention it," Popalong said, "I do seem to be ahead of myself. Everyone for fucking her?"

He held up his hand as an example. The four men put their hands up.

Popalong turned that sixteen-inch screen on me. "You're popular, what can I say. But you know, I'm going to pass. You have such a nasty disposition, I'm afraid I'd end up having to fake an orgasm. Roy, would you like to be first to crack open the box?"

Roy smiled and put the can down. He got a pair of wire cutters out of his back pocket and went over and snipped what held me to the wrecker, but this didn't free my hands. They were fastened together by a separate bond.

"You going to record this?" Roy said.

"Whatever I see is recorded," Popalong said. "Bring her out from the wrecker, please, get her pants off, and get started. I'm sort of in a hurry to see her burn. Rest of you get that tarp down."

The three in the back went straight to the tarp and pulled it up and flipped it over the antenna in the middle and tossed it onto the wrecker.

Roy led me so that I was in front of Popalong's antenna. Popalong stepped up on his spokes and hung his arms in the rods. He looked at me and smiled his dials.

"Showtime," he said.

9

There was no wind and the dead air had turned warm and humid. Sweat poured off of me and my hair stuck to the back of my neck. I needed to go to the ladies' room.

Roy wasn't taking me real serious. After all, I was a girl. Maybe I was supposed to beg and scream like in the horror movies.

What I did when Roy reached out to take hold of my pants was swivel on the ball of my left foot and whip my head around and get my hips shifting, and I brought my leg up fast and loose and snapped it back so that the heel caught Roy directly behind his right ear and made a sound like big hands clapping.

Before Roy filled his teeth with dirt, I was moving. One of the men tried to stop me, but I jumped up and snapped out my right leg and caught him in the throat with the edge of my foot. I could feel something in his neck give, then I was down and running, hitting the jungle hard as I could go, keeping my balance as best I could, which wasn't easy with my hands tied the way they were. Then I was out of there, boys, prehistoric history.

10

At first I felt like Brer Rabbit in the brier patch, then I didn't feel so good. This was where the film crawled and sucked on you, where the bad storms blew shadows and trees moved.

But nothing of the sort was happening then. The film lay still at my feet and still in the trees. There were no shadows and no storms. I supposed those things were reserved for night.

I heard footsteps behind me and I only paused long enough to jump up and pull my knees to my chest and whip my bound hands underneath me.

I saw that my hands were tied with a piece of wire that had been wrapped around them three or four times with the ends twisted together. I pulled at the wire with my teeth as I ran and got it loose. I crunched it up and put it in my pocket so I wouldn't leave something on the ground for them to mark my passing.

Eventually I didn't hear them anymore, but I kept running. I don't know how long I went, and I had no idea which way I was going. I followed the path of least resistance.

When I felt certain they were no longer behind me, I stopped and found a tree with low branches and swung up in that and climbed as high as I could.

I was shocked. I had looped back until I was almost to the highway. In fact, I probably wasn't far from where I had been captured. If I had kept running, I would have been out on the highway again in a matter of minutes.

I could see the wrecker at the edge of the highway and I could see Popalong's antenna, but he wasn't on it. I could see the Galaxy too. I couldn't see Popalong, his men or Timothy or Sue Ellen. I could see some dark smoke, but I couldn't tell what it was coming from. Its source was near the edge of the woods though.

I felt poorly, so I found a forked limb that had a lot of leafy cover and wedged my butt in the fork and put my back against a bigger limb and clutched a smaller one with the crook of my right arm. A wind began to stir, and that was all I needed to send me off to dreamland.

When I awoke my back hurt and my arm was stiff, but I felt rested. I had no idea how long I slept. It was still daylight.

I got out on the limb where I had been before and looked at the wrecker. Popalong's antenna cross was in the back of the wrecker, fastened to the wench post somehow and Popalong was on it. He had this TV head turned in my direction, lifted slightly up, but I didn't think he could see me. One of his men was coiled at his feet like a house cat.

The wrecker started to move. I watched until it was out of sight.

11

At this point, some of this is bound to be obvious. Yes, it was Timothy that was burning. I found the guy I had kicked in the head dead in the bushes. The one I had kicked in the throat had been impaled on a piece of television antenna. Popalong didn't like failures much.

I guess I should have killed Timothy. That's what he asked for. But I got the keys out of my pocket and opened up the trunk of the Galaxy and took the gas can and poured it into the tank. I got my arms under Timothy and got him loaded in the backseat of the Galaxy. His flesh came off on my hands and I had to go out to the side of the road and wipe my palms in the grass; it was as if I had been holding greasy pork chops.

I got the car going and made a U-turn and drove us away from there. I talked about anything that came to mind, and Timothy when he did speak, said, "Kill me."

I didn't seem to know how to do anything but drive, and I did that through the day and through the night, finally stopping to rest. I kept going like that, kept talking and singing and reciting poetry to myself, and I don't remember eating or drinking at all.

There's not much to tell after that. My throat got hoarse. The road pulled me on. When I was nearly out of gas I saw the lake—your lake—and I guess it made me realize how thirsty I was, and I went for it.

Next thing I knew Jack here was pulling me out and then I was in the back of your camper. I woke up and had to pee, and when I came back from that, you guys were here.

Illustrations by Nikita Knatz, Copyright (c) 1989 Silver Sphere Corporation

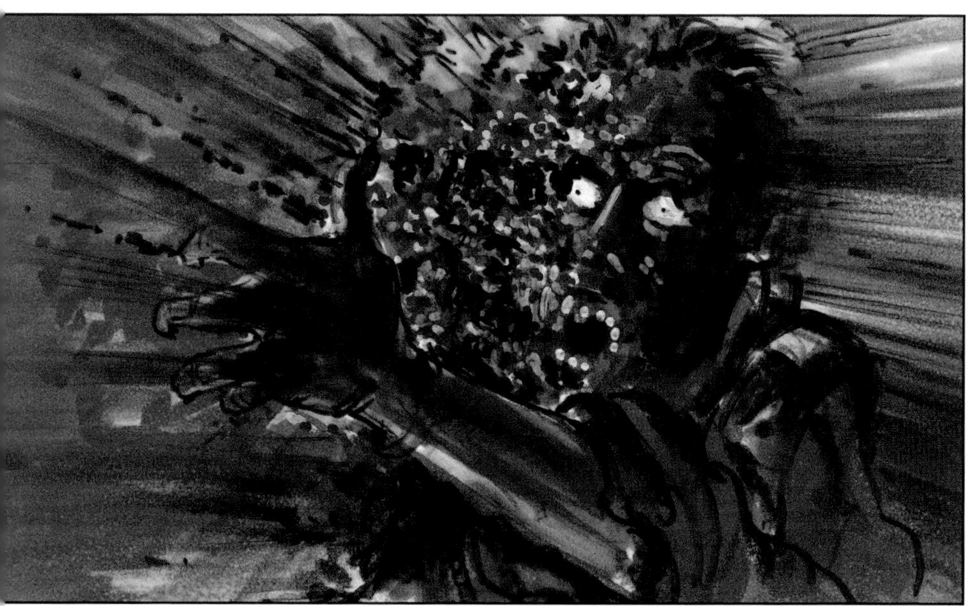

PHANTASM I+II
I DISMEMBER MAMA
THE EVIL DEAD
THE TOOLBOX-
MURDER

PHANTASM I+II
I DISMEMBER MAMA
THE EVIL DEAD
THE TOOLBOX-
MURDER

PHANTASM I+II
I DISMEMBER MAMA
THE EVIL DEAD
THE TOOLBOX-
-MURDERS

PHANTASM I+II
I DISMEMBER MAMA
THE EVIL DEAD
THE TOOLBOX-
-MURDERS

PHANTASM I+II
I DISMEMBER MAMA
THE EVIL DEAD
THE TOOLBOX-
-MURDER

NIKITA KNAT
1989

FOURTH REEL

Titties Even Closer Up, Pants for Jack and Bob, and On Down the Road

1

Bob said, "You're welcome to stay with us."

"Thanks. I appreciate it. But tomorrow, or day after tomorrow, when I'm rested, I'm going to start after Sue Ellen. I owe her that. I went sort of nuts when I found Timothy, panicked, took off in the opposite direction. But I've got to go back now and find her."

"You don't have a car," I said.

"If I can get to Shit Town, I think I can get a car and some gas. If not, I'll go on foot."

"I'm going too," I said.

"What?" Bob said.

"I can't sit here the rest of my life."

"See a set of titties and you go all to pieces, don't you?" Bob said.

"If what she says is true, we know what's at the end of the highway," Crier said. "So why go?"

"Let Grace be the White Knight," Bob said. "She's into that kind of shit. Kung fu lady and all that. We're into surviving."

"I may have to do some ugly things when I catch up to Popalong," Grace said. "It won't be an easy trek, especially if I end up on foot."

"Listen to her," Bob said.

"This isn't living," I said. "This is existing. It's giving up. I did that once before. Won't do it again. You're the one made me do something last time, Bob. You're the one pulled me of out just getting by."

"But this isn't so bad," Bob said.

"Maybe we can find a way home at the end of the highway," I said. "Maybe there's something more than what Popalong told her about. And there's that little girl, Sue Ellen."

"I'm not asking anything of you," Grace said.

"Not much you're not, lady," Bob said.

"Shit," Crier said. "We've been through some things together, the three of us. I feel like we're the three musketeers or something."

"Oh hell," Bob said. "Here it comes."

"We're all we got," Crier said. "I'd like to see us stick together. Hell, fellas, you're the first real friends I ever had."

"Well, fuck," Bob said. "Guess we could use a change of scenery. We can take the camper to Shit Town and get some gas there."

"Hey," Grace said. "I'm not asking—"

"Hush," Bob said. "I might come to my senses."

2 Up in Jungle Home I tried to sleep, but no dice. I got out of bed and slipped on my blanket and left Bob and Crier sleeping and went out on the deck where a warm breeze was blowing.

I went on down and walked over to the camper and touched it. It was cool to my touch and I got a mild sexual charge out of it, which made me feel pretty damn silly. I thought about what Grace had said about fucking the ocean in case there was a shark in there that had swallowed a girl, and suddenly it made a lot of sense.

I went around to the end of the camper. The tailgate was down. My mouth filled with saliva. I knew then that I was going to at least look inside.

I looked.

She wasn't there. There was just a basket of fruit. I guess my sexual charge had come from that or a horny spare tire.

Then I heard splashing. I think I had heard it before, but now it registered.

I walked around on the other side of the camper and looked out at the lake.

The moon was high and bright and it made the lake slick as a mirror. Not too far out in it, halfway submerged, was Grace. She was slapping her arms on the surface of the water. Playing.

I went down there, and when I was fifty feet from the water, I stopped and looked at her sleek, marble-white back sticking out of the water like a flooded Grecian statue.

She looked over her shoulder and smiled.

"Out for a walk, Jack?"

"Sort of."

"Excited about tomorrow?"

"I guess."

"You saved my life today."

"That's all right."

"Of course it is. I got hot in the camper. Funny, Timothy's down at the other end of the lake and here I am playing in the water at this end. I never made love to him, you know."

"Did you want to?"

"I think I saw him as a brother."

"You telling me this for a reason?"

"I don't know."

She turned and started to shore. She came out of the water like Venus being born. The moon hit the sheen of water on her breasts and made them bright as moons themselves. The little pink stripes on her skin looked like birthday ribbons.

"You're going to go blind," she said.

"I don't make you go naked."

"I didn't make you come down here."

I put my hands in front of me and clasped them together.

She came to me and kissed me lightly on the lips. Her breath smelled of fruit. She took hold of my arms, lifted them over her head and around her neck, said, "You'll have to pull out, you know. I don't have any birth control. And don't make more of this than it is."

I pulled her to me and kissed her. Our tongues made war.

She looked down. "Goodness, Jack. There's something in your blanket."

"You've already seen it. You weren't much impressed."

She took hold of the edges of the blanket and pulled it over my head, knocking my arms off of her. She threw the blanket down on the grass and took hold of me.

"My," she said, "how the little fella's grown."

3

After we made love on my blanket, we stumbled giggling to the camper and smeared fruit on one another and licked it off. Between licking and giggling, we made love again. Every time we moved apart our bodies made a sound like two sheets of flypaper being pulled apart.

When we finished we went down to the lake and rinsed off again and tried to make love again, but neither of us was up to it. We went back to the camper and fell asleep in each other's arms.

I dreamed good for a time. Kind of dreams a man dreams when he's holding a woman in his arms. But the dreams didn't last. I thought about my aliens and I thought about Grace's story about Popalong Cassidy and the Producer and the Great Director. I thought about all that movie junk on down the highway. I tried to make everything add up but nothing would.

It all went away and folded into a cloud the color and texture of Grace's pubic hair.

Next morning Bob woke me by pulling on my foot. I got my head out from between Grace's legs and looked up.

"That's disgusting, you know," Bob said.

I picked up Grace's shirt from the floorboard and draped it over her. I got my clothes and sat out on the tailgate and put them on.

"Well, I hope we enjoyed ourselves," Bob said.

"We did."

Bob went away and I woke Grace up and she got dressed and we helped Crier and Bob load some fruit and bamboo water containers in the camper. Then we were off.

After a few days we came to Shit Town. The post Grace had told us about was gone, and now there was an official sign made of crude lumber. On it was: SHIT TOWN, POPULATION: WHO GIVES A FUCK.

Civic pride.

Shit Town wasn't much. Some shacks made of sticks and crooked lumber mostly. It looked like a place the Big Bad Wolf would blow down.

Out next to the road was a line of cars, and people were living in those too. Some of the cars were fixed up with huts connected to them. Snazzy stuff.

We parked on the opposite side of the highway, locked up and walked over to Main Street, which was a dirt track, and went down it.

A few people ogled us, and we ogled them back.

No one offered us the Key to the City.

In spite of Shit Town not looking like much, I suppose by present standards it's pretty prosperous. There were a lot of people moving about and there was an aura of industry in the air.

Down at the end of the street was a well house. Most likely it had been built over an open spring, as I figured that was what had attracted folks to this spot in the first place, as the lake had attracted us to Jungle Home.

Beyond this I could see a lot of stumps leading to the jungle. In a short time, with only their hands and crude tools, these people had cut a lot of trees.

I figured eventually this kind of industry would lead to Shit Town having burger joints that served dinosaur and rabbit burgers, and eventually the place might move up the evolutionary line to having a kind of thrift store where you could get shower curtains, house shoes, bird feeders and Bermuda shorts.

A lot of women were pregnant, and though I'm not good at guessing things like that, they looked pretty close to domino date to me. Of course, time here is too hard to judge.

There were little huts along the street and some of them had plank counters out front with things to trade on them. There was one that had flat-in-the-middle green bread with flies on it, and behind the counter was this woman leaning on a hut post with her dress hiked up and her butt free to the air. There was a guy with his pants down against her, and he was putting it to her. If the woman liked it, it didn't show, and the fella looked like a man called to duty.

It didn't take long, and when they finished she let down her dress and took the loaf of bread and went away. The man pulled up his pants and looked at us.

"Ya'll want bread?"

"I don't think so," Bob said.

"We went on down the street and came to another stand, and on its counter was a turtle shell turned upside down, and there was a wooden pestle in it. All around the shells were piles of fruit.

A guy with a belly that looked like a bag of rocks under his shirt got off a stump when he saw us coming and came over and smiled at us. All this teeth had gone south except one dead center of his bottom gum. The rest of him didn't look too good either.

"Want me to make you a fruit drink?" he said. "Mashed right here while you wait."

"Nope," Crier said.

Next to the fruit juice place was a hut with a sign out front painted in black mud that read: Library.

"They're kidding," Bob said.

I went over and pulled the curtain of reeds aside and looked in. There was just enough room for one person in there, and that one person had to sit on a rotting stump because the roof was low. There was one crude shelf of books, and under the shelf was a little sign that said: PLEASE RETURN BOOKS.

I went inside and looked at what they had to offer. There was a Bible covered in red plastic with a zipper on it. I unzipped it and looked inside. Saw that everything Jesus had said was printed in red so you could tell it from ol' So-and-So.

Alongside it was a collection of Rod McKuen's poetry and a copy of *Jonathan Livingston Seagull* with "This book belongs to David Webb and is his inspiration" written inside.

There were two copies of the *Watchtower*, one concentrating on the dilemmas of dating in the modern world, the other on the deterioration of the family unit.

There was also a pamphlet for raising chinchillas for fun and profit (neither the fun or profit being to the advantage of the chinchillas); a postcard with a gerbil's picture on the front and a note on the back that said they could be seen at some petting zoo; a photo-novel of *Superman 3*; and a souvenir hand fan from Graceland with a picture of the erstwhile King of Rock'n'Roll on one side (prebloat) and the words to "You Ain't Nothing But A Hound Dog" on the other. There were also a couple of poems that didn't rhyme written on some dirty popcorn bags with eyeliner pencil.

I took the Elvis fan and fanned myself, then put it back and went outside. The others had wandered down the street, not having felt the pull of the arts.

The guy with the one tooth said, "Find anything?"

"I fanned myself a little."

"It's checked out right now, but there's a pretty good Max Brand novel we got, 'cept the last couple of pages are torn out. Some fella wrote an ending for it, though. He wrote on the inside back cover, 'He rode off into the West and everything was okay.' Seems a good enough ending to most anything, don't it?"

"Does at that. I take it you're also the librarian?"

"Yeah, but people want fruit juices more than they want books. Only thing is they don't always have something good to trade. Tell you, I've had all the dry pussy I want. It's making the head of my dick raw. In the long run I get the bad end of the trade. I'd really rather have some kind of meat, fish, maybe some roots that are good to boil."

"Commerce can be a bitch," I said.

4

When I caught up with the others, they were standing beside the street looking out between a couple of shacks made of mud and sticks, staring at a man hanging from the limb of a big oak tree. He was spinning around, kicking his feet and working his elbows as if in a square dance. The elbows were all he could work of his arms, since his hands were tied behind his back.

On a bench near the oak sat two men and a woman. They looked like benched baseball players waiting for their turn at an inning.

"Suicide tree I told you about," Grace said. "Come on."

"I don't want to see that," I said.

"Me neither," Bob said.

"I'll pass too," Crier said.

"Do what you want," Grace said to me, "but they're going to hang themselves anyway and you fellas need pants."

"Pants?" I said.

"You think those folks are gonna need them later?"

"I got pants," Crier said. "They're ragged, but they're pants. I'll just hang out."

Grace led Bob and me over to the tree. I looked up at the guy. His face was purple as a plum and his neck was swollen out in such a way it was starting to spread over the rope. His tongue was flopping against his chin and he was biting through it. His eyes were crossed and the lid of one was drooped halfway down and the other eye looked like a table tennis ball being pushed out of the hole from behind.

We went over to the bench. The woman was sitting on the end near us and the men were sitting next to each other. She looked at us. The hair on one side of her head had been burned off, and the hair on the other side wasn't anything to be proud of. It was dirty-brown and kinky as wire. I've seen Brillo pads with more class. She had on a filthy T-shirt and her nipples were punching through it. The jeans she had on were thin enough to shit through. Her face wasn't any kind of special. It was covered with pimples and red welts. She was barefoot.

The two guys weren't fashion models either. They had beards full of dirt, bugs and fruit seeds. Their dark coloring wasn't the result of the sun's rays. You could have packed lunches on the pores of their skin.

I hated to think what I looked like.

"Bench is full," the woman said. "Come back tomorrow. Three's about it for a day. Them's the rules."

"We're not here to hang ourselves," Grace said.

"If you're going to watch," she said, "stay back out of the way. This bastard won't never choke. I bet he's been up there an hour."

"He looks about gone to me," I said.

The man beside her, the skinnier of the two, said, "Who can tell how long he's been up there. Time isn't worth a duck fart here. But you should have seen him just a little while ago. He looked worse than this. I think he's gotten him a second wind."

"Maybe he's changed his mind," I said.

At that the hanging man began to kick his legs vigorously. "No, don't think so," the woman said.

"Look at him," I said.

"You can't pay that any mind. It doesn't mean a thing. He wanted to go worse than the rest of us. He bit Clarence there to get first in line."

Clarence was the skinny fella. He held up a sticklike arm and pushed his short sleeve back. There was a crescent of teeth wounds.

"He called me some things I've never heard," said Clarence, "then he pushed me on the ground and bit me. I told him to go ahead. Hell, I wasn't even next in line. Fran was. But look who he bit. That's the way it's always been for me. I tied his hands for him and boosted him into the rope. More than he deserved, I'll tell you. Which reminds me, you folks around when Gene here goes, maybe you could tie his hands for him. It works better that way, otherwise you claw at the rope, no matter how bad you want to go."

"I'll make do," Gene said. He got up and went over to the hanging man and jumped on him and swung back and forth like a kid on a tire swing. The hanging man's neck lengthened.

"We probably won't be around long enough to help Gene," Grace said, "but we wanted to try and talk you out of your pants, just you fellas. Jack and Bob here don't have anything but these dresses."

"Noticed that," Clarence said, "and I'll tell you boys, you haven't got the legs for it."

From the hanging man came a sound like a semi tire blowing out at high speed.

"Goddamn," Clarence said, "there's the signal."

"Yeah," Fran said. "It's nature's way of saying '*Sayonara*, motherfucker.'"

"It's nature's way of filling your pants with shit, is what it is," Clarence said. "Get off of him, Gene. Let's get him down and get Fran up there. Come on, get off of him, goddamnit."

"About those pants," Grace said.

"Guess you want them before I hang myself," Clarence said.

"Well," Grace said, "you know how it is, nature's *sayonara* and all."

Clarence nodded and undressed. He didn't have on any underwear. He tossed the clothes at me. "Take all of it. Shoes too, if they fit. Hell, if they don't fit."

I gathered up the clothes and held them. They smelled a little ripe.

"Hey Gene," Clarence said. "Want to help the other fella out?"

Gene had finally got off the dead man, and he came over to the bench and sat down. He took off his clothes, except for some soiled, green boxer shorts, and gave them to Bob.

"Go on, enjoy them," Clarence said. "You want to thank us later, well, we'll be hanging around."

Clarence loved that. He laughed like a drunk hyena.

He was tying Fran's hands for her when we went away.

5

We collected Crier and went out to the camper. He and Grace sat up front and talked, and Bob and I tried the clothes on. I ended up with some pants too tight in the waist, but I zipped them up high as they would go and left them unsnapped and used the belt I had made for my blanket outfit and ran it through the pants loops for extra support. The shirt fit fine and I wore it with the tails hanging out. The socks were thin but not holey. The shoes were an inch too long and they made me look a little like Bozo the Clown.

Bob's pants fit him in the waist, but were too short. They were what my dad used to call high-water pants. The shirt he had was too narrow across the shoulders, and he got a knife out of the toolbox and slit it halfway down the back. He slit the sides of the shoes too because they were too narrow.

Grace and Crier laughed at our outfits, but just a little. I guess thinking about where the clothes came from took some of the humor out of it.

Crier and Bob stayed with the camper, and Grace and I took Bob's gas can and went around begging for gas. The people who were living in cars that had huts attached to them were the quickest to give up their gas; they had made a stand and they were staying. Some wouldn't even talk to us, and one guy told us he'd pour his goddamn gas on the ground and piss on it before he gave it to us. We took this as a no.

By the end of the day we had a full tank of gas, and we went into Shit Town one last time to see if we could talk someone into giving us enough to fill our can. It never hurt to have extra.

We got off Main Street and went down a little side street lined with huts and cars and we came on this tall, hatchet-faced fella wearing a sweat-stained cowboy hat. He was as unusual in that he was clean-shaven.

He had the hood up on an old red-and-white Plymouth convertible, and he had a wrench and he was fiddling with something under there. He didn't look like someone that wanted to get rid of his gas, but we asked anyway.

"I got plans for a big trip," he said. "Need all the gas I can get. Y'all want a drink? It's the local poison. Made out of fruit juice and piss. No kidding. It'll put you higher than goddamn Skylab."

We passed.

He took a swig and shivered. "Things a man'll drink. Look here, name's Steve."

He stuck out his hand and we took turns shaking it and giving our names.

"Guess y'all are heading on down the highway too, huh?"

"That's the plan," I said.

"Maybe I'll see you then. Soon as I get this buddy tuned up, have me a damn good drunk, I'll be ready to roll. I figure sometime tomorrow. Can't say that I see much to keep me here."

We wished him luck and went back to the camper without the gas. I didn't look in the direction of the hanging tree.

It was dark by the time we got back there, and the four of us talked and ate some fruit and went to bed, Crier slept in the front seat as usual, and Bob, Grace and I slept in the back.

Grace was between me and Bob, but she didn't try to molest me, and she didn't try and molest Bob. Bob refrained from playing with himself.

I lay there and thought about Grace and told myself I was too mature and philosophical and had been through too much to expect anything of our relationship other than friendship. Besides, hadn't she said not to make too much of the other night?

Some things you just had to take like an adult. What she did was what she did and it didn't matter to me. She was her own person. And a man's got to do what a man's got to do, and look and see if you're right then go ahead, and every dog has his day, and every cloud has a silver lining, and a penny saved is a penny earned, and everything works out for the best, and . . . it was a long night.

• • •

It was later than we planned by the time we got up. We had fruit for breakfast because there wasn't any ham and eggs and coffee on the menu, then we got out of there. Crier and Bob up front, me and Grace in the back.

Grace talked about some books I hadn't read and necking didn't come up.

That's how it went for a few days, and finally I quit worrying about IT every second, and cut down to about once an hour.

So when I wasn't thinking about IT, I was thinking about what in hell had possessed me to agree to go along on this little run. I wasn't any hero. I had tried to be once and I had gotten nailed up for the trouble. What I did best was mind my own business, and here I was barreling down the highway so I could confront Popalong Cassidy, who did not sound like a nice guy. Worse yet, I was the reason Crier and Bob were going too. Or at least part of it. I guess when a fella gets bored he can do some stupid things. And maybe I thought I was being macho going with Grace to the end of the highway to help her out. I was wondering how I had ever arrived at that. Grace could probably beat up all three of us.

Damn, Bob had been right when he said a set of titties made me go all to pieces. And maybe Grace had known exactly what she was doing that night in the camper and down by the lake—sealing a deal.

And maybe I was being a horse's ass. It really hurt to discover I had a bigger streak of male chauvinist pig in me than I thought. It hurt worse to realize that I was stupid and tittie blind and was probably going to get killed for it. I preferred happy endings.

But even this kind of thinking didn't last. You can only focus on your own death and destruction so long before it gets boring. You begin to wonder about more important matters, like do people who wear suspenders wear them because they like the way they look, or because they hold their paints up? Do people who work on garbage trucks see their work as important? Did they grow up wanting to be garbage men? What kind of tools are used to scrape dead animals off the highway? Who was the idiot who invented those Happy Face symbols, or those signs that read BABY ON BOARD or SHIT HAPPENS? Should those folks be slow-tortured by parboiling, or killed outright? What was the true story on green M&M's?

I tell you, I had lots of interesting things to think about.

6

That night we got some dried brush and stuff and used our flint and steel to build a little fire near the camper, and pretty soon it was a big fire because Bob couldn't get warm enough and he kept piling brush on it.

"You're gonna catch the truck on fire," Crier said.

"No, I ain't," Bob said. "We're right here in front of the fire."

"I won't burn up to save the truck," Crier said.

"Count me out too," Grace said.

"It's all right," Bob said. "I'm watching it."

After that we sat there and thought and said a little now and then, but not too much because we had our minds on some things, like the fact the highway was starting to change. The nights were getting darker, as if the air was getting thicker, and there were posters and popcorn bags and soft drink cups and the like lying about, and I figured pretty soon we'd be getting into the stormy part. Already we were seeing things in the truck mirrors, and sometimes things reflected in the windows; things like the face of King Kong, the Frankenstein monster clinging to the side of the truck, Dracula and Daffy Duck with their arms around one another.

It was pretty disconcerting to see stuff like that, then look and not find anything there to reflect it. On second thought, I guess we were glad of that. Still, it was unnerving.

Anyway, we were sitting there, and Crier said, "Got to see a man about a horse."

"Me too," I said.

We walked out behind the truck and stood in the highway to do our business. It was very dark. I looked down the road the way we had come. There was a bend in the road and it went around behind some trees and there was some moonlight on the highway, but when I looked in the other direction it was dark as the inside of a goat.

I finished pissing and put my equipment up and wandered off the highway and started walking along the edge in the direction of the dark part. I didn't go too far. It was really dark.

I turned and looked at Crier. He was still hosing the concrete. He looked at me and said, "You know, after all I've been through, bad as it's been, I think things are about to get better. I feel it."

I was going to say something to that, but around the corner came two headlights and the faintest glint of a grillwork smile.

Crier, dong in hand, swiveled in the direction of the car and then he was a hood ornament.

The car, a convertible, sailed by me with Crier bent over the hood and the driver hit down on the horn, stomped the brakes and yelled, "Motherfucker!"

Crier went under the car and bounced out from beneath it and lay in the highway with the moonlight for a shroud. He still had his dong in his hand, but it wasn't connected to his body anymore. He had jerked it off, no pun intended. Lying on his back, his fist on his chest, his dong clenched there like a frankfurter, he looked as if he were studying the universe while preparing to eat a weenie.

FIFTH REEL

Tooling With Steve, Crier Gets Some Sunglasses, Showdown at the Orbit

1

The convertible fishtailed to a stop, disappearing into the darker part of the highway, and right before it did, I caught the ghostly reflection of something in one of its mirrors, some kind of monster that faded with the car's movement. Then the driver was out of the car and running toward Crier. I knew the moment I saw his cowboy hat that it was Steve from back at Shit Town.

I got my feet out of the glue and started over to Crier. Steve was down on his knees feeling Crier's chest and neck. He looked up at me and said, "Dead as a rock."

I tried to kick Steve in the face, but he caught my foot and pulled me on my butt.

"I didn't do it on purpose," he said.

I tried to get up and swarm him. He jabbed me in the chest with his palm and knocked me on my butt again.

"I didn't see him. He shouldn't have been standing in the highway."

"You sonofabitch. You goddamn sonofabitch."

Bob and Grace came over. As they neared us they slowed down, as if taking small steps would give the reality of the thing time to go away.

When they stood over us and looked down, Bob said, "Damn. One thing after another."

"One of you get his feet," Steve said, "and let's get him out of the road before we get creamed by somebody."

Grace got Crier's feet and Steve got him under the arms and they started him off the highway. Crier's hand fell off his chest and he dropped what he was holding.

"Put him down," Steve said.

They lowered him to the highway and Steve picked up what Crier had dropped and put it in Crier's shirt pocket. It poked out the top like a periscope.

They picked him up again and carried him over to the side of the road, and Steve went and got in his car and pulled it over to our side and walked back to us. I kept thinking I'd find something on the ground to pick up and hit Steve with, but the urge was going away. There didn't seem to be any reason to hit anyone.

Grace didn't feel that way. She kicked Steve flush in the balls. He dropped to his knees and had a facial workout. When that was over and he got his breath back, he said, "Damn, lady."

"It didn't make me feel as good as I hoped," Grace said, "but it still does a little something for me."

Then the camper blew up.

2

Hot, sticky morning with the convertible's tape deck blasting Sleepy LaBeef who's singing something about how he's a boogie-woogie man, jetting along with the top down, doing about ninety plus, me in the front seat, Steve at the wheel, bugs on the windshield, Grace, Bob and Crier in the back. Crier strapped in with a seat belt, leaning to the left, head partly out the window, hair standing up like wire, eyelids blown back by the wind, eyes glassy as cheap beads, pecker in his pocket, the tip of it shriveling and turning brown.

"Oh no," Grace says, "the fire's all right. It isn't too big. No sir. Just right. I'm in front of it. No problem. It's not too close to the truck. Ol' Bob's got it under control. Ol' Bob's got it by the balls. Ol' Bob—"

"Shut up, will you," Bob says.

Steve sings along with Sleepy LaBeef. New bugs hit the windshield. Outside the scenery is changing. More popcorn bags and garish posters lying about, blowing up as we jet by. The trees are starting to fill with film. Broken TV sets and fragments of antennas clutter the side of the road. Crier's pecker continues to wither.

Steve moves the convertible up to a hundred and it's rocking a little. The sun is glinting off the hood and the tires are whining: I hope no one is standing in the road. All seats are taken.

3

High noon and we ran out of Sleepy LaBeef. Then we got Steve.

"Now the reason I'm here is my wife. Finding out your gal can work a dick better than Tom Mix could work a lariat is all right, but the bad news on a thing like that is finding out the dick she works best don't belong to you. Wrong cow pony, you know. It can deflate a man's ego."

"What about you?" Grace said.

"Oh yeah," Steve said, not catching her tone. "Especially when all I ever got was the old in-and-out and are-you-finished-yet."

"Imagine that," Grace said.

"Worse than that, her man was none other than Fred Trual, and that goddamn got me, I'll tell you. He's a real baboon's ass, all the personality of a snot rag and as loyal as a paid-for date. He also stole my song 'My Baby Done Done Me Wrong,' and that was enough for me to swear I'd kill him.

"How in hell do you figure a woman. This Fred is not only ugly, but he's been in the pen and rumor has it he poisoned his old maiden aunt for what she was gonna leave him, and he knew that wasn't nothing but five hundred dollars. I mean we're talking a greedy sonofabitch here. He even eats until he gets sick. I've known him since grade school. Wasn't worth a damn then either. But the gals always went for him. Must have had some kind of smell that got to them. Had to be that. He wasn't pretty and he wasn't smart and he wasn't nice. He and Tina Sue even stole my car."

"See you got it back," I said. "Are you sure we heard both sides of Sleepy?"

"About three times to a side," Steve said. "I got it back all right, but not because they gave it to me. I'll tell you about it."

"That's all right," Grace said. "No need to bother."

"I don't mind," Steve said, and he made a corner and the tires screeched like startled owls. "I told myself when I caught up with them I was going to kill Fred. I thought I might even kill her too. And I thought when they were both dead I was going to get out my guitar and sing the song I wrote over their dead bodies, then maybe on the back of my guitar I'd write another one in their blood, right then and there. That's how mad I was. Nasty, huh."

"You're not a nice fella, Steve," Bob said.

"Now I didn't mean to run over that ol' boy, I swear it. I'm a sensitive fella, don't think I'm not. I mean I can write the kind of songs that make the whiningest, sorriest-living, beer-drinkingest and gal-losingest sonofabitch cry like a baby with a thermometer up its ass. Kind of song that'll make women's thangs tingle and make fellas call home to make sure their old ladies aren't doing it with the next-door neighbor. Know what I mean?"

"I think you sort of summed it up there," Bob said.

"It'll make me a rich man. Or would if we were back in the real world. I'd be able to buy clothes that aren't on sale at the goddamn K-mart. Go to some place to buy stuff that ain't made out of genuine plastic and genuine cheap. I'd be able to get me a new hat made out of real hat stuff and have it be one of those with a fancy band around it with a feather fresh out of a peacock's ass sticking up in it. I'd get me some unchewed toothpicks to stick in the band. I'd move to Nashville and sing my sexy little heart out. I'd wine and dine and chase them honky-tonk angels until my dick needed a wheelchair to get around. Course, that's what I would have done. I reckon Fred's made a mint off it now. It's probably on the radio back home. Go in any joint with a juke and I bet you can hear my song coming out of it, probably sung by George Jones or Randy Travis. And ol' Fred's spending my money. Tell you, I still want to kill him. If I got the chance I'd kill him deader than the ol' boy in the back seat there, then I'd really get rough."

"I take it you don't like Fred," Bob said.

"You're getting it. Let me backtrack on my story here."

"I thought that was all of it," Grace said. "I mean that's enough to hold me. What about you guys?"

"I want to hear it all," Bob said.

I was starting to get interested too, but I didn't say anything. I didn't want Grace to kick me in the balls.

"Well, when I found out Fred and Tina Sue were doing what they were doing from this private detective fella I hired, I couldn't hardly believe it. 'Cept that he had some real clear pictures of them in action and he didn't help matters none by saying stuff like, 'That's her best shot there, the one with the whip and the Mouseketeer hat,' and 'By God, I didn't know human bodies could do them sort of things. Hell, I didn't know snakes could do them sort of things. Look at that, will you. I bet he's got his head halfway in there, whadaya think?'

"I wasn't just hurt that Tina Sue was waxing another man's rope, or that the man was stupid, greedy, and maybe a murderer. There was the fact that Fred seemed to be having a hell of a lot better time with Tina Sue than I'd ever had. I didn't even know she had a Mouseketeer hat. To put it simple, I was charmed by them sweet little eight-by-ten color glossies. Here I was busting chops and sweating gravel just to make a living, trying to write songs on the side so I could be a country-and-western singer, making the occasional trip to Nashville to try and peddle my songs—and not having much luck with it—and I find out my suspicions about my wife are true, and worse, it's old Fred and he's having a better time than me. Then to put the goddamn Howdy Doody smile on it, I found out they not only went off together in my car, but took my song on account of Fred claimed he wrote it some years back and I won it from him in a poker game. I only played poker with Fred and them other boys a few times, and I didn't never win. Come to think of it, I think Fred cheats.

"Anyway, I got all this from the note."

The wind was picking up and posters and cups and popcorn bags were tornadoing around the car and beginning to collect on the windshield and flutter into the seats and slap Crier in the face.

Steve pulled over and put the convertible's roof up and Bob took the bags off Crier's face and tossed them out. Back on the road, Steve continued his story.

"The note was stuck in the refrigerator door when I got home, on account of the bitch took all the fruit magnets with her. Even the one I bought for myself that was made like a big strawberry. The note said what she had done and that she thought the car was as much hers as mine (which was a hoot) and that the new song I said I wrote and was bragging about I didn't write 'cause her boyfriend did and she said she and the boyfriend were heading to Nashville to make the money off of it. She said she thought it was a better song than she thought before, now that she knew I didn't write it. She said goodbye and that she had popped the tops on all the beer in the refrigerator so it would go flat, and for me to take a water hose and run it up my ass and turn it on full blast.

"I tell you, there wasn't a cheerful line in that note. I of course went straight on over to Fred's. I was back a day earlier than they expected. I had been up to Nashville, see, and I come back early to check with the private detective guy, and to see if I could talk some things out if my suspicions were correct, so I figured I just might get the jump on them two before they were gone with my song.

"Thinking that I had left my convertible with Tina Sue and drove her damned old VW up to Nashville didn't make me no happier, and I tell you when I got up in Fred's yard and seen my Plymouth sitting there, the sides of it all muddy and the hubcaps covered over with the stuff, my eyes filled with murder. I slammed on my brakes hard enough to throw my hat in the backseat. I got that dude back on my head and went straight up on Fred's porch. Last year's Christmas wreath was still hanging on the door; one of them with the plastic mistletoe and those damned ol' gold-sprayed pine cones glued on it. I jerked that little buddy off the door and stomped the cones and kicked the rest of it out in the yard.

"One of Fred's old two-bit hounds come around from the back then and stood off the porch growling at me. I got hold of Fred's sandy old doormat and threw it at the dog and it ran off under the house where it could collect some more ticks.

"About the time I turned around, I saw that the curtain over one of the windows was falling back into place, and I knew then that Fred was home. The window he'd taken a peek out of had MERRY CHRISTMAS stenciled on it, and I yelled out, 'I know goddamn good and well you're in there, shit-bag. Come on out. And it ain't even Christmas, you dumb cocksucker.'

"He didn't come out so I got off the porch and got hold of the cinder block he was using for a step and put it on the porch, got up there and got hold of it again and shoved it through the window with the stenciling on it.

"He come out there then with a chair leg in his hand, and he come out swinging. We sort of run together and rolled off the porch and out in the yard. His old hound come out from under the porch then and got hold of my pants leg and started growling and tugging on it. I kicked the mutt off and wrestled up to my feet, and thought I was going to do pretty good, when Fred hit me one on the noggin with that chair leg, and the last thing I remembered was the toes of my K-mart boots coming up."

"But it didn't kill you," Grace said.

"No it didn't. I woke up and the first thing I seen when I got up on my elbow was the toes of them boots again."

"And they were still from K-mart," Grace said.

"Still from K-mart. But the knot on my head was from Fred. Next thing I see is Fred and that hound dog. The dog is sitting on his butt staring at me, his ol' tongue hanging out like he just had him a bitch and was damn proud of it, and

Fred he still has his chair leg, and he bends over me and says, 'Hurt much, Steve?'

"I tell him, 'Not at all. Sometimes when I'm home I take a chair leg to my own head.'

"He hit me again, and when I woke up, I was hot and it was dark and crowded and I could smell that perfume Tina Sue always wore."

Steve paused and pointed at the glove box. "I got a last cigar in there. Been saving it. Get it for me, will you?"

I got it out and he bit off the end and spat tobacco out the window and put the cigar in his mouth and sucked on it. "I don't care what they say, these things taste a hell of a lot better when you know they ain't made by a bunch of Cubans."

He punched in the lighter.

"All right, damnit," Grace said. "'What was this dark, cramped place that smelled like Tina Sue?"

"I'm gonna tell you." He took the lighter and lit the cigar, puffed dramatically. "The trunk of this car."

"Uh oh," Bob said.

"Uh oh is right. The greedy sonofabitch had shown his true colors. I figure he decided he wasn't gonna share any song money with Tina Sue, and he killed her. Then I come along and he had to kill me—least he thought he killed me. And he put us in the trunk of the car and drove us out to the Orbit and walked off, probably hitched home. It wasn't such a smart idea, really. I mean someone would have caught up with him. But then whatever happened to the drive-in happened, and I was trapped in there, and I guess back home in Texas there isn't even a drive-in no more. I don't know what would be there in its place, if anything. But there's no body in the trunk for the police to find, in fact there's no car. So I guess Fred did all right by accident. He's probably making money off my song right now."

"Look at it this way," Bob said. "Maybe the song wasn't any good and he couldn't sell it."

Steve sat and thought about that. The fire on his cigar went out. Finally he said, "I'm not sure how I feel about that."

"What I want to know," Grace said, "is how did you get out of the trunk?"

"Oh, that. Wasn't nothing to that. I was hot and pissed and I bent up my legs and kept donkey-kicking the trunk till I busted the lock. When I got out of there didn't nobody care, things being like they were. I ended up using some wire I had back there to fasten the trunk down."

"Is Tina Sue . . . you know?" Grace said.

"Back there? Naw. I left her there a while, but when things got real bad back there, well, I ate her."

4 After a time, even Steve played out. Course, we had gotten most of his life story, and I guess maybe there wasn't much else to tell. The story wasn't exactly exemplary. I couldn't see it as a movie. He sang us a few of the songs he'd written. Nashville wasn't missing anything. Grace said it all sounded like "Home on the Range" to her, no matter what words he sang. He got quiet then, went into one of those artistic funks, no doubt. He made corners faster than ever and he wouldn't play the Sleepy LaBeef tape.

I had a hard time relaxing, way Steve was driving. And I was thinking about Crier and his dead eyeballs getting whipped by the wind. I knew it wasn't a thing to get on Crier's nerves, but it was damn sure giving mine a workout, and I didn't even have to look at him. Still, the thought of those dead eyeballs behind me . . .

When Steve had asked for that cigar, I had seen that there were some sunglasses in the glove box, and I got those out. They were neon yellow and had little bulldogs in the top corners of the frames and the dogs had black BB eyes that rolled around at the slightest movement. It wasn't exactly what I was looking for, but it was something.

I handed them back to Bob and told him what I wanted, and he put them on Crier. It helped. Crier even looked alive. He appeared to be nothing more than an excessively cool dude with his dick in his pocket.

Course, a little later in the day he started to bloat up and stink a little, and I couldn't think of anything to help that. We had to pull over and put him in the trunk, sunglasses and all. Steve fussed about this, because he had to work at unwiring the lid, but he did it. I think he was afraid if he didn't, Grace would kick him in the balls. She had that look.

We got Crier dumped in the back without his dick falling out of his pocket, got him wired in, and we were off. It seemed strange not to have the old boy with us, after all we had been through, but it did smell a mite fresher, especially to Bob and Grace.

It got darker and darker and pretty soon we got to that stuff Grace told us about. Storms whipped posters and popcorn sacks and the like every which way. The moon looked even more false than usual and it shone like a projector light through the trees, hitting the strips of film that twisted and twined there. Film ghosts were no longer reflected in the mirror and the windows. The highway was full of them: cowboys with six-shooters, knights with swords and lances, apes and madmen, giant stalking machines from *War of the Worlds*, the smiling Brady Bunch. We drove through them all as if they were mist.

Film strips crawled onto the highway and made smashed cellophane sounds beneath our tires.

When Steve got tired, we pulled over and I got behind the wheel. I drove until I couldn't, then I swapped with Bob who drove until he had to swap with Grace.

When it got back around to me, the gas gauge showed a quarter tank.

5

Daylight, and things looked a little better. No ghosts melting through the car, and no film crawling. A little storm activity, but nothing special. The sun looked worse than ever, like a pie pan spray-painted gold.

The trees were rubbery-looking and the ground reminded me of Styrofoam. The fruit we found to eat was shriveled and bitter to the taste. Everything around us looked a little cheap and off center, like the way it is when you make a real close examination of what you bought at a thrift sale.

We found a few chocolate almonds lying about and some soft drink puddles, so I knew we were getting close to the highway's end; the place Popalong had told Grace about. It struck me that Steve ought to know what he was in for. All he knew was that he was giving us a ride to the end of the highway. He didn't know we had some idea what was there, and he didn't know what we had in mind.

Steve had a mirror in his glove box, one of those kinds with the props behind it, and he had that and his pocket knife and a little kit with a tiny pair of scissors and a toenail clipper in it, and he was working on his whiskers. It made me hurt to watch him.

"Who you cleaning up for?" Bob asked him.

"Myself. I never could stand whiskers. I still don't look so good when I finish, since I can't get close enough, but it beats looking like you boys."

"I think we ought to explain something to you," I said.

"About what?" Steve said. He finished up and folded the mirror stand and put it and the kit in the glove box.

"About the end of the road," Grace said.

Steve leaned on the car and got what was left of his cigar out of his pocket. When it died out he hadn't relit it. He didn't light it now. He put it in his mouth and rolled it from one side to the other.

"We kind of know what's at the end," Grace said. "We've got an idea what we're going to do there." And she told Steve a condensed version of the story she told us. When she finished Steve quit moving his cigar. He took it out of his mouth and put it in his pocket. I couldn't help but think of Crier's dick.

"Sound's like you folks are going to get killed, is what it sounds like to me," Steve said.

"We don't expect you to go if you don't want," Grace said. "We'd appreciate your carrying us as far as you can, though."

"What if I said this was as far as I was going?" Steve said.

"That would be it then," Grace said.

"You'd walk through this stuff at night?"

"I would," Grace said.

"I'm not crazy about that part," Bob said. "I might even be talked out of it. I might even ride back with you the other way."

"You?" Steve asked me.

"All that matters right now," I said, "is are you going to the end or not. If you go back, you know what you've got."

"Sounds like I have a pretty good idea of what I'm gonna get if I go forward too." He looked hard at me. "Tell you what else, I think if I go back and Bob here goes with me, you'll go too. You don't look like any kind of hero to me. The gal here will keep walking, I can tell that. She doesn't think she needs much of anybody."

"That's not true," Grace said. "I can use all the help I can get. But if I don't get it, I'm going on."

"I'm no knight in white armor, lady," Steve said.

"Never crossed my mind you might be."

Steve smiled and put the cigar back in his mouth. He still didn't light it.

"All right, I'll haul you on, but maybe we ought to come up with a game plan. And first thing to start with is getting rid of the old boy in the trunk. He's starting to stink all the way from the back. It bothers my driving. I don't figure we'll have to eat him, with all this fruit and stuff out there, so let's get shed of him."

6

I got Crier's legs and Bob got him by the shoulders and we lifted him out of the Plymouth's trunk. He had swelled up a bit, and he really did stink.

We carried him over to the side of the road and put him down. I said, "I told him I wouldn't do this. I promised I'd get him to the end of the highway."

"Me too," Bob said, "but a person doesn't always get what they want, and you can't always keep your promise. Besides, if he'd known he was gonna stink like this, maybe he wouldn't have asked it of us."

Crier's dick had come out of his pocket and rolled up next to the spare, and since it was past the handling stage, and looked like a big jalapeno going to rot, Steve got a couple of sticks and scissored it out of there and carried it over and dropped it next to Crier.

"We ought to bury him," I said.

"Something will just dig him up," Steve said, "and this ground isn't any kind of ground for digging. But if you want, there's a worn-down spot over there and we can throw him off in that, maybe find something to cover him up, for all that amounts to."

We carried Crier over to the worn-down spot and put him in it. He was stiff as a tire iron and lay there in the indentation as if he had fallen sideways out of a chair and frozen. Steve kicked the dick on over and into the hole and we got some brush and limbs and the few rocks we could find, and put them on top of him. We got everything covered but the bottom of his shoes. Our hands sure did smell bad.

We got in the car and drove away. Bob said, "I guess we could have at least put his dick in his pocket."

7

All over the place were these TVs and antennas and papers, and the darker it got the more those papers came and swirled and collected in the trees with the film, which was now thicker than the leaves.

Over to the right, just above the trees, you could see what looked like an inverted tornado dipping down, and all of its swirls were filled with posters and bags and stuff. And on the ground were lots of TV sets. It was like we were getting closer to the garbage dump.

It got darker and we kept driving, but now we had all the windows up because the paper storm had really gotten bad, and it somehow seemed safer from the ghosts that way, even if they weren't really dangerous.

All along the highway were people impaled on antennas, and the headlights would wink at the metal between their legs, and sometimes you could see blood and shit on the antennas. But the more often you didn't, and as we looked closer, we saw why. There were few real people impaled. Most of what was there were dummies.

A thing I couldn't put a name to began to move in the back of my mind, but whatever was crawling back there went away when I saw what was in the distance.

The Orbit, its tall tin fence sparkling in the lightning flashes like a woman's wedding band catching the fire from a candlelight dinner.

From that distance, it looked like the crumbled remains of an old castle, way the shadows fell over and moved around on it, way the lightning popped and fizzled overhead, way the paper and posters swirled around and into it like ghosts heading home.

We pulled off the road near one of the impaled dummies, turned off the lights, and talked about it.

"Seems to me," Steve said, "driving on in isn't the answer, not if it's like you say it is, Grace."

"That's how he said it was, though he called it a kind of church."

"This is your show," Bob said. "What do you want to do? Tell us, and then I'll tell you if I'll do it."

"Wait until morning. Let me sleep on it. Turn the car around and pull off near the trees on the other side, and take turns at watch. That way nobody comes up on us. In the morning I'll know what to do."

"In other words," Bob said, "you'll be ready to do something even if it's wrong?"

"Pretty much," Grace said. "One of you guys take first watch." She leaned against her side of the car and closed her eyes and went to sleep, or pretended to.

"Yes, Commandant," Bob said.

"Once they got the right to vote, it's been downhill ever since," Steve said.

"I heard that," Grace said.

We guys tried to talk for a while, but we didn't really have anything to talk about. We knew Steve's life story. I took the first watch and we took turns doing that all night, and the last watch was Grace's, I think, because I'd come awake from time to time and see who was on duty. Anyway, next thing I knew it was morning and Grace had the door open and was dumping some fruit in my lap.

It wasn't good fruit. It was kind of sour, but I ate it anyway, and lots of it. I looked at the morning and thought it looked pretty fresh, more real than usual. The papers had stopped swirling and the film lay in the trees and on the ground like burnt bacon.

Grace, Bob and Steve were over by one of the dummies and Steve had a stick and was poking it. I got out of the car and went over there.

Bob said, "Popalong sure works to make things look scary. Speaking of scary, you look like hell."

"Thanks."

"We sort of got us a game plan," Steve said. "Or rather Grace has one."

"All right," I said, "let me hear it."

It wasn't complicated. It went like this. We'd wait until near dark, then start toward the Orbit, going along the edge of the jungle until we got around on the left-hand side of the place and could work around to the back, then climb up on the fence and have a look over. After that, we could play it by ear. Locate Sue Ellen, go in there and nab her and get out of there. As for Popalong, Grace said, "don't worry about him none. I'll take care of him, come hell or high water."

Thing was, it was going to be night by the time we did what we wanted to do (provided we were able to do it), and coming back to the car was going to be some kind of dreadful, what with that blood-sucking film and those storms out there, not to mention the shadows and the ghosts which, though harmless, didn't do much for the disposition.

Still, it was the only plan we had, simple as it was.

We whiled away the day eating fruit, then when it started getting windy and the sun started its plunge, we got to walking.

It turned out to be a longer hike than it looked like, and by the time we were at the edge of the Orbit, it was dark and the film was moving.

Steve had the scissors from his shaving kit, and he used that to do some snipping, but we finally had to get away from the jungle, and more out in the clear, so as to stay ahead of the stuff.

There didn't seem to be anyone on sentry duty, and the closer we got the more dummies and real people there were on the antenna poles. The air was full of the odor of rotting bodies and spoiled candy and stale soft drinks.

We went around the edge of the fence and worked our way toward the back, and as we went, we could hear the sounds of television—laugh tracks and voices—and the thought of actually seeing Popalong began to get to me.

Around back, I got Grace up on my shoulders and she looked over the fence, sat there on my shoulders for a while, taking it in.

"Well," Bob said.

"I'll be goddamned," Grace said.

I put her down then and made Bob let me up on his shoulders. I was goddamned too.

What I saw was this vast circle of people gathering around this throne made of television sets, and on the throne was Popalong, the flickerings of some show or another throbbing on his face. And below him and to the left, on another throne of busted sets, was a young girl with her long hair loose. Sue Ellen, I figured.

At the bottom of the double throne were two men. They sat on televisions, well out in front of those behind them. They had ringside seats. I took them for two of the four thugs that had helped Popalong capture Grace and her friends.

But the thing that got to me were the people. You see, from where I was you could get a good view of that part of the lot, and after my eyes had adjusted and I'd taken in the scene, I began to realize that most of the people were pregnant women. There were a few men, but not many. Most of the crowd was not a crowd at all.

Dummies tied to antennas. Lobby cards of actors. Posters with pictures of men and women on them wrapped around stacked television sets. A skeleton here and there with clothes on, or a skull stuck on top of a speaker.

The truth was, Popalong didn't really have many followers. Perhaps he had exaggerated to Grace to sound impressive, or maybe many of them were decorating the poles along the way, or had been eaten.

Didn't his followers demand constant entertainment? What was *Father Knows Best* compared to a public burning? And even if that burning was filmed and shown again and again, could it suffice? New things needed to be filmed and shown so they could be made real. Then fresh realities had to be created. Time after time after time.

Popalong and his followers seemed to be killing themselves out of an audience. The harder Popalong worked for ratings, the fewer people he had to poll.

I got down and Bob and Steve had looks, then we huddled. Grace went over first and I followed. Then Bob. Bob got on my shoulders and gave Steve a hand over.

We began to work our way through the crowd of posters and dummies and skeletons and lobby cards, and sometimes when we came to a real person, they looked at us without curiosity if they looked at us at all; the real stuff was on the TV set.

Grace moved ahead of us, and came out at the front of the crowd and looked up at Popalong.

I saw that Sue Ellen (it had to be her) was dead. Had been for a while. Her face and hands were the color of pee-stained sheets. Her knucklebones punched out of her papery flesh like volcanic eruptions. Her eyes were holes filled with popcorn. One kernel dangled from her left socket like a booger in a nostril.

A tremor went up Grace's back. She yelled at Popalong, "Remember me?"

"It's like a movie," Popalong said. "You coming into my lair."

There was a surge of wind and a mass of paper and popcorn and soft drink slush blew through the drive-in and passed on.

When the wind was gone and the paper had quit rustling, Grace said, "You and this place look all worn out. Your church is light in the pews. I think you're nothing more than a walking TV set with a line of shit."

"It's good of you to come," Popalong said. "Of course, you know what comes next."

The two toughs got up and turned toward Grace. They didn't look as weak as the others. Better diet. More human flesh maybe.

"Good to see you boys." Grace said. "I think about you lots."

The one on Grace's left got to her first. He had a piece of glass wedged into a short stick and he tried to stab her in the stomach.

Before we could make any kind of move to help her, Grace sidestepped the glass, slapped the thug's hand down and kicked him between the eyes so hard his head went back more than his neck allowed. He folded up like an accordion at her feet.

The other tough bolted.

He was a good runner. We didn't chase him. He headed for the exit. He wouldn't last long out there. Not at night, not with the film crawling.

Popalong's followers seemed uncertain. This was the sort of thing they saw a lot of, but in this case it was short and sweet and not nearly melodramatic enough. They shuffled their feet. Maybe they wanted to see it on film.

If any of them had it in their heads to go for Grace, it was an idea that went away when she turned and glared at them.

Popalong's followers were now no more than a pack of pregnant women and skinny men, their brains no better than straw. They might as well have been the dummies that the sky kept raining.

We pushed to the front. I looked up at Popalong. A Western was playing on his face. Just as a Hollywood Indian took a bullet and fell off his horse, Popalong made the tube go black. "You're just a television set," I said. "We can turn you off anytime we want."

Grace grabbed at one of the dummies and pulled at it. It came loose of the antenna that held it. She grabbed the antenna and pulled it out of the asphalt and stepped up on the base of the television throne and poked at Popalong with it.

"Come down so I can change your channels," she said. "Come down so I won't have to bring you down. I want to see you come down, King Popalong. Come on down where you belong."

"Stop it," Popalong said. "You fools are ruining things. I've got anything you want to see. There's not a show so exotic that I don't have it. Anything happens to me and you'll be back in darkness. You'll have to talk to entertain yourselves."

Grace poked him again. He stood up. She poked his knee and his knee buckled and he went down and tried to get up again, but the knee twisted under him and he came tumbling down the sets. As he went, he grabbed out and got hold of Sue Ellen's hand. She came off her throne and tumbled after him.

Popalong hit with a crunch and a smash of glass. Sue Ellen lay on top of him.

Popalong tried to get his hands underneath him. Steve went over and straddled him and pulled Sue Ellen off, then took the guns out of Popalong's holster and stepped back.

Popalong folded his knees under him and lifted his body upright. A chunk of glass fell out of his face. There was a gap dead center of the set and dozens of hairline fractures went out from it. The entire thing pulsed like an asshole straining to shit. Something sparked in the ruined depths, and the sparks jumped about like little red rats trying to abandon ship.

He tried to get up again, but his legs weren't having it. A rope of smoke twisted out of the hole in his face and rose up. The rabbit ears under his hat pushed it back and felt the air, as if searching for signals. But nothing was on that face but wreckage.

The rabbit ears went away and the hat fell back into place.

"It's all over now," Grace said, and started forward.

I grabbed her elbow. "That's enough."

"Not hardly," she said.

"Don't be his high priestess," I said. "You're giving him a TV or movie ending. Kind where the wronged person deals out revenge on the bad guy. He's too messed up to be a bad guy. He's pathetic. He's out of it, through. Don't martyr him for yourself and these people. It won't do a thing for Timothy or Sue Ellen."

"It's not like he's got anything left to hurt anyone with," Bob said.

"Guess you got two cents to put in on this, Steve," Grace said.

"It was me, I'd take him out. Hell, I'll shoot him for you if you like. It won't bother me none. But this is your show. You name the channel."

Grace looked at Popalong's ruptured face, at the scrawny body that held up the massive head, the black cowboy suit that hung off of him like a kid wearing daddy's clothes.

She went over and picked up Sue Ellen and walked away. Popcorn dribbled out of Sue Ellen's eye sockets, sprinkled the ground like snow.

Steve sighed. "This is kind of disappointing. Kind of like a cowboy movie without a final showdown, ain't it?"

"It's exactly like that," I said.

DISSOLVE TO:

Epilogue

We used some of the drier pieces of cardboard and paper we could find and built a mound and put Sue Ellen on it and covered her with some more pieces. Then Steve lit it with a match he'd found in one of the derelict cars, and after a while, most of Sue Ellen was cremated. What was left over we scooped up in Coke cups and took it off in the woods and tossed it around.

Popalong's dead bodyguard was hauled off during all the commotion by one of the drive-in people, and I guess he got eaten.

Next morning, we went to look for Crier's body. It was gone. Something had dug him out. Whatever it was got his dick too.

As for Popalong, in time he crawled back up that stack of TVs and found his place on the throne. He sat there with his tongue of blue and red wires hanging out and the inside of his face popping sparks and fizzling from time to time. But finally that quit.

He grew thin inside that cowboy suit, and when the flesh went away, there were no bones in him, just cable wire and rods of antenna held together with tightly wrapped film.

Steve brought his car into the drive-in, and he and Grace took up together and went to living out of it. I tell you, I never expected that to happen. Maybe all those bangs Grace got on the head had clouded her sense of judgment.

Bob and I built our place out of TV sets. Walls and ceiling. We used antenna pieces and part of an old car to make it work. In the mornings we wake up and watch Grace come out of the Plymouth and do her martial arts exercises. In the nude.

The bending over stuff is dynamite.

She's got a big round tummy now. She says I didn't pull out fast enough and the baby's mine. She says it's pretty far along, but isn't showing much because she's tall. Since I didn't eat the King's popcorn and neither did she, she thinks the baby has a good chance to be healthy. I don't know how I feel about that.

The other women have had their babies and—

Yes, I'm talking about you guys. But hold up, I'm almost through here. Just be polite and let me get through this.

—they look like the Popcorn King. Two bodies welded together, one on the other's shoulders, to make a single unit. Unlike the King, they are covered in eyes. The eyes look like the eyes that were on the corn the King puked up. Each eye blinks at a different time. I feel like I'm constantly receiving Morse code.

They're all sexless. I mean there's no equipment that I can see. Keeps from having to wipe a lot of asses. They came out of the cannon practically walking. They can put simple sentences together already. They're almost as tall as me. They like to listen to me read, and though they understand a lot of the words, a lot of sentences, I don't think they get the gist of it all—

Okay, Leroy. I take it back. You do understand. That's all for today, guys, girls, whatever. Go find a car to tear up. I was kidding about there being a test at the end of this . . .

What test?

Forget it, Leroy. Bye now.

That was about all I had written. I'm back inside the hut now and I'm sitting here finishing this out as best I can, which is just as well. I'm running out of things to write with. I've looked everywhere, glove boxes, the concession stand over in B Lot, you name it. I've written this in pen and pencil, crayon and eyeliner.

But it doesn't matter, I'm also running out of things to say. I guess I can mention that the mothers of those kids, or whatever they are, don't love them. But I'm not sure that's all their fault. How can they be mothers after all they've seen and done?

I see some of the drive-in people looking up at the corpse of Popalong, almost wistfully, I think. At night they wander about in the storms, nothing to do. They've forgotten how to talk to one another. It's a good thing those weird kids were born practically grown.

Sometimes I take the kids hunting with me. They chase down the game on foot. Bob says he thinks he saw one throw a stick without touching it the other day. Kid just willed it up and there it went, hit a rabbit in the back of the head and killed it.

Bob admits he saw this out of the corner of his eye, and it may not be like that, but I wouldn't be surprised.

Well, like I said we hunt a lot. Thought a better diet might help the people here, help them get a better frame of mind. But all it does is help them get around faster.

Sometimes I think I'll start back down the highway, but I'd have to go on foot and I don't like the idea of those storms or that film out there at night. Still, I think about it. Shit Town might be a better life than this. Hell, getting back to Jungle Home wouldn't be too bad.

Let's see . . . Oh yeah, Grace has a shadow now, and Steve is starting to have one. Bob and I still don't. I'm not sure what this means, but it worries me a little, especially when I see Grace working out and popping the air with her punches, and right behind her, capering like a chimp, making fun of her moves, is her shadow. Maybe I'll stop getting up in the morning to watch her. That shadow takes the joy out of it.

Book Three

THE DRIVE-IN

The Bus Tour

Introduction

I never expected to write a *Drive-in 2*, so I darn sure didn't plan on writing, *The Drive-in: The Bus Tour*, which is The Drive-in 3.

Not long after the first two came out, I was asked by a small publisher to do just that, and thought, well, okay. But there was nothing there. Just wouldn't come, so I had to pass on the deal.

A lot of years passed. A lot. Fifteen, seventeen. I'm a little uncertain. Enough that now I was certain there would never be a Drive-in 3. Besides, the other two, considered humorous books, hadn't been that much fun to write. Not all writing is supposed to be fun, but as I have said before, I'm not one of those writers who loves having written. I love writing. I can't wait to get at it. When my feet hit the floor in the morning I take our dog out, have coffee, look at the email, and then, better than nine out of ten times I'm on my work like syrup on a pancake. Oh, there's a day here and there when my mind is as limp as an octogenarian monk's dick. But that's rare, and is really my mind telling me to take a rest, or that the subconscious hasn't been quite up to par, or whatever. But nearly every morning I go downstairs and go to work and turn out three to five pages a day, and some days more. Well, some mornings more. I usually work about three hours in the morning, and that's it, five days a week. But now and again I work weekends, and every now and again, I work more than those hours in the morning. Now is an example. It's after two thirty in the morning on the day of my birthday, October 28, and I'm writing this because I have to leave town in the next day or so and need to get it done, along with some other writing before I head off to a film festival where *Bubba Ho-tep* is showing, and then the Texas Book Festival.

So, here I am, telling you this: I had no plans to write a third novel about the Drive-in world, but Bill Schafer and I began to discuss it. He wanted me to do it for Subterranean. And then, one day, out of nowhere, the novel caught fire and I was back in that world. It was easier this time, and fun.

I wrote the novel very quickly.

It had been so long since I had written the last, I didn't realize I had left out one of the main characters from the other novels. Just plain forgot him. A couple of readers called me out. I solved that problem with a small revision.

I'll let the novel speak for itself on that matter.

Also, I realized when I finished this novel, I didn't give a pure and perfect answer to the world of the Drive-in, and it's left open for yet another that need not exist. I left it that way for the reader. But I won't go into that anymore. My telling you that doesn't spoil the book or have any effect on the reading of it, but I won't explain beyond that. I will say this. What I've said about the other two.

Enjoy.

—Joe R. Lansdale, 2009

"God bless the children of this picture, this movie book. I'm going on into the Shade."

—Jack Kerouac *(Doctor Sax)*

"God ain't nothing but the mind working overtime."

—Anonymous

Fade-in Prologue

In which the Great Jack, during a hypoglycemic high, ponders the universe beneath God's asshole while writing The Drive-in Bible and contemplating a journey by school bus.

1

They all lived in the great Orbit Drive-in beneath a hole in the sky that swirled with shadows and on occasion squeezed out, sphincter-style, dark sticky goo.

The goo reeked.

The goo stuck to your feet.

Some thought it edible, because once upon a time it had rained chocolate almonds and such, but this wasn't chocolate almonds. Not by a long shot. The eaters grabbed their bellies and screamed, and they were outta there.

For awhile their bodies lay stacked by the drive-in fence, ready to go. And go they would, but not far.

(More on that later.)

The stuff, the god turds, was finally shoveled with makeshift scoopers made of car hoods, deposited up against the drive-in fence to reinforce it. This worked well. Turned hard as cement. When you piled fresh stuff on the old stuff, it stuck. And so the wall grew.

But back to the hole in the sky.

Those who lived beneath this hole in the sky in the Orbit Drive-in called it God's Asshole. Or rather Jack did, and it caught on.

Jack was the man. Leader of all that was Drive-in, baby. Like everyone else, he hadn't aged a day in all the time he had been there. Least not physically. Emotionally, mentally, man, he was some kind of wreck. His mind needed a cane. His emotions needed a walker.

But he had become the man.

Jack, the Drive-in man.

The drive-in movies, for some inexplicable reason, played at night and all night. We're talking four big screens in four connecting lots which had become individual communities, christened cleverly: LOT ONE, LOT TWO, LOT THREE, and THE BIG LOT, which was larger than the rest (hence, the BIGness). It also had a larger screen. The four screens spread their flickering blue-white light along with images of blood and destruction. *Tool Box Murders*. *Chainsaw Massacre*. *Night of the Living Dead*. Others. Spread it across the screens like rancid butter on old slices of bread.

And on cool nights, which seemed evenly measured with those that were hot and dry, the residents of the Orbit stared in the direction of the screen, watched the shimmering images, quoted from the movies aloud as if praying in unison to Mecca, and did just a whole lot of fucking.

Along with all that movie watching, fucking had taken the place of good meals, intense conversation, and wondering what movie stars and rock stars were doing.

Yes sir, that fucking be helping something serious, brethren and sistern. It gave the drive-inders community as well as unwanted pregnancy and sometimes big red swellings. Fortunately, sexually transmitted diseases were not rampant, or the whole damn pack of them would have been full of it and sick of it and gone within a year. Whatever a year was in the drive-in and its surrounding jungle. Time was hard to measure. The sun seemed to rise and set on its own time scale. Sometimes the drive-in crowd sat in darkness, nothing to keep them going but the drive-in light, powered by who knows what from who knew where.

Not a happy series of communities, dear hearts. No, sir. There were strains at the seams. Always had been. True, they were no longer surrounded by a constant twenty-four hours of darkness and black goo that would eat you. That had long passed. And they had driven away from the drive-in only to find it at the end of the road again (bummer). They were in repeato situation, inside the drive-in fence, surrounded by daylight and night, sunlight and moonlight, and a big old jungle. Stuck in there, flimsily barricaded from the outside world. Trying to be safe. Wanting to be safe. Hoping to be safe.

But it wasn't safe. Dinosaurs and strange things roamed about and dotted the skies. Showed teeth. Showed claws. Sometimes they knocked down the fence and came in for a drive-in dinner. Jack and his people had learned to run the eaters off with spears of wood and car metal, fire-licked torches, rocks slung from slings made of shoe tongues and fan belts.

Even the water hole where they had to go for the wet stuff was a dangerous place. Critters waited there for them.

Finally great catapults made of jungle wood and twisted vines were fashioned and cocked and made ready behind and along the fence. Got loaded up with car transmissions and engines, old tires, batteries, anything worn out and real damn heavy.

Sometimes, when a person died (remember those eaters stacked by the fence, dear hearts?), they were catapulted into the jungle for the scavengers to take. It got so scavengers, smaller critters, lurked there all the time, in beg position, hoping for an offering. This dead-body launching was decided not to be a great idea. But burying was no good. Outside the drive-in they got dug up anyway, and inside . . . Well, the smell of the dead wasn't a good idea. Critters could smell them even if the gravel and asphalt were scraped back and they were buried way under. Once, after Jack and others slaved to bury a body beneath the asphalt, a great pterodactyl, beating its wings faster than a teenage boy can beat his meat, swept into the drive-in and clawed the body from the ground. A brave woman, some friend or relative, tried to protect the corpse, but the winged beast took her and the body away, one in each claw. Dinner and dessert.

In an unknown year, the Great Jack died, and the drive-in tribes divvied up, and the ones who had known Jack the best, the Yippie-Ki-Pussy tribe, struck off on their own.

Jack had founded the Yippie-Ki-Pussy tribe himself, after an especially flavorful event that involved the poking of two women. Upon emerging from the old bus, in which he now lived, his privates wet with sex, he yelled, "Yippie-Ki-Pussy."

This seemed like a good and humorous idea, and thereafter, the tribe, looking for some identifying name, called themselves the Yippie-Ki-Pussy tribe after their leader, Jack.

Jack, now there was a good looker. A fine specimen of manhood made of bones and a hank of hair, dressed in rags, the flappy remains of shoes on his feet. He walked fast. He looked like a tired and perhaps alcoholic Bozo the Clown coming into the center ring to do some stumbling trick.

But still, he was arresting, ole Jack was.

Yes, I am.

Well, there goes the third person, and here comes me, the first-person narrator. I can't keep me out of it. I should. But, hell, this is all about me and all about them, and that means it's all about us, but mostly, since I'm telling it all, writing it down, it's about, you guessed it . . .

Me.

I wanted to mention that me part again.

But now and then, when you're raving in a near hypoglycemic semi-comatose state, you want to stand back and leave the me, the I, the yourownself out of the picture.

You can't do it.

You think you can, but you can't.

No matter what you think, or try to think, or try to do, it's always about, guess who?

You.

Or, to be more exact. Me.

Me. Me. Me.

But I said that already. Hypoglycemic or not. It's always about me.

I'm merely telling you what Republicans already know. To hell with everyone else as long as I got mine.

What I'd give for a steak.

From a cow, of course.

Besides, hell, I didn't die. Everything I've written down so far, except the part about me dying, is the truth, no shit, as if there's anyone here to argue with me (well, there's myself, but I'm not up to it today).

Oh, all right. There's another part that's a lie. But we'll hold off on that and come at it a short time later.

I guess, I should confess to you, Oh Journal, Keeper of the Goddamn Truth, that maybe I wish I had died. I've thought about dying. You know. A do-it-yourself job, but, baby, it ain't in me.

I like living too much.

Even if you can't call this living, it's the excuse for living I'm living, and I don't know no other way to do than to keep on trucking.

Which brings up something.

Trucking.

Gonna be doin' me some.

Tomorrow (and I'll have to decide when tomorrow comes, 'cause, baby, in here, who really knows), but tomorrow there will be time to evaluate, lay some stock, and maybe some pipe if any female that isn't scary looking is willing! And with any volunteers I get! I'm jiving on out of here, bouncy-assin' in a big ole ride, headin' for—

—well, that part ought not to be discussed or considered or contemplated or too far planned.

Because, I'm not sure there's anywhere to go.

P.S.

I really didn't emerge from a bus after having banged two hot women with my snake flapping and my lips jackin' with, "Yippie-Ki-Pussy!"

But, I wish I had.

Actually, I complained of my back.

I avoid sex now.

Mostly.

I mean to anyway.

Sometimes you can make a woman pregnant and not know it. Not know if it was you, I mean. There are so many sharing in the festivities, you see. And then, if the women get pregnant, well, there are the babies.

And, of course, so many are eating their young, and though it has begun to have its appeal (so soft, so pink, so bakeable—though most go in for raw, as fire is difficult to create), we are trying to keep some semblance of civilization.

Or at least I am, goddamnit.

So, our declaration is simple.

No eating babies.

Raw, anyway.

Keep your top button buttoned.

And pee at the far end of the fence. Over where it already stinks.

2

That night (and it has been night for a long time, I am sure; well, pretty sure) it rained goo.

Black goo.

This was nothing different. It did this frequently. Most likely it was from the sewer dump deposited by whoever was in the heavens above.

Aliens, it was believed. Up there behind the night, behind the clouds, ass cracks perched for delivery.

Least that was my theory, backed up by certain events.

But I've written about those events already. Of the Popcorn King and the long road to nowhere, the dinosaurs, and Popalong Cassidy, of the beautiful Grace who took up with the goofball Steve (how could she even consider such after having such a manly stud muffin as myself?), and of poor Crier, dickless (actually, he carried it in his pocket) and dead, toted off and eaten, his dismembered dick as well. Perhaps the critter that got him used the dried up dick to pick his teeth. On this world, in this world, wherever this world was, you thought about things like that because you had a lot of time to think.

I sit here and think about the children born here, many of them fathered by the Popcorn King. They look like the Popcorn King. Two bodies welded together, one on the other's shoulders to make a single unit. Unlike the King, they are covered in eyes that look like the eyes that were on the corn the King threw up. Each eye blinks at a different time.

They are sexless. Smooth as Barbie dolls without the attractive build. No ass cracks either. Here's the scoop. They don't shit. They eat, but they don't shit. Their pores ooze something that substitutes for that. They stink, by the way. But, I suppose you have guessed that.

Whoever *you* is.

They used to be kind of sweet. As they've grown older, they've banded together. There are few left, actually. Most have gone off into the forest to survive on their own. When they reached what I suppose could be called adulthood, they lost interest in us.

A side note. They can move small things with their minds.

Creepy, baby.

Speaking of children,

I had one. Grace, who went off with Steve, she was carrying my child. Or so she said. The baby was born dead. Good thing, really. Steve and Grace ate it. Being the father and all, they offered me the placenta.

I passed.

I regret that now and again when I'm hungry.

But you have to draw the line somewhere.

Bad things. Bad past. Bad memories.

Oh, and my buddy Bob died. Just up and died. No reason that we could see. Maybe some kind of disease. Maybe a flawed heart. I don't know, but one day he's fine, and the next day, not so much. His body disappeared quickly. Rumor is, someone, or several someone's ate it. I may have been one of the ones. I don't know. Really. If I did such a thing, I've blocked it out. I liked Bob . . . I mean when he was alive. But, hey, you can get so hungry sometimes, and I'm sure if it had been me, he wouldn't have wanted me to go to waste.

So, I'm not saying I took a chew, but I'm not sayin' I didn't.

But enough of the bad memories.

There's always the new stuff to worry about.

I'd like to have less new stuff.

Jesus. I'd like to go home.

All this, it's one hell of a tale, my friends, a whale of tale, and a ho, ho, ho, and a bottle of rum, which I don't have. But, the writing. I got that. It helps me focus, except when it doesn't.

Course, my writing all this down is most likely a waste. Who will ever read any of it, anyway?

I'm sitting up watching *Chainsaw* like I might even like it. Sitting here in the driver's seat of the bus, my diary on the dash, me with a dying ink pen that has "Get Your Car Lubed at Willies" printed on it, writing to the light from the drive-in as flashed to me between plops of alien shit, or whatever it is. My left hand is in my pants, and I'm cupping my balls like they're a sweaty, hairy teddy bear. They comfort me.

But, I really think I will catch the rhythm of this stuff, the plopping of the shit I mean, and when I do (Listen to the Rhythm of the Falling Shit), I'll go to the back of the bus and lie down, and I'll really sleep, listening to the cadence of the falling crap, lulling me into slumber, pulling me happily down into the arms of Hypnos and Morpheus.

I read that in a book once, those sleepy gods of Greece.

Yeah, sleepy time, baby.

Really.

I hope.

I wonder about the bus I live in. I think about driving it down the single highway again, setting out once more, but what's the use?

I did that in another vehicle once.

It didn't work out.

I done said that. Shit. I'm so tired I don't know what I have said or haven't said, or even if I remember how to say it. I sometimes struggle with my letters. You know, like, which way do the B's bumps go? To the left or the right?

This place changes you. Doodles with your mind.

I'm going to go back and lie down now. Thinking about all this, my head is starting to hurt.

Please, Sleepy Time, come to me, oh sweet love. Open unto me and swallow me and hold me down in the deep dark and make me happy.

Or at least a little less miserable.

3

I awoke feeling like David Innes, a character from a novel I read by Edgar Rice Burroughs. I liked feeling like David Innes because he was strong and brave and true, all the things I wanted to be, and wasn't.

In the Burroughs book he lived at the center of the earth, and at the center of the earth there was eternal sunlight, the sun being a ball of lava or something, hanging at the top of their world, which was the center of the earth. So, this being the case, they never knew how much time passed since their sun did not move and there was no night.

Did they sleep eight hours?

Or eight years?

You never knew in Pellucidar.

(A side note which breaks my light and day and night and dark discussion, but shit, it's on my mind, so here it is:

Like here, in Pellucidar—way down there at the center of the world—you had to watch out for man-eating beasts. Consider this a reminder and another reason I can relate to good old David Innes.)

Back to how hard it is to know a true day from a false day, like in Pellucidar.

Something like that.

So, pick up with—

It felt the same here on the Drive-in World, where there were changes in light, but no measure of time. This is something that has become more and more confusing, as if some device is playing out, a fuse needs to be replaced or something.

And this is kind of scary (and what isn't here?), there's a sputtering from time to time, and suddenly there's no light (the films stop instantly), and it's dark and it's a dark beyond dark, it's so goddamn dark. Then someone pours some light that would never have been thought light before into the darkness, and what was so black it was beyond black, just becomes black. Just good old night's black.

(Hot damn. Glad to see it. Hands are visible there in the dark, shadows coiling between the gaps in the fingers when you hold your hand before your face, where before, you couldn't see your hand before your face.)

What if (that age-old question) the fuse does go and the light doesn't come back, and, well, here we are, nothing left but the sound of each other breathing, the touch of each other's hands, the sharing of lice, the sharing of fleas.

I think bad things would happen.

And, hey. What if the fuse kills the climate altogether and there's nothing but void?

V-O-I-D.

My take on that is it wouldn't be good.

But, as it stands now, you can start a fire and cook a meal, and the sun could rise and set and rise and set again before you finish your ration of dinosaur egg on some kind of gooey weed, or your fistful of grubs with a dirty root.

And next time you cook, the day or night seems to go on forever.

When it's night, there are the movies.

Films, as we intellectuals call them.

They show from the moment the darkness falls to the time it goes away. Throbbing light displaying horrible deeds, chainsaws, and power tools. Once I found it entertaining. I see too much real life in it now, even if it has become as familiar as the flat brown mole on the top of my dick. Well, maybe that mole is on the left side of the old cable. But, you know what I mean, Mr. Journal. Old Bitch Diary. Whatever you are, made up of composition notebooks and pages here and there and backs of envelopes and such, written in pencil and ink and crayon and charcoal and mascara, all wrapped up tight and stuffed in a knapsack found in the back seat of a car, next to the remains of a dead body.

Skeleton actually. Small. Some idiot took a child to see an all-night horror show. That skeleton wasn't entirely a skeleton. It was a body of rags, and the rags were flesh, the bulk of it having been ripped from the bones and eaten. The bones had been cracked open and the marrow sucked out, and it was no longer a horror to see that, and I knew, just a slight push, a slight change of the emotional weather inside my head, and I too would be snatching flesh and cracking bones, chewing up meat, sucking up marrow like chocolate sauce through a straw.

But the movies. There's no way to turn them off. We've thought about tearing down the screen, but frankly, we find this a scary idea. If the screen is gone and there are no movies, then, at night, there is very little light, depending on if the moon comes up (when it comes up some nights, we can hear what sounds like a crank, like someone is jacking it up from the horizon on chains and pulleys), and if it should cease to come up, if the machinery, which I think must be getting old up there behind that curtain of sky, should cease to work, then we will have no light at night, and in this place, no light, that's scary, baby.

I mean, what if the light never comes again? And here we sit. In darkness. The occasional fire, but mostly, darkness.

Not good.

And there are the sounds.

Wouldn't want to lose them.

I have become accustomed to the screams and yells and stupid dialogue from all the films.

They are like a mama's lullaby at night.

If they cease to play and cease to light and cease to sound, there is only emptiness. And ourselves. And all that we have done, nestled in the backs of our minds, moving around to the front. Most of those memories are bad. Being completely inside yourself without outside sounds and interference, that is very hard for the very weak, and that be us, baby. The very weak.

Did I mention the dark?

I did, didn't I?

It's on my mind. The darkness.

Now that I think about it, except for that part about not knowing how long I've slept, I don't feel that much like David Innes at all. I'm not only weak, I'm always scared shitless.

But let's talk about the bus.

If I can focus on the bus, get something to eat soon, maybe I'll be all right. As is, I'm rambling, I'm free associating, I'm all over the place, and if I'm not careful, I'll once again talk about the dark.

I need to pee. And shall, out by the drive-in fence, in that special spot where the aroma of a zillion pees rises up and overwhelms and bullies and makes one hasten the act. But, hey, it ain't nothing compared to a little farther down at what we call the Shittin' Section. Now there's some smelly business . . .

The bus.

The bus.

Focus, Jack.

The bus.

Will it run?

It starts. It runs. But will it run great distances?

Must pee.

4 I've peed. I've eaten. Had some boiled fruit. I had to go outside the drive-in, in the jungle, to pick it, and I was scared, doing it by moonlight, but I was more hungry than I was scared. I brought back a stick with the fruit. I wrapped the fruit in my ragged shirt and tied it to the stick and toted it back that way. Later I put the stick in the community fire and got it ablaze, came back to my bus, and using wood I had carried from the jungle and stored in the bus, I boiled water in a hubcap—the water taken from the community water—put the fruit in the hubcap and cooked it down and made a kind of goo, ate it with my fingers, which I burned. It gave me strength (fruit power, baby), and now I feel better. Less hypoglycemic. More organized.

But my fingers hurt.

Now, here are my plans. I write this feeling better, less loopy. I can write now without feeling like the script itself will come off of the page and dance.

This is what I am going to do:

There is a trail that leads into the woods. An animal trail. It's fairly wide. It has to be to accommodate dinosaurs.

Once, while hunting down the trail, looking for something weak, looking for eggs or edible roots, me and Steve and a couple of the boys, as we call the "Popcorn Kids," came across—now get this—

—a school bus.

That's right.

Just off the trail, parked between two great trees, out there in the weeds. Vines had grown around the tires and twisted up under it and through cracks and under the hood. The vines held it tight to the ground like they owned it.

There were other things around as well, all of them just as inexplicable. A large pontoon boat. A World War II plane, not to mention a Confederate flag on a flagpole, just stuck up in the dirt, and lying about, a bunch of beer cans, a pack of rubbers, and some cigarette butts.

Above, in the sky where a break in the trees let us see it, was a great funnel.

No shit.

The small end of it dipped down out of the sky, and the rest of it flared wide and gray and up into the heavens, and all we could figure was the bus and all the other stuff had come down that great funnel, come to rest here in the jungle.

I've thought on it a lot, but I've never come up with any explanation that satisfies, but then again, this world is full of unsatisfactory questions and few if any revelations.

But, anyway, we found this bus, and we came across the bus many times after that on our treks, and finally we managed the door open, and began using it for storage. It was a pretty good place to hide from critters chasing us, as well. A kind of halfway station. We got the front door to work and the back door to work, and one day, just for fun, I turned the key, which was in the engine, and—

—it started.

No shit.

Fired right up.

The gas gauge rocked forward. A near full tank.

Like everything here, it didn't make sense.

Where did it come from?

Had it come another time?

Who had been in it?

Kids on their way to school?

A band trip?

Football team on its way to or back from a game?

We didn't know.

Over the next few . . . days? weeks? months? years? . . . Steve and I, and a couple of others, have been working to free it of the vines. The tires are all flat, blown out and ripped up to be exact, and the bus looks to have run on the rims, driving like crazy, pursued by . . . who knows what?

That comet that sucked it in?

Giant aliens with tweezers, ready to grab hold of it and fling it down the funnel?

Who knows?

But there were a few tires on a few vehicles in the drive-in lot that fit, so we jacked it up and loaded it down with rubber, and, with handmade bellows and the remains of a bicycle pump, we inflated the tires.

One day, I drove it back to the drive-in, and they opened the great barrier we had made at the fore of the place, and I steered it inside. I closed it off, began living in it.

So when I determine tomorrow has come (keeping in mind I say this often), I am going to drive out of here in my sacred little home.

Not down the highway, but down the trail where the bus was discovered, just drive off into a new mystery.

And perhaps a short existence.

It has to beat this.

THE THIRD FEATURE BEGINS

"On the road again. I'm so happy to be on the road again . . ."

—Willie Nelson

Part One

TRUCKIN', BABY

In which Jack and friends venture out into the great world which turns wet, and they see strange beasts in the shadows, an odd ghost, and, in the distance, shiny in the sunlight, the stairway to heaven. Maybe.

1

And so the sun came up, and I called it tomorrow. I hitched up my mind and my resolve, and I said to myself, Self, I'm driving out of here.

Today, baby, is the day.

So I went to Grace and Steve, and I said, "I'm leaving."

"Yeah," Steve said. "Hunting. Foraging?"

"Leaving," I said.

Grace, long and lean and beautiful, and quite naked, stood up and stretched (I could smell that they had been sexin' it up), and said, "You asking us to go?"

"I'm telling you I'm going, and you want to go you can. It's up to you. There's a couple others I'm gonna ask, and then I'm gonna go, without folks or with folks."

"We have been here a long time," Grace said. "I think. I really don't know. But it seems like we have. Shit, I say we go, Steve."

Steve nodded. "Beats nailing your dick to a two-by-four."

The day was as bright as a rich man's day, and I had all the world before me.

Such as it was.

Stuffed with dinosaurs and monsters and strangeness.

But, I didn't want to think about that.

The sun was bright. The trail was clear.

So, what we did was this: We found a few others who wanted to go. Most were afraid to go. Afraid if they got away from the drive-in with its relative protection, they would surely be on their own.

It was amazing. Once they had all been mostly young partygoers out for a weekend night at a four-screened drive-in, and now they called it home. And didn't want to leave. Did not want to go out into the world with a New Big Bad Wolf, but wanted to stay with the Wolf They Knew.

I guess it was best to have only a few with us. Less to worry about. Fewer personalities to mess with.

Me, I wanted to go to my real home.

Didn't know how.

Didn't know if I could.

But I had to find out.

We managed to take a gas tank out of a car with tools found in the trunk of another car, and we put that tank in the bus, filled it with gas we siphoned from vehicles, and we corked the spare tank with a wooden plug, as the exterior screw-on cap had been long lost, and we put it in the back of the bus for reserve. We put some fruit back there, as well. Steve and Grace had some meat that wasn't too rancid (dead critter found in the forest the day before, ants part of the treat), some water in gourd containers, a few odds and ends, and then we gave each other our best wishes and were off.

Or we would have been, but Steve came up with an idea.

"If we're gonna be traveling about, and we don't even know where we're going, I think we ought to be prepared."

"We got fruit and a dead thing we can eat. If we don't wait a long time."

This was from a guy named, and I shit thee not, Homer.

He was one of our volunteers. He looked like what you thought a Homer ought to look like. Kind of tall and lean and goofy with hair the color of watered-down shit that fled over his head in good patches, but showed through in spots and was as shiny there as a dog-licked dinner plate.

"Right you are, Homer," Steve said, "but that stuff will run out. We'll need new food."

"I knew that," Homer said. "You think I didn't know that?"

"I know you do, but what I'm talking is strapping them goddamn pontoons on either side of the bus, and if we need to float across a river, we can do it. I think, if we work on the backdoor window, we can fix it so we can take it out when we want. And we can make a rudder, stick it out the window there, and though we can't motor this baby across a river, maybe we could guide it some."

"It's a thought," I said.

"Hell, it's a good idea," Steve said.

We spent another day transferring the pontoons to the bus and making the rudder. We rigged the glass on the back door so we could take it in and out; rigged it so we could poke out the rudder and hook it on the window frame with some wire Steve found somewhere in the drive-in. Steve also rigged us up a tape player and we took tapes from all the cars we could find, except for Barry Manilow or similar shit, and then we were ready to go.

We put the box of tools inside, and just before we were to leave, a young woman came up the trail. She was short and pretty nice looking, or would have been, had her clothes not been made of an animal hide with a hole cut in it, draped over her head and cinched up with an old belt. It might have helped too if her hair had been clean and she wasn't so scratched up on the legs, and she hadn't had a look in her eye that made you think maybe she could see something just to the left of her nose no one else could see.

She was carrying a pack made of an animal skin. Wild dog. The head was still on the pack, and so was the tail, which she had turned into a kind of strap.

She said, "I want to go, too. I brought some dried meat and some dried fruit. I dried them good on the roof of my car. They're a little chewy, and the fruit has got some bugs in it, but they make it a little tastier."

"Protein is good," Grace said.

Grace, who today was wearing clothes (more of a bikini, really) made of animal hides, looked marvelous. Considering the rest of us all looked like scarecrows, I don't know how she did it. But she wore those skins great, like Raquel Welch in that movie, *One Million Years B.C.* Her hair was as shiny as the chrome on a brand new motorcycle, and that came from the fact she wasn't afraid to go down to the river out back of the drive-in and bathe and wash her hair, and use some kind of weed that if rubbed together made a pretty good excuse for soap. Her hair was all combed out too, was real long, and when she moved, it moved, flowed around her, and was the color of scorched honey.

Looking at her, dressed like that, I thought about the time me and her hooked up, and right then I was thinking on how I'd like to do the trailer hitch thing again, and damn if she didn't look at me and catch my eye, and give me a kind of grin, like, you know, you done had yours, and I pitied you, and it's probably the best pussy, if not the only pussy you ever had, so you best think back on it a lot, 'cause it's not a repeater, if you know what I mean.

I got all that out of that little smile.

I smiled back, kind of a thank you, ma'am. Ain't nothing else I'd rather have had, and in fact, it is my favorite present to date, and in memory sense, it's a gift that keeps on giving. Then she turned away, and the old bad world came back, and there was Reba, looking at me like a dog confused by language.

"What's your name?" I asked her, my mind still on Grace, fearing my thoughts would show on my forehead, or that she might notice my pecker had moved to the left of my worn pants, as if in search of prey.

"Reba."

There were also James and Cory. They were buddies. Good ole boys meet Heavy Metal types. Cory was bulky. James was wiry. Cory said he wished we had some Black Sabbath cassettes.

Steve said it was a shame we didn't. But he didn't mean it.

When we were ready, I, as tour guide, I suppose, said to everyone: "Well, climb on in, and let's shag ass on out of here."

2

The trail was as bumpy as a teenager's face, and there were places where there didn't seem to be any trail at all.

The woods, or jungle to be more accurate, grew thick on both sides, and the vines wound in amongst the trees, and things moved out there. Sometimes we saw them, sometimes they watched us, and sometimes it was just shadows, falling between the trees, but fostered by nothing we could see.

There were lots of sounds. Cries and strangles, barks and growls, grunts and groans, and once, I thought I heard a fart.

I read a story once, a funny story, and I don't remember who wrote it or what it was, but it had a line in it that I remember. It went: Somewhere, a toad farted ominously.

Out here, bumping along the trail, that kind of thing didn't seem so funny anymore.

That fart from the bushes—larger than a toad, I might add—did seem ominous.

Hell, the wind, which had picked up our first day out (I call it a day because the sun went down and came up again), picked up even more, and it whistled through the jungle and shook the limbs and leaves and vines like dry peanut husks.

We drove and drove, and finally stopped so that we might take a bathroom break.

The seven of us hadn't spoken much, had just bumped along, trying to figure on what the hell we were doing, but now, we began to talk.

There was me and Grace and Steve and Homer and Reba and the two rednecks, James and Cory. James talked about beer a lot, about how he'd like to have some, and about how he had brewed some from fruit, but it had just tasted like nasty fruit, and what he'd give for a Budweiser, that sort of thing. Cory was quiet, didn't say much, except, "I got to go take a shit," and wandered off into the jungle to do just that.

Grace and Steve seemed to have handled this whole lost in another world thing better than anyone else.

I think that's because they had each other.

I don't know if they loved one another, but they had each other, and it seemed to be working. It kept some bloom on the rose, especially on Grace's rose, 'cause like I said, she was the only one amongst us who looked fresh. Steve looked okay, though he had recently lost a tooth on the left side of his mouth, and if he grinned real big, you could see the gap.

"I get the creepy feeling," Steve said, as we sat around, cooking up some of the dead animal he and Grace had brought, listening to the ants pop in the fire that we had stoked with flint and steel and bits of tinder, "that somethin' is followin' us."

"Something always is," I said. "You can count on it. If it isn't following us, it's running ahead. There's things in the jungle. Both sides. I can feel eyes all over me."

"I don't mean like that," Steve said. "Something weird even for here."

"Considering the Popcorn King," Reba said, "I don't know how weird it could get. I ate some of his popcorn, and shit eyeballs, I did. I had a kid too. He was stolen from me and eaten. He was eaten raw. The savages. I guess it was for the best. I really didn't want a kid covered in eyeballs."

The maternal instinct is a lovely thing.

"Well," Homer said, "long as we're talking weird, how's about them dinosaurs and such?"

"And Popalong Cassidy," I said.

"I ain't saying this ain't the warehouse for weird," Steve said, "just saying I been having this feeling something is following us that I don't want to have catch up with us."

"That could still be most anything," I said.

"I was out with this fella that came to the drive-in with me," Cory said. "Out with him looking for food, and no shit, he bent over and a little dinosaur rammed a dick through his cloth pants and got him some ass, and while he was gettin' it, he bit my buddy's head off. Blood went everywhere, and if that wasn't bad enough, the dinosaur jerked, sprang around in happy circles, shooting his jism all over the place. I got some in my hair. I figured I was next to get butt-fucked and ate up, so I hooked ass to a tree and climbed it. And damn if that critter didn't scuttle up after me. He was small enough for that. So, I kept climbing, and finally I got to the damn near top of that tree, where it was thin and starting to bend, and I was thinking, well, it's either jump and get it over with, or get eaten while up in a goddamn tree, and maybe butt-fucked—though I couldn't see that critter doing that while balancing on a limb—and damned if that critter didn't miss his footing. Fell. Killed his ownself. When I got down he was lying in a puddle of blood and shit. I cut a big portion of meat out of him and took it home. I would have took my buddy home, but something had already dragged him off. Now, tell me that isn't weird."

"We've all seen shit like that, or sort of like that," Steve said. "Though, the butt-fucking and head-eating simultaneously is high on the Holy Shit meter, but I mean something else. I've started having me some visions."

"None of them have come true, by the way," Grace said.

"Maybe they just haven't had time, dear," Steve said.

"Or maybe," Grace said, "you're full of shit."

"I suppose it's possible," Steve said. "I always have been pretty full of it. But, I tell you, I've got me a feeling, and it's not a feeling I like."

"Is it a feeling or a vision?" James said. "If you just feel it, it could be the flu."

"It's a feeling," Steve said, "but it isn't any kind of flu."

"It's probably this meat," Homer said, pulling a piece on a stick from the fire. "It's just two degrees short of having gone full south. The ants on it are fresher than the meat."

"You don't have to eat it," Steve said.

"Actually," Homer said, "I do. There ain't that much we got to eat, and this has to go first. Then it's the dried stuff."

"Maybe we'll come across a grocery store," Reba said. "Seems like this place has got everything else. School buses. Pontoon boats and an airplane."

We ate, and finally Cory came back from the woods.

He said, "Hope I didn't wipe on nothing that might give my ass a rash. I picked me some big leaves, and one of them started crawling off. I was glad I wasn't wiping with it when it started to crawl."

"We're all glad your ass is clean," Steve said, "now, much as I hate to mention it, we got food, but you don't touch the meat outright. I'll put it on a stick for you, and you cook your own."

"I could tear it off with my right hand," Cory said. "I wiped with my left."

"Use the stick," we all said.

3

When eating was done, and everyone else's bathroom needs were attended to, we all packed in the bus and set out, the Big Boys blasting on the tape deck. We hadn't gone far when it grew dark as an oil slick inside of a coal mine at midnight.

What I'm trying to tell you, dear hearts, is it was dark.

Steve, who was driving, turned off the music, turned on the lights, and we eased on slowly. I saw several things—I know no other way to describe them other than to say they were things—rush out of the jungle and cross the road.

I didn't know how safe we really were, but it made me feel better to be in that big bus, and not out there on foot. Maybe, most likely, there were plenty of beasts who could peel us out of the bus like sardines from a can, but it gave me a greater feeling of security to be inside something big and metal that could move.

To top things off, it began to rain.

It came down in little drops at first, seemed it would pass. But then the wind picked up, and so did the rain.

It was a strong wind, and it rocked the bus. Soon water was flowing across the trail in dark rivers. The trail went down, dipped into the jungle, water rode up about halfway over the tires.

"I don't think it's such a good idea to go farther," Steve said, leaning forward over the steering wheel, trying to peer into the darkness, attempting to see what was before us in the light of the two pale head beams.

All that was visible was stygian water flowing through the jungle, washing hard against the bus.

"Turn it around," Homer said.

"I don't know," Steve said. "We done got kind of committed here. The trail's small for that, and it being so wet and all, we try, we might get stuck. "

"Then what's the alternative?" Grace asked. "If we keep going forward, we could get washed off the road."

"I guess I could try and back it out, but them tail lights ain't much in this rain and dark. Inflamed hemorrhoids would give more light."

"I'll go to the back window and look out, be your guide—"

"Hey, what about the pontoons?" Reba said.

"Damn," Steve said. "I forgot they were on the bus."

"And it was your idea," Grace said.

"I'm lucky these days," Steve said, "if I can remember to shit out of my asshole and piss out of my dick. Sometimes I get kind of confused on which hole is which."

"That doesn't happen much in the middle of the night when you're sortin' my holes out," Grace said.

"You can say that again, baby."

Steve jerked the bus in gear, and we sat. "Look here," he said, "the water picks us up, and we can't control things, it could wash us into the trees. I think backing is still the best thing."

"All right," I said. "We'll do it that way."

I went to the back of the bus, and Steve put it in reverse, started gassing the vehicle into retreat mode. We had gone about a dozen feet, slipping a bit on the mud, when suddenly there was a sound like someone had stuck a water hose in my ear and turned it on. Out of the jungle came a dark rush of wet, and I do mean wet, baby. It hit the right side of the bus and knocked it into the trees on the other side, and kept washing against us. The bus hung up in the trees, limbs wrapped around it like arms.

The water spurted in through the closed windows, finding every weak spot imaginable. Pretty soon it was all over the bus.

I could feel water vibrating under us, lifting us, and pretty soon it toted us up and out of the tree where we had gotten hung up, and shoved us down the trail in a rush.

"This ain't good," Steve said.

The bus floated down the trail, banging against trees. I feared the pontoons would get knocked off. But just when I thought it was all over but the drowning, we were lifted up, and we began to flow fast downhill.

All of us were now seated, hanging onto the seat in front of us, and through the windshield, in those weak head beams, we could see the dark flow of water. The bus dipped down, and it looked as if we would be lost, down there at the bottom of the rush, somewhere deep in the jungle, waiting for the water to subside so crawdads or some such could eat on us. Then, suddenly, we rode up on a wave and were floating evenly on top of the gushing darkness, sailing down the corridor between the trees at about the rate of a goddamn speeding bullet.

"I think I saw a big bird in the water," said Cory.

"No," Steve said, "that there is a big stick. A goddamn log, if you want to get technical. I figure it'll hang up under the bus, and maybe fuck something up under there."

"Quit thinking negative waves," Grace said. "We're in a flash flood, and I don't know about you, but it's my first, and I'm trying to enjoy it."

"Yeah," Cory said, "and it's wet outside and dark, and we might drown. And the fun just keeps on coming."

4

We were carried along in the dark like that for a good piece. It went on so long, I finally drifted off, first leaning forward on the seat in front of me, and finally lying down in the seat.

You wouldn't think with something like that going on, you could sleep, but the truth was, you could. Or at least I could, and I was doing me a good piece of that when I was yelled awake by Grace.

"Water's rushing harder," she said.

"What?"

She repeated herself, and I sat up.

"Do what now?"

"We got to put out the rudder, we need some guidance, we're gonna smash up. We're trying to turn sideways."

I hurried to the back, slipped out the rigged window, and got the rudder. I had James take hold of it with me, and we stuck it out.

When it hit the water, it was like hitting cement. The rudder rode up, and the end we were holding hit James under the chin. He was knocked unconscious, and crumpled to the floor.

I screamed for help. Cory, Reba, and Homer all leaped forward, grabbed at the rudder. We tussled with it, and it fought us. But we held on and went along like that for a bit, then the water got reinforcements. Probably some high place got overrun and gave up its water, 'cause it came down through the jungle in a blast of dark bully wetness, and that rudder, it snapped like a toothpick.

When it did, we were all knocked loose and thrown to the floor or into bus seats.

I think I yelled something about Mama, and the next think I knew the bus dipped down, and we plunged into the rushing wet; it pounded over the windshield, and there was water on either side of us, up to the side windows. Some of it (too goddamn much of it) spurted inside. Then, as if some kind of a miracle took hold, the bus was pushed upward by an undercurrent. It shot up into the night like a goddamn porpoise, came down on its pontoons, and was shoved along down the trail, which now, to complicate matters, had begun to wind about like it had been laid out by a cross-eyed drunk with inefficient tools.

But things started turning for the good. The water slowed, and we were flowing along comfortably now, dead center of the trail, winding around those dark jungle curves like we were driving.

And Steve was pretending to drive. He had long cut the motor and lights, but he held to the wheel, which, due to the force of the water on the tires, he couldn't turn anyway. I reckon it made him feel as if he were in control, clutching like that, leaning forward like he could drive on this watery highway, when, actually, all he could do was do what any two-year-old in a car seat with a plastic steering wheel and a horn could do.

Pretend.

And honk the horn.

Actually, with the engine turned off, he couldn't do that, but he managed to make some very convincing honky noises.

Several times.

And then an amazing thing happened. The trees on either side of us grew short. In time they disappeared. Were covered by water. The rain was gone, and there were no clouds, just this great, strange moon above us, and this other moon—the reflection of the one in the sky lying on the water like a big old silver serving platter, minus meat, minus taters, just lying there, waiting for Mom to pile it up.

Before us, or at least as far as our eyes could see in the moonlight, was water.

Water . . . water . . . water.

Sail on, sail on, sail on.

5

One of the tapes we had was a classical one. Steve started up the engine, and we played that, listened to Moonlight Sonata and such, and finally I fell asleep.

As a defense against reality I have learned to snooze under pretty dire circumstances. Had to learn how. Or, considering the events of my life, I would have never slept. I have learned to sleep very deep. Down there in the bowl, with dreams, of course, but not so many as before. Least not that I remember, unless it is a good one (usually a lie or something good long past). The bad dreams I try to forget.

That doesn't always work.

So it was that I awoke, there in the darkness, fearing it would be one of those times when the night went on forever, or when maybe my dream-shit filter was on the goof, and might in fact be clinging to the nasty remnants of an unforgiving dream, or a truth tied up in a dream, a bad memory wrapped in the sack of a nightmare.

But no. Nothing clung to me.

It was quiet in the bus. The music had long been turned off, and so had the engine, and Steve was asleep against the steering wheel. Grace had stretched out on a seat, and everyone else was asleep as well. The bus bobbed up and down on the water, but the pontoons held, and I could hear and feel the water wash up against the side of the bus.

The moonlight had turned very bright, and it glistened on the water and made it shiny as a poor man's suit. There in the moonlight, I got a good look at Reba's face. I couldn't see the dirt so much in that light, and she looked pretty good.

Of course, it might have been like they say, they all look better at closing time, or in my case, near-dying time. But she did look good to me, and I watched her sleep for a long time, and I had some fantasies, all of them nasty, and I liked how her chest rose up and down, and the way she lay there, her legs drawn up, her hands tucked between her thighs, smiling. Maybe she too was thinking of something good, though most likely it wasn't me.

Perhaps she had just finished practicing the maiden and widows dance of fingers, and it had thrown her free of bad associations, knocked her out of the dark and into soft light where she could sleep and savor some good emotions and feel all right.

I hoped so. We all deserved to feel all right.

When I looked up and out at the water, it was still calm out there, and daylight was starting to seep into things, covering up the pearly edge of the sky, turning it rosy, and though it was still a bit chilly, I felt that the air had warmed.

Not too far out on the waxy-looking surface of the water with its little waves, I saw a dark fin break the surface. It was huge. It cruised for a bit, then dove out of sight, and there were wide ripples for a long time before the water went smooth again, and when it went smooth it was completely smooth, like a fresh-buffed floor.

No ripples. No waves. Just the morning sun on water, making it pink and proud as the nipple of a fine girl's tittie.

6

The day did not come off hot, but it came off warm, and we worked the windows down so we could catch a breeze.

We still couldn't see land, not even a dark line of trees. Just all that water. And I thought: we could float here until all our food played out. Just float here until we were all dead in our floating bus coffin.

I have never liked great expanses of deep water, and at that moment in time, I liked them even less, and this particular section of water I hated even more.

We ate some of the meat and some of the fruit. The raw meat that Steve and Grace had brought on board we had cooked up completely at last stop, and now we ate that and some of the fruit. We decided we should eat all the meat, because it was going to turn bad soon, and we best have our bellies full of it, lest we get hungry and decide to eat it when we shouldn't.

Though, I figured if we were starving, it didn't really matter much. It might be better to die of a belly full of rank meat than have your belly chew on itself until you were dead.

Course, neither were appealing alternatives.

Some water splashed up at the bottom edge of the door and came inside, but the pontoons held us up pretty good, so it was no biggie. I figured if this body of water, this great lake, this sea, this whatever it was, ever grew stormy, we would be up shit ocean without a paddle. Enough water could wash in to sink us like a stone.

I wondered what all was down there, in the deeps. Other dead folks from the drive-in. That great fish and all his companions, down there in the deep dark wetness.

It gave me the goddamn willies just thinking about it.

Steve managed to slip his body out of one of the windows, and by rocking the bus only a little, he climbed on top and looked around.

He lay over the edge of the bus and yelled back through a window.

"Nothing but water."

"Well, I didn't think a few feet up was gonna cause him to see land," Homer said.

"No," Cory said, "but it would have been nice."

We had a stick with us, and we tied a pan on that and stuck it in the water and pulled some of it in. I tasted it. It wasn't salty.

"Well, I don't know how clean it is," I said. "I mean, it don't taste bad, and it isn't salty. We can drink."

"Parasites could be all in it," Reba said.

"We could boil it," Grace said.

"We got to make a fire," Reba said.

"We could build a small one right there on the floor. Maybe tear out some seat cushions and burn them. Open the windows and they'll work like a chimney."

"When we're all out of seat cushions?" Reba asked.

"Then we drink it straight," Grace said.

"Hell, I think I'd take my chances drinking it straight right off," James said, "rather that than build a fire in the bus. Besides, them seats are pretty comfortable. Comfort might be a thing. We could drink the water out there when we run out, shit out the window after we drink. Maybe get some kind of rig to catch some fish. Back home, in the Sabine, I used to catch little fish with a line and a hook and a sinker and a colored piece of cloth. You got to be good, and you got to know how to pull that hook just right when they grab the cloth, but it could be done."

"We could be like that Flying Dutchman," Reba said. "I read about him in school. We could eat and sleep and drink and shit and just be here on this bus until we died of some kind of disease or old age."

"Damn," James said. "That's a creepy thing to think about. Think I'd rather slip off in that water and drown than sail on forever, or until I just naturally died."

"A natural death don't seem likely," Reba said.

We heard Steve calling.

"Look," he was saying. "Look over there."

When he made clear where over there was, we looked.

It was an amazing sight.

7

Way in the distance was a great ladder, or rather a bridge. I mean it was huge, like the goddamn Golden Gate Bridge. It was silver, and at its bottom there was a cloud of mist, so you couldn't see to what it was attached, but it rose up high and shiny and chromey, rose up and went up into the sky and into the thick white clouds that surrounded it at the top like shaving cream.

You couldn't tell where it began or where it ended, but it was wide, and though similar to the Golden Gate, instead of stretching across something, it was rising from somewhere at a slant, going up, disappearing into some place unseen.

"Well, I'll be goddamned," Homer said.

"I wonder how far away it is?" Cory asked.

"Hard to say," I said. "Out here, on this big piece of water, it could be close, or it could be way far away. You can't really judge how big this water is, so that bridge—ladder— it could be close and small, or far away and huge."

"I can tell you one thing," Grace said. "It ain't real close. It's big. I get the impression that it's goddamn big."

"How can you tell?" Reba said.

"Well, I guess I can't. But I'll bet you. If I had something to bet."

"You got something to bet all right," Homer said.

"So do you. You bet against me, I'll kick your goddamn nuts off," Grace said.

"Let me think on it," Homer said, "and I'll get back to you."

"But what is it?" James asked. "Where does it lead?"

"Heaven," Homer said. "That bridge leads to heaven. It has to, 'cause everything down here has got to be hell. And look how shiny and pretty it is. God would want a shiny bridge."

"There isn't any god," Grace said. "It's just us and whatever is behind all this."

"Well, that's god-like enough," Cory said. "'Cause something is sure strange, and I don't think it's government work. Not all this."

"Aliens," I said. "I know that's what it is."

"Well, whatever it is," Homer said, "there it is, shiny as a metal tooth."

"We seem to be drifting in that direction," Grace said. "Very slowly. Current stays with us, we'll know soon enough how close or how far away it is."

"It's some kind of place we can want to be," Reba said. "I don't know it will be good if we get there, but I like a goal, some kind of place to go. I haven't had a goal since I tried to get Phil Senate to fuck me, and he turned out to be queer. That wasn't a goal I made, getting a mercy fuck from a queer, so I had to let it go. So I'm going to make a pretty modest goal now. I hope we wash up at the bottom of the bridge, and that we get to climb it, and that it leads somewhere where someone would want to be. There's got to be some place here that's some place someone would want to be. There's just got to be."

"Sounds like a plan," I said.

Grace was right. We weren't even close to the bridge.

We drifted for a long time. Nights and days, half nights and half days and fragment days went by, and though we flowed with a current that carried us in the direction of the bridge, it was a slow current, and I noted little if any progress.

No land appeared either. There was just that great shimmering water all about.

But one evening, the day fell, and the moon came up, cool on the horizon, like a blonde-headed giant poking its head out of the water. And shortly after its rise came a mist.

There was something odd about it, and as it came to rest behind the bus and float there, we saw (for everyone had moved to the back of the bus) that it was not a mist at all.

It was a specter.

It took us a bit of time to really see what we were seeing, as it was so large. It was a ghostly outline of the drive-in lots, and we could see gray versions of the screens, the shapes of cars, and there were spectral folks moving about. I recognized them as the drive-in people. They were going from car to car, and the specters looked happy. Slowly but surely I realized why.

The mist was a specter of the drive-in all right, but it was as the drive-in had been before the comet, the great red comet that had come burning out of the sky, hung over the drive-in, and smiled.

Showed teeth, baby, that's what I'm trying to tell you.

And this was as the drive-in was, just before the comet swerved away, changed the drive-in and all of us inside forever. This was the drive-in when it was a fun place, a gathering place, a ritual shrine to the youthful. There were women in bikinis, and there were folks in monster suits, barbecue grills cooking away. Everyone looked so happy in the misty drive-in world, you could almost hear them laugh.

We all watched carefully, not a one of us speaking. Just stood there and looked out the back bus window, glared into our past.

I saw the lot where my friends and I had parked, and there we were, poking one another, laughing.

Oh, Jesus. All my friends.

Gone now.

Just me left.

"Ain't that some shit," Homer said. "It's a haunting."

8

I don't know how long we stood at the back of the bus, watching, but I know it was a long time. I felt sad. Tears kept running out of my eyes, and when I looked around, I wasn't the only one. Only Grace still had it together, centered inside somehow, and maybe, just maybe (because it had occurred to me more than once) she was in her element now. Strong and needed, lusted after and feared. A kind of shiny queen bee in a hive of colorless drones.

But I didn't think on that long. I turned away from Grace and kept on looking at that ghostly drive-in.

In that spectral world we all looked so happy, and healthy. And though we had not aged in any classical way, here in the present drive-in world, we had, to put it mildly, gone to seed. It was obvious looking at our ghostly shapes. Even in their transparent grayness, they looked so much better than we looked now.

Again . . . except for Grace. Still strong and clean of limb, with hair like a shampoo commercial.

So there we were, looking grimly back into our past. And as we watched, a gray version of the great red comet appeared at the top of the misty ghost of the drive-in, smiled, and things went bad.

I realized I could stand there forever, watching our past lives unfold.

I said, "You know what, gang. I don't think this is healthy. The past is the past."

"Besides," Steve said. "This story seems to have gotten to the bad part. We've seen all the good we're going to see."

"I can see myself," Reba said, pointing.

"We all can," James said.

And this was true. The spectral shape twisted and misted and reformed, and showed different parts of the drive-in, like cuts in a movie. Faces. Close-ups.

Medium shots. Long-distance shots. Dissolves. Fade-ins. Fade-outs.

"Something is fucking with us," I said. "Something has always been fucking with us."

We all made a deal to stop looking at the misty drive-in.

As much as we could stop looking, that is.

We still looked. Just not as much. I just looked now and then when I didn't have anything else to occupy my mind.

Which, of course, was all the time.

It was a little easier to stop looking when the misty events moved forward in time and showed me the horrible things that had gone on, back when the food first ran out and there was nowhere to go and everyone was so hungry. I knew the Popcorn King and his horrid activities, the blood corn events, were coming up, and that helped me not look. I didn't want to see that. I had lived that, and I hadn't liked it much.

So, I quit looking.

As often.

As the night passed and we dozed and the sun came up and the light that was our day wore on and became really hot, the mist evaporated, and we had a break. There was just the ocean now, and it was flat and smooth, as boring as watching your mama peel potatoes.

We ate and climbed on the roof and swam around the bus, hung to the pontoons, did this and that. Made up games, sang songs.

It was like a real bus trip.

You know, like when you're a kid and you go to camp, and you got songs to sing and things to talk about. Only thing missing is we didn't know where we were going or when we would arrive.

Actually, a lot of things were missing, but for that short time, we found some happiness, and we concentrated on it.

When we wore out on the songs, Steve started up the engine from time to time and we listened to tapes. What we had to talk about would always turn grim. Tales of the drive-in. So doing things like songs and swimming was better.

The swimming was really pretty nifty, because all of us stripped naked to do it. Grace was dynamite. I loved that triangle between her legs, how it looked when she climbed out of the water, stretched out on the pontoon, knowing full well we were all looking, perched atop the bus, hanging over the sides, drooling. She shook out her long golden hair and arched her back, showed us what lay inside the taco, all pink and inviting. A smorgasbord of goddess.

And let me tell you, Reba looked good too. Tiny, ribs showing from lack of food, well built, and more modest. She stripped and stood on the pontoon too, but she wasn't trying to give us an aerial view of the canyon, so to speak.

She just did what she had to do, shook out her shorter, darker hair, pulled back on her clothes, climbed on top of the bus, lay in the sun, and dried herself and the damp clothes she wore.

Steve lay with us, hanging over the roof looking down at Grace, and he said, "Grace is such a tease."

Homer said, "You know, I wouldn't ask this in the real world, and you may hit me, but you got to understand, what I'm seeing there, and not having had any in awhile, 'cept this fella's butt hole (pointing toward Cory, who raised his hand in admission), but it wasn't the same, you know, so can you tell me, for entertainment's sake. Is she good?"

Steve pursed his lips, made a kind of smacking sound, looked at Homer, smiled, said, "Now, let me ask you this, Homer, my man. Looking down on that young woman, all ripe and spread out and brown, and being all uninhibited like, and you having had, at best of recent, some shitty ass off Cory, what the fuck do you think?"

"Oh, yeah," Homer said. "That's what I wanted to hear. That's exactly what I wanted to hear."

"Male chauvinists," Reba said.

We had sort of forgot she was there.

"Well," James said, "this here is a new world, and it's got new rules, and, shit, we don't mean nothing by it. Besides, how much of a chauvinist is Homer. He fucked Cory in the butt."

"I don't like him though," Cory said. "It was just one of those things. Me and him, we wouldn't even hang anymore if he hadn't gotten on this bus."

"Maybe you ain't chauvinist," Reba said, "but I wanted to mention, I've seen you all swimming, and each and every one of you have what can only be described in euphemistic terms as having real small dicks."

"Hey, now," James said, "that ain't right."

"It certainly isn't all that euphemistic," I said.

"You don't mean me," Steve said. "You couldn't mean me. They used to call me Horse in P.E."

"I think they were just calling you by your first name," Reba said.

"What's that mean?" Steve said.

"You know," she said, "Horse Ass."

9

Night came, and we all climbed back inside the bus, and the misty world of the drive-in floated up out of the ocean, first in a cotton candy twirl, then the twirl spread, and figures began to form, coiling and uncoiling, eventually taking shape.

The drive-in ghost floated behind us for a time, then it moved forward, melted right through the walls of the bus and was part of us, our own ghostly wraiths moving past us and through us and around us; all of the events of the drive-in unfolding silently and overlapping and passing one through the other.

For awhile we watched in awe, but in time, some of us anyway (I was one) had had enough. I coiled up on one of the seats and covered my face with my arms and tried to sleep; my trained ability to do so kicked in, and I drifted off. I dreamed I was on a great rocking horse, and it was bucking, baby. I mean up and down, even side to side, and finally my head banged against something, and I found myself lying on the floor of the bus, and the bus was churning about. I climbed onto a seat and looked out the window.

Great sprays of water and splashes of white foam were striking the windows, and the bus was washing precariously to one side, then the other. Out there in the frothy splash of foam, I thought I saw large dark creatures move. Then the water slashed the bus, and anything I might've seen was gone.

The others were up and watching as well. There was nothing else to do. A bit of water came through the cracks in the windows, washed under the bus door, and foamed in the driver's section like soapsuds.

But still we floated.

Someone vomited. I didn't even look, but I could smell it. All I could think was, when this stops, that will have to be cleaned up. I visualized us at the bottom of this . . . ocean? Monster lake? Whatever it was. Just settling down to the bottom, the pressure of the water squeezing the bus, shattering the glass, the water rushing in. And then I thought, what if it's not as deep as it seems, and we go down? We could hit the bottom and there wouldn't be the pressure to crush us, the quick rush of water to drown us. It would be a slow seep. Just sitting there on the bottom with water leaking in through the windows, slowly filling the bus.

I knew if this body of water were that shallow, I would just open a window and let it all rush in.

It seemed to me you should be able to open a sliding window. Underwater pressure wouldn't keep that from being done, would it?

And if it did, maybe I could break it.

There were ways.

All this went through my mind as the bus washed about.

One good thing, though, the misty past adventures of the drive-in were nowhere to be seen.

As I sat there in my seat, Reba slid in beside me. She took my hand. "You don't mind, do you?"

"No."

"I thought, we went down, you know, we could go down together. Someone with someone."

"Someone with someone," I said. "

"We don't have to like one another," she said.

"I know . . . We don't have to dislike one another either."

"That's true," she said, and squeezed my hand hard. "I thought I wanted to die a few times, but I've lived so long now, been through so much, I don't want to die anymore. I just want to find my place. Isn't that a strange thing to think? That I just want to find my place."

"No. Not at all. I know exactly what you mean."

The storm tossed on, and once the bus lay almost on its side, but the pontoon rig Steve had made held. The water waved us back, and the bus settled and turned, and soon the rush of the storm was no longer pushing the side of the bus, but the back of it, and that little twist of fate may have been what saved us. We washed forward, the storm propelling us like a motor.

Why the bus didn't spin and take it on the side again, I can't say. It was as if the storm were the hand of great child, and we were its toy, and the child was motoring us forward, on down a wet highway to who knew where.

10

The storm subsided.

We didn't sink.

The day came up quick and hot, and there was no mist and no ghostly drive-in.

Reba and I lay down in the seat together. It was a narrow seat, so she had to lie on top of me. She rubbed against me. She put her mouth close to my ear.

"I didn't think I could get juiced again," she said. "I thought that sort of thing had all dried out. But I'm wet as outside the bus. And hot, and I hurt, you know, in a good way. Down there."

"I feel like I have a crowbar in my pants," I said.

Not exactly romantic, I admit, but we were not living in romantic times.

She pulled up the rag of a dress she wore and rolled to the side and undid my near worn-out pants, and out I came, popping up like a jack-in-the-box.

"We shouldn't," she said, holding my dick in her hand.

"No?" I said.

"I don't want to get pregnant."

"I'll pull."

"What if you don't?"

"I will."

"Famous last words."

"Really. I will."

She slid over me and spread her legs, and in I went, and she said, "You lie still."

"Everyone knows what we're doing."

"Maybe not," she said, "and even if they do, let's try and keep it private as we can. Let's have this between us . . . Oh, God, that feels good."

And so we went at it. She made a little noise even though I was silent like she asked, and very quickly she opened her mouth and showed her fine white teeth, then made a squeak like a mouse that had just gone to Cheese Heaven, leaned over, and touched her forehead to mine. After a moment, she sat up and went at me again, and when I was close, not so close that I knew it would happen, but close enough I knew it wasn't far off, I pulled and shot on her pubic hair. She made with a little purring sound, spat on her fingers, rubbed the sperm into her dark triangle of hair and over her lower belly.

She licked her fingers.

She looked down at me and smiled.

She said, "I needed that."

"It didn't hurt my feelings any either," I said.

She climbed off of me, patted my balls, and said, "See you later," as if she were about to drive off to work.

She pulled her ragged dress down and moved to the back of the bus.

I pulled my pants up and lay there both satisfied and confused, felt just a little cheap and used and maybe not all that well respected, and wondered if everyone had been watching.

Part Two

In which the great bridge is nearer, a catfish appears, and the gang takes up new quarters.

1

The days went by slow, and we got good at fishing. Using a piece of cloth cut off one of our rags for bait, dipped in blood from an open wound Cory got from snagging his elbow on the side of the bus while out swimming, we attached that strip of cloth to a long length of twine (it had come with a kite found in the trunk of a car). Actually, we had a roll of it, the twine, and we cut several strips and made a strong cord by braiding them. We made a hook carved out of a bone from the meat Steve and Grace had provided, a sinker made out of a bolt we worked out of one of the seats with a screwdriver. With our rig we sat on top of the bus, taking turns, catching fish.

The fish we caught were mostly small, but now and again we'd catch something a little bigger. We found that a way to prepare our catch for food was to gut them and cut them in strips and lay them on top of the bus for a day and a night, then turn them over and do it to the other side. We tied them up there with string, running cord from one window, across the top of the bus to the other window, tying the cords off on seats inside.

The sun didn't exactly cook them, but it dried them some, and that was good enough. Trust me, when you're really hungry, you get a whole lot less persnickety.

Slowly, we started making not only a home of that bus, but a pint-sized community.

The only thing that was really terrible was when we wanted to go to the bathroom, we had to climb out a window—which made the bus lean heavy to one side—and work our way to the roof and hang the old moon over the side.

This however, in the number two department, didn't work so well, as there were dark streaks on the windows, as our loads didn't go smooth into the water.

Finally, it was determined the best thing to do was to climb down on the hood of the bus, near the front, and let it fly. This way, you didn't quite hit the water, stains on the front weren't so noticeable, and the way the bus nodded itself forward into the waves, as it was wont to do, it washed off the old dookie, became a perpetual self-cleaning machine.

Compared to how things had been, it seemed downright hygienic.

When I could, I got out my little possessions, which were all in a backpack I'd found in one of the cars—you wouldn't believe the stuff we found in cars—and inside I had paper and composition writing books I'd taken from different places, and in those I tried to keep a running diary of everything that had happened. I also had a Louis L'Amour book, *Hellfire Trail*, that I read from time to time, even if it was missing a few pages, and I had a copy of an old Ace Double science-fiction book. It had a cover on back and front and half of the book was a novel called *Masters the Lamp*, and the other half—you had to turn it over and open it from the other side—were short stories under the title *A Harvest of Hoodwinks*. The writer was some guy named Robert Lory, and it was pretty good, though a little less interesting when you had read it about twenty times. I liked the story "Rolling Robert" best, and I could tell it pretty good, and I did that for Reba quite a few times, and though she had read it from the book its ownself, she liked me telling it best, because I added what she liked to refer to as embellishments. I put fucking in it. She liked that. And if you've read "Rolling Robert," dear nonexistent reader, you know what a goddamn accomplishment that is, putting in the fucking, I mean.

So our biggest battle was not food, or drinking water, though we did call a moratorium on pulling up water in our buckets any time close to when one of our esteemed crew did their number one or two.

So, all things considered, life was tolerable. But there was all that water.

Water. Water. Every goddamn where you looked.

Water.

And more water.

Did I mention the water?

Alas, our greatest opponent was . . .

Boredom.

Boredom set in with a vengeance. We made up games. I Spy was out. That was easy. Uh, I spy . . . Water.

Me and Reba, we spent more time together. I shared my two books with her. We talked about this, we talked about that, did some serious drilling and heaving anytime it was night, and sometimes when it was day, and it got so, after awhile, the other guys, the ones not getting any, started to eye Reba in a way that made me nervous.

I didn't like the way they were looking at me either.

Of course, they looked at Grace that way too. But Grace, they'd have had to have come on to her fast and en masse, 'cause she was one badass. All that karate, or tae kwon do, whatever it was. And Steve, he was her man, and he was a pretty tough nut too. So, it was me and Reba they eyeballed.

In time, Cory took to fucking James in the ass now and then. Then they'd reverse it. I don't think it was a big homo thing, though I was hoping for that, so they could get their mind off what I was getting, and off who was giving it to me. But, you know, they were guys, and they had discovered there were holes they could use; did it out there right in front of everybody, just tapping the cork in the upturned jug. Course, out there and in front of everybody was pretty much how everything was, you know, being on the bus and all, but, man, they weren't even trying to pretend they were hiding it.

One of them would lift his pale, shit-holed whiteness to the other, say, "Okay, it's your turn, and don't look at me, 'cause that beard you got is throwing me off," and then James would say to Cory, "Like fucking you in the ass and looking at that cut-up head you shave with your pocket knife is any kind of goddamn turn-on," and Cory, he says, "Close your goddamn eyes, and just imagine it's your mother."

Then there'd be a fight, fists flying this way and that, then they'd make up, pat each other on the shoulder, say something nice, and it was Ass Fuck City all over again. And later on, just to show there wasn't any hard feelings, they'd hold each other's nuts while the other stroked off.

It was kind of sweet, really.

But the sweetness only went so far, and they kept eyeing Reba. And Homer. He eyed her too, 'cause he wasn't even getting his ass end worked. They all eyed her so much she didn't go back there with them, not even to get her food rations. I had to bring her food out, and I'll tell you, I was not feeling too good going back there myself. I think they wanted to beat me up and eat me and keep Reba.

And maybe they liked me for what they wanted to like each other for. I had good long hair and I kept shaved with my pocketknife, so there was just the now and again shaving rash to remind them of my masculine features.

And, hell, I'm gonna say it. I've always kind of prided myself on the shape of my ass, so I'm sure it was a factor, that good ass of mine in rags, which, though not a fashion statement, did show, in spots, the meat.

Nervous times, dear hearts. Nervous times.

2

One time when it got dark and I was nervous from the way James and Cory were acting, and Steve and Grace had moved to the front, trying to stay out of it all, and Homer, he was practically oblivious, just stretched out on a seat, not knowing that at any moment he could be lunch or ass-poked.

I started telling stories from the Lory collection aloud. You know, like I was just telling Reba, but really loud, and pretty soon, they were listening. Cory and James, and then Homer, who sat up and listened with his mouth hung open. Up front, even Steve and Grace quit groping each other, as that was available to them on a regular basis, and took to listening. Reba sat by me, worked her arm around mine, leaned against my shoulder, and listened to me tell the stories from the book.

I think I told three of the tales, and I told long versions, adding in stuff not in the stories, but stuff I thought ought to have been there, though I went light on the sex stuff, no use heating up the natives, and those stories, way I told them, it held them.

I felt the way I figured cave dwellers must have felt. Felt like the Grand Poobah of the cave, the storyteller, sitting there by the fire (minus the fire, of course) talking into the night and everyone listening carefully, and gradually scooting closer, more engrossed in the stories by the moment. And that was a good feeling. Having a kind of control. Even if it was with a story. Because for a long time now I had felt totally out of control, a random leaf blown by a savage wind.

And I thought in the back of my mind, as I was telling these tales, here we are in a tale ourselves, an incredible adventure we didn't want to be living, but we wanted to hear stories anyway, tales about others in strife and joy, but not our own strife and joy.

It was kind of weird, really.

But it worked.

And when I finished that night, everyone seemed calmer. Happier. Not so much aware of the ghostly drive-in that pursued us and floated around us and tried to become one with us.

I felt I had taken some of the pressure off the teapot. And Reba, she was sweeter that night, and slower, and I felt respected, and when I came, I opened my eyes and saw over Reba's shoulder the ghostly shades from the drive-in drift by. An old acquaintance, Crier, was looking my direction, not really seeing, just standing there ghost-like, looking at the spot where I lay on my back, Reba astride, and I felt a strange fondness for him. But in that moment of pleasure, I was quite fond of everyone and everything.

And when daylight came, it was a little better in there.

No one was singing tunes from *The Sound of Music* or giving me the high five, but it was better. Calmer.

Nights came, I told more of the short stories. And as the nights passed, I told the Lory novel. Then the Louis L'Amour novel. Then I began to make up things. I felt like Sheherazade from the *Arabian Nights*, and like her, I feared if I ever slowed down or bored them, I was dead meat.

Then, when I felt I was maybe out of tales or losing my energy to tell them, was hoping my ass could take a lot of loving and not be too unhappy with it, and, in fact good at it, so I would have something to barter besides being turned into jerked meat, a strange thing happened.

And considering our lives have been a list of strange things, this was a very strange thing indeed.

3

The day had turned out hot, and the water was still, and it hardly seemed we were flowing with the current at all. We were mostly becalmed. There was, of course, nothing but water to see, and the great bridge, clouded at bottom and top, but visible. It seemed no closer than it had seemed many days before.

I climbed on top of the bus for a bit, took in the sun with my shirt off, lying face down. But there was so much of old Sol, and I didn't have any way to protect my skin from the rays, and the idea of some terrific sunburn without so much as a bottle of calamine lotion didn't appeal to me, so I decided to climb inside and take in some shade.

As I turned over to go back in the bus, I saw Grace climb out, stark naked and brown as a walnut. She didn't fear the sun and spent much time in it. And though the sun's rays might be rough on her in the near future, right then she looked like a brown jungle savage, a regular Sheena. I watched her dive from the hood of the bus and swim about for awhile, then I climbed back through the window with my shirt.

It was a good thing too, and it was a good thing that Grace became bored and came back inside, because Cory pointed out an open window, yelled out, "Look there."

We looked out the window where he was pointing.

The great fin again.

"That is one big fucking fish," Cory said.

"There's enough meat there to dry and feed us till this big old waterhole goes dry," Homer said.

"Well, I don't know about that," Steve said, slipping an arm around Grace's nude body, "but there's a lot of meat there."

"I'm gonna get my line and such," Cory said, "get up there, see if I can catch it."

"You're gonna need more than a few twists of twine and a bone hook to hold that one," I said.

"You can catch a big fish on small line if you know what you're doing," Cory said, snatching up his fishing gear. "And I got some fish guts for bait. They've been hitting good on that one."

He climbed out the window with his gear, boosted up by James.

We could hear him on top of the bus, and we saw his line flash out in the direction of the fin.

The fin surfaced and the water rippled. Then everything was still again.

James said, "Shit, he's done gone to the bottom."

About that time we saw the string go taut, and Cory yelled, "Goddamn. String cut my hand."

James stuck his head out the window. "Hold him, Cory."

"Get up here and help, James."

James climbed out the window, worked his way to the roof of the bus. He clumped around up there for awhile, then we heard them both cussing.

"Maybe they need more help," Homer said.

"Damn," Steve said, letting go of Grace, grabbing a seat back for balance. "That little cord and that fish are causing the whole damn bus to rock."

"They need to forget that fish," Grace said. "The thing could swamp us."

About that time the twine snapped. James and Cory cussed and began to jump up and down on the roof.

"Stop that, you idiots," Grace said.

I felt a tug at my sleeve.

I turned. It was Reba. She had her mouth wide open. She was clutching my sleeve with one hand and pointing at the water with the other.

The fish had surfaced.

And, to put it simply and honestly, it was a big motherfucker.

"It's a catfish," Homer said. "It's like a blue cat, only a whole hell of a lot bigger."

"It's big as a Great White," Grace said.

"It's coming right for the bus," Homer said, as if this might not be obvious to the rest of us.

The great head split, and the mouth was wide, maybe six feet, no teeth, but there were whiskery growths sticking out from its broad face, and its eyes were black and bottomless.

It dove, showing only its fin, which split the water like a razor slicing paper.

Then the fish hit the side of the pontoon.

The bus shook and I heard Cory and James cuss again. I was knocked back into the seat behind me. I scrambled to my feet, made it across the bus, to the window, called out, "Get back inside. Now."

But the catfish hit again, and I heard a splash on the opposite side of the bus.

I turned for a look just as Reba said, "It's Cory. In the water."

And it was.

He yelled out for help a couple of times, and I was about to work myself through the window to go for him, when Grace said, "Oh, my God."

I turned.

The catfish that had rammed the bus rose up out of the water. Its tail flashed, and it seemed to heave like it was being pumped with a bellows. It sat there on the surface, looking at us, giving us the evil eye.

But he wasn't nothing.

He wasn't nothing at all.

Not anymore.

There was something new.

Something that made our concern about the ramming catfish seem like a silly notion.

In fact, the idea of leaping into the water and wrestling with it seemed less scary than what was about to happen.

4 The water, as far as the eye could see, foamed. Then it lifted in a sheet of sun-shimmering silver, and beneath the splashes and lapping of the water was a darkness. At first it was a line, like a black storm on the horizon, stretching way wide.

The line widened, became a maw, and the maw became a great black cave. Slowly, the cave condensed, and there was just the fine line again. Then the line dropped below the water, and there was a dark hump rising, making a brief waterfall to either side. This was followed by a faraway flick of a finny tail. I don't know how far away that tail was, as it was impossible to tell distances, but if I were a betting man, I'd say, and no shit on this, it was a half a mile away, and even that far away it was considerably bigger in appearance than any fishtail I had ever seen, no matter how close to my eye and how large the fish.

The body rose up higher in the water, and there was a massive head, about the size of six city blocks, and there was a glimpse of one eye the size of a spotlight, and a whisker, big as bridge cable. The whisker flexed.

I looked and saw, down a distance and to my left, the other eye (way down there it was, dear hearts) and another whisker (also way down there), and it was then that our finny friend opened its mouth and showed us the cave again.

In that moment, of course, I knew what it was. A catfish. And not the sort you'd catch and toss in the back of your truck to be weighed at Wal-Mart for a fishing contest.

This watery denizen would have made Moby Dick look like a fucking anemic minnow on a runway model diet.

The mouth stayed open, and the fish dropped slightly in the water. A whisker whipped the wind like a black snake whip, and the other catfish, the one we had thought was big, turned and swam slowly toward the greater one, a willing sacrifice.

It swam right into that cavernous mouth, splashed on in and out of sight. The maw continued to widen and expand and the water rolled and foamed as the monster swam toward us.

We just sat there, our thumbs up our asses.

Wasn't any place we could go.

Nothing we could do.

No one said a word. Not even a Holy Shit, look at that size of that motherfucker.

Nothing.

We didn't even notice that Cory had worked his way back up on a pontoon and had climbed dripping wet through a window. Well, that's not entirely true. I had noticed, but it hadn't registered deeply. How could it. Not with that Leviathan out there.

Water ran into the fish's mouth like being poured into a funnel, and way to the left, and way to the right, I saw a shiny spurt of spray, and knew water was rushing through the great fish's gills, shooting out against the clear blue sky like geysers.

The bus began to move. Rapidly. Flowing behind the formerly large, now less impressive catfish, into the darkness of the maw that must have swallowed Old Jonah.

Finally, someone spoke.

It was Grace. She said, "This sucks."

Steve said, "I just want to say goodbye to my dick. It's been good to me."

The water moved fast and went into the fish and we went with it; there was a rush into the great mouth as the bus straightened itself, fled down the throat of the beast, and behind us the light faded.

I turned to look.

The dark line was lowering, and the bright blue of the outside was going away as if a blind were being slowly pulled closed. Water lapped in and with it came a total blackness like the end of all things.

There was a thud and a jerk as the water the behemoth gulped slammed up against the back of our craft. The bus began to flee along at breakneck speed, like a roller-coaster ride, on down, dropping our stomachs out. Water spurted in through the bus's cracks, and someone, James I think, yelled, "We're gonna drown like rats," and from the back window came a confirmation, a blast of black wetness (should have closed that fucking window up), and away we went, water gushing to our knees, causing us to climb into the seats, only to instantly feel the water rise up to touch us.

Away we went, faster and faster, propelled into the pitch dark moist nowhere toward the nucleus of the Lord of the Fishes.

5

One thing you don't expect inside a fish is light.

Soon there would be other things unexpected. But, for the moment, let's just consider the light.

Lights actually.

A row of them.

But let's not jump too far ahead.

Let's roll back and talk back and go up the throat of the fish, and let me tell you how we came down.

We came down in a stink, baby. The water nearly filled the bus. We bumped our heads on the ceiling, and the water smelled bad, and there were things in the water, and the bus went fast, and then it slowed. There was a feeling like being a mole in a water hose. And somehow I knew we were in some piece of gut, making our way to the center, where, I figured, stomach acid, or whatever fish use to digest (is it rocks? no, I believe that's chickens that get pebbles in their craw), would be our final destination.

Seven for the soup.

Dinner served.

A little later that day it would be out the ole sphincter, blown through the asshole into the deeps, an acid-pocked bus full of skeletons.

If that much was left.

Just so much fish shit.

But, I was saying about the lights, and now we come to them again. So, we're jetting along through the guts and into the stomach, hanging onto the seats, drenched in water, not quite drowned, but in a position that we in the business of being swallowed by fish like to call, seriously wet, and then—

—SQUIRT—

—right out into—

The light.

A muddled light, I might mention, as if shown through thick wax paper, but it was light. The bus came down with a smack, right side up (thank goodness), and the water in the bus sloshed back and forth across us, and the light shining through the windows, piercing the water that was now almost to the ceiling, burned our eyes.

Water fled from the bus the same way it had come in. Only took a matter of minutes before it was to the point where we could stand in the seats and have the water about our waists. At that point it slowed its drain. The windows, though lit up with light, also were splattered with all manner of dark business I would rather not consider, and so was the floor of our bus. There were even small fish flapping about, and I found leeches clinging to my body like day commuters grasping the handholds on a subway car.

All our food supplies were ruined, soaked up with that water, and possibly the water and fuel were fucked too, depending on how well the corks held in the containers. But, at that moment in time, that didn't seem like a big concern.

Steve dove under the water and worked the bus door, and it came open. The water rushed out, and so did Steve, Grace, Cory, and Jim. Homer, Reba, and I clung to seats and waited for it to wash away.

Then we too slipped and slid along the sopped floor of the bus and out into the lights.

They hung from long cables at the summit of the fish, which was pretty far up there, dear hearts. And the fish itself was like a great aircraft hangar in size, but its sides heaved, and the meat and bones moved with the pressure of its breathing. In the sides of the fish were great pockets cut into the meat, and in the holes of this meat, high up, we could see people. On both sides of the fish, extending back for a goodly distance, as far as we could see before the rows of lights played out and there was only darkness.

Occasionally, as I observed, I'd see a spark emit from the fish's insides, pop out like a firefly, crackle like cellophane. There were a few metallic ladders on wheels and runners, like in a great library. The ladders were narrow, but they went high up. Down into the dark spot at the tail of the fish, where the lights played out, my eyes adjusted enough I could see there was a pile of cars, both old and new, and one small airplane. All of this was mounded up together in what could almost be called a wad. The paint was off the cars for the most part, and there were holes in the metal, like termites the size of motorcycles had been at work.

Our bus was resting on a grid, long and flat with drainage holes all through it. The grid began at the pulsating gut gap that had launched us here, and a sewage aroma came from that gap as it irised open and closed. We wobbled slightly, not having gained our sea legs, as the great fish propelled itself through the depths. Beneath the grid, I could see a boiling green mess that gave off a fart odor that blended with the special smell that puffed out of the sphincter. The catfish that had swum before us lay flapping on the grillwork, its mouth opening and closing as it gasped for water.

People in the meat caves started down the ladders. There were a lot of them. Some wore rags, but most were raw and wet looking, covered in fish blood, their hair matted. Many were covered in puckered scars.

As they came down to see us, Steve said, "You know, I caught many a catfish in my lifetime—well, not that many, I suck as a fisherman—but, I never found no folks inside of one. Or any lighting equipment."

"How about old cars or airplanes?" Homer asked.

"Nope," Steve said. "None of those either."

Grace said, "I just hope the natives are friendly."

6

"How y'all doin'," a big naked man said. He was holding his limp dick in one hand like it was a symbol of authority, and there was enough there to look authoritative. I was glad I was clothed, otherwise I would have been mucho big-assed embarrassed. A wiener like that belonged in some kind of museum, or maybe peeking out from under a circus tent in the snake section.

As an added note, a leech hung off his left thigh in a decorative way.

"I don't know we ought to welcome you or not, seeing as how I figure you weren't just driving through. But, I reckon some kind of howdy is in order, so, Howdy, goddamnit."

He opened his mouth in a big grin at this comment, and showed us just how many teeth he was missing.

Men and women, and even one child, were amongst the crowd. I guess there must have been fifty or so. A number of them leaped on the large catfish that had washed in ahead of us, and with fists and bone clubs they were carrying, they beat it about the head until it stopped thrashing.

The naked man never even looked at this business. He just kept twiddling with his dick.

"That's some cannon you got there," Grace said to the naked man, "but I don't know I like it pointed at me. And, now that I mention it, it seems to be a larger cannon than a moment ago."

"I just try and display a little at a time," the naked man said. "I don't want to scare nobody . . . You look so good."

"Thank you," Grace said. "I try to take care of myself."

"And you look good too," the naked man said to Reba.

"You're hurting my feelings," Steve said. "I just had a hell of a bath, and no good words about me?"

The naked man grinned. "I'm down here much longer, and you'll start looking pretty good too. My name is Bjoe. It's really Billy Joe, but everyone called me B. Joe, so I just shortened it to Bjoe, one word. I could tell you all kinds of fascinating things about me and my life, but I think you probably got other interests."

"That's the truth," Homer said. "Where the fuck are we?"

"Why, silly," said Bjoe, "you're inside a giant catfish."

"As Steve here said," I said jerking a thumb at Steve, "I've never seen a catfish like this. How come it's got all this rigging? The lights and such? The caves up there in the meat?"

"Sometimes," Bjoe said, "I think about it and my head hurts."

"I feel sick to my stomach," Homer said. He turned from us and vomited onto the grillwork. We all stood there watching it leak through the holes, down into the bubbling mess below.

"You got a mite of sea sickness," Bjoe said. "Had that myself at first. No telling how long I had it. We can't tell one day from another down here. Not even false days. I mean, they're ain't no real light, just them bulbs. And there ain't no night. Ain't nobody wants to turn off the light. There's some dark up in them caves we cut into the meat, and there's dark down there past them wrecked cars and such, but, hell, you don't want to go down there. There's things on the other side of them cars you wouldn't like to meet in a dark fish ass."

"Things?" Cory said.

"We don't know what they are, but they're fucked up and goofydoofy."

"Goofydoofy?" Grace said.

"Yeah. They don't like the light though. You see, they was here before the lights."

"How do you know?" I asked.

"I just reckon it. Well, I kind of know some things, but it's a long story."

"Got a feeling we ain't gonna be catching no train or nothing," Steve said, "so, we ought to hear it."

"You will," Bjoe said, dropping his flesh hammer so that it flopped against his thigh like a pale eel. "But first thing we got to do is eat. Got to eat when you can eat. We'll show you the ropes, since I figure you're gonna be permanent."

"Now there's a word," Grace said. "Permanent."

Reba said, "I never knew how permanent the word permanent sounded, until just now."

7

They pulled the skin off the catfish using sharp pieces of bone, their hands, and their bare teeth, bit into the skin near where the head had been—it got chopped off with bone tools—scuttled backward, stripping the skin off in dark bands, revealing the clean white meat, still pulsing.

They cut into the meat or tore at it with their hands, and pretty soon they were through the meat and into the guts. Blood and fluids ran out of the fish and through the holes in the grating, hit the bubbling mass below, and disappeared.

"I think that's stomach acid," Grace said, nodding down at the stuff below the grate.

"Yeah," I said. "I think you're right."

"I think we better get in the chow line," Steve said. "That catfish, big as it is, is going fast."

We hustled back to the bus, where we had knives, and, slipping and sliding over the goo on the floor, we found them.

My knife was in my backpack, which I had appropriated from a car where the kid who had owned it had been eaten by her parents, and along with the knife were some other items, most of them ruined. But my journal, which I kept in a plastic bag I had found long back, appeared to be in tip-top shape. That was good, but right then I would have traded it for a ham sandwich.

Back at the fish, we cut off slabs of meat and ate them raw. It was surprisingly good, but then again, most anything to eat had become a gourmet treat as far as I was concerned. I had known folks back at the drive-in to peck undigested berries and such out of piles of dinosaur shit, had sworn that it having passed through the stomach of a critter made it more delectable.

When we finished eating, we looked about to see all the others wiping their oily hands on their clothes or bodies or in their hair. I used my ragged pants to take care of my etiquette.

Finished, the Fish People eyed us for a long while without speaking. Finally, Bjoe, having rescued his dick from lonely abandon, and having picked the leech off his thigh and eaten it, said, "Up there. That's where we ought to go. That biggest cave. That's where we have our community meetings."

"What kind of meeting we talking about?" Steve asked.

"I don't like heights," James said. "Fact is, I don't like being inside a goddamn fish either, but I can take that better than heights."

"You need not come," Bjoe said. "None of you need come. But that is where we can drink. We have drink there."

"You mean like booze?" Cory asked.

Bjoe nodded.

"Where would you get that?" Homer asked.

"Made it."

"Oh," Cory said. "And may I ask out of what?"

"Spoiled things."

"Of course."

"This fish, our swimming home, he eats what I guess is algae. Some kind of weed anyway. You add water, let it set till it smells, which takes, I don't know . . . who knows down here . . . Too long, anyway. But when it smells worse than the inside of the fish here, then you know it's ready. You got to hold your nose on that first jolt, but after that, it's all right. Besides, it beats all the bourbon and beer we don't have."

"There's a point somewhere in all that," James said.

"Does the fish ever do any acrobatic type swimming?" Grace asked. "I mean, anything that might make all this goop beneath us slosh up through the grates?"

"It does," Bjoe said. "Now and again. Mostly, just a bit of side-to-side movement. Not bad. The Big Boy is quite steady, actually. Most of the time. I do advise not being in the area of your bus, however. Lots of water comes through his gullet there, washes through. Sometimes, enough of it comes through, the goop as you call it, swells over the grates, and then we all got to stay cavebound. You really should get your own cave. You got to cut it into the meat. But not too deep. You do that, you could injure the fish, or cut through the outer skin, then it would all be over. Which, sometimes we think might not be such a bad thing. A quick rush of water, and down we all go to the bottom, our lungs wet as Noah's flood."

"I guess we can come up," I said. "To talk."

"And have a drink of that rotten fish swizzle," Cory said.

"I'd like to try that," James said, "but once again, heights. Ain't for it."

"I might can bring you some back," Cory said.

"That would be great. Just like the rest of my life. Great, great, great."

8

With the exception of James, who decided to stay with the bus, we followed Bjoe and his band up one of the rolling ladders. I tried not to look up, as the fella in front of me didn't have on any pants, and a nastier asshole you could not imagine, and when he stepped high his grapes swung wrinkled and ugly on their vine.

Behind me came the others, Reba, Cory, Homer, Steve, and Grace last in line.

It was a precarious trip, as the rungs of the ladder were damp from wet feet, and I had to hold on tight. I cautioned the others to do the same.

When we reached the summit, we stepped off the ladder and into a very large cut in the meat; a pulsating cave that went some distance back. The walls were wet with thin stains of blood from the fish, and you could see veins throbbing in the wall of the cave. One rib bone had been exposed and was visible. I could see skin over the rib and wondered just how thick that skin was, and how much it would take to pierce it, bringing in all that water; thought too about these folks, and what Bjoe had said, about how they sometimes thought about ending it.

I didn't like my life, but as I had come to realize, it was the one I had. I wanted to play out its string as long as I could, and I preferred to not have anyone cut it short for me just because they had had enough and wanted to go.

There were skulls in the caves, or rather the tops of skulls. They were split from the eyes up, and had been turned over to be used as utensils.

"How'd you come by your tableware?" I asked.

"Folks that died," Bjoe said. "We ate them. Waste not, want not. You have a problem with that?"

Actually, I didn't. I didn't like it, but in this world, you did what you could. It was okay by me. Cannibalism has its place.

If they had in fact died, and not been helped along.

I had a tense sensation that we might have just climbed a long ladder to unwillingly accept a dinner invitation.

"I know what you're thinking," Bjoe said. "And no. We're not going to murder you."

"I could have told you that," Grace said, looking ready to fight.

"We may not look like much," Bjoe said. "And I may play with my dick more than a rap musician, but we don't mean you any harm. Long as you abide by the rules and get along and such."

"That's good to hear," Steve said.

"What about that booze?" Cory said.

"We'll come to that," Bjoe said. "Please. Make yourself at home. Guys, play with your dicks if you want. We don't discourage it. Ladies, you can plunk your pudding if you like. We don't consider it vulgar here."

And they sure didn't. Three of the women had revealed themselves and were slapping their meat in a savage manner, grunting like pigs to trough.

"Maybe later," Grace said.

"Suit yourself," Bjoe said.

We sat down cross-legged, and I could feel the great fish's flesh vibrating beneath me, taut as a harp string. The meat against my ass was warm, and I could imagine going to sleep quite comfortably in this cave.

The women who had chosen to explore their valleys were still at work, and even though only one of them was moderately attractive, I couldn't help but watch. There was nothing really sexual about it for me. It was just interesting to see. Sort of like midget wrestling.

Bjoe went over to a row of skulls against the fleshy wall and picked one up. He brought it over, set it down in front of us, squatted to join us.

"So," Cory said. "You just get some weed the fish ate, let it rot and such, and it's ready to go."

"We spit in it too."

"Whoa, now," Cory said. "I didn't need to know that."

"Saliva blends with it, makes it ripe."

"I bet," Steve said.

"You really should try some," Bjoe said. "It'll set you free."

Cory leaned over and sniffed it. "It smells like a dead animal," he said.

"Indeed," Bjoe said.

"You just hold your nose?" Cory said.

"First sip, yeah. After that, probably won't need to."

"Oh, shit," Cory said. "I'm a fool."

He took hold of his nose with one hand, lifted the skull to his lips, and sipped.

Carefully, he put the skull back down, removed his hand from his nose.

"That. Without a doubt. Is the foulest motherfucking thing I have ever put in my mouth. And I got to tell you, I once ate a turd because it had some kind of nuts in it. I think it was shat out by a bear or something. But that right there. That is some nasty shit. But . . . it kind of grows on you."

"What happened to your head?" Bjoe asked Cory. "Knife fight?"

"I shaved it. But not too well. I'll have another jolt of that fish brew, if you don't mind."

"Help yourself. There are plenty of bowls of it. Would any of you like to try it?"

"I'll pass," Grace said. "I haven't even had a bear turd yet, so I'll hold out."

Everyone else passed.

Cory grabbed two more skulls, drained them down. Then he burped, fell over backwards, unconscious.

Homer leaned over and looked at him.

I said, "He isn't dead is he?"

"No, but his breath is really something," Homer said. "And strong. It could hold up a tea set."

"Would you like to hear how we came here?" Bjoe said. "And maybe I can clear up some things for you. About the fish, I mean. I know some of it, or rather I've noodled out a lot. Rest of it is guesswork. And some, shit, I don't got a clue. Maybe you can fill in some holes."

"Tell us," I said.

Part Three

In which Bjoe, while playing with his tallywhacker, recites a tale of woe, boating, fish intestines, expert lighting, the Scuts, and such. And, in the meantime, Cory stays drunk.

1

"I won't begin where it began, because we all began there. The night of the drive-in and the big red comet with the hot white smile.

"Forget that."

"I'll begin where it began for us. The all of us here except you newcomers. There have been a few other newcomers, folks eaten by the fish, but they were all dead when they came through. And, frankly, we ate them.

"When the comet came back, like so many others, perhaps all who were in the theater, we started down the long road. We were among the first to leave. At the end of the road we found what you found. The goddamn drive-in again. We were on a loop, and we arrived at where we had left.

"Folks were coming into the drive-in to stay, but a caravan of us decided to strike out down a wide trail, bump our way along, and see if it went anywhere else.

"We went for a long time. Some of the cars conked out. People died. People got eaten. There were a few murders, rapes, and acts of depravity along the way, not to mention creature attacks, and that accounted for some loss. You know the drill. Been there done that, I'm sure.

"Finally we came to a wide break in the woods and found ourselves on the edges of great sea. Or so we think. Maybe it is a lake so great it seemed like a sea. But we found ourselves there, and there was no alternative but to stop.

"Critters were thick along that lake, and we decided to make tools from bone, plus use what tools we had. It's amazing how much in the way of odds and ends can be found in the trunks and back seats of cars. Even car parts could be made into tools.

"So, what we did is we circled the cars, vans, and trucks in a double circle, to make a kind of wall—remember, there were a bunch of us, so it was a big circle—and inside that circle we began to build.

"During the day we cut timber and dragged it with pickup trucks. One of the cars served as a door to the circle, and the driver would pull it back and we would bring the logs in. Here we cut them and shaped them and coated them with clay to keep out insects as best we could, then we built them up into what can only be called one large goddamn home. Around the home we built palisades, tall, cut with sharp points on their ends. Beyond those, we slanted logs in the ground with points sticking out like angled porcupine quills. It wasn't a bad job at all.

"In time, we used clay to cover the log walls. This not only kept out bugs, it better kept out the wind and insulated us from the cold and the heat, whenever it came. After a time, we built great chimneys on either end of the structure. Here community meals were cooked. Wild animals and roots and greens and such we found. Occasionally, one of our band would die and we would eat them, and let me tell you, if you haven't had the old long pig, it can't be beat. Now, I'm not suggesting anyone eat anyone here—unless they die—but, if you get the opportunity, don't be squeamish. And I'll tell you, it don't taste like chicken. Or pork for that matter. It is a unique and sweet taste unrivaled by any meat. Damn. My mouth is starting to water just thinking about it.

"But we built this great place, and we called it home, and let me tell you, after all we had been through, it wasn't so bad.

"Fact was, it wasn't bad at all, and we should have stayed there, and we might have, but along came Noah.

"That wasn't his real name, but it's what we came to call him, at first derisively, and finally, respectfully, and then . . . Well, let me go back to the story.

"Noah, actual name Tim, said we should build a great boat.

"He wasn't preaching religion, wasn't saying it was going to rain. He wasn't even saying life was too hard, because, actually, all things considered, it wasn't. He was saying we should build a great boat because he knew how, and it would give us something to do, and we could sail across the sea.

"Now, he did have one idea. He thought that on the other side of the sea we might find home.

"I don't know if this was a silly idea or not. I suppose it was, knowing full damn well there were no seas or great lakes like this in East Texas, but it was hard to know what to think, and finally, what I think made us all decide to build it was a simple factor.

"Boredom.

"I kid you not. There we were, plenty of food from the forests. Small animals, the nuts and berries, wild greens program, and we were catching small fish from the freshwater sea. We had plenty of water. Our fort was pretty safe, even from dinosaurs. It was clean and dry and warm, cool on hot days, and we were fornicating pretty much at will and babies were being born, and most of them were living, looked like they'd grow up and our community would swell.

"What I felt like was this. One time I saw a cow on the side of the road, behind a fence, but she had her head through the fence and was eating grass growing on the other side, near the highway. I remember thinking, silly cow. She had a whole pasture full of fine green grass, and there she was nibbling at some scrawny grass growing by the fence that had been dosed with the fumes from thousands of exhausts.

"How stupid. If she could break through the fence, pretty soon she'd be on the highway, and maybe get hit by a car.

"Looking back, we were that cow with our heads through the fence, but we didn't have grass to nibble. All we had was Noah's idea.

"We called him Noah because he said he was a builder, and he had proved this by helping to design and construct our fort, which, by the way, we called Fort Drive-in.

"He said, we can build a boat, like Noah's ark, and we can sail out and see what there is to see. And maybe, he said, we can expand what we have here. Find better food, build greater forts, and form a kind of community of forts. Sail the waters. Establish trade between forts. I mean, he had the whole nine yards laid out and marked off and ready to cut.

"He drew up plans. First in the dirt, then on animal hides. He marked this, he marked that. He drew an overall picture of the boat. It was to be huge. It looked like Noah's ark. We began to call him Noah.

"Now, I got to tell you, there is to me no dumber idea than to think that ever there was a man that built an ark that held all the animals of the world, and a family too, and that they sailed on the ocean for forty days and forty nights. Dumb. I don't care who you are or what you believe, that's just goddamn dumb.

"But, you know what? This Tim, this Noah, he was almost telling us the same thing. Build this big-ass boat, stick in a few of the wild birds we had caught, a few of the wild animals (pig-like critters mostly), and all our nasty asses, and we would set sail on water so big we had no idea if there was an end to it anywhere. Just get on out there and sail around and see what happens.

"Let me tell you, in retrospect, I consider it one of the dumbest ideas since people came up with and believed the story of the original Noah, and the only thing dumber is pet rocks and an idea I had once about a portable pet called porta-kitty, legless and in a sack that hung on the wall and mewed when you turned on the lights. But I won't go into that.

"I'll just say, we built that boat.

"The boat was very big, because it was decided that everyone but a handful of us would go. Some would stay and hold down the fort, so to speak, while the rest of us went adventuring. The idea was to come home with plenty of exotic information, foods, and such, and since we weren't being assailed by wild Indians at the fort, it was thought all that was needed to hold it was a skeleton crew. I suppose they are there yet.

"The boat took a long time to build, and it was hard work. But I found it a wonderful thing to do. Boredom was on the run. Adventure was in the air, and I was banging regular tail, two women who didn't mind sharing me, and I didn't mind sharing them.

"We were clean and well fed and spent the nights, sometimes the days when we were too tired to work, talking about our quest.

"Yippie. Out there on the water. Sailing about. Adventuring. Yeehaw.

"Again, I never even liked the deep end of the pool back home, so what was up with me and the boat and Noah? It's hard to figure. Life certainly turns you some spins, that's for sure.

"So there came a day when the boat was finished to Noah's specs. We had driven wooden pegs into wooden ribs and swollen them up with water and poured tree sap into cracks. Noah said this was the thing, the sap, the resin, and that it would hold tighter than an eighteen-year-old virgin's doohickey on her wedding night.

"We used our trucks and cars to pull the great boat up on a ramp, and then we built another ramp below the front end of the boat, and we greased it with animal fat and dung, and with all of us pushing, we were able to make it slide out and down and into the water. There it was held by ropes made from vines and strips of bark. Big and broad and ready to go.

"We cheered.

"I distinctly remember cheering.

"Yeehaw. I'm a dumb ass. I'm going to leave a nice home on the banks of a beautiful body of water, surrounded by great trees, with plenty of food, and a lazy lifestyle, to climb onto a boat and sail off to . . . Nowhere.

"Seemed like a good idea at the time.

"Anyway, we swarmed aboard. The boat was already packed with food and stuffs, and there were, in fact, a dozen long lifeboats on that sucker. It stood high out of the water like it was proud of itself. We were ready and eager to set sail.

"The sails went up. Made from animal hides and vines, they were, but they were solid and they caught the wind, and we set out. And the wind was good that day, strong and blowing harder than a whore at Mardi Gras.

"About one day out something that should have occurred to us before, suddenly became prominent. Noah may have known how to build a boat, and we knew how to hoist sails, but frankly, none of us, Noah included, knew how to actually sail.

"And the good wind went away.

"Another problem. The boat was so big, that the only way it moved was s-l-o-w-l-y. Out there far from land, we became becalmed.

"This was okay for a day or two, you know, benefit of the doubt and all that, but within a few days we were pissed. All of us.

"We went to Noah, and in polite words, told him to turn that motherfucker around and take us back to Fort Drive-in, and from now on he could live in the fucking boat.

"No, someone said, the boat would become a second fort, up a ways from the first, and those with children, they could live there, make it a giant nursery.

"But, the bottom line, thing that counted, was this. We wanted to take our asses back to Fort Drive-in.

"'No,' said Noah. This was just the sort of thing that ruined a good adventure. Sailors always grumbled. The becalming would pass, and with it would come a good wind, and we would sail on into adventure.

"Besides, he made a very good point.

"Without any wind, becalmed as we were, we weren't sailing anywhere. Home or otherwise.

"Did I tell you this Noah was a good speaker? He could talk the pork off a pig. He was that kind of guy, had that kind of voice. Held himself firm and high, had a beard. Reminded me of Charlton Heston in that Biblical movie, *The Ten Commandments*. So, to make it short as my hopes, I'll just say we were famboozled again and hung in there.

"He had even given us a little fire in our bellies, made us think it was a good idea.

"So, finally we did catch a wind, and it was a good one, and it carried us far, far out, and land was no longer a distant line of brown. It was lost to us. There was only the sea and the sky, and once again, guess what? No fucking wind.

"Died like a politician's promises.

"Let me tell you. I just thought that I was bored at Fort Drive-in. That big boat soon seemed like a fucking canoe. I paced it daily, as did a lot of others. Noah, he stayed away in his cabin. Sight of him made us angry, and he knew it.

"It was also obvious to us by this time that if we wanted to go home, we wouldn't know how to do it. We had been turned and moved by that last good wind, and in fact, felt as if we were doing little more than spinning about like a top in pretty much the same place, so no matter which direction we decided to go, it would be a crapshoot.

"You know how it is here on this world, this place, this dimension, whatever it is. The sun might come up in one spot one day, in another the next. Same with the moon. And the stars. They move about like fireflies.

"These, of course, are things we should have thought of. But, like a lot of fools, we had put our fate into the hands of one person. Someone who KNEW THE ANSWERS. It wasn't until we were on the ocean, becalmed, going a little crazy, starting to go short on supplies, and catching no fish, that we determined Noah didn't know his dick from a grub worm.

"So, and I'm a little ashamed to tell you this part—but not real ashamed—there came a time when we had had enough, and we pulled him from his cabin and cut off both his ears, his nose, his dick and balls, tied him to the rigging and hoisted him up.

"He lasted a long time, hanging up there, bleeding to death, screaming and cussing, wiggling with his hands tied behind his back, his feet tied together, as big white birds pecked out his eyes and took off chunks of his flesh. He was plagued by insects too. Big mothers. They tore at him as well.

"It was horrible to see.

"All that meat going to waste.

"So after a time, on a dark night, we brought him down and beat his head in and cooked him up and he was good. And might I add, we ate him by his own light, having used some of his fat which was not much at that moment in time, him having lost weight up there on the ropes—to stick in bowls to light as lamps. So there's an irony, or at least if it isn't irony, it's a strangeness, to make a light of him to eat him by.

"When we were finished, we beat in his meatless jaw with clubs, knocked out his teeth, gathered them up, and in a kind of ceremony, tossed them into the dark waters, one by one. And for a long time, I kept a toothpick made of a snapped and fragmented bone from his skull, stuck it in what were then the remains of pants and/or now just so much fiber dust somewhere inside this fish.

"But, shit, I lost the pants, I lost the toothpick."

2

"Well, there we were. Out there on the vastness of the wetness, having eaten our captain, who was about as seaworthy as Captain Crunch, in a boat that looked like a giant Noah's ark with a rudimentary sail, and we weren't sailing so good.

"We cursed the drive-in world, and we cursed the lack of wind. We cursed Noah, and we cursed the ship. We even got around to cursing ourselves. I missed the college classroom, teaching, which is what I did for a living, gentlemen and two ladies. Liked teaching fine. Spreading knowledge. Meeting young women. Truth be told, I fucked a lot of my students. I know that isn't ethical but, as you can see, I'm sort of dick oriented, and I, like my students, am young, in my twenties. I just couldn't help myself. Hear what I'm saying?

"So, I liked to do what they did. Go to the drive-in being one of those things. I took one of my students as a date. She was fine. I mean fine. But when things got bad, shit, had to eat her. And, not the usual way that word is used. I mean, you know, I did that too. Before I got hungry. And then, I actually ate her. Cooked her. Had matches in the glove box and a lighter on my person.

"God, I miss my cigarettes.

"I miss her as well. She was pretty special. I think we might have gotten married when she graduated. One thing for sure, she was gonna make an A in my class, she did the work or not.

"Not that she couldn't do it. She could. She was smart. Hell, she even cooked up good. Sometimes I think I can still taste her. You haven't eaten until you've had human flesh . . . Did I mention that? A tittie, it fries up good.

"Oh, yes. The boat. We were on the boat. And I'm thinking, where the hell are we, really? I'm sure we've all thought that. I know I have. Where are we?

"Another planet?

"Another universe?

"Up a duck's ass?

"I sort of like that idea. Not the duck ass. The different universe idea. You know, all that stuff about multiverses. Expanding out beyond our own universe, and the laws of physics not applying in the same way, or at all, and the laws of physics here being nothing more than bylaws. You hear what I'm saying? Bylaws. What applied where we were, our world, does not apply here. Someone has laid out a whole new list of what does and what don't.

"But, I think on that, and I think, shit, to believe that, I got to make a real leap of faith, and finally it's just so much guess work.

"Yet, here I am. Some goddamn place. The inside of a fish, that much I know. But, this world, can it be? Why yes, I tell myself. It can be. For here I am. So I be, and you be, we all be.

"But still I wonder, and the wonder confuses my head.

"It also causes me to veer from my story. I'll throw out a mental lifeline and tug it back. I should know how to tell a tale better than this, a tale that ends up with me inside a fish's tail, which makes a hell of a tale indeed.

"So there we sat on our boat inside this branch of the multiverse, or wherever the fuck we are, and finally we got some wind.

"We had been becalmed for some time, and we had prayed for that wind, begged for that wind, longed for that wind. And when it came, we didn't want it.

"It started out calm and cool and fine enough, but in short time it was less calm and turned cold. The water frothed like meringue on a pie, and then it was not so much frothing as foaming, then not so much foaming as white with fury, like a mad dog frothing.

"At first, before it went psycho-wind on us, it filled the sail in a single puff, and we decided to turn the boat, for no good reason than the bulk of us voted to do that, thinking we had come from that direction, but not really knowing, you see, just guessing.

"But we decided to turn it, gentlemen and two ladies.

"And the boat began to move. The wind picked up, and the boat moved faster, and then an interesting thing happened, and this was even before the wind turned savage.

"Parts of the boat began to fall off.

"The glue we had made to stick between the boards, after being damp for so long, was coming apart. Noah had designed the boat in such a way that not all of it was tightly pegged. Some of it, heaven forbid, was held together by no more than resin and hope. This sort of shit, my gathering of little dirties, is exactly why Noah should have been eaten.

"He had duped us.

"He didn't know glue from cow shit. And hadn't that motherfucker ever heard of a nail. A bunch of nails. Not just a peg or two, but real nails. Maybe we would have had to have made them from wood, but they should have been made. Some kind of way. Hear what I'm saying?

"Glue is okay for paper hats and homemade valentines, but it's shit for holding together big-ass boats after they get good and wet and end up in a storm.

"The waves and wind lashed us and slammed us, and washed into that weak-ass glue and made it thin, made it come undone even faster. We rode the waves, this way and that, and our sail got wadded up like a snotty Kleenex. Folks were going crazy, they were so scared. They were fighting and yelling, fucking, leaping over the side of the boat. It was like someone had touched us with a crazy wand.

"Finally, I took control. I didn't know I had it in me. I had to stab a couple folks, make them quit running around like assholes, make them shut up, but pretty soon, I'm yelling ideas, and then the ideas are orders, and folks are listening.

"Stabbing a motherfucker or two will bring another fella's mind around quick-like.

"I yell out about the lifeboats, say let's get those goddamn lifeboats filled.

"About the time we're trying to do that, the whole goddamn great boat, or ship, or whatever the fuck it was, came apart. Just collapsed like a Republican tax cut. Looks good on the outside, and works fine up front on the short run, but boy do you pay for it in the back end. And, my little dirties, we were paying for it.

"Thing was, the lifeboats had been filled. About a hundred and ten of us in those boats. There were a few folks left over. We had to give them our best wishes and a couple of knife wounds to keep them out of the lifeboats. When the big boat came all the way apart it left us floating, and those unfortunates who hadn't been fast enough to get their nasty asses in the boats, that hadn't been stabbed, well, they were just out there, hanging to lumber or going under, or getting finished off by boat paddles to the head. It sounds cruel, but it was better than just leaving them there. Especially the little ones. The three- and four-year-olds who were struggling so hard. You can't stand to see that, I will assure you, so we beat them down.

"The wind kept up, and we had to bail water out of the lifeboats, and there wasn't much room to bail, so we put some of the mothers and children over the side and wished them luck. We had to stop hitting them with the paddles, due to the fact we had shattered one and cracked another. That wouldn't do.

"I know that sounds cold, and I suppose it is. I got to come back to that, me saying how cold it was, but how necessary it was. You see, for the bulk of us to survive, we had to rid ourselves of the weak. And most of the mothers and children were weak. We hung onto the stronger women with the plumper babies (food should always be considered), and kept at it.

"The night came and that was bad, but at least the wind had stopped and the moon had come up. During the night, some of the folks in the boat disappeared. I don't know what happened. I think someone must have cut their throats and drank the blood and put them over the side. It had to have been seen by just about everyone (not me, though), but no one was complaining. Not when the bailing buckets had warm blood in them to drink.

"When the sun came up, we checked our boat, took a head count, and determined how our survivors were doing. There were some who had been injured when the big boat came apart, you see, and now, in the daylight, we could see they weren't doing so good, so we put them over the side.

"Except for one. We cut him up and ate him.

"I might also mention, that the ones we put over the side that morning we didn't let drift and we didn't bust them with boat paddles. We drowned them, pulled their bodies close to the side of the boat, and tied them off with rope. They were our larder. We had come to that, and thank God we were wise enough to do just that. I only regretted that we had thrown so much fine meat over the side the night before. I remembered one of those women quite well, seeing her ass in the wet moonlight, bobbing up and down like a round-ended barrel. She would have provided us with rump roast for days. She had been a volunteer. Someone who just couldn't take it anymore. She bobbed about for awhile, that ass up in the air, and then she dove in and went down with hardly a splash, and didn't come up. My guess is she swam down till her breath played out and the water filled her.

"The other boats floated nearby, and they too had gone through a thinning. I suppose with our experiences in the drive-in, this kind of ruthlessness was to be expected. Sentimentality had long passed us by, and though for a time, there in Fort Drive-in, I thought we might be gaining our humanity, I learned quick-like we had not, and thank goodness for that, or I, and the bulk of us, would not be here today.

"Considering we're all inside a giant fish, that might not be such a good thing in the long run, but I suppose the best any of us can hope for these days is extension of life, and not quality. In the past I often thought, quality, not quantity, is what's important. Until I was faced with the big sign-off. The idea was unappealing to me. I didn't have the courage of the fat-assed woman who went over the side and swam deep down.

"I am still ready to grab at whatever bit of life I can get, no matter how sour it might taste, how foul it might look. I still wish for better food and cleaner pussy and having my ass outside of this fish and back at my house in East Texas.

"Hell, I'd settle for being back at Fort Drive-in. It was a pretty good deal. You could bathe regular, fix meals that didn't stink so bad you had to hold your nose, or worse, just get used to.

"But, I was telling you about the boats.

"Drifty, drifty, drifty, that's me.

"We went a couple of nights and some days, and then one night, in the moonlight, all of the boats floating close together, the dark water rose up high and broadened. We thought it was a freak wave. But it was not.

"The darkness froze for a moment, then opened up into greater darkness, and the boats, even though we paddled hard to not let it happen, flowed into the big ole darkness of the black hump, and down we went.

"You know what's next. You experienced it. We shot out of a gut or throat, or whatever, and landed here on the grid, splashing water behind us, shattering our boats and spilling us willy-nilly, this way and that, breaking some of us up. As a side note, I should add that those poor unfortunates got eaten. That was their unintentional contribution, but, I think, if their ghosts could be here to discuss it, they would tell you they were proud to share, considering they weren't going to recover from their wounds.

"The lights that hang above us, went way back. Not to the tail. But way back. They are starting to play out now, but then, they were bright and far. Not like now, where there are almost less than half the lights there used to be.

"And, so here we were, where you are now. In the fish's belly, lit up and stinky, all of us lost causes."

That was the first part of Bjoe's story. And we're going to pause there.

When he finished telling us all that, Cory rose up, asked for more grog, fainted dead away again.

I thought, this guy, this Bjoe fella, decided he wanted to eat one of us, or all of us, because he always seemed to find some justification for long pig preparation, and that ladder was going to be hard to navigate with us running all over each other's asses.

And, Cory, shit, way it looked to me, he was first on the menu. I wasn't going to try and drag his big unconscious ass down that ladder. He was on his own. Pickled and ready to serve.

I said, "So the lights were here?"

Bjoe nodded.

I scooted back closer to the ladder, tugged on Reba's sleeve a little. She looked at me and slid back too.

I looked at Grace and Steve. I could tell from the way they looked at me, they too were hip. Thinking: this guy could go snacky-whacky at any moment.

"Wow," Grace said. "The lights were here, right?"

"Yes," Bjoe said. "Yes, they were. Brighter than they are now, and they went way down the fish, and for awhile . . . But I said that."

"Okay," Steve said. "Tell it all. Tell some of it over if you have to."

Bjoe nodded.

"We lived back down there as well, at the back, away from the big rushes of water, not up here on the scaffolding and in the caves. But that was before the Scuts."

"The Scuts?" Grace asked.

Bjoe nodded. "Yep. The Scuts."

3

"Oh yeah. The lights were here. And that was a mystery to me, at first. Then I began to put some things together, draw what we like to call in mathematics some goddamn fucking conclusions.

"I'll begin with the robots.

"Don't look so goofy. Really. Robots. Fuckers made of metal with lumps for heads and a single light for an eye. Tentacles instead of hands. All cabled up and ready to go. Guess there were six cables, flapping this way and that. Reckon there were twenty or thirty of them metal, multitentacled doohickeys. Don't know for a fact, didn't count them, but it was in that range.

"Maintenance.

"Bless their little electric hearts.

"Place was a hell of a lot neater then."

"So," I said. "What you're saying is, the grill was in place, all this was in place before you came."

"Do I look like a fucking electrician? A carpenter? A metalworker? And where would I get the tools? Yeah. It was all here."

"And you think you know why?" Grace asked.

"I do, you good-looking thing. And, hey, I'm really talking to all of you. You all look good to me. But, shit, you lady, you're, I don't even know where to begin."

"Begin with why all this stuff was here," Grace said.

"All right, doll. You see, I think the robots were finishing up this baby. Making this fish . . . Don't look that way. Let me explain, let me go into what we in the mathematics business like to call one big ole fucking goddamn shit-eating hypothesis.

"This world is hand and machine made, gents and two ladies. I shit thee not and fuck with you not at all. That's what I believe. You see, this fish, it was water workable, and the robots, they were here to finish up its insides. Do maintenance while it was operating, and at the same time being built. Maybe whoever was building this fish, having it made, forgot all about it and set it adrift before the robots were all done. They had a built-in wear-out time. Like those dissolving stitches you get in your head. They stay in so long, then they dissolve. That's what happened with the robots. They were supposed to do maintenance for so long, then the fish was supposed to go obsolete, like a Ford, you know.

"Why, I don't know. Maybe there's no real reason. Maybe it's just that these work-on-stuff robots can only last so long before they go nutty-bolty. That being the case, they—whoever they is—decided they'd build them with this go-to-butter clause in their wiring. Finish up a certain span of work, then goo-out.

"Ain't that a possible?

"Sure it is. Don't think on it long. Sure it is.

"So they got the grid to not get eat up by the stomach acid they made. And they have lights above, 'cause they're doing work inside a way-down-in-the-dark structure, so therefore gentlemen and two ladies, you got to have some old-fashioned illumination, lest you think you're sharpening your pencil and it's someone's dick.

"They didn't even take note of us when we came, those robots. Not so much as a howdy-do, or, oh-shit, you done found out the fish is electric and we ain't the Partridge Family. They were programmed, hot-wired and motivated, chip-headed and blueprint driven."

"But, the fish has flesh," Reba said.

"Oh, yeah. It's got flesh and it's got veins that pulse with blood. But, I'll tell you another thing this big old finny motherfucker has got, and that's wires, sweet baby cakes.

"I know you must have noted now and again that the dinosaurs seemed to crackle and pop, spark and sputter. Yet, they died or got killed, we ate them and didn't find wires in our teeth, so, it was like what can only be called one big fucking mystery.

"My belief, and you can just quote the living dogshit out of me on this, is that the wires were too small. No shit. Too small even in dinosaurs. To understand the wires, how this alien-built world works (I know, I said aliens, and I'll stand by that remark), is you got to understand the wires are minuscule, as in small little bastards. You can't see them with the undressed eyeball, and, before you go where I know you're gonna go, let me run ahead of you.

"You're gonna say: Yeah, but Bjoe, we done ate the meat off these critters, and we didn't eat the wires, and what I'm going to tell you, now grab hold of your balls—I already got mine, and those of you who are ball-less may clutch anything at will—I'm gonna tell you flat out, you did eat them too, my little hungry folks.

"They're edible. They dissolve. I mean, shit, they can make women's panties you can eat right off the snatch and have them taste like fruits and such, so you think some way-advanced alien motherfuckers can't make some edible iddy-bitty goddamn wires?

"They can.

"And inside this fish, in which you could stuff several dinosaurs and our worn-out asses, except you baby blonde, goddamn you are fine and movie-star-like and not even partially worn out—"

"Tell it," Grace said. "Just go on and tell it."

"Yeah. Okay. Look at the wall of the cave. See the flesh of the fish pulsing. See those cables of veins. Well, when we cut this dude apart, just dug chunks out of it on the inside, touched bones in some cases (the scaffolding is what I call the skeleton), I found wrapped around them, running through the meat, veins, I could see were wires. Red and blue, green and white. You can cut through them and not get shocked. Remember what I said about physics here being bylaws. Things are different. Bring that little thought back to the fore.

"And now I'm gonna go all Serbian guy Nikola Tesla on you, and we're gonna talk alternating-current power transmission, rotating magnetic field principle, and polyphase alternating-current system and induction motor all over the goddamn place, and let me quote B.A. Behrend, 'Nature and nature's laws lay hid in night; God said, let Tesla be, and all was light.'

"That's from my schooling, gents and two ladies. In math and physics and such, I was just schooled all over the goddamn place, although I regret to say I'm all theory and no action, or not much action anyway. I once fell off a chair screwing in a light bulb. That's my electrical work career right there, in the proverbial motherfucking nutshell.

"Now, you're looking at me funny, like I've gone north and am waving at you from afar, shouting out stuff the wind is carrying away. Let me put this where you can fucking understand it. Get your mind jaws around this, gentlemen and two ladies.

"This electricity comes up from the ground, the water, out of the atmosphere, drawn in by . . . Well, shit, I don't know. Do I look like a fucking Einstein? I just quote people, I don't really understand them. Except to say, There ain't no plug-ins, Jack, there's just the electricity, and it's on its own, pulsing through the wires, the veins, the edible cables. And the fish, it lives off the electricity, just like we humans live off electricity. At birth, BAM, there's a spark, jumper-cable time, my little dirties. Our batteries are charged. We got that crackly stuff running through our veins. Call it chi if you will, and if you want to go Japanese, call it ki, and, if like me, you want to stay on the planet Earth (though we ain't, I don't think), call it elec-goddamn-tricity.

"Call it string cheese for all I care.

"You see, the robots, they were finishing up this little fucker, and whoever owned it set it a'sail and a'dive before it was done, and the robots, they were trapped here, and they just kept working while we were here. Not bothering us at all, but restoring lights and fixing stuff, shining the grid.

"So, like I said—and we've come back to it gentlemen and two ladies. Finally, those robot gentlemen just wore down and dissolved. Went to silver-metal goo, they did, and that goo just went right through the grid and into the goop, and sayonara robot fellas. No shit, pilgrims. That's how it went down.

"Their work was done, their time was done.

"But I done told you all that. I tell you now, we got a new phase me and my pals are latching into.

"We used the robots' ladders to climb up here, and there was no place to really rest, so we ventured to cut into the walls of the fish, just so deep, so we could make caves.

"And caves we made, and that's when I found in the walls the veins, so big 'cause the fish is so big. All just one big train-and-fish set this motherfucking world is. Here we are, adrift out there in the hooty-hooty with nothing but our own goddamn selves, and maybe now and again a peek at what this real world offers: aliens seen in dreams—yeah, I see your face, you got them dreams—and wires seen in fish-meat caves.

"I might also add, that the meat we cut out to make the caves, oh, my goodness, it was sweet as pussy fresh with the pubescent bloom, salted down with excitement sweat and the juices that cause it to make smacking sounds in the deeps of the nights.

"But that was one of the few good things, that meat. 'Cause, down here, it wasn't grand. The water the fish gulped was drinkable, if not exactly Evian, and the food the fish swallowed kept us with bellies full. And we, of course, could borrow from the fish itself from time to time. And we had the light, and because we did, well, we couldn't sleep good at night.

"So, early on, we lived at the farther end of the fish, not down in the dark part of the tail, but farther than here. This was before the caves, I should say. You see, there were the cars and such down there, stuff the fish had scooped up somehow. We would go down there and sleep in the wrecked cars to get away from the light. But the lights started to die out down there, and that's when we began to appreciate them. Unlike stars that wink out, their light did not travel long and far while dead or dying. Just being lights, they winked the fuck out and left that part of the fish as dark as the inside of a wolf's ass.

"This darkness, it produced another problem.

"I mean, it was there before. Way down in the tail where there were never lights and it stayed dark. Way down there bad things moved, my little dirties. We didn't know what they were, though some folk went that way to explore (and let me point out I was happily not among them), and they didn't come back. We couldn't yell them up, and the parties that went to search, carrying fire from car metal sparked against dried seaweed and such, didn't come back either.

"We could see their little lights, all Prometheus and such, and then, gentlemen and two ladies, they were gone.

"Here a moment. Gone the next.

"No one else went down there. We yelled a lot, whistled some, but no folks come up.

"Let me add this, though. Just before one of those weak-ass torches went out, I thought I saw something shaped like . . . well, something shapeless, you know. Like shadows that got no shape, like that. Figured I saw it under hot lights it would have shape all right, but not a pretty one.

"Then what light there was got stolen and there wasn't even a flutter of shadow, just this snatching sound like a bullwhip cracking and wrapping itself around something there in the pitch-ass darkness, and that was enough to tell me, don't worry about staying away from the light like those I'm-going-to-God sonsabitches. No sir. Go the other way. The way you've known since you were small. Since cavemen first lit torches and poked them in caves. Stay the fuck away from the dark. Dark bad. Dark final. Stay away from the dark. In the dark, it's dark, gentlemen and two ladies. Dark. Just plain ol' dark.

"Anyway, I think it—whatever the fuck it was—nabbed the torch guy. Hell, I know it did. 'Cause there was a grunt, then the light went out. We scampered quick as frightened mice back toward the hottest and brightest part of the light, all us sonsabitches who had been watching at the edge of light and shadow. And when we arrived beneath the bestest lights and their warmy, not quite toasty yellow, we was goddamn proud to be there.

"Now, that wasn't bad enough, there being something down there in the dark, and it not being good, another concernful-type thing happened.

"The goddamn lights back there started going out a bit more regular.

"That was bound to have made the things, the shadow guys, the Scuts, happy. Unless they are fifty feet tall, they can't reach the lights. Like here, there must be ladders back there. And that may be why it's all dark to the rear of our fishy boat, them beasties, the Scuts, having climbed up there and done those lights in. But their sliding ladders, they don't come this far. Their ladder rails play out about where all them cars are piled, so they can't just keep taking them out, not unless they're willing to come into the bright lights for any time at all. Find their way to the ladders."

"What are they?" Reba asked.

"Not sure. But I think they are built-in disease. You know, the robots were maintenance, and these guys, these shadow motherfuckers, they are dis-maintenance. Just like us, gentlemen and two ladies. We are built in such a way that cells repair, and all manner of such shit, but, we are also built to age and go obsolete-o, baby.

"These Scuts. They are the Big Boy's Obsolete-o team.

"Someday, they win.

"And the fish, he's all done in.

"And so are we. And now we're here. And we just might give them a fight."

"Why did the lights last as long as they did?" I said. "I mean, why didn't they put them out early on? And if they put out the ones they put out, why didn't they venture into the light to get rid of these?"

"I can't answer that. I don't know. Maybe they were happy back there in the dark, eating fish shit, and then one day they find out we're here, get a taste of long pig from our little torch-carrying adventurers. And being so delicious—and it is delicious—they decided shit wasn't quite the delicacy they once thought.

"And it's different coming up on a light from the dark, reaching out quick-like and banging it. But to get these, they got to come seriously into the light for some time before they can even get to a ladder. That gap between us and them is enough to hold them, I think. Unless all the lights go out. You know. Just play out without help. It could happen. I've seen a couple die, no Scuts needed."

"Is there anything in those cars that's useable?" Grace said, always the utilitarian.

"In those cars, in one of them, I found a lady. A beautiful lady. She washed in one day while I'm up here watching the water flush, and her car washed in with it. Washed along the grid and flowed to the back and banged up against them other cars. I went down to investigate, 'cause I could see someone was behind the wheel.

"She was all drowned, her blonde hair pushed tight against her head, her lips purple. But God, did she look good.

"And the water, well, it had tenderized her.

"So, of course, we ate her.

"Rest of the cars yielded skeletons, tires, and greasy jacks. Nothing special. I figure they were folks drove off from the drive-in, tried auxiliary trails, same as us, but it hadn't worked out. Flash floods may have got them. Or they could have died in their cars, and in time, rain would slippy-slip-slip them down muddy paths twixt great trees and hungry critters toward the great body of water under which we are now, doing the Nautilus shuffle, only to be swallowed by our larger-than-average-and-then-some fish. Who, by the way, we affectionately call Big Boy or Ed. Let me tell you something about Ed. Sometimes the plumbing backs up, and what can only be described as about a whale's ass-load of fish shit, flows back this way on a real serious schedule. You can smell it before you see it. It usually gets to just this side of all them cars and such. It ain't pretty, and whatever it is that lives down in there must be tougher than a Christian lie, because when it washes back, now and again, you still see those creepy-shadow-shapes moving amongst the cars, all shitshined, I guess.

"Nasty as we are here, back there, man, we got to be talking nastier than you want to be times ten. Know what I'm saying? And when that fish fart smell comes sailing back this way, it's so solid, you had a club, you could beat it back.

"Oh, Lord. What kind of life is this? Here we are. Jonahs all, with electric lights and bad fish plumbing.

"I need drink. I need love. And figure what I'll get is a drink from yonder skull.

"Let me stop for a drink."

4

Okay. Enough of this guy's story. We'll get back to him.

It's me, diary. You know, Jack. Me. I'm talking here.

Writing here . . . Whatever.

I've come to tell you this Bjoe's story, but, seeing how my world, our world, is a weird movie, and I'm writing this down, and I'm sleepy, I think at this moment in time I'll pause Bjoe's story and pick up on it when I feel less tired.

Also, this pen is playing out, and it's harder to get a dark inky impression . . . shit, I'm starting to sound like that insane nut Bjoe, wandering this way and that with thoughts and pen.

I think this world does it to you. Scrambles the brain waves, dear hearts. Sometimes I feel as if my mental impulses, like a ball, bounce off things, ricochet, and are caught by a catcher not intended, so to speak. And that when he! she! it! throws the ball back at me, it's not the same ball first thrown.

Too tired. Too hypoglycemic.

God, what I'd give for a glass of iced tea, a fine fresh dinner salad with ranch dressing and that little crumbled-up bacon stuff, a medium-rare rib eye, and afterward, a big clean bed with crisp sheets and a nice soft pillow.

Going to stretch out on a bus seat, alone. Reba has already stretched out on another, and these seats are not roomy. It's one thing to be seriously doing the dirty deed, 'cause you want to do that, you'll do it on a goddamn toadstool. So the seats are not too small for that, but for sleep, it's nice to have a bit of room.

So, I'll lay me down to rest, and call for—

INTERMISSION

And now, refreshed, somewhat,
we return you to your movie—

5

After resting, as well as one rests here, I started my day. No matter if it is day or night, I call anytime I'm awake and functioning a day.

There is really little left of Bjoe's story worth telling, so all I'm going to write down is this:

We woke Cory up, and Grace slapped him a bit, and he was sober enough then to climb down the ladder, our friend Bjoe lurking above us, calling down for us to go ahead and sleep up there with them, in their fishy cave.

My thoughts were: I do, I might not wake up. And the last defiant thing I might ever do is give Bjoe or the others a spot of indigestion and then pass turd-like out of existence. On the other hand, I might be nothing more than a warm pleasant feeling in their tummies. Couldn't have that.

So we climbed down. Quick. And once in the bus we slept, after having made sure all the windows were closed and the door was good and locked, and we kept knives by our sides.

Bjoe's story got me worried. I think there's good reason to worry. I'm awake. So I should worry. I also worry in my sleep, now that I think about it. At least most of the time.

Reba is worried too. She climbed on me this "morning," and we had sex so desperate and savage and unsatisfying, I wish I had just pulled my pud or maybe stuck a stick up my ass.

We spent the morning flushing out our bus by backing it even closer to the exit from which we entered the fish's belly. We stood outside and let the water that the fish swallowed flush through the back window and cleanse it.

It isn't exactly clean smelling, but it got rid of all the muck, washed it out the door.

That done, we considered driving the bus closer to the piles of cars and the darkness, which lay thick, like something stacked.

James, who had wiled away his time in the bus while we were visiting with Bjoe, said, "If what you told me about the dark things is true, wouldn't it be smarter not to go that close to those things? The Scuts?"

"Yes," I said, "it would be smarter. But, it's a kind of trade-off. Bjoe, he's not coming right out and nailing us. I figure they don't want to fight if they don't have to. But, you can see he's starting to think of us as lunch. He can't help himself."

"And maybe more than that," Grace said. "I think he had other plans for Reba and me."

Reba nodded. "Seemed that way. Especially you."

"Yeah," Grace said. "He wants to screw us, skin us, eat us, make pouches out of our tits."

"Yours would certainly be utilitarian," Steve said, and Grace slapped him in the back of the head.

"It was a compliment," Steve said. "Sort of."

"So, we can be near a spot that they don't like to go," I said, "or, rather we hope they would rather not go, or we can be right out there in the brightest part of the light, where they feel safe."

"I could tell he's got the willies about those shadow things," Grace said. "He tried to play it pretty deadpan, but he sure was massaging the old sausage when he got to the part about the things in the dark. The Scuts, for scuttle, I presume. I thought he was gonna toss the old mayonnaise from one end of the cave to the other, way he was getting down."

"Sure sorry I missed that little trip and conversation," James said.

"I don't think you really mean that," Reba said.

James grinned.

"Here's the way I see it," I said. "Last night, we just locked up. And I guess that was enough to save us. But in time, the more they think about it, us down here, them up there, their bellies gnawing, and this Bjoe with a love for human flesh, I think a day will come when they decide to try and take us."

"I agree," Grace said. "I get the feeling they aren't trying to add new members to their group. Not really. Just lunches. Here near the darkness, if we have to, we can retreat into the shadows and deal with those things as they come."

Cory had been silent, trying to get over his hangover, but now he spoke. "Big question I got, is how do we get out of here? It's cozy all right, but I'd rather not stay here."

"That one," Grace said, "we're still working on."

"And, if there's a solution," I said, "I suggest we find it. Not only because of Bjoe and his companions, or because of the Scuts, but because this morning I noted that some of the lights that had been just in front of the cars, they went out. My guess is, in time, all the lights will go out. And then we're going to have to deal directly with the Scuts. We won't last long inside of a fish where we can't see how to move about."

"Another thing," Reba said. "Have you noted that it's temperature controlled in here? A little warm, but there's something keeping a fairly balanced temperature. The lights go, maybe it goes. For that matter, maybe whatever powers the fish will play out."

"Can I say something?"

It was Homer. He went through spells so quiet, it was easy to forget he was there.

"Sure," I said.

"One way out might be we wait until the fish is close to the surface, and then we exit like turds and float up, taking something to hang onto with us. There's wood lying about, stuff the fish has swallowed. We might could do that."

"Good as far as it goes," Steve said. "But how would we know how deep down we are. We go out when we're way down deep, we'd drown before we made it to the surface."

Homer shook his head. "Catfish like to get along the bottom, that's no lie. But don't you feel it?"

"Feel it?" Grace said.

"Pressure in your ears?"

Now that he mentioned it, I had to admit I did. It came and went. The others agreed that they too felt it.

"When the pressure goes away," Homer says, "I think Ed's at the surface, or close to it. That would be the time to go. I mean, there was a door, that would be when to go out of it."

Everyone was silent for a moment.

"It's a thought," Steve said.

"It isn't much," Grace said, "but it's more than anyone else has offered. Homer, you just might be a genius."

"You think?" Homer said.

"No," Grace said. "Not really. But even a blind pig finds an acorn now and then. And I think you may have found an idea."

"Well," Homer said. "Wow. An idea. Me, of all people. Uh, what kind of idea did I have really?"

6

"It was a thought," Homer said. "But I didn't take into consideration that there isn't a door."

"There are two ways inside this fish," Grace said. "We got the mouth, and we got the asshole. We try to go through the mouth, well, water rushes through there all the time. We'll drown. Maybe, if we go to the rear we can find an exit. This thing may eat and shit, but it doesn't have real fish intestines. I think Bjoe is wrong about some things. I think this fish is, or was, a work in progress. The robots were supposed to finish it all up, give it fish insides, but, for some reason, they played out."

"Leaving the fish not quite complete," Steve said.

"Yep. I think that whatever built this world, the things in it, is losing its grip. Maybe mentally, maybe it, or they, or whatever, just got bored with the whole thing."

"So it's falling apart?" I said. "Our gods are going insane?"

"Yeah. Or it's not being finished. It's like a dream I used to have when I went to bed at night, elves would take up the rest of the world and fold it away. But they were quick, see, so if I got up to go pee, looked out the window, they were always there with a backdrop. And they built things instantly, before I could get to them. But sometimes, in my dream, I'd look out of the corner of my eye, and there would be nothing.

"I remember the dream well. Gave me this feeling that the world was all a lie, and that I made it up as I lived and breathed. And sometimes, my daydream broke down."

"So in the dream, you dreamed you were daydreaming?" Steve said.

"Yeah. And now I may be living in just the sort of world I dreamed about. But, a lot more unpleasant."

"My head's starting to hurt," Homer said.

"About escaping?" Steve said.

"Yeah," Grace said. "I was going to say, could be, in the back, there's a way out."

"Great," Cory said. "We go out the asshole riding on a turd. And drown."

"That's where Homer's idea comes in," Grace said.

"What idea was that?" James said. "I still don't think I understand all I understand about that idea."

"It's about listening to the inside of our heads," Grace said, and she let that hang in the air like a fart.

"I get it," I said. "We work our way to the rear, hang around until we feel the change in our heads, in our ears. Then, it's the asshole escape. Homer's idea, but without a conventional door."

"That's right," Grace said. "But we have to prepare ahead of time. We have to be sure there's a way out back there. It may be there's real fish guts to the rear. We might need floating devices of some sort."

"Maybe the Scuts got life jackets," Steve said.

"Funny," Grace said, "but it's some kind of idea. Otherwise, we live our lives in the belly of a fish. Just hanging around until an overwhelming crowd of hungry folk descend on us ready for dinner."

"It's possible we could get along with them," James said. "We've seen and done some pretty strange stuff ourselves. I mean, shit, I can't believe I've been fucked in the butt. That's not something I'd do on a Saturday night back home. I even ate a dead baby once. Maybe twice. All right. Probably three times. And I saw two of them killed. So what makes me better than them?"

"You have to make yourself better," Grace said. "We all do. We've all missed a step. We've done what we had to do to survive. But, I know me and Steve and Jack, we've tried to keep it together. Tried hard. Now we can keep trying, and the rest of you can try with us. If you want to stay here, that's your choice. All of you. Me, I'm looking for a way out of the exhaust pipe."

James nodded. "Guess so."

"Hell," Homer said. "I'm for it. It's my idea, and I didn't even know I had one."

"How about everyone else?" Grace asked.

"I'm in," I said.

"Me too," Steve said. "I go where you go, honey."

Cory raised a hand. "Count me in. But, maybe we could make some kind of deal with those guys up there. For some of that liquor. It tastes like boiled dogshit, but it makes you feel pretty good."

"That's one thing we don't need," Grace said. "Distractions."

"So what's the exact plan?" James asked.

"That's a bit of a problem," Grace said. "An exact plan hasn't exactly come to me yet."

"Then we all put our heads together," I said, "come up with a more detailed plan."

"It sounds iffy," Cory said.

"Actually," James said. "It sounds fishy."

He looked a bit disappointed when no one laughed.

"It does," I said. "But, I'm tired of being pushed around by this world. I want to push back. Let's rustle up something to eat, then put our heads together and figure how to do what we want to do."

7

We scrounged up some food. A few fish Ed had swallowed. We cut them open and ate them raw. I wondered if they too were lined with little wires, a combination of flesh and electricity.

After eating, first order of business was to see if the bus would start.

It wouldn't.

Steve and Homer opened the hood and checked around under there.

"I think it's just damp," Homer said. "We got to get something to dry the inside of the carburetor, and such. Some rags would do it."

"We're wearing them," I said.

"Everybody shuck," Grace said.

We took off our clothes and stood butt-naked while Homer and Steve took our rags or animal wrappings and used them to dry the inside of the engine.

Well, we weren't all butt-naked. I had shoes. And so did all the others. Grace's were made of dried animal hides, as were Reba's. I'm sure I looked ridiculous standing there wearing only shoes, and shoes where the soles would have flapped like tongues, had they not been tied up with twine and vines I had scrounged during our stay in the drive-in.

This drying business went on for awhile, and in time, our clothes, now greasy, were returned to us. I put my rags on, as did the others. Grace, however, decided her top was too greasy and threw it away.

It was enough to make me want to believe in a good god.

Almost.

After a bit, we all tuckered out, and I was feeling queasy on top of everything else. Sea sickness. I guess Ed from time to time swam faster and deeper, and perhaps slightly off-center.

We decided enough was enough, closed up the hood, and tried it again. It fired up. We drove it up close to the pile of cars, decided to rest. I went right to sleep. As always, there were thoughts and worries and dreams. I dreamed about the ghost of the drive-in. Where was it? Did it only mist about on the sea above us?

I dreamed of aliens with devices that seemed to be cameras, and maybe special effects instruments. Were they filming us? If there were lights inside this fish, why not cameras? Were we some form of exploitation film? A documentary on strange life placed in odd circumstances; a kind of reality show for the quivering, tentacled, green-faced masses that slithered above our sea and above our sky?

And then, in an instant, it came to me, like the flash of an old-fashioned camera, one of those kind that made the eyes go bright, then see white, then turn one temporarily blind. In that instant, I knew for a fact that a truth was thrust upon me. Something inside me put it all together, worked it all out, took hold of it and held it and saw the insides of everything that was, and there was a revelation. I knew how the universe worked. To be more precise, I knew how my universe worked. I was astonished. I was elated.

And then I awoke, it was lost to me, fleeing fast from my memory like dark water down a drain. I felt as empty as a eunuch's nut sack. I lay there on the hard bus seat and tried to call it all back to me, but it was like calling a deaf hound dog. That buddy had done run off and was gone.

I pulled my arm from over my eyes and sat up in my seat, and was startled.

The bus was surrounded by the fish cave folks. There were even a couple on the hood, their faces pressed up against the glass, looking in.

One of those on the hood was Bjoe. He was on his knees with both hands on the glass, sort of cupped, and his forehead was pressed up against them, and he was looking in.

I must have let out a startled sound, because Reba, who was lying on the seat across from me, sat up, saw them, and let out a loud noise herself. Pretty soon we all stirred.

Grace, who was in a seat near the front, rose up and looked around. Her naked breasts took my mind off of the fish cave folk for a pleasant moment. She didn't look self-conscious at all. "What do you want?" she said loudly to the glass.

Bjoe put a hand to his ear.

Grace repeated herself.

Bjoe stuck the tip of a finger against the glass. It was pointing in her direction.

"Why?" Grace said.

Bjoe just smiled.

Grace shook her head. More of the fish cave folk climbed onto the hood and pressed against the glass, thick as a grape cluster. All of us were out of our seats now.

Cory said, "Maybe they just want to talk?"

"They don't look as friendly as before," Steve said.

"They've had time to think about us," Cory said. "Probably been comparing long pig recipes."

"Ain't no different than the rest of us," James said. "I've eaten dead bodies. I've cannibalized."

"Yes," Reba said, "but those bodies were dead. We aren't."

"Yet," Homer said.

"Is the door locked?" I said in a soft manner.

"Yeah," Steve said. "It is."

We watched them for awhile, then sat in our seats and watched them watch us, their faces and hands pressed against the window glass.

"I feel like one of those lobsters in a tank," Steve said, "you know, the ones where you pick your own."

"And I'm the prime lobster," Grace said, without one hint of modesty.

"I think we're going to need to start the bus up," I said, "drive deeper into the darkness. This bit of shadow doesn't worry them like I hoped it would."

"I believe you are right, Brother Jack," Steve said.

"I say we wait," Cory said. "They're just weird. We're weird. They haven't done anything else."

"One of them has a large bone," Reba said, "and he's trying to work at the edges of my window."

We looked on her side, and sure enough, one of the guys had a big old bone, sharp on one end from having been broken, and he was sticking it in the edge of the window, trying to work the glass loose. He wasn't looking at what he was doing. He grinned at us. He had very yellow teeth.

They began to beat on the windows, all around, with their fists.

"Yep," I said, "No question in my mind. They want to eat us."

"Well, fuck them," Grace said, turned her ass toward the front glass, and pulled down her little fur shorties and gave them a moonshot.

They beat on the glass harder.

"I think you're just encouraging them," I said.

Steve climbed into the driver's seat, hit the key. The engine sprang to life. Steve jerked it in gear and punched it. The bus seemed to leap. The folk on the hood went flying backward, and there was a sound like someone stepping on crackers in cellophane. The bus bumped twice.

I looked out the back window. A couple of the fish cave folk lay in a bloody wad on the grating, and Bjoe was up and limping after us, shaking his fists. The others were coming at a run, passing him.

We were going pretty goddamn fast for a large bus in a small space with a short length to run. Also there was another problem. A large pile of cars in front of us, and no time to stop, and really, no purpose in stopping.

And there was the little problem of the Scuts, whatever they were, waiting in the dark.

The bus slammed into the pile of automobiles and the darkness that surrounded them.

8

The bus hit the pile of cars, hit them hard, knocked our asses about, tossed me over a seat and into another. When I clambered to my feet and looked out, the bus was no longer moving, but it had moved the cars a mite. The darkness had fallen over the front of the bus and covered it like a drop cloth.

Glancing out the back windows, into the light, I saw the fish cave folk were closing from the rear. I could already envision myself being ripped open, my guts pulled out for an appetizer.

Steve jerked the bus in reverse, backed it with a full-throttle wobble, hit a couple of the fish cave folk and drove them down beneath the bus, smashing them like walnuts. Then he gunned the bus forward again, but at an angle. This time he hit one of the cars and really moved it, pushed it back deeper into shadow. He put his foot down hard on the gas, and there was a sound like metal grinding, and smoke rose up from the tires. For a long time the bus just held its spot. Held long enough the fish cave folk reached us and leaped against the back of the bus, up on the bumper and beat at the glass and metal wall there.

The cars began to move, began to slip backward. The bus began to creep forward, taking us and the bus and the pursuing fish cave folk into the darkness.

Steve drove on, the cars parting like the Red Sea, rolling up on either side of us, tumbling along the grate floor. After a few moments, we were deeper into the darkness and the fish cave folk began to fall back.

"They don't like it here," Reba said.

"Neither do I," Steve said. "I just saw something that didn't look like anything, but like all kinds of things, rush by the hood."

We were still moving, but we had slowed down. We looked out the windows and saw nothing.

"You still see it?" I asked.

"Nope," Steve said. "It went by fast."

"Maybe it was just a shadow," Grace said. "I didn't see anything."

"You weren't looking straight ahead," Steve said. "And no, it wasn't a shadow. Unless they can pull themselves apart from the darkness and . . . well, I don't know what it did. Run? Flew? Tumbled? I couldn't tell you. It was there, then it moved, then it wasn't there anymore. It was like it fitted itself into the darkness again. It was . . . I don't know, darker than the dark."

"Stop the bus," I said.

"You sure?" Steve said.

"They aren't coming anymore," I said.

Steve geared the bus down, brought it to a halt. Looking back, it was as if we were down in a dark hole staring up at the sun. Against the light the fish cave folk moved. They grabbed up their dead, and pulled them to the side, set upon the bodies with knives. Fights broke out.

Bjoe appeared from the midst of the fleshy wad, slashing at anything in his way with a bone knife. A throat was cut. A man fell at his feet. The crowd parted around him, scuttled back. At his feet the man whom he had cut thrashed and squirted blood from his throat.

Bjoe looked toward the bus, knife in hand, hair disheveled, dick and balls hanging like some kind of withered fruit. I guessed he could see our shape. He didn't come toward us though. He just looked at us for a long time, then turned and said something to those around him.

After a moment the fish cave folk moved toward Bjoe, slowly, respectfully. They set about cutting, mostly tearing, at the bus-crushed bodies. Bjoe leaned over and stabbed the quivering man he had wounded a couple of times, ripped him open from gut to gill.

Intestines hissed up steam, and blood gushed. Fish cave folk dropped to their knees and dipped their faces into the bloody body. Some ran off with meaty pieces, like dogs.

Bjoe, realizing his prized long pigs were being taken from him, settled down over the man he had killed, bared his teeth. I couldn't hear him from there, but I could sure see those teeth. Could even imagine him growling like some protective wild animal.

"I think it's a good thing we didn't stay back there," I said.

"Yeah," Reba said. "Bjoe has done run all out of nice."

"He was so friendly the other night," Cory said.

"Hell," Grace said. "You wouldn't know. You were drunk. You ought to be glad we didn't leave your intoxicated ass lying up there. We thought about it."

"I'm glad you didn't," he said.

"I don't believe it takes a ton of thinking," I said, "to know that Bjoe is off his nut. He was friendly, and maybe he thought that would work for him. With the girls."

"Yeah," Grace said. "He saw you and me as maybe a willing carnival ride. Then, an unwilling lunch."

"It didn't turn out so easy for him, though," Reba said.

"No, it didn't," Grace said. "And I wish he'd put something over that big old ugly thing of his. It looks like a turkey neck. You know, cut up for boiling in soup."

"Don't make me hungry," Homer said.

"Course," James said, moving his head from right to left as he looked out the window. "Bjoe and his bunch may turn out to be the least of our worries. I just saw what Steve saw."

9

No one else saw it, but none of us doubted there was something out there to see.

"We got some food still," Steve said. "And water. We can settle in for awhile, think things over."

"And if we need to go to the bathroom, do a one or a two?" Cory asked.

"Hang it out the window," Steve said. "Have someone watch so whatever those things are don't crawl up your ass."

"It's the bathroom part I hate the most," Reba said. "Not having privacy and some place comfortable to go. And, you guys, you may do number ones, but you don't do number twos. Way some of you smell, those have got to be number fours."

"On that note," Steve said, "what say we hustle up something to eat?"

"And might I suggest we eat small," Grace said. "We want time to figure on Homer's plan."

"I just love that part," Homer said. "Me with a plan."

After eating, we decided on lookouts. We started with Steve. Way we worked was we let the ones who felt the least tired do the watching. There was no way for us to know how long a watch was, so we just had to go by instinct. If someone felt they wanted to watch for awhile, they took over, replacing whoever was on duty at the time.

The plan was, everyone got a watch.

The rest of us, though not sleepy, tried to sleep anyway. It wasn't that hard, really. Boredom, fear, depression, it all helps you sleep. Only problem for me is, it didn't really give me freedom. In my dreams I thought about the same things I thought about when awake.

As for the plan to escape, nothing more was mentioned about it for a time. But, I did feel my ears pop a couple of times, and I reported it to Grace.

We were sitting up front of the bus, me and her and Steve, and she was speaking softly. She said, "Homer's plan gives hope, such as it is, but I don't know it will actually work."

"It was really your plan," I said.

"Of course," she said. "Thing is, could be our ears pop when we go down, *and* when we come up. Trick is to know which is which."

"Ah," I said.

"I think I can tell the difference," Grace said. "There's a real pressure when we go down. It's subtle, but it's there. When we go up, or when I think we go up, I feel . . . well, lighter. Thing is, I'd like a few days to really get used to feeling it."

"I get you," I said.

"We go off half-cocked," Steve said, "we'll drown like rats."

"We'll probably drown like rats anyway," I said.

Later in the day, a new problem presented itself.

It was on my watch. I was at the back, looking out the window. Bjoe's minions had carried off the bodies and gone away, but from time to time they showed themselves, moved as far down the grid as they dared, right at the edge of light and shadow.

Bjoe came once. I don't know if he could see me well or at all, where I stood at the back window. I'm sure he could see the outline of the bus, surrounded by piled cars on either side, but one thing was for sure, I could see him, out there beneath the bright lights.

From what Bjoe had said I could be assured he wasn't a Christian, but, by golly, he had all the makings. Narrow-minded, mean-spirited, judgmental, and hypocritical. He may have been a little too well educated, but on all other fronts he would have made a hell of a fundamentalist, even if he was coming from the opposite end of the spectrum.

All he needed was a suit and a tie and a pulpit. He was just the sort to have a choir boy bent over a spare pew, or his hand in your pocket when you weren't looking, all the while telling you how he knows the truth and you got to get with the program, Brother.

In a way, he had his own congregation. The fish cave folk. We were to be their source of wine and wafer, flesh and blood. I'd had a run-in with that type before, when we were originally in the drive-in.

But, this wasn't the problem. At the moment, this was an annoyance.

The problem was Cory.

No one was sleeping now, we were just taking turns at the back of the bus, and Cory, he went to the center, said, "I think we're all going to be together, then we got to share better."

"How's that?" James said.

"The women."

"Hey," Reba said. "I think the women get a say in that."

"Listen here, now," Cory said. "Under normal circumstances, I'd agree. But I'm tired of bumping James in the butt. It ain't satisfying."

"And there's that shit-on-your-dick factor," James said.

"That too," Cory said.

"Then stop doing it," Reba said.

"Well now, I'd like to," Cory said. "Me and James have talked about it. We don't like it none. We ain't homos, but we do want to get off."

"Jerk off, and shut up," Grace said. She was still at the front of the bus, and now she rose from her seat, stood in the aisle. She stood with her legs spread, her naked breasts rose with her deep breathing. She looked formidable, but she also looked good, standing like that, her breasts revealed.

Steve said, "What she said."

"It don't have to be nothing special," Cory said. "And you girls wouldn't even have to care or like it. We could do it from behind. You could look out the window. But I say we all get a turn. It ain't right that we shouldn't. We got needs. We're human, and this ain't like at home. Social business and manners, they ain't no good here. It ought not be that Steve and Jack here are the only ones getting their pudding tossed. I say, right now, we make a deal: you gals give it up. I don't know we can measure time on whose turn it is real easy, but we can work something out. Grace, you and Reba, you can take turns, you can—"

It was quick, I'll say that.

Grace, who must have been twenty feet away, was suddenly running down the aisle, very fast toward Cory. I knew in my heart of hearts she wasn't hastening to give him some nookie.

I was right.

She leapt in the air.

Cory tried to step back.

He threw up his hands.

Too late.

Grace's foot snapped out, and she made with a loud yell, and her leg sliced right between his lifted arms and caught him in the face and there was a cracking sound and his head turned quick and he made a noise like someone who had just stepped on a tack.

When Grace hit the floor of the bus, Cory was already there.

I forgot all about my turn at the watch. I moved forward, stood over Cory. His mouth was open, and blood was coming out of it. His head seemed awkward on his neck. His eyes were open, but they had a kind of "I'm wearing milky contacts" look.

Homer eased up, bent over, and touched his fingers to Cory's neck.

"I don't feel nothing."

I bent down and checked him out as well. I'd seen enough of it now to know one thing for certain. I was looking at death.

"Dead," I said.

"No, shit," Grace said.

"Yeah," I said. "No, shit. You kick a guy in the neck like that, it ain't just gonna modify his speech patterns. A kick like that, back home, wherever that is, I bet his family pictures fell off the wall."

"I'm not bothered at all," Grace said. "I'd like to make him that way twice. James. You still with Cory on this share-the-wealth thing?"

"No," James said. "I mean, I could see his point. But not a lot . . . Not at all . . . It was a bad idea."

"Damn," Homer said. "You killed that man with a kick."

"I certainly did," Grace said.

"Cool," Homer said. "Not only are you hot, but you are deadly . . . And, remember: I wasn't in on that . . . you know, plan."

"Good," Grace said.

She bent over and grabbed Cory by the arm and dragged him to the front of the bus.

"Open the door, Steve," she said.

Steve, briskly, I thought, stepped to where the door device was, grabbed it, and pulled. The door hissed open, and Grace, being not careful at all, bumped Cory down the steps of the bus and tossed his ass out into the dark.

There was a rustling noise, and then out of nowhere the darkness became darker and Cory was snatched up. I saw his feet flap once or twice at the air, then he was absorbed by shadow.

Steve pulled the bus door closed quickly, and something dark slammed against it.

"Just in time," Grace said.

She walked to the center of the bus, said, "I'm serious. Dead serious, as you saw. Anyone else have any kind of plans for me or Reba? Come on. Anyone want to talk pussy?"

No one raised their hands.

"I don't go for any shit," Grace said. "Especially if it has to do with me. And if you think I feel bad about Cory, I don't. I meant to kill him. It worked a bit better than I thought. I figured I'd have the pleasure of beating him to death, but it didn't work out. James, now you ain't even got Cory's warm butt to wrap around your little old pecker. I better not so much as see you look in my direction or scratch out a picture of a vagina on the back of a seat with your fingernail. Hear me?"

"Yeah," James said, standing very stiff at the back of the bus. "I do."

"Good," Grace said. "Now stare at the floor."

James looked at the floor.

"Keep looking down for awhile. Don't look up anytime soon. I don't want to see your ugly face. Got me?"

"Got you," James said, without lifting his head.

Grace said, "Jack. I'll take the next watch."

And she did.

10

"They keep working their way closer," Grace said.

Grace was still at the back of the bus, at the back window, and when she said this, we all took notice. Fact was, we were paying Grace very close attention.

"I hope you don't kill me for having an opinion," Homer said. "But, what happened to my plan? We sit here long enough, either Bjoe and his bunch will get us, or these . . . shadows will, whatever they are."

"The bus's lights work, don't they?" I said.

"Yeah," Steve said. "I didn't exactly have time to think about them before, but yeah, they work. I mean, they should, all the dampness didn't short out a wire."

"I say we turn on the lights, drive in deeper," I said. "There isn't any going back, and we're going to try and make our way to the rear of the fish anyway, so, crank it up, turn on the lights, and drive on."

"It's a start," Grace said.

I looked to the back of the bus. Bjoe and his followers were standing out of the light, just over the line into the world of shadow.

Bjoe was worrying his pecker as he glared at the bus. He stepped into deeper shadow, and I couldn't make out his features, then he eased toward us slowly. His minions followed.

"They're getting a hell of a lot braver," Grace said.

At that moment, one of the female minions came forward, bent to the ground there in shadow, and made a movement with her hand. There was a spark. She went at it again. More sparks. Then a blaze.

I realized what they were doing. Striking metal to get sparks, knocking it into some tinder. Dried seaweed probably. The little blaze struggled at the shadows then was lit to a torch, most likely coated in fish oil or fish fat. The torch tore a bright hole in the darkness.

Other torches were lit.

Soon there was a crowd of torches moving our way.

"They really want you, Grace," Homer said.

"They want us all," Grace said. "We're nothing to them but a big old dinner."

Steve said, "All right then. Now we find out. Hold onto your asses."

He started the bus, hit the lights.

They came on.

A cheer rose up inside the bus.

I know. No big thing. But, hey. We took our victories, small as they might be, where we could get them.

The bus lurched forward, began to pick up speed.

Behind us Bjoe and the others ran after us, their torches bobbing in the shadows like bouncing balls.

Steve put the hammer down, and in a matter of moments they were nothing more than bright pinpricks, and soon the little pieces of light quit moving, but we didn't. We rolled on.

"Won't be long," I said, "and they'll all eat each other. It's bound to come down to that eventually."

"Glad to not be part of the feast," Reba said.

We slowed and rolled on. The darkness became darker yet, and there started to be a kind of thumping against the side of the bus, against the glass.

Shadows, like large black pieces of construction paper, but with heft, blew about the bus and rocked it, crawled all over it. We could hear them on the roof, scuttling from one end of the bus to the other. Where they had hit the glass was dark, oily slime.

When the glow of the headlights hit them, they scattered. They were ragged in shape. Not one like the other, just torn black curtains of night, the tears all different, all irregular.

Once I saw a split in what could only be described as the dark face of one, and there was something not so dark there. Teeth. Shiny. Almost silver.

"What the fuck are they?" Homer said.

"Parasites," Reba said. "Maybe some kind of crazy cancers. With dentures. They may be killing our giant fish host as well. Only more slowly than they would kill us."

"I think they're just pure pieces of evil," Homer said. "You see, I finally figured out where we are. It took me some thinking—"

"I bet," Grace said.

"—but I come to a conclusion. It was our time. We died. And we went to hell."

"Why the fuck would I go to hell?" Reba said. "Bad language?"

"Me," Grace said, "I did some serious fucking. But, hey, would that count? There really isn't a commandment that says no sex. Just no adultery. And besides, I don't believe that shit anyway. Which part of the Bible you gonna believe. The mean-spirited, mean-assed God of the Old Testament, or the sweet philosopher of the New Testament?"

This didn't faze Homer.

"That's where we are," Homer said. "Hell. We're being punished."

"I don't deserve punishment," I said. "Well, I didn't. I've done some things since coming here that might be debatable. But to get here, if it's hell, hey, I must have got in the wrong line somehow."

"I suppose it could be that," James said. "The wrong line."

He had been real quiet up till now, possibly not wanting Grace to leap in the air like a fucking Ninja Turtle and kick his head around in a three-sixty.

"We thought we was all in the line for drunken fun, movies, sex, what have you, and it was a trick line, so to speak. We got in the wrong line . . . Wrong place at the wrong time."

"There isn't any hell," Grace said, "and if there is, this isn't it."

"It's bad enough to be a hell of sorts," Reba said.

"We get to make choices still," Grace said. "I figure that's hell, when you can't make choices. When you can't struggle or strive anymore. Can't choose to be who you are no matter what the circumstances. We get to that point, then we're in hell. Right now, we're still alive."

About that time Steve brought the bus to a halt.

"Shit," he said.

We moved to the front of the bus, looked out over the hood. Shadows washed over the hood like floods of ink, but finally they parted long enough for us to see what Steve saw.

A drop-off.

A place that just went . . . down.

"We won't be driving any farther," Steve said. "We've come to the end of the trail."

11

"What now?" Homer said

"Well," Grace said, "if we're going to execute your plan, we're going to have to start using our heads. Here's what I suggest. We all relax. Just relax. We keep someone awake at all times. Say two of us. What we do is we start being real quiet. We only talk if we have to. Boring, I know. But what we got to do is be quiet inside ourselves, and listen, and feel for when things change."

"The pressure in the ears?" Homer said.

"Exactly," Grace said. "If at least two of us are awake at all times, and two of us feel it, we try to decide if it's oppressive pressure, you know, going down, or relaxing pressure, surfacing, or being near the surface."

"Uh," James said, holding a hand out to Grace, "not to be kicked to death or anything, but near the surface, wouldn't that be as bad as being way below?"

"Depends on how near the surface," Steve said.

"But how can we know for sure?" James said.

"You can't," I said. "We judge the way Grace says for a time. When we feel we can recognize the way it feels when we get close to the surface, then we plan for the next time and go for it."

"Don't your ears adjust after a time?" Steve said. "Get so they don't pop?"

"You better hope not," Grace said. "And another thing, we're going to have to go out there."

"Outside the bus," Homer said. "I don't even like to hang my ass out the window anymore. I got to go, I go damn quick."

"Yeah," Steve said, "the bus is starting to stink, all that stuff on its sides."

"We have to go out," Grace said. "We got flashlights, and those things don't like the light."

"How bad do they not like it?" Homer said.

"It's the chance we have to take," Grace said.

"She's right," I said. "We have to go out there and find the way out of Ed. The flush, so to speak. And when we do, then we got to figure how to ride our way out, and hope for the best."

"We could just stay right here," James said, "inside the bus. It's not so bad."

"For how long," I said. "We'll run out of food. We'll end up eating one another—"

"Maybe it wasn't such a good idea throwing Cory away," James said. "I mean, he was already dead . . . I'm just saying what I think others are thinking."

"I wasn't thinking that right then," Grace said. "But I could. We all could. Some of us have not only thought it, we've done it."

James's hand went up.

"No shame in that," Grace said. "If the meat is available. It wasn't too good for Olympic hopefuls crashed in the snow, and it wasn't too good for pioneers crossing the Rockies, caught in blizzards, so, by God, it isn't too good for us. But, I must admit, I wasted some not-so-prime meat."

"Yeeewwwwww," Reba said.

"You just haven't got hungry enough," James said.

"Could be," Reba said, "but I don't want to start being a cannibal any time soon. I might start to like it the way Bjoe likes it. And then I might not want to wait for the food to die. Or, I might even think how nice it might be if someone did die, so there'd be the meat."

"At the time," Grace said, "I was thinking I wanted that bastard out of my sight, not how I could prepare him for dinner. If I really thought about that sort of thing, wanted that sort of thing, I wouldn't have thrown him out there for the shadows to snack on. Thing is, we can't sit here. We have to find a way out, even if it kills us."

"I don't like that 'kills us' part," James said.

"You have no real say," Grace said. "You shouldn't have sided with Cory."

"I only sided a little bit."

"Get quiet again," Grace said. "Thing is, you can stay if you want, but you won't decide for the rest of us. Look here. I'm not going to decide for any of you, for that matter. All I'm saying is I'm going to try and find a way out. You can work with me, or do your own thing. But, me, I'm going."

"I'm in," Steve said.

"Me too," I said.

Reba and Homer agreed. James was silent, the way Grace had asked him to be.

"All right then," Grace said. "I say we start the shifts, for feeling the changes. Up and down. No one has to sleep, but someone, two of us have to stay awake. No talking. Starting as soon as we lay things out. Unless it's necessary to survival. You want to sit up and look about, or try and help the ones assigned to feel the change, go for it. But if it's not your turn on deck, so to speak, either sleep or shut your mouth. We'll record what we find. Jack, I've seen you writing. You got paper, a pen in that pack, right?"

"I do. The pen is starting to run out of ink, but I have an eyebrow pencil and some mascara that I found in a car. Have to, we can write with that."

"Good. As I was saying. A couple of us need to go on an expedition. Outside. See if we can find the exit hole."

"I'll go," I said.

"Me too," Reba said.

"All right," Grace said.

James raised his hand, looked at Grace. "I know this is something I shouldn't ask. But who made you captain?"

"I did," she said. "Problem with that?"

"No. That works fine for me."

We still had a few flashlights, and there were even a couple of matches Grace had produced from somewhere. And there were knives, of course.

Grace, me, and Reba moved to the front of the bus. I took one flashlight, Reba the other. We each took a knife. We spoke quietly.

"Thing to do," Grace said, "is go out there, see if you can figure where Ed relieves himself, and can we get out that way. This critter, he isn't going to be like a normal fish—"

"No shit," Reba said.

"No telling what you'll find," Grace said. Then almost too soft to hear: "But you got to find something. Some way out."

"Those things move awfully fast out there," I said.

"I know," Grace said. "I can go instead of you."

"I didn't say that."

"I can, though," Grace said, "but the problem is James. I don't trust him, and with me out of the way, well, Steve could handle him, but I like having him double-teamed. I may just go on and kill him. That would be the smart thing to do."

"But it wouldn't be the right thing," I said. "We start doing things like that, then Homer is correct, we'll be like a lot of other folks on this world, and with no one acting as room monitors, this will be hell."

"I'll try to remember that," Grace said. "Now, you remember Bjoe's story, about how the torches his folk were carrying went out, and they were nabbed. I think that's exactly what happened. The torches burned out, and the light went out, and when it did, they were nabbed. Once you turn your flashlights on, don't turn them off. No light, and they come. You've got light, they won't bother you."

"You're sure?" Reba said.

"Of course not," Grace said. "I'm trying to make you feel better. All we know is they don't like light. They might be strong enough to have put those torches out themselves. They might jam those flashlights up your asses. I don't know. I can go, you can stay. One way or another, someone has to go out there and look around."

"We could all go," Reba said. "Isn't it a bad idea to divide? You know, we've all certainly seen enough horror movies."

"If we all go, and it goes wrong, none of us make it," I said. "I wouldn't like that. I want some of us to survive, if for no other reason than I'm stubborn. We don't make it, then we still got others who can."

"You could send James," Reba said.

"He wouldn't be worth a damn if I did send him," Grace said. "I don't like him, and I don't trust him. Besides, I'd hope he would drop his flashlight. Here's the bottom line. We got to find a way out. We all go, we wouldn't have a chance. There's only two more flashlights. There would be a wad of us out there without enough light. The two of you, you can fend for each other. I don't know what to say you're looking for. A way out. That's it. We'll all probably drown anyway. But I'd rather do that than sit here and hope there's a god who notices and sends us individual scuba suits."

"I got you," I said. I turned to Reba, said, "Think the way we do this, Reba, is one of us takes up the rear, sort of back to back, and we wave the lights around a lot. Let them know we're armed with bits of sunshine."

"I'll have Steve turn on and flash the lights every now and then. I can't tell time, but I'm going to wet a string, hang it from the ceiling, when the drips fill a paper cup—"

"You don't have any paper cups," I said.

"I'm going to fold one out of a piece of paper from your pack. I'll make it a small one. When it fills, I'll flash the lights. Then I'll flash them again. Three, four times. Then we'll wet the string again, let it fill the cup."

"And if the string dries out before the cup is filled?"

"I'll keep it wet," Grace said, "if I have to pee on it."

"All right," Reba said. She took a deep breath, called over to Steve. "Open the door."

12

Even with the lights it was very dark, and my first thought was that those little pale yellow beams of ours weren't worth anything when it came to the big bad things out there in the wilds of Ed's belly; those dark things all het up and fast and nasty and full of teeth.

Reba actually put her butt to mine and backed. We rotated our beams like search lights looking for Kamikazes. We hadn't gone far when we found the little shadow dears.

They whispered past us, rattled and fluttered there in the dark. I shone my light this way and that, felt something at my elbow, snapped the beam over there, only to have a chunk of the dark pop away.

"Oh, shit, don't fall down, Jack. Don't trip. Don't fuck up. And, for heaven's sake, I hope the flashlights don't go out."

"I've been trying not to think about that," I said. "All I've been thinking is, I ever get hold of the director of this picture, boy is he gonna take a bitch-slapping."

"Oh, Jack," Reba said. "It hit me."

"What?"

"Those things. One of them hit my arm. It's bleeding."

"Get the light off yourself. Keep it searching. Keep moving."

"I shouldn't have come. I sounded so brave when I volunteered. But I shouldn't have come."

"Neither of us should have. Do you want to go back to the bus?"

"Yes. But guess what? I can't see it anymore."

I looked back the way I thought we had come. And Reba was right. There was nothing but the dark to see.

The things moved around us as if we were the center of a hurricane. They swirled, crinkled, and cracked, like an old film negative being wadded. As we moved forward, flashlights extended, waving this way and that, the things scattered.

But it seemed to me they were getting a bit more testy, coming ever closer. Pretty soon, we both had a number of cuts from the edges of the things as they flittered by.

"Look," I said.

So she could look, I turned right and she followed around until I took her position and she took mine.

"My God," she said.

"Yep."

What she was looking at was a narrow metal bridge. A grillwork bridge. It went across into a darkness the flashlights would not cross.

The bridge spanned what looked to be an abyss.

"Let's scoot onto the bridge," I said. "One of us can point our light, get a better look at what's down there while the other watches for critters."

As we made our way onto the bridge we were confronted by a foul smell.

"God Almighty," I said. "We must be at Ed's sewage plant."

"Or a way out," Reba said. "It goes down a ways, but it also veers to the right there, to what could be Ed's rear end. Though, with just a flashlight, it's hard to tell what I'm seeing."

"Let's change roles," I said. "You flash about, I'll have a look."

Reba was right. The hole beneath the bridge dropped way down, and there were worker ladders on either side of the pit, something the robots used for maintenance. But there was a kind of tunnel that went off to the right. I noticed too that it was moving. As I watched, it irised open, then closed. Then repeated itself. Again and again.

It was a sphincter. I saw a mass of something dark rise up from the pit and reach the tunnel, flow into it as if sucked, and disappear.

I lifted my light and joined Reba in flashing mine about.

"I think it's a sphincter that exits Ed's waste. We might could get out that way."

"Boy, won't that be shitty?" Reba said.

"Frankly, I don't see how we can do it. Not and live."

"Grace is right though. We have to try something. We can't just wait here. We'll die anyway. I'd rather go out trying."

"I could go down there and investigate. I think I can swing over the bridge and get closer for a look. Can you stand being here by yourself?"

"Oh, Jesus . . . Make it quick as you can."

"Kiss me," I said.

She did. Quickly.

I went to the base of the bridge and started climbing over. Reba's light hit me.

"Shadow," she said.

I jerked my head and my light. My carnivorous shadow friend fluttered away from me.

I got my foot on the ladder and started climbing down. It was hard to do with my flashlight, and I knew if I dropped it, I was dead meat. Maybe the things wouldn't come down here, but even still, if I dropped the light, when I went up, they'd be waiting.

The deeper I went the stinkier it got.

What had seemed like depth from the bridge, darkness in the light, was something moving, gurgling, and stinking.

Ed functioned as a fish, but had never been completed. Like Bjoe said, someone forgot, or the mechanisms just played out too soon. Still, Ed was working all right, and his innards were working satisfactorily enough to manufacture what we in the bathroom business (which is pretty much all of us), would describe as pure-de-ole-identifiable-for-a-fact—you-bet-your-smelly-ass—

S-H-I-T.

No question there.

13

I shined my light down there. The tunnel was pulsing, sucking in that nasty goo. I thought, well, I die this way, it isn't a death I ever expected. It was, to put it mildly, a unique way to go. Had to be better than cancer or some sort of horrid disease, going slow, like being gummed to death by protein-deprived octogenarians.

In a way, it was no less dignified than aging and lying in your own shit and being eaten away slowly from the inside. Of course, if I were home, who was to say I wouldn't just die quick of a heart attack at the age of eighty while in bed with a twenty-five-year-old hooker with her little finger crooked up my ass.

So, that thinking business, sometimes it was better not to do too much of it. It could get you in trouble.

I was pondering this to the point of almost feeling that hooker's little finger in my tail, when suddenly, above me, there was light.

Not heavenly light, but light. And it was too much light for Reba's flashlight. Light from a distance, filtered through something the consistency of a gunnysack. It held for a long moment, then went out.

"The bus," Reba said. "Oh, God, Jack, come up."

I carefully padded my way up the shit-slick ladder onto the bridge, somehow maintaining my grip on the flashlight.

When I was standing beside her, she said, "Wait."

I waited. The birth of the universe couldn't have been any slower than that wait.

Then, the light.

When the beams hit, the darkness shredded like something dark tossed into a fan. There was a sound like a baseball card in bicycle spokes, the bicycle being peddled fast.

"The darkness," Reba said. "It's absolutely alive with them."

"They may be the dark," I said.

When the bus's head beams went out, I made a swooping movement with my light and Reba flashed hers about too. After a moment, I used the light to nab the direction of the bus, though I couldn't actually see it in my feeble beam, and pulled the flashlight over my shoulder. I did this repeatedly, signaling for them to come.

"Oh, Jack, behind you."

I turned with the light. The darkness sucked back a bit, the bridge trembled.

"Sorry," Reba said. "I had the light on it, but it was still coming."

"They're not as afraid now," I said. "They're getting brave."

"Look."

We could see from a great distance the bus beams moving toward us, two headlamps that looked to be the size of the tips of our thumbs.

Seeing the light grow and brighten was as hypnotic to us as it might have been to a moth. Soon, we stood on the bridge in a bath of yellow. It was heartening.

We worked our way back to the bus, and to get in the door, we had to step momentarily out of the glow of the bus's head beams and into shadow. Our flashlights seemed less bright than before, and I could feel those things all around us, closer, touching, almost tasting us. Steve, sitting in the driver's seat, worked the door lever and let us in. As the door slammed behind us, Steve, eyes wide, said, "You don't want to know what was right behind you, almost up your asses."

Inside, everyone gathered around, and we told what had happened. Steve drove the bus right up to the edge of the divide. He let the bus idle. The lights struck across the chasm like a golden honey bridge.

"It's ugly down there," I said. "Once you go in, you might be wadded up with the turds. If you aren't, you'll be stuffed with turds, won't be able to breathe. I don't see a way to make it work."

"We haven't got but one choice," James said. "We got to go back into the light. Maybe Bjoe will let us stay with him. He might do that. Or we have to fight him.

Hell, Grace can kick Bjoe to death. We can become the leaders. We can't get out without being killed, and we can't stay back here in shadow, so seems to me, that's the only way to go."

"In case you haven't noticed," I said, "we're a little outnumbered. Not even Grace can fight all of them. Not even with our help."

"Bjoe might listen to reason," James said. "I mean, we'll be in the bus. We'd have some protection, and we could fight them if they try and come in. I think we got a better chance that way instead of waiting for our fucking ears to pop, diving into that shit, and hoping we aren't made into turds or stuffed with them."

"He's got a point," Homer said.

"Much as I hate to admit it, he does," Grace said. "But I'm not big on going back. A place I've already been that isn't good, doesn't seem worth going back to."

"Fucking news flash," James said. "We've already been here, too, and it ain't for shit."

Steve had killed the engine while we were talkin'. Now he turned the starter and fired it up again.

"Hey, man," I said, "what's the scoop?"

"I don't want to go back," Steve said, "and we're at the end of the line here, so why don't we go forward?"

"You been sniffing glue, doing the bag?" James said.

"Do you feel it?" Steve said. I had, but it hadn't really registered. "We're surfacing."

Everyone was silent for a moment, then Homer said, "Yeah. We are. But for how long? It may have been kind of my idea, but I'm liking it less all the time,"

"We can't go back," Steve said. "There's only one place to go . . . Into the shit."

"Oh, man," James said, "you don't mean it?"

"The bus is our only protection," Steve said. "It might survive the process."

"And if it does," Homer said, "we'll squirt out the fish's ass and into a whole hell of a lot of deep water. We'll sink like a goddamn brick tied to an anvil tied to a Cadillac transmission."

"We have to be ready," Steve said.

"What the fuck does that mean?" James said.

"When we shoot out—"

"—you mean if we shoot out. And if we do, we'll sink, like the way Homer said."

"—we have to be ready to open windows. They slide down, so the water pressure ought to allow that. We slide them down, and we swim out."

"Oh, that's a good plan," Homer said. "And why don't we find something heavy to tie to our dicks to make it just a little fucking harder?"

"We haven't got much time," Steve said. "My ears are clearing. We're reaching the surface."

"Count my ass out," James said. "Give me a flashlight. I'll take my chances back with the cannibals."

"It's now or never, folks," Steve said.

I gave James my flashlight, said, "Good luck, man."

"It would be best if we all went back," he said. "Best all around."

"Not gonna happen," Grace said.

Steve opened the door as James turned on the flashlight.

"Goodbye, asshole," Steve said.

"You're all gonna do this?" James said.

"I guess we are," Grace said. "Anyone that isn't, go now."

"I'm crazy, but I'm sticking," Homer said.

The rest of us nodded.

"Goodbye, dumb shits," James said, waved the beam at the pulsating shadows in the door, made them scamper.

He went out.

Steve closed the door.

We moved to the back of the bus and watched James and his light. Actually, just the light. The shadows were too thick to see anything else. The light bobbed quickly as it raced away from us.

"Think he'll make it?" Homer said.

"He can't make it either way," Grace said, fastening the back window down tight. "If those shadows don't get him, the dinner bell is waiting for him on the bright side. Frankly, I don't care if they use his balls for tennis. He made his own goddamn bed, now let him lie in it."

"I hate to just let him go like that," Homer said. "I mean, I did let him fuck me in the ass. It wasn't that much fun, really, but I let him. I feel like me and my ass owe him something."

"You've heard my thoughts on the matter," Grace said. "I'm all done thinking about him. Your ears still popping, Steve? I can't feel it."

"I think our buddy has surfaced."

"I think it's time to do the big deed, baby," Grace said.

Steve made with a wild rebel yell that shook me to my bones.

"My mama always said I was a little turd," Reba said, as we filed into a seat next to one another, our hands gripping the seat in front of us. "I guess she was right."

"Grab hold of something, and good luck to us all," Steve said, and with the beams on high, a fresh yell on his lips, he punched the gas, and we jolted forward, and Reba sang at the top of her lungs: "We all live in a yellow submarine."

"With bad insulation," I said.

Part Four

In which a yellow school bus is the vehicle for a bizarre exit and becomes a kind of projectile turd that won't float. The great shining bridge is seen again. Ghosting is experienced. Dog urine fruit is digested. Chicken Little rules. Toys are found.

1

Let me tell you, time can stand still.

It stood still as the bus went over the lip of the shitter. I envisioned us perched on the edge of a giant, dark toilet bowl full of someone's little dividend, and we were about to dive in as if we had good sense. Shit-busters to the rescue.

Our own rescue, we hoped.

But, BAM. There we were, on the lip, frozen in time.

We just hung there.

Or so it seemed.

Then all of time gathered up and pushed, and we came unglued.

The bus, a long brightly lit, yellow, pontooned turd, dripped over the edge and took just two days south of forever before it hit that mess.

I was in my seat, facing down at the dark doom below us, my butthole biting at the upholstery, clutching the seat in front of me so hard my fingers ached.

And the shit hit the windshield. Hard.

I thought:

With our luck the windshield will blow and that pile of fish turds will smash us all the way to the back of the bus, fill our lungs with digested refuse, then, if we have a chance to live, if any one of us might be a survivor, that fish's asshole will chew us up like a mole in a lawn mower, and out we will go.

Down we went, and the light was extinguished by the black goo, and I could feel Reba next to me, but couldn't see her. I could hear her breathing hard, and there was a sensation of being like a BB sinking down into a vat of chocolate pudding, minus the nice smell and the fine taste.

Then the bus started to twist and turn, and I knew it was that weird digestion process that the Powers That Be had constructed, maybe left unfinished. The bus began to spin, and next thing I knew I was knocked into Reba hard. Was bouncing about the bus like a ricochet shot. The smell was terrible, and I could feel that mess on my hands, which meant it was easing in through the cracks in the windows and the doors, had possibly shoved through the window Grace had latched up in back.

But, no, I consoled myself. If that had happened, the bus would be full of that nasty stuff.

Then, as if thought were the catalyst, I felt the horrid mess press up against me like foam, filling my nostrils with its stench, pushing me either forward or backward, down the aisle. I was uncertain which, though I could feel myself bouncing between the seats. There was a loud crunching sound, like a smartass wadding up an aluminum soft drink can, and someone screamed, a loud horrible scream that could not be identified as man or woman. Then I was pushed up against what I realize now was the windshield. The shit shoved me. The windshield made a cracking sound, and I blacked out. But the blackness into which my mind fell couldn't have been any blacker than the world that was already around me.

I came awake.

I was surprised at that.

I was still alive. I could still breathe.

But I was surrounded by wetness. Not the thick mess that I had felt before, but wetness. I was bobbing about in the water, and I could see the water rippling, and there was great white foam, and sticking out of the foam was the nose of the bus, the windshield gone, the roof crushed in, the front right tire blown.

I had been shoved through the windshield, and the bus had shot to the surface, if ever so briefly. Perhaps the pontoons (which had come loose of the bus) had done it, or as we went into the fish's ass sphincter and he let us fly, the force of it had driven us out and up. Trapped air in the bus, maybe. I didn't know. In that moment, nothing made sense.

Reba was clinging to the front of the bus. I could see her pretty well lying in a pool of what I realized was moonlight, silver as mercury. I could see a dark patch on her face where blood had bloomed like a flower, the moonlight made it appear to be a large black rose.

She clung to the bumper, lay across the hood in what could only be described as a dazed state. She looked in my direction, but I couldn't tell if she was seeing me or not. She lifted her head a little, like a turtle sunning itself on a rock, then lowered her head against the bus, continuing to cling.

The bus started down, quickly. I tried to yell Reba's name, beg her to let go, but all that came out was a hoarse croak. The water foamed around the bus, churned the fish turds that had come up with it, then the bus dove. Water lapped over Reba and rushed into where the windshield had been, then it was gone, taking Reba with it, leaving only a wide band of chrome-colored ripples that pushed me up and down in the water like a fisherman's cork.

I dove after the bus, but I was too weak. My lungs wouldn't hold the air I had swallowed. It was so dark I couldn't see a thing below. Huge turds bounced against me.

There was nothing I could do.

I fought my way to the surface, screamed as I broke the roof of the water and saw the moon above me. I began to cry. I felt something touch me. A vast patch of water disappeared, and in its place was a great gray wall.

The wall rose higher.

And higher.

It was Ed swimming by.

He dove. The dive pulled me under. I fought with everything I had to make the surface, even ended up putting my foot on Ed's back and shoving off.

I broke the surface and looked in the direction Ed had gone. All that could be seen was a great fin knifing through the dark water. As I watched, something struck me hard in the head, almost knocked me unconscious.

I grabbed at it.

It was one of the pontoons. It had snapped in half, but it still floated. I grabbed hold of it and clung, tried to climb on top of it. It rolled with me, and I lost it a couple of times, but finally I had a solid grip on it, straddled it, latched my legs around it tight.

Across the water I saw a white mist. And then I saw it was not a mist at all, but the ghost of the drive-in. It slowly floated toward me. Floated until it was over and around me. And inside the drive-in I could see everything that had happened while I was there. I could see me and my friends, all dead now, in the camper, tooling along the highway, heading for what we thought would be a great weekend.

There were dinosaurs and such, and all the events that had happened after we escaped the drive-in theater—or so we thought. All that and more. Overlapping, running together, seen simultaneously like a bad TV connection, one program blending into another.

The mist stuttered. Was followed by a sound like electricity shorting out. A snap of light and shadow, a crackle like cellophane being chewed by a goat, and the mist was back.

The Popcorn King.

Those dinosaurs.

Poplalong Cassidy and his carnivorous film.

Grace. Shit Town.

The bus. All gray and ghostly and us inside. Outside the bus. Inside the bus. Every view you could imagine. All that had taken place. Reba and I making love. Grace kicking Cory to death. All of us, looking like some kind of ride at Disneyland, a bus full of escaped specters from the Haunted Mansion.

The past and the present rolled in and out. Everything was caught up in that white mess of memory.

I closed my eyes and tried to scream, but my voice was still too hoarse.

I dropped my head against the pontoon, stretched out on it as best I could. And clinging like I was riding a rocket to that silver moon above me, to escape the mists and all it contained, I fell into a stupor as the water rode me up and rode me down.

2

"It's okay," I heard Reba say, and I could feel her stroke my hair.

I awoke to find she wasn't there. There was only me and the pontoon, and it was a breeze moving my hair, not Reba's soft fingers. The moon was gone, and the sun was warm but not too warm, and the water was a bright sheening blue. Beyond, there was a great cloud bank, and in little patches, like glimpses of car metal as seen through clouds of white dust in a dirt-track race, I could see the great silver bridge.

I thought of Reba again, bright eyes, fine face, skin made hard from life, her navel like the end twist on a gut-stuffed sausage, the tangle of hair between her legs.

I thought: That's about right. Here I am floating on what is essentially a goddamn log. I've lost all my friends, and my lover, and what I'm thinking about is not her sweetness, and kindness, but the fine wet thing between her thighs.

Men. They ain't worth killing.

And I be one of them.

As I clung to the pontoon, I was thinking: This might be my chance. Just to let go. Just to drift down, the way poor Reba had. Drift down into the great deeps and fill my lungs with water, and end it all.

Wasn't drowning supposed to be pleasant?

Or did I read it was actually very unpleasant, and the idea that it was pleasant was a myth? Which was it?

Just the thought of unpleasantness was enough to make me dismiss the idea. It was never anything I was in love with anyway.

"Jack," a voice called.

I thought: Here I go again.

But this wasn't Reba calling.

It was a man's voice. Sounded like Steve.

Then came Grace's voice calling my name.

I rolled my head to the other side, and out there on the water, floating up and down, were two heads and a body. The body was between the two heads, and they were hanging onto it. It was not floating very well, and I slowly deduced it was Homer, face down. On one side of him was Grace, on the other, Steve.

I tried to yell at them, but my voice came out in a bark. I realized then that the rushing water had gone into my throat and filled my belly and caused me to throw it up at some point, scalding my throat with stomach acid.

"We'll come to you," Grace said, and they let go of Homer and swam to the pontoon. Homer's body floated lower in the water, so there was really little to nothing left of him to see.

They gripped the pontoon at the front and back. I continued to straddle and clutch the pontoon like a spider on a stick; I began to cry.

"You're okay," I said.

"More or less," Grace said.

She was at the end where my head was, and I lifted my eyes and looked at her. It was really the first time I had ever seen her look the worse for wear.

There was fish shit in her matted hair. Her face looked haggard. Her flesh was waterlogged, her lips were purple. There were patches on her face where the fish's stomach acid had burned her; red spots like flung paint. The look in her eye, for the first time, appeared distant, that hundred-yard stare. She too had finally felt the bite of fear.

But, it was still a beautiful face to me.

She said, "Reba?"

I shook my head.

Steve reached out and patted me on the foot, said, "Can we all share this thing a little better?"

So, the three of us, one at either end of the busted pontoon, one in the middle, shifted positions throughout the gnawing hot day to prevent boredom, floated about on what by late afternoon looked like a wine-dark sea.

I noted that the skin on my arms was burned, and I could feel it on the back of my neck, and on my face as well, and I knew soon I would burn even more, and by tonight, or early the next day, I would feel it and not like it.

Grace and Steve were burned as well.

I was thinking about all this, when I saw something that made me croak out. I could hardly make the word.

"Lund."

"What?" Grace said.

I cleared my throat.

"Land."

And so it was. There was a dark line of greenery and a fine line of brown shore, and way beyond it we could see the dark bridge, or ladder, rising up into the fluffy white clouds. We kicked our legs and tried to work the pontoon in that direction.

We paddled all day, and finally night fell, and we didn't look any closer to me than when we had first spotted the shore.

We paddled throughout the night, one taking turns straddling the pontoon, sleeping a bit, then swapping out to let another do the same. The mist came back and surrounded us all night, and it was hard to see the land there in the dark, even with the moonlight (and tonight there were two moons), and on we paddled, like angry beavers, and when daybreak broke, we were still some distance away.

The current was carrying us toward the shore rapidly now, and so we merely clung for a long time, resting.

When land seemed truly within our grasp, we began to paddle again, and it was just growing dark when we made the white sandy beach, abandoned the pontoon, and crawled up on shore to rest.

We didn't make it any farther than that, and I awoke to the water lifting and tugging at me, realized if I didn't get up and move, that it would take me out to sea.

The mist was floating about again, but I didn't even look at it. I shook Steve and Grace, and the three of us staggered farther inland, found a spot beneath a tree with limbs hanging so low and thick they almost touched the ground.

We crawled under them and lay near the tree's thick trunk. It was good and dark under there, and there was plenty of room, and the sand was soft and warm. We couldn't see the mist. There was only the sound of the sea crashing against the shore, and a smell of healthy greenery.

Almost immediately, we were asleep.

3

Next morning I awoke to light slipping under the thick tree limbs. I pushed my way from beneath them and out into the sunlight, staggered toward the beach and the sea.

The water was blue and the sky was blue, and the blues were dark and rich in color and blended one with the other. In that moment, it gave me the impression of being at the bottom of a china bowl. The sun, in all its warm glory, was like a bright yellow flower painted on the bowl's insides, and the beach sand beneath me was some fine ingredient, flour perhaps, and here I was standing on it. Probably waiting to be mixed into some kind of cake if my current bad luck continued.

I blinked and turned and looked toward the inner shore.

Trees. Huge and green and beautiful. Beyond it all, rising up into the blue and disappearing into it, as if poking a hole in the sky, was the bridge, or whatever the hell it was. It was the closest we had been to it, and I could see now that it was gold and silver, and there were black lines running along the sides of it, and slowly, it came to me that they were massive cables. I had a sudden hot mental flash that savage lines of electricity were being channeled through those cables, and that the whole thing was plugged into the ground, and if the plug were pulled, the world would be sucked into a vacuum, all that was here: sand and trees, sky and sea, us, we would all go, SsssssssssssssssuuuuuuuuuuuuuuuuCK!

And we would be gone. Like spilt paint pulled into a wet vac.

When I turned back toward the sea, I saw a curious thing. The great sky sagged. Like someone above had poked it with a large finger. It sagged low out at sea, almost touched the water.

"Shit," I said.

I was standing there looking at it, when I heard Grace say, "Well, you don't see that every day."

I turned and looked at her. Steve was crawling out from under the tree limbs, starting in our direction.

"No," I said. "But you do see something every day that you didn't see the day before. That something is something new, and this is today's new thing."

"Perhaps one of many," she said.

Steve stood next to us, said, "Holy shit. What happened to the sky?"

"We were just contemplating that," Grace said.

We shopped around for food and found some fruit growing on a strange-looking little tree. Steve tasted it, pronounced it sour as dog urine (I don't know if this evaluation was from personal experience or not), and we passed on it.

We walked along the beach, looking for other foods, a dead fish maybe, and then I saw her.

Reba.

She lay on the shore on her back.

We ran to her.

She wasn't looking good.

Her face was puffed out from the water, and her hair was pushed down over her eyes.

"She's dead," Steve said.

I knelt down and put my arm behind her head and lifted her to a sitting position.

When I did, she coughed, and water projectile-vomited from her lungs. It went all over her legs. She coughed some more, opened her eyes, and tried to focus.

She almost smiled.

She tried to speak, but when she did, no words came out. Only water.

I picked her up and carried her inland, set her down so her back was against a tree.

"You don't look much like the Little Mermaid," I said.

"Don't feel much like her either," she said.

"We thought you were gone," Steve said.

Reba actually smiled this time. "Not yet. This is it? This is all of us?"

"Homer made a pretty good float," Grace said, "but I think he was dead before the bus reached the surface. He was at the back. The mess came in through the window there, smothered him."

Reba stared off at the water, said, "My God. What's happened to the sky?"

We looked at what we had already seen, but now, there was a portion of the sky actually dipping into the water. That piece moved when the water moved.

We sat there for awhile, and while Steve stayed with Reba, Grace and I went down the shoreline looking for something to eat. We finally did find a dead fish or two, chose the one that was in the best condition, and carried it back. It wasn't a large fish, but it was something. We tore it open with our fingers and shared the cold innards among us. Had I not been starved, it would have been disgusting.

It wasn't much, however, and Grace and I walked back to the dog-urine fruit, which was shaped somewhat like a large golden pear, and took a few from the limbs.

We brought them back and had dog-urine fruit for dessert. It really wasn't so bad once you got past the smell. And the taste.

Reba, being in as bad a shape as she was, wasn't able to go on. We decided to stay a night on the beach, but did manage to help her back to the low-hanging boughs where we had spent the night before.

It was very nice under there. Cozy.

Walking back I saw something I had overlooked before, floating up between some rocks.

My backpack.

I went over and got it. Inside was my journal. A few loose pages had come out of it and had washed up on the shore. I gathered them, and while Reba rested, I spread them out on the beach and let them dry.

We spent the night under the tree boughs, and in spite of everything, or perhaps because of it, we all slept deeply.

4

"I don't remember much," Reba said.

We were under the tree boughs, and it was daylight outside. I was pretty certain time had been working consistently over the last few days, because they had felt exactly like *days*. My inner clock seemed happy with the timing.

Still, for all I knew, we could have been sleeping for days before the light came.

We had meant to move on the very next daylight, but we hadn't. We decided to let Reba regain her strength. It wasn't like we knew where we were going, anyway. Or if we should go. Or if it mattered if we did go.

"All I know was the bus came up, I was clinging to it," Reba said, continuing her tale, "and I think I saw you in the water," she said, indicating me.

"You did. I dove after you. But couldn't find you."

"I lost my hold on the bus," Reba said. "It came to me that it was taking me down, and I knew it was best if I didn't hang on, but I don't know if I let go, or the force of the water pulled me loose. But I came loose. "Still, I was too weak to swim, and I just knew I was a goner. Then I was lifted up."

"Ed," I said.

"Yeah. He surfaced, and as he did, he brought me up. I rode on his back for a moment. Long enough to get my breath. Then he dove again.

"I was sucked under. I thought, well, this is it. I blacked out, came awake as I surfaced again, got a gulp of air. Then, guess what? I blacked out again. Next time I woke up you were standing over me, Jack. And, believe me, that was a pretty sight . . . What's the plan now?"

"We kind of loosely thought we should go along the beach a ways, just to see what's about. Then cut inland toward the bridge. We don't know why, but—"

"Why not?" Grace said.

"Yeah," Reba said. "Why not?"

We abandoned the idea of walking along the shore. It had seemed like a good idea at first. Dead fish could be collected. We might even find a way to fish for fresh ones.

But, now that we had learned to eat the dog-urine fruit, we decided to break it open and let it dry, pack it in my pack, along with my de-sodded writing goods, and carry it as food.

We wanted to go straight for the bridge.

Another thing. We thought it might be the safest place.

The night before, while sitting out on the beach, a star had fallen from the sky and landed in the water, washing a large wave nearly all the way to our sleeping tree.

The next night, we had seen the moon sag.

And that morning, much of the blue sky on the horizon was hanging low and being washed and moved by the water. The sun was almost in the wet itself.

"I get the feeling," Grace said, "that those who put this whole thing together aren't home anymore."

"Or they've lost interest," Steve said.

The jungle was dense, but we found a trail, an animal trail, I presumed, and we went along it as fast as we could go. It was strange. We had no idea where we were actually going, but we were damn well getting there fast.

I suppose I could say the bridge was our goal. And being as how I had become very goal oriented, because staying in any one place on the drive-in world soon led to depression, it gave me a feeling of motion and accomplishment.

We stopped several times to rest. We found plenty of water in nice gurgling pools, and there was a lot of the dog-urine fruit. We kept our dried fruit and ate the fresh stuff, and when night fell, we slept beneath trees. That is, until one night we heard a cry from the island forest so frightening that we took to the trees after that.

I thought of the trees as Tarzan trees. They were large with broad limbs, and there were enough smaller limbs about, coated thick in leaves, you could find natural hammocks to sleep in.

I felt good about this, until I thought our screaming predator might be able to climb trees.

In our nice tree hammocks, twenty to thirty feet off the ground, Steve and Grace tucked up in a bundle of limbs above us, Reba and I talked about all that had happened, about all that had been before the drive-in, about what we would do if we ever escaped this world and returned to our own.

We even discussed the idea of staying where we were.

The island was beautiful, and if we could find something better to eat than the dog-urine fruit—fish maybe—we could stay here for a long time. Maybe forever. Eventually, Reba said, either she or Grace would become pregnant, no matter how careful we were, and there would be children.

It was a thought.

A nice island.

Cool winds. Lots of water.

Plenty of dog-urine fruit . . . Well, that wasn't so good.

Most likely we would learn to catch fish, and maybe there was other food on the island. Had to be. From the sound of that scream, that was a predator, and predators had to have something to eat besides dog-urine fruit.

And maybe this wasn't an island at all. We had come to call it that because of the way it looked. But it could have been the edge of a continent. A place away from all the weird movie worlds and strange occurrences; an oasis in a morass of what Reba called Weirdity.

And, of course, for me, there was Reba.

She was pretty and smart and we didn't seem to age.

How would that work for children? The children in the drive-in hadn't aged a lot. They grew, but, come to think of it, none of them ever made adulthood.

Then again, how long had we been here?

The oldest the kids had been was three or four, and most of them died. Or got eaten.

And there were the weird creatures. The results of the Popcorn King's poisoned sperm. They had grown very fast, to a kind of retarded adulthood on one level, and on another, to an advanced childhood where they could move things with their minds.

And there was the drive-in mist. When we were close to the sea, it would come out of nowhere, floating along the black water. But it never came to shore.

Never. It was a seagoing thing, or so it seemed. And Grace had a theory about what it was.

It was similar to my own idea. Television ghosting. If this was a movie world with different stories going all at once, perhaps our past and our present were colliding; different channels and episodes running together; movies mixing and misting, and falling apart.

It was a disturbing thought.

My mind rambled like that, going from this to that, as Reba and I lay in the boughs, she cradled in the crook of my arm, my eyes on the sky.

And I thought: What a pretty thought. To stay here. To have children. To live naked and free and full of piss and vinegar to the end of our days.

Lots of lying about in the sun.

Lots of fucking.

Lots of doing nothing and needing only something to eat and drink.

Life was really simple if you let it be.

But life was never simple here. You could never let down your guard. My arm had gone to sleep, and I wanted to move it, but hated to for fear of waking Reba and disturbing the wonderful fact that I had a fine-looking woman on my arm. For she had recovered fast. The puffiness was gone. Her hair had lightened. Her body was lean, but not starved, and her skin had developed a glow. She also wasn't wearing much in the way of clothes. Always a plus.

Yet, even with that wonderful thought to consider, we were still here.

On the drive-in world. And this was a world where Chicken Little would be right.

The sky *was* falling.

5

On the morning after my night contemplating, thinking maybe this place was as good as it got, and that was good enough, I awoke and climbed to the top of our tree and saw an amazing and disturbing sight.

First off, the world was blood-colored; the sun had sunk halfway into the sea, and great clouds of steam were rising up from it.

The water was drying up, running away from the shore. Fish were leaping about as they were boiled alive. All of this I could see, and when I told the others, we made the decision to hasten our pace, to see if we could reach the great bridge to the sky.

Steve said, "I was thinking, wouldn't it be nice to go back there and get some of those boiled fish."

"And I was thinking," Grace said, "the time we spent doing that might be a bad idea. We too could soon be boiled. And if the sun goes completely down into the sea, will it rise again? Will there be only night? Will the moon come out? Will it fall too? Will the stars drop off? Time, however it works here, is not on our side."

So we went along swift in the blood-red light, and in time that light turned stranger yet as night fell. The sun didn't want to go away, so there was a red stain across the night sky. The moon shone silver, and full, and the stars were dots of fire, and if you looked real close, there seemed to be creases in the night, as if dark velvet cloth that had been stretched was no longer taut, but was in fact drooping.

We ate the dried dog-urine fruit, and kept pushing, and just as the moon dipped away, and the day came on bloody-dark, we began to smell the odor of death. It was a stiff odor that shoved at us, but we ignored it. We could see the bridge clearly above the trees, and we pushed on in that direction, the stench growing strong enough to cut and make bricks.

It got so stout, that each of us took turns puking, but we kept on keeping on. In time, though the smell never went away, our nostrils and our stomachs accepted it.

By the time night had come, and we had slept, and risen again before the moon fell down, we came upon the source of the odor. The tropical forest had disappeared, and there was just a bleak stretch of ground, and a great mile-high (I'm guessing here as to the height) pile of something we couldn't identify. We stood there looking at it, and as we did, slowly, the moon fell off, and the dying sunlight was all we had, giving us a rusty glow and a view of the clearing and the pile in the middle of it.

"My God," Steve said.

"If God had anything to do with this," Grace said, "then he's just as big an asshole as I've always thought."

I had to agree.

It was a great black pile, and the pile buzzed and flexed and moved.

6

When we came closer, an immense cloud of crows rose up against the red sky with a caw and a savage beating of wings, and with them rose a swarm of humming flies.

The bloody sunlight, formerly shiny on the dark wings of the birds and the bright green-and-black bodies of the flies, now shone on a pile of human shapes. Some of the shapes were of wood, some of metal, some of plastic. There were crudely whittled soldiers with tall hats and chin bands, painted up red and black with big blue eyes and Groucho Marx mustaches. There were less crudely molded metal soldiers with turnkeys at their backs. There were women, too, and unlike the male soldiers with painted-on clothes, they were roughly shaped with blonde and red hair and big bow mouths and wide blue eyes, pink knobs for nipples and quick swipes of black paint for pubic hair. Some of them, like the soldiers, were made of metal and were slightly better formed with windup keys at their backs. Their flesh tones varied: there were white, black, and yellow, and even green; there were all manner of shapes and sizes. Amongst these human-sized, crudely whittled, and sophisticated windup toys, were what looked like mannequins with perfect-painted features and real hair on their heads, male and female. And on these were truer anatomical features; missiles for the men, grooves for the ladies, patches of what looked like real pubic hair.

Twisted in amongst them were long green tentacles and bulbous heads and huge pop-eyes. Rubbery-looking aliens and some that looked to be made of flesh; flesh going gray and dripping with slime. I had dreamed of such beasts from time to time. Up there in the sky somewhere, twisting dials, moving cameras, proceeding along dolly-runs. Making movies, with us as their reality show. And here they lay.

Further up the pile were what appeared to be real human bodies, rotting, arms dripping off like melting plastic, legs falling free of the bone, heads twisted, coming loose, the eyes plucked out. At first I thought some of the bodies were moving, but soon realized it was the maggots squirming amidst the real corpses and the termites chewing about in the wooden figures, the crows flapping about, giving the glancing illusion of the human shapes making movement on their own.

"My God," Reba said. "What place is this?"

No one had an answer.

Beyond this pile was one great beam of the bridge. And it was very wide. We couldn't see the edges of it. All we could see was the gold and silver metal that made up the bridge, and those huge black cables, twisted thick and numerous as armpit hairs on a French lady.

Way up, dead center of the pile, was a dark hole in the sky, like someone had burned the tip of a cigarette through red construction paper; a hole like the one that had pulsed and shat its refuse above the drive-in.

"It reminds me of some white trash fucker's yard," Reba said. "Throwing shit out the window. You know, food and cans and such. But here we got a waste disposal of giant toys and dead bodies. Still, the attitude, it's the same."

Grace moved over close to the pile. She said, "Look at this."

We eased next to her. The stench was so strong I wasn't sure I was going to be able to stand in front of the pile another second. My stomach did a flip-flop, gathered itself, and the feeling of nausea and light-headedness passed.

Grace reached out, took hold of a rancid, blackened arm, said, "This one has been here awhile. Look at it. Look close."

The arm had rotted, and the crows had been at it, and though the arm was clearly meaty, inside it I could see a flexi-metal rod that served for bone, and twisted around this "bone" were wires—red, blue, white, and yellow.

"Part human," Grace said. "Part machine."

"Holy shit," Steve said.

"Question now," Grace said, "is do we still want to go up there?"

She pointed up at the wall of metal, the jungle of wires.

"I don't know what else to do," Reba said. "The world is caving in on itself. Whoever runs this crazed-ass shithole must be up there. I think it's time to confront him. Beard God in his own goddamn cheap-ass Naugahyde, cheetah-skin-decorated den, and kick his ass."

"Hear, hear," Steve said, and stuck out a hand.

We piled our hands on top of his.

"Up, up, and away," Grace said.

"By the way," I asked, "how do you know if there's a God he's got Naugahyde shit up there?"

"It fits his toss-out-the-window, white trash image," Reba said.

"Ah," I said.

Part Five

Complexities are contemplated. A bridge is climbed. Toy soldiers get funky. Experiences with rubber, wood, and flesh. Aliens are found. Bad things happen to good people. The world is folded, and our remaining heroes travel through a glass darkly.

1

Let me tell you how we did it, took that climb.

We decided, as we always knew we would, to go up that great beam, which was slanted slightly and had those multitudes of cables to cling to. From a distance those twists of wires had looked like one big dark cable on either beam of the bridge. Now, I could see it was not a bridge at all, but what it was, I was uncertain. The metal beam and its skin of tangled wires ascended into the red sky, disappearing, not into the waste hole, but advancing to the top to be wrapped in clouds like a precious possession in fluffy balls of cotton.

It was not a short trip, dear hearts.

It might not have been Everest, but it wasn't a hill back home either. It was WAY THE FUCK up there.

So, we took the dried fruit from my pack, laid it out, determined it was not enough. We went about picking more fruit and drying it. It was a scary decision. Every moment we wasted meant the sky could fall, doing us in. But, if we were to take the climb unprepared, and if it was as high up and difficult to travel as we suspected, then we could die of thirst and starvation. Not to mention we might fall off and smash our asses.

Maybe that's where the bodies and shapes of humans had come from. They had fallen, not been pushed.

But, shit, man. Did those wooden critters walk?

Or were they just prototypes?

And how were those great potato chips made so thin and vacuum-packed in a can without crushing all of them?

I wished I were home with a can of them, sitting in front of the television set watching a rerun of *The Lone Ranger*. Guns snapping, bad guys falling. But no blood, man. No blood. No real terror.

Of course, when we got to the top, we could find ourselves in worse shape. But again, it was that goal business, dear hearts.

The goal.

The reason to strive.

It's what made us want to climb, and it beat standing around with our thumbs up our asses, waiting for the world to fall apart and the sun to blow down on our heads and cook us.

Steve found some gourds and we labored at hollowing those out by twisting off the narrow, blackened, umbilical-cord tops and working a sharp stick down into them. We wormed the stick about until we liquefied the gourd's guts, then we poured the goo out. There were numerous pools of water about, and we dipped the gourds in those and rinsed them, filled them with sand and let them dry while the fruit dried.

We even went back to the beach and found some of the boiled fish. We ate some, and found that they were pretty good, considering we had been living off dog-urine fruit, which made for a very real and very regular bowel movement, dear hearts. I figured, way we had been eating and shitting, the woods were full of scat.

We cut the boiled fish open with scoops made of sharp sticks, wrapped them in leaves, and stuffed them in my pack. We made spears by twisting off limbs in such a way that a sharp piece was left on the end. It wasn't a great weapon, but it was all we had.

On the day when fruit and gourds were dry, we packed my pack full of the withered dog-urine produce, filled the gourds with water, corked them with pieces of wood, made slings of vines to carry the gourds, made similar straps with vines so we could fasten them to and carry our spears on our backs, then we started out.

Our plan was to take turns with the pack. We all carried our own water gourds and spears. As for the pack, I carried it first. We took a hike around the pile of busted toys and rotting bodies, made our way to the shiny beam that rose up to heaven.

And with the red-stained sky dripping down frighteningly low, we did the pile-on hands thing again, made with a little one-for-all grunt, and started up.

It went well enough at first. The wires were thick, and they gave you something to cling to. The beam slanted enough you weren't just hanging out in space, but it didn't slant enough for you to be comfortable. It didn't take long before I was tired. I thought it was just because it was my turn to tote the pack, but when Grace took it over, I found I was even worse off, as if the weight of all that food had given me what strength I had.

Finally we came to a great bolt in the beam, and the wires were nestled about it in a wad. We found we could crawl up in that wad, and the wires were bundled tight enough, very little light got in. We crawled in there and pressed up together, mostly in a sitting position, opened the pack, ate and drank sparingly, then rested.

Resting turned out to be a full-bore doze.

When I awoke, stars were in the sky, and I watched two of them drip off and fall. I could see way out there, dear hearts, and I watched as the stars hit the sea and the water rose up big-time, came crashing down on the island, washing trees away like matchsticks with a garden hose.

The drive-in mist, which was cruising the water below, was hit by the waves and disrupted. It curled and coiled and broke apart.

Reba, who I didn't know was awake, said, "We left just in time."

"It's not going to wash the whole thing," I said, "not this time. But what if the moon falls?"

"It's all over," she said. "Davy Jones' Locker, baby."

The moon was out and it was bright, but that old lunar wad nodded from time to time, as if it might doze off and drop into the waters below. We watched for awhile, until the drive-in ghost had regrouped and began to float over the waters, then we decided to wake the others, keep climbing, making time while the moon was up and its light was high.

As we climbed, Grace and Steve in the lead, Reba (carrying the pack now) and I lagging slightly behind, Reba said, "What do you think about all those bodies down there, the toy soldiers, the mannequins, and such?"

"I don't know. I'm having some thoughts, but they aren't altogether formed, and what thoughts I'm thinking I can't express, but, baby, somewhere back to the rear of the old bean, I'm not liking what I'm thinking at all."

"Want to share?"

"I meant what I said. I don't know how to explain it. It's more a feeling than an expression. But it comes to me, you'll be the first to know."

"I think I do know what you mean. Something is nagging me, too. And it feels uncomfortable. Like a pretty bad thought is trying to burrow out, and I won't let it."

"I hear you," I said.

Many days and nights passed, and sometimes there was no place for us to really rest, so we had to keep on climbing. And sometimes, when we found a bolt, where the wires were always clustered, we decided to stay for a day or two, if anyone could in any way decide on what a day was.

In time, more stars fell, and the water rose up way high, and soon there was no land or trees below us. Oh, for a few days it was there, in patches, and the water would roll back and show us at least the tops of trees, and now and again a patch of mud, but eventually that went away too. And then one night the thing we had feared happened.

The moon came up and went down fast and furious. Striking the sea so hard it sounded like an atomic bomb had gone off. The great beam vibrated and the metal sang with a sound like a scream from a robot's lungs.

The ocean yawned, and the water went all about, then it gathered itself together with what sounded like a moan and rushed forward. All the waters of this drive-in earth appeared to have loosened their bounds, and they had gathered together in one great wet flood; it thundered below us with a gush, and it began to rise, like a plugged toilet, and in a time so short as to be somewhere between our taking a deep breath and cutting a fart of fear, the water charged up and around the beam, rose nearly to our feet.

Well. Okay. That's an exaggeration. But it rose up as high as we had been two drive-in days before. Had we decided to hang out a little longer down there, we would have bathed the big bath, baby.

The flood brought with it a bullet-hard rain and a cloud of mist, and the mist collected itself and became the drive-in ghost. We looked down on it and I saw within it the island and us on the island, and then I saw us and the pile of corpses, false and neat, and I quit watching then. Feared it might show me our future. And, frankly, I didn't want to know.

2

"All these wires," Steve said, "I think they run the drive-in world. They travel along these great beams, and the interconnecting parts that look like ladder rungs. They run through those. They go from the sky to the ground. They're worked into this world's fabric. They give it light. They make the sun, the moon and stars, night and day work. Or did. They're starting to go bad. Shorting out maybe. No maintenance. The whole goddamn thing is breaking up. I don't know, maybe it's on purpose. But down there, it's all over. I'm sure of it. From sea to shining sea, from one end of the jungle to the other, all the way down that single stretch of highway, the drive-in at either end. It's done, companions. Done."

We were resting in a mess of wires by one of the huge bolts, and Steve, he was running on, talking ninety miles an hour, as if he were on some kind of caffeine high, which he wasn't, unless the dog-urine fruits were naturally rich in it.

And maybe they were, because we were all in one of those late-night type of conversational, philosophical moods that one usually associates with coffee houses or university lifers or chat-it-up smart guys trying to score pussy.

Only thing was, it wasn't late night, it was day, but the day wasn't much. The sun was down low, literally, and it was leaking its light over the water, making it the color of rich bourbon. There was a lot less water now. Much of it had been steamed away. But still that sun dripped into the sea, and our version of Sol had begun to lose its shape, like a rotting fruit going quick-fast to liquid. On the seabed all manner of creatures, giant squids, fish, and even our great catfish friend, Ed, squirmed in the mud.

From where we were, we could see the great fish clearly. The dark things, the ravenous cancers, or pissed-off shadows, whatever they were, those hungry things that had been inside of Ed, had exited the old boy's ass. The shadows fluttered about the muddy seabed like crickets. There was too much light for them, fading or not, they hopped and twisted and fell about like dying locusts, came apart in little black pools that ran into the mud and were absorbed.

The people who had been inside Ed exited as well. They were very small from our position, the size of termites. But we knew they were people. They came out of the gaping mouth of the fish and disappeared into the mud. It probably went very deep, that mud. Maybe miles.

If anyone was still in the fish, they might stay on the surface for awhile, as Ed covered a lot of space and was sinking more slowly, spread out like that, but he was sinking. We could see that big buddy going down.

Goodbye, Bjoe, if you're still there. Goodbye you man-eating, dick-jerking asshole.

The horizon had become a charcoal gray band, and it was broadening. Soon, all the world below would be dark.

Above us, the clouds were near touchable. Puffed up and white as a Jesus robe.

I said, "I think, tired as we are, we should start moving again, while we can see to climb. If the sun holds out just a while longer, I think we'll reach the clouds."

"And if we do," Reba says, "who says that means anything? It can be just as dark inside a cloud as out. The sun goes, what the fuck does it matter where we are?"

"I'm thinking the beam leads somewhere," I said. "Remember Popalong, he climbed up here, through that hole over the drive-in, and it was nearly as high as this. He saw things. He told us a little about them. This world has an attic."

"But there's no guarantee this leads to it," Reba said. "This world, in case you haven't noticed, lacks logic."

"Doesn't matter," Grace said, "we made this decision, and now we're stuck with it, we either ride the dick or use our fingers."

"Say what?" Reba said.

"It's an old saying I just made up, meaning, we've made a decision. We don't know if it's the real thing, the big cosmic fuck, or just us playing with ourselves. We won't know till we get up there."

"There really isn't any other way to go," Steve said. "Well, other than down. And if we climb down, I don't think we're climbing down to much. A lot of mud, dead fish, and such."

"You're right," Reba said. "Of course you are. I'm just tired."

We started climbing again.

There was something I hadn't mentioned to the others. The clouds. I feared our oxygen would thin. But it didn't. Truth was, the sky, the clouds, the whole arrangement, was way lower than back on earth. But it was a bit chilly. As we climbed through the clouds, they felt wet and sticky, like cotton candy.

And then we broke through a bank of clouds so thick you could swat them with your hand and knock them about. When we rose above them, struggling our way along the wires on the beam, we saw it.

A hole at the top of the world, the beam traveling up through it like a knife through a wound.

3

When we came to the top of the beam it began to narrow dramatically, and eventually we had to go one at a time. Grace was the first inside, followed by Steve, then Reba and myself. Behind us, the sun dimmed even more as it dissolved into the mud.

We climbed over the lip of the sky and stood in a room.

A dusty goddamn room.

A big room, I might add. But, a room.

Dimly lit, but lit. The source? Unknown.

There were all sorts of things there, and many of them were things I remembered Popalong Cassidy describing. There were backdrops of all sorts and tins of film, and loose film scattered helter-skelter, piles of television sets, all sizes.

Looking up, I could find no ceiling. Just darkness. In fact, I couldn't see any walls. There was just a floor and lots of junk and lots more for as far as the eye could see in the dim light.

"There seems to be some kind of path along here," Grace said.

And there was. A break in the backdrops and tins of film, forming a little corridor. Dust clouds rose and floated as we walked. We were all soon coughing, but in time the dust ceased to bother us, and we proceeded at a brisker pace.

"I remember Popalong Cassidy said he could walk into the backdrops," I said.

"Yeah, I remember that too," Grace said.

"We find one of home," Steve said, "we're set."

And as if wishing would make it so, we found just that. A huge backdrop hung down on chains attached at the top to . . . Who knows what? The backdrop was so long it curled on the floor. It was a painted outside view of the pool hall back home, the street out front. It was where my friends and I had conceived our plan to visit the Orbit Drive-in; it was where Willard had kicked some ass protecting Randy, the two who were later welded together by a lightning strike, welded in such a way they became one mean creature, the Popcorn King.

"If we can step through that," I said, "we will be in my hometown. Everyone can find a way home from there."

I turned for an answer from the others, saw another backdrop across the way. The Dairy Queen in my hometown. A tear abruptly dripped out of the corner of my eye, ran down my cheek.

"We could search about," Grace said, "but if we can step through it, if we can go back to East Texas, close enough for me."

"You said it," Steve said.

"I'm up for it," Reba said.

I walked slowly toward the backdrop, stuck out my hand, and ran up against canvas.

I pushed again.

Harder.

Nothing.

I hit the canvas with my palm. Then my fists. Hard as I could. It rippled a bit, but I didn't pass through. I fell to my knees and pressed my forehead against it.

"The lying sonofabitch," I said. "He didn't go anywhere. Popalong said he could go through the backdrops. He said it."

Reba bent down and put her arm around me. "Come on, Jack. It's okay."

"No. It's not okay. I've had about all I can take."

"Get the fuck up," Grace said.

I turned and glared at her. She stood there in all her glorious, topless beauty. I had turned and was prepared to be angry, but looking at that woman, her face full of confidence, all I could do was make myself stand. I said, "Sorry, I had a moment."

"Okay," Grace said, "but now the moment's over. Popalong, who knows, maybe he did pass into these things. In his mind. And what works one time, may not work the next. We aren't whipped yet. We're never whipped till we say we're whipped."

"I don't know," Steve said, "I'm feeling a little whipped myself. I just don't have the energy to fall down and cry, or I would."

"Me too," Reba said.

"We can rest, or we can search," Grace said. "And, another thing, something important, I think . . . Right over there. A wall."

It was. A nice brown wall that ran way up into the darkness, out of sight. There was a standard light switch on the wall. I hit it. The lights in the great room brightened. There was a creaking noise, and the backdrops began to move about on their chains, changing positions. They locked in and were still.

"Now there's something cute," Grace said.

It was a door, revealed by the movement of the backdrops.

Grace strolled over, took hold of the knob. "When I turn," she said, "be ready for whatever."

She turned the knob, pulled the door open.

Nothing leaped on us.

No whatevers.

Inside the room were all manner of mirrors, and looking into them, we looked different in every one. Not just short or fat or tall or wide, but we had different faces. I could recognize them as our faces and bodies, but they were different.

Even Grace showed discomfort, started moving along quickly. For in many of the mirrors her shape was not so attractive. Her breasts drooped, and she looked tired and scared and old.

I looked weak, bent over, my fingers almost touching the ground. Steve's face was blank in many of the mirrors, and Reba was chunky and big-legged and exhausted.

"It's how we really feel," Reba said.

"I don't feel that way," Grace said. "Not at all. I think it's how this world wants us to feel."

"Whatever, I'm for going back to the other room," Reba said. "At least some of the backdrops are pretty."

But we kept moving, and soon the mirrors were gone, and there were these rows and rows of what we had seen in a pile on the ground beneath the hole in the sky. They hung on cables from the ceiling we couldn't see. There were crude-cut bodies and nicer ones, and really fine ones, some with windup keys at their backs, many without, all the fleshy ones nude and shiny. No one stunk here. They looked fresh. And there were aliens. The ones in our dreams, and in the pile below the sky.

The aliens were in great chairs in front of enormous cameras that were poked through holes in the floor, and the chairs, they rode up in such a position that the aliens' filmed-over, bulging eyes were pointed down into the cameras, and the creatures were held in place by belts and straps so they wouldn't fall from their chairs. They didn't move.

We walked slowly toward them, threading our way between the hanging figures. A tentacle dripped over the side of one giant chair, and I reached out to touch it. It was slick with decay and smelled.

"Dead," I said, "all dead."

We moved between the chairs that held the many aliens, came to a canyon in the floor. We looked over the rim, all the way down. All we could see was a dim red glow. We could feel heat coming up through the opening.

"This must be the garbage hole, where the bodies are dumped," Grace said.

"My guess is," I said, "that red glow is the sun. It has fallen onto the drive-in world, heated it up. I bet all that's left now is lava."

Looking across the vast expanse on the canyon to the other side, I could see cars and buses, planes and trains. They looked small and were all heaped together in the manner of toys tossed aside at the end of the day by an exhausted child.

"I bet we're looking down the funnel from the sky," Steve said. "It could be that, instead of the waste hole."

"The funnel was far away," Grace said. "The waste hole was just below us."

"Maybe," Steve said. "But time and distance . . . Nothing makes sense here. And there's some of the same kind of stuff that was thrown down the funnel over there," he said, pointing at the autos and planes and such on the other side of the great gap.

"But who, and why?" Reba said.

None of us had an answer.

We went back and looked at the hanging bodies, and Steve said, "You know, I think these human shapes haven't gone rotten because they've never had the spark of life. The ones below, I bet they had it, and they didn't work out, had to be discarded. The others, they can be wound up, but these . . . Look up there, see, the more human ones have wires going into their heads."

I looked, and sure enough, I could see the wires twisting down and into the tops of their skulls.

"Oh, God Almighty," Reba said. We rushed over to where she stood, and what we saw made us all gasp and go weak.

Hanging in a row were a number of alien and human bodies. We recognized the human shapes. There were several copies of each. There were crude, carved wooden copies, and windup copies, and I suppose there could have been copies in the pile below, and we just hadn't seen them, or they were too rotted, or too mixed together.

It was all the members of the drive-in.

Replicas of them.

I saw my old friends, Randy and Willard . . . Crier . . . Many others.

But there was something even more stunning.

Us.

Figures of us.

Rows of us.

Hanging there. Mouths open. Wires running into our heads. Windup versions. Crude wooden versions. Naked little suckers letting it all hang out.

"Ain't this the shits?" Steve said.

"I think my tits perk higher than that," Grace said, looking down the row of replicas.

"Damn, Jack," Steve said. "Are you really that well hung?"

"He is," Reba said.

"I second that," Grace said.

"I wish I hadn't asked," Steve said.

4

Grace had Steve boost her up to the top of one of the hanging figures of herself. She put her hands on its head, said, "The cable has a little hook, and it fits into a thin loop around the bodies' necks. The wires, they . . . seem to be just pushed into the tops of the skulls."

Grace yanked at the wires. They came free. "Yep," she said. "I'm going to unhook this one."

She did, and swung down, and Steve managed the copy down. We pulled the body away from the hanging rows and out into an open space where there was a little more light.

We all bent over and pushed the inert figure's hair around, felt where the wires had fastened into its skull. There were these little bumps, and if you looked close, really close, you could see the holes where they had gone in.

"What the fuck could this all be about?" Steve said.

"I have an idea," Reba said. "And I don't like it."

"What?" I said.

"Bend over, Jack. Put your head toward me."

I did as I was asked. Reba ran her fingers through my hair. She said, "I found these before. I just thought they were birthmarks . . . They look like the marks from the wires in the Grace figure head."

"Now, wait a minute . . . Coincidence. They're just little birthmarks or something. I didn't even know I had them."

Reba didn't answer. She just bent forward, offering me her skull. Reluctantly, I ran my trembling fingers through her hair. There were little bumps.

"The same," I said.

Grace ducked her head forward. I ran my fingers through her beautiful, blonde hair. Same bumps.

Steve ran his own fingers through his hair, said, "Me too."

"I don't think I like what I'm thinking," I said. "The catfish," Grace said. "Ed. Remember, there were edible wires inside his flesh. They were so big, we could see them. But with us . . . They're small. They could be . . . must be inside us."

"No," Steve said. "I'm human. Can you make a machine hungry, make it want sex and Coca-Cola? I don't think so. Shit, man, I had a life before this crazy place. It sucked, but it was better than this. I got all kinds of memories. I got a divorce, for heaven's sake. I mean, what robot wants to shit or pee?"

"We all have lives," Grace said.

"No," Reba said. "Think about it. The windup versions, the woodcut versions. It's like whoever made them was learning. Advancing."

"But, couldn't they just be models based on us?" Steve said.

"We all have the place for the wires in the tops of our heads," Reba said.

"It's too crazy," Grace said. "You mean, all our memories are . . . false."

Reba nodded. "Could be."

"We're just goddamn robots," Steve said.

"Technically," I said, "I think we're androids."

"But East Texas. Our homes . . . You mean, they never were? We never left this world? Or rather, we've always been here?"

"I don't know," I said. "But, I'll tell you what. I'm pissed. We've been fucked . . . Jesus. That means Mom and Dad. They never were. Or they were machines. Like everyone else."

"Like us," Reba said. "What I'm thinking is they may never have been your parents. It may be all in our head. In our . . . Jesus . . . in our wires and circuits. We were given past histories, tossed into this world for something's entertainment. Even the aliens, they're false. They're just bodies. Rubber at first. Then devices like us. Something someone was playing with until he figured out how to do it better, and then, he/she/it grew bored."

"That would explain why the world is coming apart," Grace said. "Our creator. He just doesn't give a shit anymore. I always thought, you had a creator, he had to be better than some egotistical Christian god, wanting everyone to love him and worship him while he killed people with diseases and made them suffer . . . But, you know, compared to our god, that Christian god is looking pretty good . . . If there ever was a religion called Christianity . . . My Lord, everything is in question."

"All of it must have been based on some truth," I said. "Our creator's truth."

We all sat down around the Grace shape on the floor. Just sat there. Quiet. For a long, long time.

Finally Grace said, "I say we find this creator, and kill the sonofabitch."

"Sounds good," I said.

"Wouldn't that be a bad idea?" Steve said. "He is, after all, our Frankenstein . . . And how do I know that? Is there really a character called Frankenstein? Or is that just part of the whole brain implant, probably a chip in my head of some kind. Man, everything we know or have learned may be a big old fart-smelling lie."

"We're each different," Grace said. "Where he fucked up, is he gave us free will. We can do what we want. And that means killing him. Hell, wanting to do that. Have some kind of revenge. That makes us human, don't it?"

"If there ever were humans," I said.

It took a long time for us to make our way around the funnel, to the other side. We ended up sleeping a lot, and eating all our fruit. But finally we made our way to where the planes and buses and such were.

Some were real, or looked real. Some had windups at their backs. One of the planes, a little two-seater, had a propeller in the front that was attached with a tightly wound rubber band.

The machines were average sized. One of the cars was a 1966 tan Chevy Impala. The window was down. Grace stuck her head inside, said, "The keys are in it."

She got inside, turned the key. The car started.

"Now there's something neat," she said. "Low on gas, but I say we try it."

We climbed in, Grace at the wheel. She wheeled around the automotive and aerial debris, and we were off again, tooling along a great tile floor.

5

We found a wide gap in a wall, a mousehole, and we drove through that. There were trees in there, but they were prop trees, the sort that looked real front on, but at their backs were little stands that held them up.

We passed towns made the same way. Towns we knew. It was Interstate I-45, or so said the road signs, and the towns were the right towns, but they weren't real. There were even people standing about, at the sides of the road, but they too were false, with little stands at their backs. False cars. False dogs and cats.

Everything a plywood and cardboard lie.

We drove on, and the little towns fell away and gave place to more woods. The woods grew darker and we could see huge sets of glowing eyes out there.

"Man, what could that be?" Steve asked.

"I don't think we want to know," Reba said.

We hadn't gone much farther when suddenly a set of the eyes rushed forward.

A mouse.

A big fucking mouse. Bigger than a horse. It darted for the Impala.

Grace gave the Impala the gas. I glanced back through the rear windshield. The mouse stood on its hind legs and waved its paws in the air in frustration. As it tracked back into the woods, I noted there was a windup key in its ass.

"It isn't even real," I said.

"Neither are we," Reba said, and she began to cry.

At one point, we saw beside the road a whole row of tin soldiers. They had rotating keys at their backs. They were dancing together, and it was funky stuff, that's what I'm trying to tell you.

"Who winds them?" Steve said.

"That would be the motherfucker we're looking for," Grace said.

We drove in dark silence for a long time, and I know that each of us was thinking of our lives, wondering if any of it was truly our lives, or if we had even lived the drive-in lives, let alone the before-the-drive-in lives. Just driving along, thinking all this, feeling hollow as a chocolate Easter bunny, remembering sweet moments and sad, thinking, did any of this shit happen or did all our ideas and memories run through chips and wires hidden in our bloodstreams. And is the blood in us blood, or Karo syrup, or is there such a thing as blood, or even humans, and which or what are we, and did this mean someone other than George Lucas made up *Star Wars*?

Sometime during our drive, the lights were cut off by someone or something. They just snapped off. We turned on the car lights and proceeded. We pointed the car at a silver glow we could see on the horizon, on down that pseudo I-45.

We drove until we came to an end of the highway and all the props, and still we drove on, across a flat expanse of nothing, almost as bleak as the highway into Amarillo, Texas, if there is an Amarillo, Texas or a highway in that direction, if there is a direction. My God, was there north, east, west, or south?

It made the chips and wires and such in the goddamn plasti-flesh skull ache, is what it did.

Not long after me thinking all of this, wondering where this highway ended up, the Impala ran out of gas. We got out and walked toward the glow on the horizon.

We walked and came upon . . . tools. Giant screwdrivers and pliers, and there were wires and tubes and dials tossed about. We weaved in between them, kept going toward that glow.

The goal the glow, baby. The glow the goal.

Finally, we arrived at the only place we could arrive.

The End of It All.

There was just the table edge. Nowhere else to go but back, and that wasn't appealing. The dim light in the distance was not so distant now. It was a huge television, nothing on it but a white glow and an Indian head test pattern. We could hear it hum. And in the TV's projected light, we could see a great room. On the white-sheeted bed was an elderly man, and there were metal stands by his bed, and they held bottles of liquid, and tubes ran from the bottles into him. They were affixed to his arms and head. Around him were machines with lights and dials on them. To the right of the room was an open window, and moonlight seeped in quietly to rest on the sill like drift-down glitter. To the left of us, sitting on the table was a toy, a rubber band windup plane and a checkerboard with a box of checkers next to it.

There were shelves in the room, and they were covered, or perhaps the word is littered, with all manner of old toys and books.

"By now," Steve said, "I've seen everything but a pig doing the hula while wearing a tutu and a top hat with a cork in his ass, but, I got to admit, my little old brain, or computer chip, whatever, is doing the dipsy-doodle on this here shit."

"I'll second that," Reba said.

"Thirds," Grace said.

"Oh, hell, count me in too," I said.

"I don't know if you have noticed," Grace said, "but what we're on, isn't quite as wide as it was. And now that I can see better about the room, I spy a chair, a couch, and guess what, we're on a table."

"I'll be goddamned," Steve said.

"I see a lot of test tubes," Reba said. I can see them over there, near the bed . . . Goddamn, look at that."

We looked where she was pointing. The TV set. The set crackled like Rice Krispies, and lines appeared and met in the middle, and out of the lines came an image, and the image moved across the room toward us.

It was a young, thin, pimply man with unruly hair and glasses thick as goggles. He wore blue jeans and a white shirt with a pencil and pen pack sticking out of the pocket. The pants were a little too short, and you could see his white socks with little blue clocks on them. He wore brown loafers.

As he moved across the dark expanse of the room on a beam of light, he said, "Hi. My name is Billy."

The beam from the TV brought him down on the edge of the table, and there he stood, looking as solid as us.

"A lot of people call me Little Billy, or used to. I am your creator."

6

"Then we're going to kill your ass dead," Steve said.

"Actually, you can't," Billy said. "Or, you won't have to. I'm not me . . . Really."

"That figures," Grace said. "Nothing is real here."

"Oh, yeah. Some of it's real. This room is real. The things in the room are real. To me, anyway. The little toy plane on the edge of the table is a real toy plane. I'm not really coming out of the TV set though. I just thought that seemed cool. I'm coming out of him."

Billy turned and pointed to the old man on the bed.

"And who is he?" I asked.

"Me. The older me. The creator of the creator, me creating me. The younger me."

"I think we ought to just walk back and get eaten by the windup rat," Steve said.

"He's a partial," Billy said. "The rat, I mean."

"Do what?" Grace asked.

"He's a partial. Part flesh, part machine. But, not really."

"Glad that's straightened out in a confused manner," Steve said.

"We want to kill you," I said, "but, you know what, since you're just a beam of light, I'm gonna guess that isn't going to happen."

"No. It won't. Told you that. Besides, what you want is not to kill me—"

"Oh," Grace said, "I assure you, that's what we want."

"What you want," Little Billy said, "is to know the truth. Every one wants to know the truth. And the truth is this. The world is bigger than you, and you are on my bedroom table, in my lab. And I'm eighty years old. This is how I remember myself. As a kid. But, I'm eighty, and my time is nigh."

"That's why everything is breaking down," Grace said, "you're not maintaining it anymore, because you can't."

"That's right."

"So, you built prototypes," Grace said. "Until you got something more lifelike, discarded the old ones in a waste heap, then gave us, the keepers, false memories and turned us loose in a horrible world. Gave us memories so we thought we had a past and could long for going home?"

"Sort of," Billy said, taking off his glasses, cleaning them on his shirt.

"You're a fucking monster," Grace said.

"No. I was just playing. I'm not even really very smart, so I didn't exactly do that."

"What did you do?" Grace said.

"Philip K. Dick asked once, Do Androids Dream of Electric Sheep, and the answer is, they do dream."

"Okay, now I really want to get eaten by the windup rat," Steve said.

"On the bed the man is not a man but an android. He is a creature and creation of this world, which is a creation by human beings. Maybe. I don't even know that answer. Humans. Androids making androids. Androids making humans. God making humans, a single cell of thought floating in ether, imagining it all? Whatever."

"So we are the android's androids," Reba said.

"No," said Little Billy. "You are the android's dream. The android, Little Billy, is a beautiful creation like his mother and his father and his now-dead sister. He could procreate. He was as human as a human. And like a human, he dies."

"Can't you like jump him off?" Steve asked. "You know, battery cables or something?"

"He is an android," Little Billy said, "but he is too human to be fixed like a machine. He ages. He dies. That's the short and the long and the abbreviated middle. He created your world and all of you to give him life inside his head, since life no longer exists outside of it. On the bed, inside his head, he knows the truth now, that he is an android. He didn't even know, until now. All the secrets of the universe, his own and others', are revealed. And he sends me to you, in his younger form, to talk to you. He's sorry you've been through what you've been. But not really. He had fun believing it all. Believing for a time he was a great creator of aliens and androids and of a marvelous dark world. In his head, images nestled in a little speck of chip smaller than a virus, he enjoyed the idea that he carved you first, and wound you up, then wired you up, and made you all, put you in the drive-in world, created problems, and let you go. You see. But he did that all in his head. He never put a knife to wood or a wire to chip, flesh to machine. He/me loves movies. A man of unseen wires and parts loves the dreams of the machine, the camera, the devices, the effects. And you, are in fact, the dreams of a machine."

Little Billy glitched, cut out, came back.

"I haven't long. Old age . . . or what we think of as old age, has caught up with us. Me/him. And when I go, the world as I know it goes, and the world I have created goes. And our knowledge of who we are and why we are, goes with us. And by the way, Grace, three points for not wearing a top."

"Now let me get a handle on this shit," Steve said. "We ain't really androids neither. We ain't nothing but a dream?"

"You are what you are," Little Billy said, and there was a glitch, and his image jumped away, jumped back, then faded.

And was gone.

We stood stunned, and when I looked back at the way we had come, there was only the table, and I could see the end of it, and beyond it, the dimly lit wall of the room. Finally, I said, "I'm as real as I want to be, friends. And I say we do what we've always done. Charge on. Live what life we have for as long as we have it."

This was considered. Grace stuck out her hand, palm down. I put mine on top of hers. Steve and Reba joined in. We said, "Hooyah!"

"Now," I said, "might I suggest transportation? The toy plane? It's a four-seater."

"What the hell?" Steve said. "Why not?"

We made our way over there. The plane was pointed toward the back wall. Steve and I had Reba and Grace climb up on the checker box and step inside the plane. Grace took the little wheel in her hands.

"Do you think it works?" she said.

"Don't know," I said, peeling off my tied-up clutch of spears, tossing them on the ground. "We're gonna turn it so it faces the window. Then we're gonna wind it up, climb in, and let it go."

"How?" Grace said.

"I have an idea. A spark inside my little brain that is neither flesh nor computer chip, but the makings of an old man's dream. His brain is my brain. And that brain tells me we are going to turn the plane around, me and Steve."

We struggled to do it, but managed, then shoved it up close to the checker box again, pointed it in the direction of the window.

Steve and I went around front, got hold of the propeller, and began to wind it, grabbing each new propeller blade as it came to us, winding it tight.

"When we have it wound tight," I yelled up at Grace, "take your bundle of spears from your back, and stick the whole bundle between the blades, and you and Reba hold the propeller in place till we get inside."

We kept winding, and soon it was as tight as we could wind.

"Now," I said.

Grace stuck the bundle of five spears between the blades, and with Reba helping her hold them, we let go. One of the spears snapped, the propeller moved a bit, then held.

Steve and I scrambled on top of the checker box, slipped into the back seat of the plane.

"When I say," I said, "jerk up the spears and toss them away."

Grace nodded.

"Now," I said.

She and Reba jerked them back and tossed them loose of the plane, and the little toy rattled and roared and wheeled across the table, came to the edge of it, and launched. It dipped at first, then rose up and glided, wobbled a bit, then headed straight on toward the open window.

"How long do we last?" Steve said.

"As long as the old man," I said. "As long as life gives us. As much as life gives us. Hell, nothing's promised to human or android or dark little dream, so goddamnit, we'll live what's there."

The plane sailed smoothly out of the window and into the moonlight and into a cool fall breeze that swept under the plane and lifted it higher. White moths burst in front of us and beat wings to the sky and became white flakes in the darkness. Above us, stars—real stars as my false memories remembered them—shone above us, bright and sharp. And there was the moon. A great silver plate lying on the black fabric of night. The air smelled of fresh-mowed lawns, and there were warm lights in house windows and a long dark yard where grass grew, and I knew instantly, that this was the world I had come from; this was my East Texas as created for me by my android sire who lived here in his East Texas created for him by . . . Whoever.

I took in a deep breath of cool night air and felt good and strong and strangely alive.

I thought: There's no reason to write anymore, so I will not. I tore open my pack, took out my journal of composition books and pages, tossed them high to the sky.

The fluttering pages evaporated in the air like cotton candy birds licked wet, then the front of the plane faded, and I laughed, and I saw Grace and Reba fade, and Steve looked at me, and smiled, and faded, and so did—

EPILOGUE

The end ain't the end, and the mystery ain't the mystery, and the grooves of the pseudo-mind are dark and, well . . . groovy.

FADE OUT

FADE IN, DEAR HEARTS.

We were back.

"What the fuck was that?" Grace said.

"I thought the old man died," I said, "taking us with him."

"He must have had a moment," Reba said. "A mild stroke."

"Don't matter," Grace said. "Tree!"

The plane, which really had no guidance system other than windup, aim, and point, went straight for a large oak. I threw my hands over my face, and the plane hit the tree and knocked me loose of the seat.

I woke up lying on the fresh-cut lawn.

I sat up slowly. Nothing seemed broken. I eased my pack off my back, tossed it aside, made it to my feet, staggered toward the wreckage. I saw Grace crawling out of the cockpit. There was a thin line of blood across her forehead.

"Shit! Shit! Shit!" It was Reba, calling from the other side of the plane.

When I got there, Reba was on her knees, bending over Steve.

"He's dead," she said. "His neck."

Steve's neck was twisted in such a way it reminded me of a neck-wrung chicken. His teeth littered the moonlit grass around his head.

Grace came around the plane slowly, her forehead bleeding more now, running over her pretty features like a flood. She looked at Steve, then eased toward him. "Goddamnit," she said. "Goddamnit."

She dropped down on her ass, cradled his head in her lap. It rolled over as easy as a sock puppet's head. Blood ran out of her mouth and onto her bare legs. Her naked breasts heaved in the light.

I looked away, back at the house. The lawn was littered with my journal papers.

"And the fun just keeps on coming," I said.

"Yeah," Reba said, reaching down to touch Grace's shoulder. "Look."

She wasn't excited, just stating a fact. The distance was squeezing in. The yard was constricting, the houses were fading. It was like an invisible fire had surrounded us and was burning toward us, taking everything in its path. Where there had been something to see, lawn and trees and houses, now there was darkness.

Above us, the moon and the stars winked out.

We, me and Reba and Grace, the body of Steve, our plane, were at the center of a long, narrow, valley. The walls that rose on either side of it were dark and bumpy, pulsing and sparking. Wires ran along the bumpy walls like veins. The sparking gave off spotty, strobe-like light, so it was hard to see how far the valley, or to be more accurate, the trench, ran.

"Now what?" Reba said.

"His brain," I said. "The old man's brain. Made of flesh and wires and micros smaller than virus-sized chips, made of this and that and things we don't know. His brain's business, my friends, we're inside it."

"That makes less sense than being part of an android's dream," Reba said.

"He can't create the world out there anymore," I said. "Can't project his thoughts the way he could before. He's dying. It's all pulling into the source. We're inside his head. We're impulses in the grooves of his mind. He's probably in a coma. We were never part of any kind of dream. We were invented. And we are real. What happened to Steve is real. How I feel about it is real. He has sparked us to life. He is God, and we are his creations."

"You don't know that," Reba said.

"No, but it's as good a theory as any, and it's my story, and I'm sticking to it."

Grace rose up slowly and laid Steve's head carefully on what served as ground—pulsing meat.

"I wonder if there's anywhere to go," she said.

"One thing I've learned from you, Grace," I said. "Don't be a quitter."

"That's the goddamn truth," she said, taking off her ragged fur bottoms, using them to wipe the blood from her face. She tossed the rag aside, stood there in all her magnificent naked glory.

"Look there," she said.

It was the drive-in world mist. It was flowing down the brain-corridor, white as a geriatric's head.

"As Steve would say," Grace said, "ain't that the shits?"

She turned to us, put out her hand.

"As long as it lasts," she said.

"He could be in a coma for moments, or years," Reba said.

"Or there may be more to it than we know," Grace said, "if as soon as we peel one layer off the onion, we find another. My guess is there are plenty more layers, more truths to discover. Fact is, we don't even know how true our recent truth is."

"It's really nothing new," I said. "It's just like the way we thought life was, and certainly must be. Unknown. Unfocused. Unpromised."

"You are one fine-ass philosopher, Jack," Reba said.

"How long do I hold my hand out?" Grace asked.

I smiled, put my hand on top of Grace's. Reba placed hers on mine. We said, "Hoooyah!"

Slowly, we gathered ourselves, then, standing shoulder to shoulder, we started down the long, dark, sparking corridor through the mist and all its specters, moving onward to someplace or no place.

It was our mystery to discover.

THE END

UNDERLAND PRESS

Who is Underland Press and what do they want from us?
—Fangoria

**We want you to get lost in our books.
We want our fictional worlds to overtake your real ones.
We want you to be delighted, fascinated, and entertained.
We want you to love us so much you come back for more.**

Jeff Vandermeer's
Fantasy Noir

FINCH

In this powerful and poignant novel by a World Fantasy Award Winning author, the past and the future, the cosmic and the gritty, collide. What will happen if Finch uncovers the truth? What will happen if he doesn't? And will Ambergris ever be the same?

Brian Evenson's
Dark Masterpiece

LAST DAYS

By the author of *The Open Curtain* and *Fugue State*, *Last Days* questions what it means to be human, and how far you can go before you become lost even to yourself.

Will Elliott's
Award-winning Debut,

THE PILO FAMILY CIRCUS

Winner of the ABC fiction prize, *The Pilo Family Circus* begins with a nightmarish chain of events that finds Jamie stalked by a trio of gleefully sadistic clowns who deliver a terrifying ultimatum: audition or die.

www.underlandpress.com

BUY NOW FROM UNDERLAND PRESS and GET 10% OFF
Listed Trade Paperback Price For A Limited Time With This Coupon
Code: BAFKM

We want you to get lost in our books.

We want our fictional worlds to overtake your real ones.

We want you to be delighted, frightened, and entertained.

We want you to love us so much you come back for more.

LAST DAYS